D0951407

tart

Jody Gehrman

RED
DRESS
INK
™

First edition July 2005

TART

A Red Dress Ink novel

ISBN 0-373-89526-7

www.RedDressInk.com

Printed in U.S.A.

Acknowledgments

Thanks to the professionals in my life who help keep me focused, specifically my agent, Dorian Karchmar, my editor, Margaret Marbury, and my Web designer/all-around girl genius, Rosey Larson. My continually supportive and enthusiastic colleagues at Mendocino College deserve huge kudos, especially my cohorts in the English department for their flexibility, warmth and humor, and Reid Edelman for sharing with me his favorite tales of directing disasters. Thanks to the Ukiah Writers' Salon for helping me with my fledgling attempts at PR. An enormous thank-you to Bart Rawlinson for reading an early draft of this and for talking me down during revision-induced panic attacks. Thanks to Tommy Zurhellen, one of my most generous readers and best friends. It goes without saying that I'm completely indebted to my family for their love and inspiration, as usual. But most of all, thanks to David Wolf for helping me to believe in and laugh at myself in equal measures.

PROLOGUE

It's midnight in Austin, and I'm starving, but I refuse to indulge in French fries at the all-night diner; I've got a bus to steal.

The air is warm and rich with jasmine in an upscale, arty neighborhood near the university. It's a Saturday night, and I can see a girl in a white halter top smoking a cigar in the kitchen across the street. I feel a pang of envy; I want to be her, a carefree chick in a skimpy ensemble, playing the tart at a party, preparing to start the school year with a hangover. I used to be her, but things have changed. Just look at me now: sweaty and furtive, crouching behind an SUV, psyching myself up for a life of crime.

The party crowd spills out onto the porch. I watch the pretty twentysomethings clutching red plastic cups and pray they're all drunk enough to be unreliable witnesses. I inhale deeply, whisper my mantra, "He gets the jailbait, I get the wheels," and make my move.

FALL

PART I

CHAPTER 1

I'm almost to Santa Cruz when my engine catches fire. I've got my entire life savings stuffed into my bra, my hair is so wind-matted I can't even get my fingers through it, and I desperately need to change my tampon.

Things could be better.

It's mid-September, and California's crazy Indian summer is just getting started. The hundred-degree weather cools only slightly as I careen closer to the Pacific, where a slight tinge of fog is always hovering; it's still plenty hot, though, and I'm sweating profusely, cursing as my temperature gauge lodges itself stubbornly in the red zone. Highway 17 is the quickest route through the Santa Cruz Mountains, but I'd forgotten just how manic it is: the crazy curves force everyone on the road into race-car-style cornering. Three pubescent surfers in a beat-up Pinto station wagon keep swerving into my lane as they pass a joint around. I honk at them instinctively; all three towheads swivel in my direction, and the car veers unsteadily toward my front fender again. I hit my steering wheel with the palm of my hand and ease onto the brakes, praying the Jaguar in my rearview mirror won't slam me from behind. "Cunt!" one of the surfers yells. "Chill, lady," another one adds. Did he just call me *lady?* Jesus, I could use a drink.

When the engine makes a sound so primal I can no longer ignore it, I pull over onto the narrow, crumbling shoulder and get out to assess the situation. The bus is producing enormous clouds of black smoke, and bright orange tongues of flame are licking at the air vents. I haven't even bothered to check the oil since I left Austin three days ago. I knew the bus was making increasingly alarming noises, starting around El Paso, but I told myself that's what hippie vehicles do, and turned the radio up louder. The smoke is so thick now I can barely see, and I'm afraid to open the door to the engine because I've got this sinking feeling it will blow my face off. *Woman Found by Highway; Face Found 100 Yards Away.*

Shit.

Medea, my cat, is yowling a pathetic, drugged-out plea from the back seat, so I quickly stuff her into the cardboard pet taxi and carry her out onto the shoulder with me. Then I start thinking about the cat Valium in the glove box, wondering how many of those tiny pills I'd have to take before this whole scene would take on an underwater, slow-motion sheen.

Of course, there's something about the utter destitution of the situation that appeals to me. In theater, we're taught that people are only as interesting as their current crisis. Jerry Manning, my favorite professor back at UT, used to scream at us, "Disaster defines you. Where's the disaster? Come on, give me your disaster!" I feel a tiny trickle of blood as it forms a damp spot in my underwear. Medea scratches at the cardboard, her panic momentarily breaking free from the straitjacket of drugs I've kept her in. Her terrified mewling has gone from meek to murderous. "Here you go, Manning," I whisper. "Here's my disaster."

Unfortunately, my only audience is the steady stream of traffic roaring past me at breakneck speed, making the bus shudder like a cowering animal. I stole it from my boyfriend, Jonathan, who is now officially my ex-boyfriend, but I haven't managed to force him into the past tense just yet. If you must know, the bastard's a Taurus and he's got beautiful hands and he writes plays that make people swear he's some freaky genetic hybrid: two parts Tennessee Williams, one part David Lynch. He moved to New York several months ago with Rain, this nineteen-year-old acting student with slick black hair that hangs below her ass and a five-thousand-watt smile.

The flames shooting from the engine are getting more insistent.

This is not good.

I wipe the sweat from my forehead and begin fantasizing about a very stiff, incredibly cold vodka tonic: I can see the ice, smell the carbonation, taste the green of that freshly cut lime swarming with bubbles. I think again of the cat Valium and wonder if I have enough time to secure the stash before Jonathan's beloved VW explodes in a pyrotechnic burst of orange, like something from a Clint Eastwood flick. *Woman's Charred Remains Found Clinging to Glove Box*. I squeeze my thighs together in an effort to keep the blood from running down my leg.

A guy on an old dented BMW motorcycle pulls over and takes his helmet off. He's got a crooked smirk and a twenty-year-old body that looks oddly mismatched with the lines around his eyes. His hair is damp and stands up in hectic disarray like a child who's just waking from a nap. The leather jacket looks ancient enough to be a hand-me-down from James Dean himself. He looks at the bus, at me, and back at the bus again.

"Need help?" he yells over the whir and wind of the passing traffic.

"Naw. Thought I'd just hang out, watch the show," I yell back.

He shrugs and starts to swing his leg back over his bike. "I'm kidding!" I shriek.

He turns toward me again, and a grin appears from the five o'clock shadow: white teeth, substantial lips, a nose that saves him from too pretty with a slightly swerving bridge where I'm willing to guess he broke it years ago. He's the perfect Hamlet; he could play moody and build to insanity with enough sex appeal to keep the audience hot and bothered as Ophelia. He's a little dirty, but in a good way. I could tell if I took a couple steps closer I'd smell the powerful perfume of leather and sweat.

Hold it together, Bloom. You're just rebounding and road-delirious. Your cat is thrashing about in a cardboard box and you've stolen a vehicle that is about to go the way of Chernobyl.

He comes closer and says into my ear, "I don't think this one's going any farther."

"Thanks. Excellent diagnosis."

"What's in the box?"

"My cat."

He just raises his eyebrows at that. Then a huge semi comes rolling around the corner and practically knocks us over. "This isn't a good spot," he says.

"No kidding." It's a bad habit of mine: the more I need help, the more I behave like a snotty twelve-year-old. A dry, hot wind washes over us and the flames are reaching outward, like the arms of needy children. "Are we supposed to pour water on it, or something?"

"I don't know. You got any?"

"No," I yell, shaking my head for emphasis. Is it my imagination, or is the traffic getting louder the longer we stand here? "I've got a six-pack of Vanilla Coke in the back seat—will that help?"

"Not likely. What are the chances one of these assholes has a cell phone?" He watches the passing traffic with a tired, cynical expression. Jeez, strong pecs under that T-shirt. Jonathan's chest was practically concave. With his shirt off he looked six years old. Watching this guy's profile, with his once broken nose, his dust-smudged, stubbled chin and his blue-green eyes staring down each car as it blurs past, he looks a touch dangerous. It occurs to me that this could be a bad situation turning worse. *Woman and Cat Found in Dumpster.*

He starts waving his arms at the truckers and soccer moms. Medea is now yowling pathetically from the cardboard box, which I'm afraid to put down because the Valium seems to be wearing off and every five minutes she does a little body slam that nearly knocks her from my arms.

"Where's the damn CHP when you need them?" he grumbles. At this point it occurs to me that I have every reason to avoid cops right now—or anyone who might call cops. *Psycho Woman Sets Stolen Car on Fire.* I squeeze Medea's box with one hand and grab Biker Guy's waving arm with the other. "Whoa—hold on—do you think you could just give me a lift somewhere?"

He looks at me. "Well…shouldn't we…?" He eyes the flames. "We can't just leave it here."

I've got to think fast. I lean closer and speak into his ear, so I won't have to yell. "Look, there's no room here for anyone else to pull over, anyway. It's too dangerous. Plus, what are they going to do?"

He cradles his helmet between us and studies the hillside. "Lots of dry grass around here just itching to go up in flames. It could explode," he says.

"All the more reason to get out of here."

"True." I can see him assessing the situation, working the possibilities out, like someone playing chess.

"Plus, I really need a drink," I say, feeling slightly giddy at the thought of that cool vodka tonic fizzing in my throat. "Nobody's going to stop, anyway."

"Pretty grim view of humanity," he says.

"I'll brighten up soon as you get a little vodka in me."

We've just managed to bungee Medea's box onto the

back of his bike when the bus and everything I own erupts in a loud, surreal orgy of light and heat. I start to laugh. I don't know why; it's just the sound my body emits, without any consent. The whole thing's an omen of some sort, but right now I'm too hot and hysterical to guess at what it all means.

"Come on," I yell. "Let's go!" The air is alive with the smell of gasoline, and the waves of heat are so intense it's like swimming in an ocean just this side of scalding. He looks at me, puts his helmet on my head and says something, but I can't hear him now because my ears are engulfed in padding. I think I can read his lips, though; I think he's saying, "Fuck. Fuck. Fuck."

CHAPTER 2

We should have done away with marriage long ago; by now it should be a fuzzy historical footnote, like eight-track tapes.

Unfortunately, knowing this didn't save me from getting engaged last spring. I'd been a die-hard Amazon since my parents' divorce, arguing with anyone who'd listen that a girl should never trade her leather bustier for a Whirlpool dishwasher, but in my late twenties, I temporarily forgot. Having sex with the same person on a regular basis can really mess with your understanding of pertinent details, like who you are, for example. I should have known things were taking a turn for the worse when Jonathan, who always prided himself in being wildly original, popped the question on one knee in a nauseatingly sunny and not at all offbeat setting. It was April and we were picnicking at a quaint park; the trees were sparkling after a light rain and toddlers were toddling across the grass and tulips were waving in the breeze, for Christ's sake. It was mortifying, how *Sound of Music* it all was—especially when you consider that both Jonathan and

I insist musicals are the lowest form of entertainment, right below public lynching.

Why continue submitting to a proven recipe for disaster? Take two cups pressure to conform, equal amounts fear and isolation, add a dash of childhood trauma and you've got marriage. Put that in the microwave with sexual urges and animal behavior, cook on high until the whole thing either caves in with apathy or explodes with infidelity. There is no such thing as a genuinely happy marriage, there are just varying degrees of skill in the performance of one.

Cynical? Maybe. I've earned my cynicism, though. I wear it like a Purple Heart.

My parents split up when I was eleven. My father, the shop teacher—skinny and slouching, sporting horn-rimmed glasses and pants that showed his blinding white socks—started giving it to a twenty-six-year-old dental hygienist with major cleavage. Simon does Sally. It was a mess. Calistoga (think sleepy, claustrophobic, its only claim to fame a line of mediocre beverages) had a great time laughing about it behind cupped fingers.

After the divorce, my mother moved to Marin County, studied numerology, unblocked her chakras and became an embarrassingly successful hypnotherapist. Her main clients were miserable bleach-blond divorcées driving Beemers and wearing dream catcher earrings. She started marrying with a vengeance, always with an unerring eye for the clod who would make her (and, by association, me) most miserable. I called her a serial wifer. She didn't need them for their money; she was driven by something much deeper, more compulsive and masochistic. She once said to me, "Claudia, I don't marry because I *want* to. I marry because I find it impossible not to."

As for my father, he married the dental hygienist, who turned out to be a hypochondriac. She got out of her dental career, claiming the drills exacerbated her migraines, and sponged off my father, consuming his modest but carefully stashed savings, until a guy rolled into town who built swimming pools, and she went off with him. It was a weird time in my life, watching the drama of my parents' love and (worse yet) sex lives unfold with the creepy predictability of a B horror flick. At first I dug my nails into my arm and tried not to scream, but by the time I was into my teens I observed it all with cool detachment, bored by the snowballing disaster of it all.

Cynical? Isn't *observant* a little more accurate?

Anyway, now that my Jonathan-induced amnesia is safely behind me, I have every reason to be thrilled that he fell for a jailbait temptress and ran off with her. I should send them a dozen roses with a note: *Better you than me.* Let them indulge in each other's flesh until they're surfeit with sex and kisses and don't-ever-leave-me-I-love-yous and the slow, torturous monotony of the future stretches out before them like the open ocean before seasick stowaways. I'm done with it all. From now on, I'll be a warrior for non-monogamy. I'll fight the good fight, protesting the evil of the bridal industry and romantic comedies wherever they rear their treacherous, sycophantic heads.

CHAPTER 3

Clay Parker takes me to a filthy dive on Mission Street called the Owl Club. It's a Tuesday afternoon and there are only three customers, two old guys with faces like worn baseball gloves and a woman in tight cords playing pool by herself. She also appears to be having a solo conversation, and since no one's bothered to feed the jukebox we can hear most of it— something about the FBI and Walter Cronkite, but it's so complicated I tune her out after a few minutes. I'm feeling really guilty about poor Medea, who's puffed up like one of those troll dolls after too many twirls, so I bring her in with us and hold her shaking body in my lap, trying to stroke her into submission.

"I guess we should call the cops, or something," Clay says as he returns from the bar with our drinks.

"Cops?" My head swings toward him too quickly.

"It's a bad time for a fire like that—could get out of hand," he offers, but I can see by the way he's studying me that my panic is apparent.

"I can't." I spent most of the ride here trying to concoct

a good story, but I'm a rotten liar. I've been acting since I was six years old and still I can't fib my way out of a goddamn dental appointment, let alone grand theft auto and arson, so I've resigned myself to telling this hapless stranger the truth. "Look, I hate to get you involved in all this," I begin, stirring my vodka tonic quickly before downing half of it. "The thing is, I sort of—well—borrowed that bus."

"Borrowed it?" In the dim light of the Owl Club, I can't be sure what color his eyes are—somewhere between blue and green—but there's something remarkably comfortable and familiar about his face. He has a stare that makes you lose your train of thought, and for a long moment I can't remember what I'm doing here, or what I'm supposed to confess.

"If I seem incoherent, I'm sorry," I say, looking away. "I'm a little tripped out. God, this is absolutely the most delicious and the most needed vodka tonic I've ever tasted."

"You didn't steal it, did you?"

"Well…" I try a smile, but it's all wrong. The woman playing pool breaks and the smack of the balls makes Medea sink her claws into my thigh with alarm. "Ouch!" I cry, quite loudly, and everyone turns in my direction. I sink a little lower into the booth. *Psychotic Car Thief and Mad Pussycat Apprehended at the Owl Club.* "It was my boyfriend's," I whisper. "I just borrowed it, but he doesn't know."

"Aha. And where's your boyfriend now?"

"Ex-boyfriend. Sorry. I can't seem to get that right. He's in New York, having sex with a teenager."

"Charming." He leans back, looks at the ceiling, and I can tell he's wondering what he's gotten himself into.

"You don't think it'll start a fire, do you? I mean, of course it was *on* fire—the explosion and all—but do you think it'll catch?" What an idiot. Why can't I speak?

One of the old guys at the bar laughs violently at something, and this time Medea makes a break for the door. I scramble after her, but Clay's quicker by half; he scoops her up into his arms and has her purring in his lap before I've even managed to lay a hand on her. Jonathan never did get along with Medea. He claimed he was allergic, that she gave him a headache and an itchy tongue, but I always suspected it was more of a jealous grudge than a physical reaction.

Now that I'm standing, I feel a warmth spreading into my underwear again, and I realize that in my haste to get a little vodka down my throat I completely forgot about changing my tampon. I excuse myself to the ladies' room, which turns out to be a disgustingly neglected converted broom closet. There's a sink stained brown with rust, the floor is covered with miscellaneous paper products, and the single-stall door has been delightfully decorated with a vast array of rants, insults and warnings, the most prominent of which reads, *Die Puta Bitches.*

I study myself for a moment in the small, cracked mirror. My hair, even on a good day, is immune to threats with a comb. Each curl finds its way into its own contorted expression of chaos; trying to interfere leads only to excessive frizz. Today the curls have twisted to ambitious dimensions, resulting in a Medusa-on-crack look. I'm wearing this little orange sundress—the most comfortable thing I own for long drives (now, I remind myself, the *only* thing I own). It's not exactly the height of chic, especially since it's all wrinkled, the armpits are wet and the bodice is smeared here and there with the sooty remains of Jonathan's bus. I think of Mr. Indecently Attractive out there, nursing his beer and petting my cat; perhaps it's just as well that I'm so horrifically unpresentable today—there's less chance of me wandering into something I really shouldn't.

Tampon, Claudia. Focus. Oh, but goddammit, my stash of OB is now being cremated on the shoulder of Highway 17. There is a machine, thank God, but I haven't got any change. I could go back out there and get the bartender to give me quarters. But then Clay will see me and it'll be obvious or at the very least odd (think about it, Claudia—wouldn't incinerating a stolen vehicle qualify as plenty odd already?).

I know the chances that I'll create a favorable impression at this point are slim (not to mention unnecessary. Remember? On the rebound, delirious with heat, on the rag, homeless, with all possessions currently blowing amid Tuesday traffic in form of ash. Do not, I repeat, do not indulge in a messy entanglement with Gorgeous Motorcycle Boy). But still, I don't want to make things worse with one more faux pas.

There's a gentle sniffling coming from inside the bathroom stall. I freeze. It never occurred to me that I wasn't alone in here. A quick check under the door reveals a pair of pink flip-flops. A couple seconds pass, and then the toilet flushes and out comes Beach Barbie.

She's wearing a tiny tank over a bikini top and miniature turquoise shorts, cut high enough to reveal her mile-long legs. Her eyes are bloodshot and her nose is pink from too much blowing, but neither this nor the seedy setting is enough to detract from her overwhelming California glow.

I try not to gawk as she squeezes past me to the sink, washes her hands and then her face, pats both dry with a paper towel.

"Hi," I say.

She looks at me in the mirror and smiles, revealing the expected set of gleaming white teeth, then she bursts into sobs.

"Oh, no," I say. "What is it?"

"I—" She can barely get the words out. "I hate—"

"Yes? You hate…?"

"Guys," she finally spits out.

By now, there's snot dripping from one of her pretty little nostrils, so I duck into the stall she just left and get her a wad of toilet paper. "There you go," I say, patting her shoulder gently. "It's all going to be okay."

She blows her nose loudly several times, then composes herself quite rapidly, considering the extremity of the breakdown. "Oh, my God," she says, checking her reflection for mascara damage. "I'm so embarrassed."

"Don't be. If you have a quarter or a tampon, I'm never telling anyone. Deal?"

She's got a pink beach bag slung over her shoulder, and now she paws through it, pulling out a half-eaten Snickers bar, a bottle of aspirin, three lipsticks and a cell phone before finally producing the coveted Tampax. She hands it to me. Its paper wrapper is smooth and delicate from so much toting around.

"Oh, God, thank you," I sigh. "You're an angel of mercy."

She hiccups daintily and smoothes her already perfect hair with one hand. "Our little secret, right?"

"Lips are sealed," I say, disappearing into the stall.

When I emerge, my tragic little Beach Barbie is gone. As is usually the case, the blood damage was much less extensive than I'd feared—hardly more than a spot—so I'm feeling refreshed and eager to return to my drink. Clay is still stroking Medea. He appears to be engrossed in a conversation with her, as well. Her puffiness has completely disappeared and she is stretched out happily in his lap, soaking up the affection. She's always had excellent taste.

"…terrible motorcycle ride," he's telling her, as I sit down. "But you're okay. Bet you always land on your feet."

"Thanks," I say.

He looks up. "For what?"

"Oh, I don't know…calming her down. Bringing us here. Saving us from a fiery death."

"I hardly saved you." He wraps a hand around his beer and rotates it slowly before taking a swig. "You two don't look like the kind of girls who need saving."

"Anyway," I say, eager to change the subject, "what's your story? What do you do?"

"For a living?"

"Okay, sure. What do you do for a living?"

He shrugs. "I've got a record store."

"Here in town?" I ask.

He nods.

"That's cool. So you're into music. You play anything?"

"Not really. I DJ on the side, but it's slow going. The gigs I make money at are mostly weddings, which generally suck."

"Oh, man," I say. "I hate weddings."

"Jesus, if I have to play 'You Are So Beautiful' one more time I'm going postal."

"I think our generation's way too jaded for marriage. It should seriously be outlawed. Forget the whole same-sex marriage debate." I lean into the table. "Let's do away with the whole institution."

He looks amused. "Now, that's something I can drink to," he says, raising his beer bottle. We toast, and a vision of his mouth on the nape of my neck makes me feel suddenly much drunker than half a vodka tonic can account for, even on an empty stomach.

"So what are you doing in Santa Cruz, anyway?" he asks.

He keeps turning the conversation back to me. He's probably a serial killer. People who murder for a living tend to be rather private. One more reason not to go home with him.

"How do you know I'm not from here?" I ask, twirling my straw in my drink and looking coy in spite of myself. Stop. Flirting. Stop. Flirting.

"I had the dubious pleasure of growing up in this vortex. I can spot an outsider by now. Besides, your license plate said Texas."

He's an undercover cop. Oh, God. I can already feel the cold steel of the cuffs against my wrist bones.

"You okay?" He reaches across the table and gently touches the very hand I'm busy morbidly encasing in restraints. Please, Jesus, don't let him be a serial killer undercover cop.

"Sure. Why?"

"Every once in a while you get this wild gleam in your eye—"

"Wild gleam?"

"The same look Medea shot me when I unstrapped her from my bike."

I laugh, though even to me it sounds strangled. "Yeah, well, I'm a little off today. I don't routinely rise at four in the morning, drive six hundred miles, then blow up my stolen vehicle to unwind in the afternoon." Listing the events of the day makes me feel the wild gleam coming back, so I try to steer us toward safer topics. "Um, let's see, what was your question?"

"Santa Cruz—what brings you here?"

"Right. I've got this university gig teaching theater."

"Wow." He looks impressed, and maybe a little bit skeptical, which only confirms my suspicion that I am not professor material.

"Yeah, well, they were hard up," I explain. "Some guy faked his credentials so they had to fire him. I'm the only person they could drag here at the last minute. They made it clear that I'm just a stand-in—you know, one year and then, unless I turn out to be the next Stanislavski, I'm on the street." The combination of my nerves, three days on the road alone and this dreamy vodka tonic are making me babble, but I hardly care. It feels good to talk to somebody other than a pissed-off, stoned cat. "I'm a total perennial student— I fell in love with the endless adolescence of college—so I figured a university's the only place I stand a chance. Except I'm not so sure about the professor thing. I suspect I haven't got the wardrobe for it."

He waves a hand at me dismissively. "At UC Santa Cruz? You could walk on campus in a garbage bag and by the end of the day you'd have a following. Lack of fashion is a fashion here."

"Yeah. Well, good." There's an awkward pause; we end up looking at each other for too long, and this makes me so edgy I blurt out, "Christ. I can't believe I actually stole my ex's bus." He looks a little unsure about how to respond, and

I realize I'm starting to monologue in a dangerously unchecked fashion. "Sorry. Very long day, as I mentioned."

"Sounds like you could use another drink," he says, rising. Very carefully, like one parent transferring a sleeping child into the lap of the other, he hands me Medea. "More of the same?"

I suddenly realize I've been gnawing nervously at the wedge of lime from my drink; even the peel is now littered with teeth marks. I toss it back into the glass, which I hand to him sheepishly. "Yes, please. Oh, but here—let me get this round." I reach for my money, still tucked inside my bra, but he shakes his head.

"Don't worry about it. Consider me the welcoming committee." He turns and walks toward the bar. Watching him makes me bite the inside of my cheek. Has there ever been an icon steamier than that subtle sag of a man's barely there butt in faded Levi's?

I lean back against the vinyl of the booth and close my eyes, running one hand absently over Medea's soft fur again and again. The tart taste of lime still lingers on my tongue. Claudia. Please. For once in your life, resist. Resist. Resist.

CHAPTER 4

Tart is my favorite word. I love how it tastes in your mouth—sour, tangy, just sweet enough to keep your lips from puckering around it in distaste. I love what it stirs in the mind—the synesthesia of flavor mixing with colors: buxom women in reds, oranges and apple-greens, gleaming with cheap temptation, like Jolly Ranchers. It's been a central goal of my twenties to live a tart life; I want everything I do to have that sharpness, that edge of almost-too-out-there to be tasty, but not quite.

Until I met Jonathan, living tartly meant, for starters, never saying I love you. Which was easy, since apart from my cat, my gay roommate and my vibrator, I didn't really love much of anything or anyone. I'm not even sure I loved Jonathan. I think our relationship was rooted in blind panic, and that, combined with great affection for him, was exactly the brand of love I'd heard about in pop songs since puberty. Being with Jonathan was terrifying, sometimes tender and studded with misery. These are the central ingredients of love, ac-

cording to Top Forty tunes throughout the ages, so I figured I must be on the right track.

Before Jonathan and the Great Blind Panic, I used to
think monogamy was every woman's enemy, and that
promiscuity (a central element of every tart's lifestyle) was
synonymous with freedom. It's probably generational—lots
of girls I went to college with admired strippers and porn
stars the way our mothers admired starlets. It's that fuck-you
to middle-class values that inspires awe in us. We find the
sex industry and all of its incumbent seediness sort of glamorous. And tart.

But being a tart can be exhausting, and after a while its
rewards start to seem a little tawdry. Now that I'm round-
ing the corner toward my thirties, the fervor of my tart
philosophy has faded some with wear. Frankly, my right to
be wild, cheap and promiscuous has started to bore me.

I guess that's part of why Jonathan and I got so serious
so quickly. We met when I was twenty-eight. I could see
right into my thirties from there, and beyond. I knew a
change was in order. I started cringing every time I spot-
ted some woman in her late thirties haunting the junior
racks at Ross Dress for Less, sporting deeply ingrained
crow's feet and hair that's been dyed so many times it looks
like cheap faux fur. I'm not sure why self-respecting tartery
requires a wrinkle-free face and body, but it does. That's no
doubt really messed up, but it feels like a force of nature
too momentous to challenge.

It was in this twenty-eight-year-old climate of anxiety
and pending doom that I met Jonathan. He was creative, suit-
ably unconventional and so crazy about me that I could feel
a palpable confusion coming off him anytime we were in
the same room. I was directing his play, *Molotov Cocktail*, a
farce about morticians in training, and whenever we dis-
cussed his rewrites over coffee he took every opportunity
to touch me in ways that could be construed as friendly or
accidental: his elbow nestled fleetingly against mine, his knee

bumped against my thigh under the table. I was flattered but not overcome. I told myself he wasn't my type—too skinny, his hands too pale, his eyes too furtive and searching, so unlike the muscular, vaguely bovine types I was used to going home with.

But Jonathan was nothing if not persistent; he rooted himself beside me and sent exploratory tendrils into my psyche with the strength and tenacity of kudzu. I started to crave the way his black hair looked in the morning light as he rolled himself a cigarette with agile fingers. I became addicted to his smell: Irish soap, cigarette smoke, Tide. He was so solicitous, as only someone with a heart that deflates between relationships can be. Jonathan loved being in love. He was lost without someone to brew coffee for, or share his favorite scripts with, or sing to sleep with funny, black-humored lullabies he made up as he went along.

He convinced me to move in with him three weeks after we first slept together. It did make some sense, since my roommate, Ziv, was involved at the time with this German guy, Gunter, who had three habits Ziv found adorable and I found repulsive: he covered the entire bathroom with a thick dusting of tiny black hairs each time he shaved; his favorite time to practice his cello was postcoital, which usually meant 2:00 or 3:00 a.m.; and he continually, despite my protests, consumed any chocolate products we smuggled into the house, including the special Belgian hazelnut bar I hid in my underwear drawer. So Gunter was driving me away, and Jonathan had this beautiful place—the upstairs of a lovely old-fashioned Texas-style minimansion with French doors, hardwood floors and a claw-foot tub I spent most of that year floating in. A warm, stable relationship and a cool new apartment to boot made cohabitation seem catalog-perfect—a Pottery Barn fairytale.

But old habits die hard. Monogamy was quite a shock to my system, both physically and philosophically. Toward the end of that summer, when we'd been living together a little over five months, I became overwhelmingly itchy for Something Else. When you're addicted to the pursuit of all things tart, Friday night with a video and Chinese takeout is a little foreign. I'd pace the living room and blurt out nasty jabs, like a junky trying to kick.

I had lived for twenty-eight years just fine, following my sexually nomadic heart, stretching out my elastic adolescence for as long as it would last, and now suddenly half my instincts were urging me to make a nest, while the other half screamed "Flee!" Just because I'd decided to try the nesting thing didn't mean I had the slightest idea how to pull it off.

And so I did what most people do in lieu of a solution; I denied there was a problem until I could arrange for a full-on disaster. In the fall of my last year in grad school, seven months into my experiment in cozy living with Jonathan, I had a flash-in-the-pan affair with my Set Design professor. He was in his forties, with distinguished graying temples and a gruff, Tom Waits-style lecturing voice. He was nothing to me; I had no illusions that we were doing anything except blowing off steam. The guy wasn't even very good in bed; he was married, and felt terrible about me, so his rushed, guilt-driven exertions were never very satisfying. After two seedy sessions in a dank hotel, I called it off. He sighed with relief and gave me an A in the class, even though my final project looked like a kindergartener's shoe-box diorama.

Of course, I had to tell Jonathan. I may not be your classic stickler for integrity, but I do have my own idiosyncratic moral code, and honesty is a central tenet, right behind tartery. Besides, half the reason I had the affair was to loosen the stranglehold my life with Jonathan exerted; telling him was key to this loosening. I'd needed a little tart back, and I'd taken it by force, but now it was necessary to fess up.

I sat him down on a cold Saturday in December. Christmas was just a week away. I summarized with my eyes averted, peeling the label from a bottle of Corona. His reaction fell short of violence, but he did dash into the john to throw up, and afterward he stared at me with the sort of expression a baby might use on his mother as she shoves his finger in an electrical outlet. At that point I felt more than a little sick, myself.

I might be saying this just to soften the sting of him leaving me months later for Rain, but in retrospect I see our relationship from that cold Saturday on as filled with him calculating his revenge. Even proposing was just one more form of payback; he knew my promise to marry him meant I'd publicly renounced all tartness, and so when he left, he took with him not only my future, but my past.

CHAPTER 5

It's six o'clock, I've got three vodka tonics in my blood-stream, and I'm in love.

Okay, that's probably not it. It's probably just culture shock. I haven't been home to California in three years. Obviously, the ocean air is salt-rotting my brain. That's why I feel so reckless and giddy, like a thirteen-year-old at a slumber party.

"Where are we going?" I ask as Clay leads me out of the Owl Club and into the startling sunlight.

"We've got to get Medea someplace cat-friendly," he says.

"You're right," I say. "Let's strap her back onto your bike." I giggle at my stupid joke.

Clay steers me gently east and picks up the pace. "My friend Nick lives right around the corner," he says. "She'll like him. He's a spaz around people, but he's a genius with cats."

"What sort of spaz?"

"He's got a mild case of Tourette's."

"No," I say. "Seriously?"

"Mostly around customers. Unfortunately, he works for

me at the record store. One time he called this sweet little old lady a 'rug-eater cunt.' You should have seen her face."

"Oh, my God," I say, laughing. "Isn't that a little hard on sales?"

"Yeah, well, she wasn't a return customer."

As we walk the two blocks to Nick's, my eyes keep straying to the half-moon scar near Clay's ear. I can't stop thinking about kissing it.

"Everything okay?" he asks, shooting me a sideways glance.

"Mmm-hmm. Why do you ask?"

"I think you might be getting that gleam in your eye again."

I laugh. "Different gleam. You'll have to learn the difference."

"Right. Well, here we are," he says, striding through a little wire gate and up the steps of a run-down house. The tilting porch is covered in thick strands of ivy and nasturtiums. "Chez Nick." He pushes open the front door and hollers, "Nick! I brought you some kitten for dinner."

A short guy with a receding hairline and a too-tight Ramones T-shirt appears in the living room doorway. "No need to yell." He's eating a doughnut, and when he sees me a big blob of jelly slips out of it and lands on the *R*.

"Fucking-shit-whore," he blurts out.

Clay looks from him to me and back again. "What? She makes you nervous?"

"Sorry," Nick says, swallowing the doughnut without chewing. He starts to choke, and Clay whacks him on the back a couple of times.

"Maybe you should wait outside." Clay nods toward the door I've barely stepped through. "I'll be there in a second."

"Um. Okay." I shuffle back out to the sidewalk. "Nice to meet you."

In a couple of minutes, Clay reappears, sans Medea. He's shaking his head.

"All righty," he says, slapping his palms together happily. "Now we've officially begun the tour."

"The tour?"

"Yes."

"What tour, exactly?"

"The Santa Cruz Freaks and Tasty Treats Tour."

I look over his shoulder at Nick's dubious house. The windows are draped with purple, rust-streaked sheets, and there's a strange sculpture made of Pabst Blue Ribbon cans dangling from a tree. "Are you sure she'll be okay in there?"

"Positive. Like I said, he's a disaster with women, but with cats, he really shines."

He starts to guide me away, but still I hesitate. "I may not be a model pet owner," I say, digging in my heels, "but I do worry. She's sort of all I have at this point."

With both hands on my shoulders, he looks into my eyes. "Claudia. I swear, she'll be happy as a clam. Trust me."

I bite my lip, studying his face. I've known him all of four hours and am shocked to realize I do trust him. "If you say so."

"I promise. Now, right this way, madam, and I'll introduce you to what Santa Cruz excels at."

"Freaks and Treats?" I ask.

"Precisely."

Clay Parker's Freaks and Treats Tour:
1) Nick and his jelly doughnut. Freak with treat. I'm skeptical, but willing to proceed.
2) Fancy place downtown with white linen tablecloths and waitress with sparkly red thong peeking out of black slacks: wolf down a dozen oysters on the half shell and beer in frosty cold mugs. Clay confesses he's having the best day he's had all summer. I blush. I hardly ever blush.

3) En route to destination, we spy our second freak:
   long-hair on unicycle playing a plastic recorder. Due
   to high speed of vehicle, can't be sure, but suspect
   he's playing "Little Red Corvette."
4) Gold mine. Downtown farmer's market. Peaches,
   fried samosas, free samples of calamari. Too many
   freaks to name: mullet guys, drag queens, belly
   dancers, skate punks, goth girls, rasta drummers. Clay
   points out Dad in a Sierra Club baseball cap scolding toddler for not recycling apple juice bottle. At
   first we laugh, but when kid cries, start to feel depressed.
5) Manage to discreetly disappear into Rite Aid for
   tampons. Inside, more freaks: three betties in 80's
   neon and teased bangs, filling cart with jumbo Junior Mints and Pall Malls.
6) Dessert at the Saturn Café. Sullen waitress with pink
   Afro. Clay orders us Chocolate Madness and a side
   of chocolate chip cookie dough. We feed each other
   the mess until we're groaning in pain.
7) Insist on the Boardwalk. Remember visiting a hundred years ago, am seized with uncharacteristic
   nostalgia. Clay grudgingly admits Boardwalk is
   chock-full of freaks and therefore justifiable addition
   to itinerary. Ancient roller coaster nearly forces oysters, calamari, peaches, samosas, cookie dough and
   Chocolate Madness back up. Discover Clay has adorable, girlish scream when terrified.
8) Nightcap at Blue Lagoon. Lots of beefy guys in
   leather. Want to kiss Clay so desperately can taste it.

CHAPTER 6

Clay Parker lives in a yurt. Before tonight, I've never heard of such a thing. It's round and wooden and is shaped like a circus tent. It's more homey than I'd imagined. In fact, it has solid wooden floors, glass windows, running water and electricity. It's the sort of place a hobbit might live in, if he was born and raised in Northern California.

You're wondering what I'm doing here. So am I. But things are much more innocent than they sound—really—in fact, Clay's insisted he's going to lend me his bed while he spends the night at the smallish cottage down the road, where Friend lives. So far, the gender of Friend is a mystery my gentle probing has failed to pierce. Here's the paltry sum of clues I've managed to procure:

1) Cottage has a couch, which he's indicated he occasionally sleeps on.
2) Friend is "an old friend." Assuming this refers to years of acquaintance, rather than somewhat com-

forting possibility that Friend, regardless of gender, is ninety and incontinent.

3) Friend will not mind the late hour (is now 1:00 a.m.), lack of prior notice or burden of making extra coffee come morning.

4) Friend makes great coffee.

Nancy Drew I am not. Even after nine hours of drinking, gorging and drinking again with this man, I am steadfastly incapable of asking about his romantic or (God forbid) marital status. It's one of those sick dances we do: tell ourselves if we don't ask, magically no obstacles will interfere. Equally sick is the assumption that, because sleeping-with candidate has not asked *our* status, said candidate wants what we want.

Ugh. Cannot believe I'm embroiling myself in this brand of mess yet again. But Clay Parker is absolutely bristling with sex appeal. His eyes are wise and knowing, his face all the more appealing for its minor irregularities. He's got that endearing tiny half-moon scar near his left ear and a bicuspid with a minuscule chip missing. His left eye squints just a little more than the right, especially when he's smiling. And then there's the nose: that swerve toward the top, so subtle it makes you think you've imagined it, until you see it from a new angle and notice it again. Somewhere between the oysters and the peaches, I asked him about it. He blushed crimson.

"Whoa," I said. "Don't tell me—does it involve bondage and thigh-high boots?" He chuckled, but there was something wrong, and I instantly regretted asking. "You know what? It's none of my business."

"No, it's fine. You can ask me anything." *Except,* I thought, *are you currently doing anyone?* "It's just—my dad. He was a little rough on me when I was a kid."

"Oh. I see." There was an awkward silence, followed by me blurting out, "He hit you?"

"A couple times." We watched a tiny slip of a woman struggling to control her Great Dane as they crossed the street. He shrugged. "I guess nobody's perfect."

"Where is he now?"

"Dead." He swallowed and held my gaze. I felt that weird surge of maternal warmth that always freaks me out—the impulse to stroke the stray wisp of hair back from a man's forehead.

"What about your mother?"

He laughed, and though I was relieved to see him smiling again, there was something a touch hardened in the sound he made. "Oh, she's still kicking. That old girl will outlive me, no doubt."

"Do you like her?" Pop psychy as it is, I cling to my theory that boys who like their mothers are more satisfying in every way.

He thought about it a couple of seconds, which seemed like a bad sign, but when he answered I could tell it was just because he took the question seriously. "I do like her. I mean, we'd never hang out if she wasn't my mother, but she's feisty and she loves me more than anyone. That's always irresistible."

I just smiled, wondering if there's anyone who loves me more than anyone.

Now that we're here in his yurt, I'm a little daunted by the intimacy of it. I find myself standing in one big round room, lit by several candles and a brass lamp. I look around at the kitchen sink and the rustic, homemade-looking armoire and the (oh, God) king-size, quilt-covered bed all right there in plain view. We've been wandering for hours from one indulgence to the next, the ocean breeze messing with our hair, and now suddenly we're encased by his bookshelves and his record player and his barbells on a thick wool rug. His dog, an old mutt the color of caramel that answers to Sandy, pants and wags her tail in a frenzy of joy as her master runs his hands all over her paunchy body.

"You surf?" I ask, noticing a large surfboard, yellowed like a smoker's teeth, propped up next to the armoire and another, bright turquoise, near the door.

"Yeah."

I nod. Usually, I find surfers to be a bit of a turn-off; California clichés generally make me want to heave. In this case, I can't even work up to a sarcastic remark. Even surfing seems cool on him. "It's a sweet place," I say, stuffing my hands into my pockets.

"Oh, yeah? You sound surprised."

"Well…" I shrug. "I'd never heard of a yurt. The way you described it—I mean, its Mongolian origins and all—I was picturing some yak skins stretched across a driftwood frame."

He laughs. I like his laugh very much. It's throaty and resonant, sexy as hell. Is it my imagination, or is it tinged now with just a shade of nerves?

"Here." He hands me Medea, who is back in her box, probably puffed up again and pissed off. At least we did her the favor of leaving the motorcycle at Nick's and getting him to drive us out here. She couldn't reasonably be asked to put up with another death-defying ride, especially after all the drinks we've had. It was ten miles, easily, and though they were spouting off names at me—"Empire Grade" and "Bonny Doon"—I've no idea where we are. You'd think I might be wary, given my habitual fixation on mass murderers, but nine hours of continual conversation have allayed those fears. If Clay Parker is in any way homicidal or rape-inclined, then my instincts are so terrible I deserve to be strangled and cannibalized.

"I'll put Sandy out so we can let Medea get her bearings."

"Are you sure? It's her—" I struggle to remember its name "—yurt, after all."

"Oh, she's dying to get out. It's no problem." He slips out the door with her. The yurt walls are canvas-thin, so I can hear him saying soft, reassuring doggy things to her as they crunch around in the grass.

I coax Medea out of her big-haired, frantic state again, though she can't stop smashing her nose against all the canine-scented furniture with a mad, panicked expression. "Yes," I murmur, trying to make my voice as warm and reassuring as Clay's. "We're in dog territory, babe. Don't worry—they don't all bite."

The weird thing—I mean the really weird thing—is that this afternoon-into-night-into-wee-hours with Clay has got me pursuing lines of logic I've never dared pursue before. Not even with Jonathan. Studying Clay's face in the dim, reddish glow of the Saturn Café, I found myself wondering what a baby would look like with his eyes and my mouth. God, is this my baby clock talking? I spent a whole semester of Fem. Theory my sophomore year writing papers on the topic: how the patriarchy created the baby clock mythology to con women into surrendering to mommyism. At the time I was twenty-one, giddy with the right to get drunk in seedy bars and swivel my hips against this boy and that to frantic techno rhythms. What did I know about biology, except that beer gets you drunk and sex makes you— momentarily at least—something like happy? Now, eight years later, I find myself contemplating how a stranger's eyes would look in my theoretical baby's face over a plate of Chocolate Madness.

What do we know about each other? Hardly anything. I know he's an atheist, owns a record store, graduated from Berkeley and was a drummer in a punk-rock band called Poe when he was fifteen. He knows I love theater, directing more than acting, that I grew up in Calistoga and went to Austin in search of cowboys. Hardly enough résumé fodder has been revealed to warrant the swapping of spit, let alone genetic material. So how can I explain these freakishly domestic fantasies streaking though my psyche like shooting stars?

"You two okay?" Both Medea and I spin round at the sound of his voice. "Still a little skittish, huh?"

"Who, her or me?"

"Both." He's standing in the doorway, keeping Sandy from entering by gently nudging her away now and then with one leg. "Come out here, will you? I want you to see something."

For a fraction of a second I hesitate—*Dismembered Arm and Paw Found in Remote Woods*—but then I remember Clay's story about adopting a baby raccoon when he was eight. He named it Zorro and fed it with a bottle, for Christ's sake. Would a guy like that dismember a girl like me? I extricate Medea from my lap carefully and follow him outside.

He leads me down a short path in the dark, mumbling, "Watch your step." When we get to the middle of a broad, grassy meadow that smells of yarrow and pine, he looks up and I follow his gaze. Oh, my God. Above us, the stars stretch out in luxurious multitudes, crowding the sky with a million pinpricks of light. I feel suddenly minuscule and happy. I think briefly of Jonathan's bus packed with all my belongings, reduced now to a charred pile of ash sweeping off on the night breeze. Out here, it doesn't seem like a big deal. I'll figure it out. Dwarfed by the enormous carpet of stars, I take a deep breath for the first time in days.

"Smells so good out here," I say.

"Yeah," he says. "I think it's the stars, myself."

I squint at him in the dark, wanting my eyes to adjust so I can study his eyes. "The stars have a smell?"

"Yeah, I think so. Don't you?"

I look back up at the layers and layers of them, so vast they surprise me all over again. "Never occurred to me."

"I think everything's different in the presence of stars. Food tastes different—"

"Different, how?"

"Saltier, I guess. And sweeter. Music's different, too—more dreamy, and lonelier. More—" he pauses, and I can see his silhouette clearly now; his face is tilted upward "—more longing in it. And everything takes on this particular scent. You smell it, don't you?"

"Mmm-hmm," I say, thinking he'd make a damn fine Romeo if he were ten years younger—he's got that dreamy-melancholy thing going.

"Wait a second," he says, and sprints back the way we came. In a minute I hear music floating on the warm September air: acoustic guitar and a melody I've never heard, but it's like I already know it and love it. Some things are like that; sushi tasted totally familiar the first time I put it in my mouth. My parents were choking on the wasabi and I just went on chewing with the gentle smile of someone coming home.

The man singing has one of those resonant, ragged, sexy voices that comes from someplace deep and cavernous in his smoke-filled lungs.

With your measured abandon and your farmer's walk, with your "let's go" smile and your bawdy talk.

Clay returns, and he stands so close to me that our arms touch.

"You see? Sounds different under the stars, right?" he asks.

"I haven't heard it any other way," I say. "How can I be sure?"

"You're not a Greg Brown fan?"

With your mother's burden and your father's stare, with your pretty dresses and your ragged underwear...

"I could be converted," I say, smiling. "I've just never heard him before."

"Never heard of—my God. Talk about deprived."

The skin of his arm feels very warm against mine. Hot, in fact. I lean slightly toward him so that more of my skin touches more of his.

"It's good you're not set in your ways," he says. "If there's one thing I'm evangelical about, it's music." It's a good thing I refuse to analyze this; if I did, I'd hear the whispered implication that he plans to evangelize me.

"This song's been haunting me all day," he says. "I think

it might be about you. Tell me the truth, Greg Brown's in love with you, right?"

"Can't get anything past you," I say, but now I want to shut up so I can hear the song and find out what Clay thinks of me. I can only catch certain lines now and then, though, between the crickets and the breeze playfully tousling the pines.

With your pledge of allegiance and your ringless hand, with your young woman's terror and your old woman's plans…

"Uh-oh. I just realized," Clay says. "I'm doing it again."

"Hmm?" I'm still straining to hear the song. *Will your children look at you and wonder, about this woman made of lightning bugs and thunder…take in what you can't help but show with your name that is half yes, half no.*

"I'm being a DJ."

"What are you talking about?"

"I do this when I'm nervous—try to talk through music. Not even *my* music. Pathetic."

"I don't think it's pathetic," I say. "I think it's sweet."

He turns slightly, and so do I, and our arm contact becomes my breasts fitting warmly against his chest, and now the sound of his breathing is so close it blends with everything else: the shimmery pine needles and the cricket-frog chorus and the lyrics I can't quite follow anymore.

He bends down slightly, the shadow of his face moving toward mine, but instead of the expected searching lips, I feel his teeth biting down gently on my lower lip. I suck in my breath.

"I wanted to do that for hours," he says, his voice thick in his throat.

"Bite me?"

"Mmm. Taste you."

This guy's not normal, I think, and a montage of our day unfurls inside my brain with the frenetic pace of time-lapse photography: the bus exploding into ribbons of orange and yellow, the kaleidoscope of the pool balls at the Owl Club,

Nick and his jelly-smudged Ramones shirt, Clay feeding me calamari with his fingers. His mouth closes on mine now, and I can taste the day there, the effervescent weirdness of it, the unshakable sensation that I'm being marked by every minute.

You won't remember the half-open door, or the train that won't even stop there anymore, for you.

CHAPTER 7

Dawn. Sky is a crazy electric blue. Slivers of it appear when the grass-scented breeze lifts the airy curtains and reveals the morning in triangular slices. I flip over and notice for the first time the circular skylight. Human beings are made for yurts, I think. "Stars make things taste saltier and sweeter." *You won't remember the half-open door.* Clay is positioned in a slightly diagonal tilt; one leg is draped over mine, lips slightly parted as he snores a soft, wheezing prayer to the sleep gods. Medea's here, curled up close to my head on the foreign pillow, and Dog—what's her name? Cindy? no, Sandy—is curled up at our feet. Medea opens one eye, checks out proximity of Dog, goes back to sleep. I should be shocked at abruptly finding myself in this tranquil, domestic tableau.

Nothing has ever seemed more natural.

I follow Medea's lead and collapse back into dreams.

Knock knock knock. Knock knock knock.

Who's drumming? Jesus, California hippies for you. Always beating their bongos...

Knock knock knock. Knock knock.

"Clay? You awake?" A woman's voice. Edgy. Irritated.

My eyes pop open. Friend? Has Friend come to visit?

"Clay? Come on, you there? I need your help." Softer now, asking, "Can I come in?"

I look over at Clay, who is still in the position I saw him in last: stretched corner to corner across the bed, mouth open, snoring. I poke his arm urgently. No response.

"Listen, I know you must be in there, hon."

Hon?

"I know I said I'd respect your privacy, but the car won't start and I have a dentist appointment." Pause. I can hear her swearing softly. "Clay." Another pause, and then a decision: the doorknob turns. "I'm coming in, okay?"

Oh, God. Paralyzed, clutching sheets to my naked chest. I want to shake snoring Clay awake but I can't move as the door swings open, followed by a door-frame-shaped blast of sunlight and Woman.

We're both perfectly still as we stare at each other. She's so backlit, I can barely make out her features. I can tell only that she's petite, dark-haired, tightly wound, the type I'd cast as Hedda Gabler: intense, compact, ready for a fight. This is all the data I'm able to gather, blinking into the sunlight, before a whispered "shit" escapes her lips and she backs out the door, slamming it behind her. I hear her footsteps rapidly retreating.

Wanton Tart and Cat Shot by Furious Gabler. Man Says Both Just Friends.

I fall back against my pillow (not my pillow—my pillow is cremated) and close my eyes for a couple of seconds, willing the previous scene to rewind and erase. No use. Instead the scene is in a perpetual loop, playing over and over across my closed lids.

"Clay?"

More snores.

"Hey. Clay?" I'm getting louder, now, shaking him gently but firmly.

"Dad?" he asks, his eyes popping open in alarm. Again, that bizarre, maternal urge stirs in me—some eerie, foreign desire to say "Shh, it's okay" and kiss him back to sleep. I make a conscious effort to strangle this urge. There will be no shushing or kisses this morning.

All the same, I can't keep a tiny bit of warmth from my voice. "No, it's me."

A little-boy smile takes over his face. "Oh. Ms. Claudia, I presume?" He wraps his arms around me, pulling me down against his chest, and for a second or two I'm so intoxicated by the hot-skin smell of this embrace I nearly forget that his better half is currently rifling through her sock drawer for a .38 special. *Resist,* Claudia. *Resist.*

"Listen," I say, extricating myself from his arms. "There's been a little incident this morning."

"Did we wet the bed?"

"Not that kind of incident. An angry-woman-bursts-into-room sort of incident."

He looks stunned. "Shit. Really?"

"Would I make this up?"

"How do I know?" he counters. "I hardly know you."

"Yes, well, ditto," I say. "And obviously, there's a few things I should have asked. Like, say, 'Are you married?'" I'm sitting up now, hugging my knees.

"Claudia," he reaches out to touch my wild nest of hair. "Shit. I'm really sorry." Not the oh-that-was-just-my-crazy-kid-sister explanation I was praying for.

I stare at him incredulously. "So you are, then? Married, I mean?"

"Well, divorced." He pauses. "Practically."

"What does *practically* divorced mean?"

"We're legally separated."

"Is she the Friend in the cottage?" He hesitates before nodding. "Jesus, Clay, you had like nine hours of candid conversation to come clean with me, at least let me know what I'm getting—"

"You never asked."

Indeed. What can I say? I never asked.

CHAPTER 8

It's foggy and I'm shivering when Clay drops me and Medea at the Greyhound station downtown. His truck was warm and smelled like cocoa butter. I wanted nothing more than to curl up there before his heater and never leave, but my pride forced me to refuse his offers of a sweatshirt and breakfast. On the drive here, our conversation was limited but revealing.

CLAY: I know this looks really bad.
CLAUDIA: Uh-huh.
CLAY: Really, really bad. I feel like such a shit.
CLAUDIA: Okay…
CLAY: Did you talk to her?
CLAUDIA: Who?
CLAY: Monica.
CLAUDIA: No. It wasn't exactly an ideal condition for conversation.
CLAY: I'm not in love with her anymore. I want you to understand that.
CLAUDIA: Right. You're just married to her.

CLAY: Not for very long.
CLAUDIA: And you didn't mention this earlier because…?
CLAY: I know, I know. This looks really bad.
(Repeat)

So here I am, sitting at the Greyhound station with two homeless guys bundled into blankets, one of them reading GQ. Suddenly I'm living the lyrics of every old-timey down-and-out blues number. I'm still wearing this positively crusty-with-human-grime ensemble: orange sundress, sweat-drenched bra, bloodstained underwear, and I've little hope of changing into something "fresher" (as my mother would say) anytime soon, seeing as I now own no other clothing. In fact, I now own absolutely nothing.

Oh, God. My favorite Levi's, reduced to ash. Sea-green cashmere sweater: ditto. Everything—no—I mean *everything* I ever called my own is now dwelling on another plane of existence.

I plod toward the ticket booth and realize I have no idea where I'm going. My original plan was to camp in the bus until I found a place to live—hopefully before school started. Now the bus is, for obvious reasons, not a reliable dwelling. So I've got to figure out where to crash until I can rent my own little shelter from the world. I tell myself this is all very Zen, very neo-Dharma bum and therefore cool (except I keep lugging my cat everywhere—did Kerouac do that?), but when I approach the glassed-in face of the ticket vendor and I look into her kind blue eyes, I find myself fighting off tears. I fumble for some dollars, pulling them from my bra, but they're so wrinkled and wilted I can't force them into any semblance of order.

"Morning," she says. "Where would you like to go?"

"Um."

She smiles. "Let's start with the basics—north, south, east or west?"

I manage a weak chuckle. "Give me a second," I say. "I'll be right back."

I sit down on one of the benches and mop at my tears with the back of my hand. I close my eyes and try to breathe. Medea squirms in her box. I open the flaps a crack. Her eyes are glow-in-the-dark as they peer up at me from within her shadowy little cardboard cage. "Shh," I say. "I'll get you a nice treat when we get home." Home.

"Excuse me," I say to the ticket lady. "Do you have any buses that go to Calistoga?"

She consults a thick directory. "Santa Rosa," she says. "Is that close enough?"

"I guess it'll have to be."

"One way or round trip?"

"One way, please."

"That'll be eleven dollars."

I hand her a limp twenty and she counts me out my change.

"You going to check out those mud baths?"

"God, no," I say. "Just going home."

Calistoga's only about three or four hours from Santa Cruz by car, but by bus it's a twelve-hour saga. I take the Greyhound to Santa Rosa, then another bus from there, and finally walk the last eight blocks to my father's house. By the time Medea and I arrive on his doorstep we're exhausted and snappish, having schlepped across three counties in raunchy-smelling clothes with a full cast of trying characters, including an ancient man in a wheelchair who, having mistaken me for his dead wife, wouldn't stop trying to hold my hand, and a wiry little elf of a bus driver who threatened to kick us off when he heard Medea mewing.

Over the course of the day I've developed a serious obsession with showering. That first blast of cool water on my chest, leaning in to soak my face, then my hair; the gentle massage of liquid needles against my scalp. The whole experience has become my nirvana—a longed-for state I can almost taste but never achieve.

It would have been quicker to go to Mom's in Mill Valley, but thinking of her latest husband and her spoiled, Britney Spears-clone stepdaughter makes me want to yuke, so I opt for Dad's.

"Claudia," my father says, opening the door. "You're— wow. You're here."

"Yeah. Sorry I didn't call." We just stand there awkwardly, surveying each other, and for an agonizing second I think he's not going to ask me in. Then, as if reading my thoughts, he steps back and gestures toward the living room a little too eagerly, like a waiter in an empty restaurant. "Come in, come in," he gushes. And then, his tone going puzzled again, "You're really here."

"Didn't you get my e-mail?"

He just looks confused. "Oh, you know me—I haven't really adjusted to all of this technology stuff."

"Dad, can I let Medea out? She's been in this stupid box all day."

"Who?"

But I'm already releasing the poor thing; she circles my legs, blinking into the light, looking a little crazed and disoriented. "My cat," I say, and sigh. "It's been a very long day." I say that a lot, lately.

He squints down at her as she rubs against his shin. "Hello, kitty," he says doubtfully. "What's her name?"

"Medea."

"Oh," he says, stiffly. "Hello, Maria."

And then he starts to sneeze. Five times. With increasing volume and violence. Jesus, what is it with men and cats? Clay's the only guy I ever met who didn't practically disintegrate in the face of a little cat fur. *No. Don't even think about Clay Parker.*

"Ah-ah-ah-allergic," my father manages to articulate between sneezes.

"Okay. I'm sorry. Um, can I put her in the guest room for

now? I'd put her out, but she's so disoriented I'm afraid she might wander off—"

"Garage," he says, yanking a handkerchief from his back pocket and sneezing some more. So off she goes, into the garage, mewing in protest until I fetch her a bit of tuna fish and a saucer of milk. I sit there with her for a while, playing absently with her tail and watching her eat, enveloped in the cool, cathedral-like stillness of my father's garage. As my eyes adjust to the shadows, I gaze around at the meticulously organized shelves and file cabinets, the worktable with tools hanging on hooks, arranged categorically: drills here, saws there. It occurs to me that these may even be alphabetized, which I find more than a little depressing. The air is scented not with the usual grease-and-grime smell of most people's garages, but with my father's favorite all-purpose cleaner for twenty years now: Pine-Sol. Parked in its usual place—dead center—is Dad's 1956 Dodge Plymouth convertible. It gleams with spotless pride in the dark, never having known a dirty day in its life.

I find Dad in the kitchen, cutting up celery. The house, like everything in my father's life, is so clean you could eat off any surface, including the tops of high cabinets and the icy-white linoleum floor. He bought a tract home soon after I moved to Austin—one of those creepy, cookie-cutter models that scream "No Imagination."

"So," he says, handing me a glass of milk with ice in it. I don't usually drink milk, but I sip politely, anyway. "How long are you here for?"

"You mean, here, at your house? Or…?"

"When do you go back to Texas?"

"Pop, listen. I got a job in Santa Cruz."

He smiles. He has very white teeth, perfectly straight; my mom says he was still wearing braces when they got married. "You've got a Santa Cruz in Texas? Isn't that funny. I guess all those saints really made the—"

"Santa Cruz. California, Dad. I got a job at the university."

He stops cutting celery and stares at me a moment through his horn-rimmed glasses. He's got very light blue eyes and a face that is harder to read than any face I've ever encountered. He goes back to slicing. "Are you serious?"

"Yes. Of course I'm serious." I drink more of my milk and try not to think about the report I read once about cows in America being so mistreated and diseased that they get loads of pus in the product. Eugh. I put the glass down.

"What about your boyfriend? Is he moving here, too?"

"What boyfriend?" I'm unable to stop myself from this perverse response. Something about his calm, measured slicing of celery and his luminous white tile countertops are getting on my nerves. I remember now why I've only seen my father five or six times in the past ten years.

"Jason, wasn't it?"

I shift my weight and look at the ceiling. "Jonathan. We broke up."

"Oh. I see." He nods at the celery in a cryptic fashion.

"Anyway," I say, dumping the rest of my milk in the sink as inconspicuously as I can, "I'm moving to Santa Cruz. I just need to get a car and a place to live." I stand there, staring at the ice cubes in the sink. I run the water so he won't see the milk I dumped out, and that makes me remember the bathing fantasy I've been fueled by all day. I want to cry with relief when I think of my father's hotel-sterile bathroom. "Can I take a shower?"

"Oh, sure, honey. Sure." He's more enthusiastic about this possibility than anything I've told him so far. "Extra towels in the hall closet." Oh, God. My father's white, fluffy, dryer-scented towels. I almost throw my arms around him in ecstasy. Then I remember that I don't have anything to change into, and the thought of putting this wretched outfit on yet again turns my stomach.

"You think I could borrow a T-shirt, maybe some shorts?"

He lets out a snort of awkward laughter. "Honey, where's your suitcase?"

"It's a really long story. Just—anything. Sweats, old jeans, whatever you've got."

"Well, okay. I'll see what I can find. They'll be in the guest room."

"Thanks, Pop." I walk over to him and, before I can get nervous or weird about it, kiss him on the cheek. "I really appreciate being able to come here."

"Oh," he says, smiling nervously, never taking his eyes from the celery. "Well." And then, when I'm walking down the hall to the bathroom, he calls to my back, "You know you're welcome, sweetie, anytime." I think he means it, but something about the effort in his voice makes me want to cry.

CHAPTER 9

To do:

1) Buy fantastic, sexy, dependable, movie-star-quality car for under three hundred dollars.
2) Do not think about Clay Parker. If absolutely must think of yurt experience, think of WIFE and add SELF at wrong end of .38 special.
3) Find adorable, sexy, movie-star-quality pad for under five hundred dollars.
4) When did I become a home-wrecker? Argh.
5) Join gym. Go to gym. Thighs look like molded Jell-O.
6) Make friends.
7) DO NOT THINK ABOUT HIM.
8) Transform self from hideous, kinky-haired, irresponsible car-thief home-wrecker into elegant, scarf-wearing professor. (Idea: highlights?)

For several days I use my father's house as the base of operations while I continuously flip-flop between wild bursts of effort to get my life together and bouts of total despondency, during which I lie flat on my back in the guest room, stuffing my face with Pringles and watching cheesy Hugh Grant videos. This manic-depressive stretch hardly fulfills my hopes of returning triumphantly to California and emerging like a phoenix from my troubled past.

I grew up here, in Calistoga, and coming home is like facing a firing squad of ghosts. I know loads of people are carrying around childhoods more miserable than mine—hell, most of my friends' horror stories make my family look like the Cleavers—but all the same, I get restless here, enmeshed in the world that formed me.

Luckily, my father doesn't live in the house I spent my first decade in anymore. Most of my worst associations are stuck there, in the idyllic little Victorian on Swan Street where we lived before my parents divorced. That house is where my parents fought their worst battles, almost always silent ones that went on for weeks at a time. They were both very good at refusing to speak to each other. I often felt like a modern-day sitcom character who finds herself in the midst of a silent film. The easiest way to explain their marriage is by cutting to the chase: they didn't love each other. Not in the days I can remember, anyway. And though my mother was in every cosmetic way the ideal housewife, she maintained an air of aloofness, an icy edge that, paired with my father's lack of communication skills, made my growing up years chilly and lonely.

Calistoga isn't a bad place to grow up, though it's pretty small and confining when you're a hormone-crazed teen. It's wedged between two smallish mountain ranges, one of several little tourist towns in Napa Valley that's beautiful and pristine and increasingly saddled with this "wine country" label, which attracts the most anal-retentive blue bloods in the country. Unlike a lot of other towns around here, Calistoga always maintains a kind of redneck Riviera not-quite-thereness, though, which I'm secretly glad about. The tourists who settle for our town are the ones who can't quite afford our posher neighbors, though we do our best to keep up appearances. We've got these natural hot springs and more spas than citizens; people flock here from Des Moines and Denver and God Knows Where to sit around in huge tubs of "volcanic ash" and scalding water, imagining that all the toxins they've been stuffing themselves with for fifty years will magically evaporate and they'll emerge like radiant infants. Truth is, half of the time the volcanic ash is really just garden-variety dirt, and once I even witnessed the use of cement.

I know more than I care to about the Calistoga spas—I've worked in just about all of them, though in the ten years I've been gone they've probably shuffled around a bit. When I was fourteen I started raking mud and fetching cucumber water for the needy, red-faced tourists. Within a few years I got some training and moved up to massage therapist; at seventeen I was the only girl I knew making twenty bucks an hour plus tips. It was a good enough gig. People treated you like a cross between a doctor and a prostitute, which I always found amusing.

Even though I was making good money there, Calistoga was destined to spit me out. When I was eighteen I started sleeping with a guy who owned a winery, two restaurants and a spa. Of course, he was married. Actually, his wife owned a winery, two restaurants and a spa, since he was a fading Calvin Klein underwear model who'd long since pissed away any money of his own on fast cars and coke. Anyway, we got caught up in this torrid affair and the whole town knew about it, since we had a terrible habit of driving around in his convertible Fiat, dismally shit-faced and out of sorts, yelling whatever popped into our heads at people on the streets and generally behaving in the most obnoxious and juvenile fashion possible. He should have known better, since he was twice my age, but then again I should have known better, too. My parents were too caught up in their own soap opera to offer me much guidance, which only inspired more recklessness on my part. I guess I thought if I really fucked up, they'd have to act like parents for once. It ended with his wife dragging him through a very brutal and highly public divorce, citing me as the major body of evidence against him. The town was electric with stone-throwing glee; I couldn't walk down the street without twelve-year-old girls whispering behind their fingers and smug, middle-aged mothers peering over their spectacles at me while their husbands leered. Scarlet Letter city. It was enough to drive a girl to Texas.

Why Texas, you're wondering? I had vague notions of cowboys and sweet tea and big skies that could shelter me from everyone I'd ever known. When you grow up in a pretentious tourist town you get tired of all the lattes and the carrot juice and the organic aromatherapy candles. Texas seemed like the antithesis of all that. So I drove to Austin, got a job at another spa, moved in with a gay law student I immediately fell in love with, and started taking acting classes at the community college. Before long, I was a full-fledged Texan. The only thing I really missed from back home was the ocean, which was a long, winding drive from Calistoga, anyway, so I told myself there was nothing that could draw me back.

Funny, how home works on a person, though. It stays in you, dormant for periods but still living, like a song you thought you'd forgotten until it springs from your radio one afternoon and fills you with a longing you never even knew was yours.

I'm not saying I've come back to California out of homesickness. My life is more random than that. I just found myself depressed and bored and jilted, eating way too many pints of Häagen-Dazs in the brutal Texas heat; I was ready for a change. A friend of a friend told me about a last-minute opening at UC Santa Cruz. I applied, and after a brief phone interview, they took me sight unseen, emphasizing that it was a one-year deal with only the remotest possibility of moving into tenure track. A salary was mentioned; I'd make in one year what I'd lived on for three in grad school. Like most of the things I've accomplished thus far, it happened without much effort, almost by accident. And now here I am, about to teach at a university with the giddy, giggle-suppressing nerves of someone who's been admitted to a private country club using a false ID.

The truth is, no university would have hired me with a paltry M.F.A. in directing (from the University of Texas, no less) if it weren't for one lucky break that's been haunting me for years. It was a lark, really. Ziv and I, up late one night and high on his espresso, made a movie. He was a recovering film major, and he still had some really expensive equipment. We just made up a character, Zelda Klein, and I improvised a nervous breakdown in our kitchen while baking a lemon meringue pie. We called it *Meringue, Meringue.* There's actually this really great part where I try to shove about twenty pairs of spiked heels down the garbage disposal. (You're wondering why in God's name I had twenty pairs of spiked heels on hand? Art project my friend Maxine did; she glued hundreds of spiked heels to this huge wooden cross. Afterward she gave me all the seven and a halfs, though none of them was comfortable enough to wear). We shot it all in black and white, which gave it this pseudodocumentary, grainy touch that accidentally made it really arty and vogue. Like we knew what we were doing.

But the real magic of *Meringue, Meringue* was this one sequence we shot right at the end, just as the sun was coming up. It was March and there was this storm starting up—a wild, warm Texas storm with wind that made you want to do something you'd later regret. Caught up in the moment, I ran outside, and Ziv followed, dragging his expensive camera equipment awkwardly. I stood on our porch, staring up at the swaying tree branches tinged with gray dawn; the wind caught hold of my cotton nightgown, pressing it flat against one leg and whipping it wildly away from the other, like a flag. There was a clothesline in the neighbor's yard with sheets and T-shirts flapping this way and that. It was the last moment of the film, and I have to admit it was beautiful. We couldn't have planned it; it was just the right light and the right wind and the right night-gown, the right laundry in the background. It was just—well—right. Sometimes you get lucky.

So I edited the film and added credits and sent it to Sundance—more on a whim than from any serious aspirations. Goddamn if it didn't win second place in the short-film category. Ziv and I were blown away. For years after I enjoyed this unspoken Girl Genius status at UT, and it was more than obvious to me that's why I got hired at UC Santa Cruz. *Meringue, Meringue* was an accidental coup, but it earned me more career points than anything I'd ever labored at.

But I digress. Today, I'm congratulating myself on actually having accomplished number one on my to-do list: buy car. Well, okay, it's not necessarily sexy, dependable or movie-star quality, and it did cost closer to seven than three, but it seems to run and there are no flames just yet, so I'm feeling fairly smug. Beaming behind the wheel of my very own 1964 acid-green Volvo, I imagine I look very retro and Euro-chic. I bought it off a Swedish architect who had to leave the U.S. abruptly for a new job in Singapore. He also unloaded an ancient laptop, four ferns and a stainless-steel teakettle in the process. Frankly, the whole transaction was highway robbery on my part, but I figured maybe the gods were trying to make up for my first two days back in California. Conflagration, calamari and sizzling sexual exploits aside, my return to California's been pretty brutal, so far.

But today is promising. The air is unseasonably cool, having been moistened by morning fog. I've got a mocha in a paper cup perched precariously between my thighs, and I'm heading south on Highway 1, letting the wind whip my hair into a hectic bird's nest. I feel good.

There's just one little problem with my buoyant mood: it's making me cocky. As I get closer and closer to Santa Cruz, I can't keep my slutty, disobedient brain from making a beeline for Clay Parker. I feel his teeth closing around my bottom lip, hear my sharp intake of breath. I can taste the sweet dribble of peach juice I licked from his thumb at the farmer's market, smell the incense and hear the insistent racket of hippies playing bongos.

And now is not the time to be thinking of Clay Parker. Now is starting-new-job-in-six-days-better-get-ass-in-gear-and-find-apartment time. Nay, starting new *career* in six days. Oh, Jesus. Can you order lesson plans from Amazon?

I turn up the radio louder (okay, there's no car radio, but I've commandeered my father's petite yet powerful boom box, which is now riding shotgun and blasting Ani Di-Franco—the momentary rebellion of some pierced DJ, no doubt, so sick of the prescribed playlist she's gone mad). This is when I love California: the sun is too low yet to be treacherous, the sky is a delicate blue, and twists of fog are nestling in the creases between hills. On my right, the ocean is undulating; her vast green expanse sparkles with gold specks, and the waves hit the beige stretches of beach in fits of white foam. The blond grass that covers every surface is giving off a wet, wheaty smell and a bad-girl bisexual has commandeered the airwaves.

Maybe I really have come home.

Day six of grueling apartment hunting yields results: I find a place I can unapologetically refer to as a flat. In case you haven't noticed, I'm a total Anglophile; I long to say "bloody hell" and "knickers" and "sod it" with all the cool reserve of Helen Bonham Carter, but of course each of these phrases sounds stilted and absurd in my American accent. I have managed, on occasion, to pull off "shag." It's one of my favorites, so I just can't resist. It sounds so much hipper than our American options: "screw" is so pedestrian, "bang" is way too aggressive, "hump" is for fourth-graders. God knows, I'd never use the gooey mess of a phrase "make love" without feeling like a cheesy seventies tune. I mean "fuck" has its own poetry, since it's all hard angles and no backing down, but it has no warmth, and could never have the cozy yet unsentimental, offbeat appeal of "shag."

Anyway, the little studio I just put a deposit on is definitely a flat, and so this gives me an excuse to become one syllable more British. The rent is almost reasonable—okay, *not* under five hundred (forgive me, to-do list), but I had to be flexible and double it. I suspect the landlord is fortunately unaware of just how slick and trendy the place is. It's an upstairs unit in an old brick building downtown. It's above a hair salon, and the smell of perms *does* seep through the floorboards, but not in a terribly noxious way. Speaking of floorboards, that was a major selling point: after all the hideous brown shag and orange linoleum I'd looked at for four days, these hardwood floors, freshly buffed and sweetly golden, took my breath away. In short, it is precisely the right place for a bohemian, scarf-wearing professor to dwell. As soon as I become that bohemian, scarf-wearing professor, it'll be perfect for me.

CHAPTER 10

Things I presently own:
1) Adorable 1964 Volvo. Green.
2) One laptop computer from Swede. Very sleek, but have not yet managed to turn it on.
3) Hand-me-down futon from Dad. Smells like Pine-Sol.
4) One pair of shorts from Goodwill. A little tight. Discard after first paycheck.
5) Three T-shirts borrowed from Dad. Burn horrifying Nascar shirt after first paycheck.
6) Four Swedish ferns. Dying.
7) One stainless-steel teakettle. Perfect.

Thursday afternoon I move my precious possessions into my lovely little flat and survey the results. I tell myself the effect is wonderfully spare and chic, with that glam-Zen minimalism so many urban hair salons strive for. I don't quite buy this, but I tell myself I do.

As the sun starts to glow orange in my western windows,

I make up my mind to go for a walk. For a week now I've been so completely consumed with the hunt for a car and a home that I haven't had much time to stroll around aimlessly. It feels good to get the sidewalk moving beneath me and to breathe in the greasy perfume drifting inland from the burger joint down the street. The heat of the afternoon is giving way to the cool evening chill sliding off the Pacific. A wayward branch from an apple tree is hanging over the sidewalk; I look around, pluck a nice green one and munch as I stroll.

I meander past the shops on Pacific Avenue, peering into each window: a bookstore, used clothing, a surf shop. And God—oh, Jesus, a music store: *Viva Vinyl*. The glass door is propped into a wide-open position. It's held in place with a terra-cotta pot filled with cement, sprouting a tall, iron-stemmed LP with the words Come In splashed recklessly across the glossy black surface in red paint.

Come in.

Don't. Go. In.

Maybe I should go home and change. Except I haven't got anything to change into, and I won't until my next paycheck.

It might not be his—I mean, come on, what are the chances?

He said his store was downtown. He specializes in vinyl.

Yeah, but this is Santa Cruz—college town, hipsterville. There must a record store on every block.

Do. Not. Enter.

My feet are real fuckups. They operate independently, like little rogue states, and yet it's the rest of me who's got to face the consequences.

The store is deserted. It's filled with a dusty, warm attic smell. There's a wall of decorative vintage guitars on display toward the back; I scoot past the rows of records and CDs to stare up at them. They remind me of dead butterflies pinned under glass: beautiful, perfectly preserved, but eerie when they're so still.

"Can I help you find something?"

I spin around and there he is, barely two feet from me. His question reverbs off the walls of my mind. Can he help me find something? What am I looking for?

Of course I've thought about this moment. In a town the size of Santa Cruz, running into him was inevitable—I knew that. I'd planned a cold shoulder: aloof, busy, pleasantly cruel. I wasn't going to get caught up. Now I bite my lip shyly and say, "I'm just looking, thanks," with all the coolness of a starry-eyed groupie dying for an autograph.

"Claudia Bloom," he half whispers. I see him swallow, and he folds his arms across his chest, pins his hands in his armpits. We stand there, staring at each other for a dizzy five seconds, until an astonishingly fat woman and her three kids come barreling through the door in search of *The Little Mermaid* soundtrack. I gnaw on my apple and flip through the bluegrass section aimlessly, trying not to be nervous.

Why am *I* nervous? He's the one with the wife. I flash on a memory of myself digging frantically under his covers, trying to locate my panties amid the tangle of sheets and watching the door for his gun-toting wife at the same time.

After they leave, a thick silence falls over the store like snow.

"I was just about to close," he says finally.

"Oh, okay—sorry I'll get—"

"No." He laughs. "I mean, you know. Do you mind if I lock the door?"

"With me on this side of it?"

"Exactly. If you don't mind." Oh, God. He's just so damn *attractive.* There's some sort of heat coming off him, I swear. An image of our bodies braiding together and tumbling to the floor flashes through my mind. Brain, do not *think* like that. He's waiting for an answer. Scoot out the door. Plan of cold, disinterested shoulder is not happening. Abort. Abort.

"Okay. I mean, sure," I say.

I watch as he walks to the door (that butt—it slays me), moves the flowerpot inside and turns the key in the lock. "So," he says, coming back to the bluegrass section, where I'm nervously teething on my apple (the thought of actually eating it now seems repugnant, but the tough skin is comforting between my teeth). "I wasn't sure I'd see you again."

I force myself to stop gnawing on the apple and shrug. "Small town, I guess."

He nods. We both start to say something at once; we stop, laugh, start again, interrupting each other once more. "Go ahead," he says. "I didn't mean to—"

"Nothing—no, I was..." I've totally forgotten what I was going to say. "G-go ahead," I stammer. "You go first." *Claudia, you've got a terminal degree, for Christ's sake—can't you do better than this? This is thirteen-year-old girl waiting for an invitation to ice cream social, okay? This is not scarf-wearing queen of intellect.* That reminds me: must buy scarf.

"Um...I'm just really embarrassed," he says. "About what happened last week. You know? It looked really bad and everyone was put in an awkward spot and I just...I'd like a chance to explain."

"Okay..."

"Well, do you want to talk here or...are you hungry?" He nods at the apple. "Is that your dinner?"

I smile. "Sort of. Yeah, well, I've been pretty busy—I guess I am a little bit hungry. Except..." I glance down at the too-tight Goodwill shorts I've been wearing for days and my father's ancient, grease-spotted Calistoga High T-shirt. Did I even comb my hair today? "It can't be anyplace even remotely nice."

"Why—what do you mean?"

"Look at me, Clay. I'm a mess."

He lets his eyes wander on a long, slow trip down my body; I start to blush furiously. By the time he's looking at my face again, I feel like an overheated tomato. "You look great," he says, an impish glee in his eyes.

"Well, whatever," I reply. "Maybe there's a taco joint or something?"

"Mmm, there's a great place just a few blocks from here. Best carne asada you ever had in your life."

We get five minutes into Operation Chance to Explain and things are going all right, even if I am more shy pubescent than icy sophisticate. He's messing with the cash register and gathering up his things and every move he makes telegraphs that he's infected with precisely the same prom-night jitters I've got. Bizarre. Here we are, full-grown adults (how old is he, anyway? Twenty-seven? Thirty-seven? I have no idea), and we're bumping into things and forming incomplete sentences at the prospect of going out for tacos.

Then the phone rings. He gives it a blank stare. It continues its soft electronic bleating twice before he says, "Let's let the answering machine get it," and reaches for his coat. On the fourth ring the machine picks up and something deep in the pit of my stomach knows who it'll be.

"Hi, Clay? You there? Pick up, okay? It's Monica." Long, poisonous pause. Clay hovers near the phone but does not touch it. "I need to talk to you." There's a quick sniffle. "Clay, please. I really need to talk."

Clay snaps the phone up. "Hi," he says softly. "What's up?" I walk away from him, feeling strangely numb. Seconds ago, I was struggling against the heat in my blood just looking at him, and now there's ice water in my veins. I try the door, but it's locked. I lean my forehead against the glass and will myself not to listen, but his words float across the small shop to my ears. "I know…it's not easy for me—don't say it's…I just mean I've had my rough days, too, you know? Okay… no, I was just closing up."

After he puts the phone down he stands there a couple of seconds; I stay perfectly still, waiting for a cue, wishing the door was unlocked so I could just slip outside and let the air clear my head.

"That was Monica," he says, and his voice seems very far away. "My, um, wife. Except she's not really—we're not really…anyway, she's having a rough day. It happens."

"Of course," I whisper, still not turning around.

"What?"

I turn and face him. "Yes. Okay."

"Claudia…" He takes a couple of steps in my direction, but I stop him with my voice.

"Obviously, you're busy—"

"I wanted to see you. I wanted to explain—"

I laugh, but it's not a pleasant sound. "I don't think there's anything to explain."

"The situation's complicated, okay? I'm not trying to lie to anyone."

"Married is married," I say. "Divorced is divorced." Finally, my voice has all the icy conviction I'd dreamed it might. Where's this moral fervor coming from? How many times have I slept with married men—guys I didn't even care about? "I think this whole thing is just—" the word is slow in coming, because it's not one I ever use "—wrong."

I try the door again, ruining my little speech with a futile shove. "Can you please unlock this?"

"No."

"No?"

"I want to explain to you where I'm coming from."

I lean my forehead against the glass, suddenly tired, and say, "Please. Just unlock it, okay?"

He crosses the room and I give him plenty of space. Proximity is dangerous right now. Already I can feel the sick emptiness brought on by the phone call giving way to an urgent need to smell his skin. Once he's got the door unlocked, he turns to me again. "I wish I could just tell you how hard this is," he begins, but he interrupts himself in alarm. "God, your face is *white*—are you okay?"

"Yeah," I say tersely. "I'm fine."

"Do you feel sick? You're really pale." He moves closer, and I back up.

"Look, don't worry about me, okay? You've got a wife who obviously wants you back. I just don't understand why you had to drag me—a total stranger—into your little domestic mess." My voice rises on the last two words and my lower lip trembles slightly; I need to get the hell out while I can. One problem: he's in front of the door.

He's staring at me with a stunned expression, and then he gets a hold of himself and steps out of my way. "You're right. I'm sorry."

"Yeah, me, too," I mumble, and bolt.

That night, lying on my Pine-Sol-scented futon, watching as the occasional headlight sweeps ghostly shapes across my cracked ceiling, I think about Clay Parker. I think about his hands and the almost imperceptible half-moon scar on his left cheek. I immerse myself in elaborate recollections of his tongue sweeping across my clavicle; I play that moment over and over, like I used to do with my *Saturday Night Fever* 45, never tiring of the repetition.

I'm so paralyzed. I can't pursue the guy with his desperate, grieving wife trailing after us all the time. And yet I can't stop thinking about him: his gentle laughter, his easy way with cats, the dad who hit him and the mom who loves him more than anyone.

I think of our Freaks and Treats Tour, how exhilarated and young I felt. The roller coaster at the Boardwalk made my stomach drop in the same delicious, terrifying way it does now when I replay his tongue on my clavicle.

Infatuation. What a country.

It's not just that he's married. That's part of it, yes, but there's something else I can't quite put my finger on.

God knows I've had affairs with married men. It never

really bothered me before—at least, I told myself it didn't. There was the fading underwear model in Calistoga, then Roger, a fellow massage slut at Lake Austin Spa. He kept trying to "release my tantric energy," which meant I had to lie there forever while he performed the worst cunnilingus I've ever experienced. There was Jerry Moss, the professor with the Tom Waits voice. That one nagged at my conscience, not because he was married, but because it was the only time I'd ever cheated on someone myself.

That was how I rationalized it: in all but one case, they were the ones breaking their vows, not me. Cheating on Jonathan with Jerry was the only time in my vast decade of tartery that I actually betrayed someone's trust. I have a peculiar moral code, yes, but I do have one. I told myself that the institution of marriage was, in itself, a scam, so it's hard to get sentimentally attached to other people's vows. It's like asking a Marxist to give a shit when a capitalist goes bankrupt.

This time, with Clay, everything's different. It's quite sickening, really. I think about the moments before his wife burst through the door with all that sunlight behind her, when he and Medea and Sandy and I were all lying there peacefully, listening to crows cawing outside, watching dawn turn the windows and the skylight an electric blue. I wanted that moment. I wanted to keep it, live inside it again and again. And now I see somebody's gotten there first.

I guess when you don't really want the whole person, when you just want to borrow him for an illicit afternoon or two, an affair is easy. You never meet the woman you've borrowed him from and you forget about him soon enough, caught up in the next fleeting pleasure.

But when you really want him—or at least a chance to try him out—things change. You find yourself stammering incoherent, guilt-tainted speeches in record stores and shoving at doors you know are locked.

You find yourself studying the shadows on your ceiling, wishing he was studying them with you.

Oh. Bourgeois coupling crap. Good God, what have I gotten myself into?

CHAPTER 11

The first day of school should be outlawed. It's late September, the peak of a California Indian summer, and the earth is about to crack open, it's so parched and overheated. Of course, Texas wasn't exactly a mild climate, either, but at least there I was a student and, since students are granted permanent adolescent status, was therefore expected to show up in tattered cutoffs and slinky tank tops or tiny sundresses that left vast expanses of skin exposed—uniforms that eased the discomfort of stuffy confinement in idea-filled rooms. God, I miss being a student. Today it takes me well over an hour to get dressed, despite the fact that my wardrobe contains exactly six frantically purchased items to choose from. By the time I walk out the door, I've spent so much time with an old, melted eyeliner trying to add sophistication to my ill-fitting secondhand skirt-and-blouse ensemble that I look like a cross between Mary Poppins and Courtney Love.

Approaching my office, keys in hand, the crisis in confidence brought on by my sucky outfit gives way to a moment of speechless awe. There, printed in block letters across the glass panel on my office door is something I hadn't anticipated: C. BLOOM. Right there, in plain sight. I've officially become official. I no longer skulk about in the hallways or set up camp in library nooks like all the nomadic students wandering here and there, looking lost and abandoned. No. My ship has a port, my port a name, and that name is C. BLOOM, Theater Arts Professor.

I stand there for a long moment, gazing at the letters. Then I reach out and trace the *C* with one finger, half afraid that it will smudge away under my touch.

"It's a trip, huh?"

I turn to see a woman with dark hair and medieval eyes watching me. She looks about forty; she's wearing a red wraparound skirt and a black T-shirt that says Runs with Scissors on it. "You must be Claudia," she says, reaching out to shake hands.

"Yes."

"I'm Mare Marquez. I teach dance. First time I saw my name on a door I couldn't decide whether to cry with happiness or run the other way."

I smile. I like this chick. She's got turquoise rings on every finger and she looks like she's never worn lipstick in her life. Her cheekbones are high, and her skin is the color of summer spent on beaches eating fresh fruit with brown fingers. "So which did you do?" I ask.

She laughs. "Neither. I just got out my keys and acted like I was born with my name on doors."

"Good advice," I say, and try my key. Miraculously, I choose the right one and it slides right in. "Hey. So far so good."

"My office is down the hall, if you need anything," she says. "Welcome."

"Thanks."

I slip inside and look around at the bare bookcases, the beige phone, the corkboard sprouting an assortment of brightly colored pushpins. I pull up the blinds and sunlight floods my wood-veneer desk and the sleek black computer. "So far so good," I repeat in a whisper.

I pull out my roster and look at the names for my first class: Beginning Acting. Looks like an okay group. Couple of Brittanys, a Miranda, one Misty Waters (yikes), a handful of Waspy-sounding boys. Let's see…class doesn't start until ten-thirty. I've still got twenty minutes—plenty of time to figure out a lesson plan. I'll just quickly check my e-mail, then get right to it.

TO: Claudia Bloom
FROM: Ziv Ackerman
SUBJECT: ccccclllllaaaaauuuuudddddiiiiiaaaaa.
Oh, my God, dollface, I'm lost without you. Can't believe stupid X (refuse to record despicable name here) forced you back to California—I blame everything on that prick. Now my apartment is barren, my outlook manic on good days, Kafka-esque otherwise. The refrigerator is so horrifyingly bachelory; none of your precious little curries or Trader Joe treats in there.

To top it off, new roomie moves in tomorrow, and he's one hundred percent testosterone. I swear he eats boys like me for breakfast, washes us down with a swill of battery acid. He's Transylvanian; his accent sends chills down my spine. Okay, okay, you know me too well—yes, he does look a little like Jude Law (okay, he's a dead ringer—yum), but that doesn't mean I'm going to put up with little hairs on the bathroom sink. It'll either be a total nightmare or a dream come true. Any predictions, my Bloomie?

How I miss you. Tell me California's crumbling into the sea, and you're on your way back home to our little Texas nest. Mr. Transylvanian Jude Law is so out of here, I swear.

Ciao, my Chica,
Ziv

Ah, Ziv. A soft, weepy sigh escapes me before I can stop it. Remember how I told you about the law student I moved in with and subsequently fell for when I got to Texas? That's Ziv. He's very sexy in a Johnny Depp, pierced-nipple, can talk about Nabokov until three in the morning sort of way. Lucky for me, he hasn't slept with a girl since prom night back in Chattanooga, and so we became best friends. After Jonathan moved to New York with Rain, I limped back to my old room at Ziv's—a drafty little hovel I hadn't lived in for years. I only stayed there about four months, but it was precisely the right place to nurse my torn heart and battered ego. Ziv can dish on enemies with an almost pathological fervor; he also doesn't tolerate moping beyond a set statute of limitations (about four minutes). At that point he scoops you up, pours his rich, velvety espresso down your throat and then he drags you off to glamorous bars where he magically convinces the hunkiest men on the premises to flirt with you until you feel you can go on.

Staring at the screen, I feel a distinct pang of homesickness, thinking of the quirky little apartment we shared on and off during my decade in Austin. I remember the sound of the train from my window, the glass-and-marble shower, the wicked, bitter tricks he and I planned to play on Jonathan—pranks we'd never really try, but oh how we savored our plots. Once we spent two hours detailing how we'd humiliate him at the premiere of his new play: we dreamed up everything from Ex-Lax in his cocktails to announcements over the loudspeaker of his most intimate measurements. Everything about life with Ziv suddenly seems golden: the sound of his espresso machine whirring to life in the morning, his appearance on the edge of my bed, serving me delicate little eggshell-size cups full of deep, dark magic, his eyes already gleaming with the buzz from his first double of the day.

I hit Reply and let my fingers fly across the keyboard.

TO: Ziv Ackerman
FROM: Claudia Bloom
SUBJECT: Man, you don't even know...
...how much I miss you. So far I've managed to incinerate X's
bus, become hopelessly entangled with a yurt-dwelling sex
machine (married—help—murderous wife still attached at
the hip) and am on the verge of losing my job as we speak
due to hopelessly frumpy fashion funk. Ziiiiiv. Where is my
life? Now am desperately trying to pull off teacher thing and
have zero idea how to proceed. Please advise.

My eyes wander down the screen dreamily; when I notice the numbers there, they set off a screeching siren of
alarm in my brain. Oh, my God. Ten forty-three? How?
How did that—?

Happen. Jesus. Okay, breathe. Where is class? Grab roster,
paper, pen (teachers always have paper and pen, right?).
No—wait. Grab snazzy fake-leather binder with notepad
given to self at new-faculty orientation. There. Much better. Now: bag, pencil, coffee cup, um...should have syllabus,
but no one really has those on the first day, do they? Think,
Claudia, think: will create effortless and convincing excuse
about missing syllabus, or better yet, not mention at all and
let them think this is How We Do Things in College. Lipstick? No time. Will get all over teeth. Hair poofing out in
back? Hell, it is. Oh, well, just don't turn around. Never want
students looking at ass, anyway.

I sprint down the hall and turn a corner at breakneck
speed. Looking for room 812...let's see...690...692...turn
another corner, still running, and *whack*. Sudden impact:
coffee explodes, snazzy fake-leather binder propels across
hall, scattering rosters in all directions. Looking up, I see a
small, dark-haired woman recovering her balance, and I
realize I've fallen flat on my ass. *Get up, Claudia. Christ.* I
scramble to my feet and a burst of ridiculous, self-conscious
laughter erupts from my throat; when I see the look on the

woman's face I ineptly disguise my nervous giggles as a coughing fit. She's got a handkerchief out now and she's violently jabbing at the fist-size splotch of coffee spread amoebalike across the breast of her snow-white blouse.

"I am *so* sorry—I didn't even see you," I stammer, hovering awkwardly as she continues to scowl and scrub at the stain. "Can I help? Do you need some water or something?"

"It's not coming out—I think I'm burned."

"Burned. Ohhh. I'm such an idiot. Listen, let me help—do you need some ice?"

"Forget it," she says. "Just—forget it." She stands there in her crisp, formerly perfect outfit: navy blue skirt, neutral stockings, suede pumps, freshly ironed blouse, her dark hair impeccably smooth and silky; the stain looks so out of place, it has the same childishly comic effect as a mustache drawn on a supermodel. I stifle another giggle.

She studies me for a moment. Surprise, recognition, and then—what? Irritation? Rage? They all register in her eyes in rapid succession. She strides away from me abruptly, as if it's my face, not my coffee, that's burned her.

Weird, I think. Well, shit, she can hardly hate me just for bumping into her, whoever she is. Hopefully she's a traveling book rep and I'll never see her again. I look at my watch. Aargh—10:50. I'll be fired.

Please, *please,* God—I'll never ask for anything again—just let me get through this day.

Striding into the black-box theater, I force my face into a semblance of confidence. The chattering gives way to a deafening silence, and I feel fifty eyes on me, inducing a powerful sense of vertigo.

"Hello, class. My name's Claudia Bloom. Any questions?" Delete. Delete. You're supposed to actually *teach* something before you ask for—wait. Someone's got a hand up. Okay, here we go; this is easy. A girl sporting a wild tuft of indigo hair is looking at me with cranky indolence. "Yes?"

"Wasn't this class supposed to start, like, half an hour ago?"

"Every day but the first day." Twenty-five bewildered faces look at one another skeptically. "Acting is all about waiting. Timing. Patience tempered by instinct. It's about grueling hours spent hovering between worlds. You people—you're the ones who stuck it out. I like to know who my hard-core actors are, right from the get-go. I can really only focus on a select few."

"Half the class left already," a boy in overalls offers. "Some of them went to Westby's office."

"You see. You think they're going to make it? Huh? If they can't stand a measly twenty-something minutes waiting for their instructor, you think they're going to tough it out when their agent hasn't called in months? You think they'll have the stamina for those long hours of nervous fidgeting when they've got a couple lines in act one, scene one, and they don't have their big deathbed soliloquy until act three, scene four? If they have to go running to the dean's office whenever things don't go precisely as planned, you think they'll tolerate the wild, passionate life of the thespian and all of its incumbent bull—"

"Oh, Claudia." I spin around and Ruth Westby, the department chair, is watching me from the doorway. "You *are* here."

"Yes. Of course I am," I answer innocently.

A bony, middle-aged woman in enormous pink glasses files in with a handful of disgruntled others in tow. "Well, she *wasn't* here," the woman tells Ruth. "She must have just—"

"It's fine, Ruth," I say. "It's an exercise I like to do on the first day. Nothing to worry about."

She hesitates for a second; her dark eyes linger on my face, and I feel my stomach knotting up painfully. Then she nods and smiles pleasantly. "Happy first day, then."

She disappears. And suddenly it's just me. And them. With

no lesson plan. The woman in pink glasses is staring me down like a babysitter who just watched her ward tell a bald-faced lie to the clueless mother. "All right, then. Let's see. Why don't we start by learning each other's names?"

"Where's the syllabus?" Pink Glasses asks.

"Syllabus?"

"Yeah. You know. Piece of paper. Says what we can expect, how to get an A, all that. Frankly, I'm just shopping around."

"I see." There's an awkward moment of silence. I clear my throat. "Well, frankly, I don't offer a syllabus until after the first week. So, as I was saying—"

"Why not?" Pink Glasses again. She reminds me of a praying mantis, folded at hard angles into the too-small chair. Her real eyebrows have been completely plucked, and she's painted new ones into high arches above the rims of her glasses, Wicked Witch style; she would be terrifying if she weren't so annoying.

"Tell me your name, please," I say in my coolest, most collegiate tone.

"Ralene Tippets."

"Well, Ralene, I don't want to call this an *audition*, precisely, but I need to know who's serious before I commit. You understand? Once I know who's staying, I'll hand out a syllabus."

"That's not even legal," she says. "You can't discriminate."

"I'm talking about a series of exercises, Ralene. A get to know you week, during which we will determine who is serious and who is not. You're shopping around for classes. I'm shopping around for students. I think that's fair, don't you?"

"It might be fair, but it's not *legal*," she scoffs, looking around her for support. The others are noncommittal; they study their fingernails or keep their eyes on me obediently.

"Okay," I say agreeably. "So phone the police."

Her spidery eyebrows arch halfway to her hairline, but she shuts up.

"Now then," I say. "Anyone care to review what we've covered so far?"

Tuft of Indigo raises her hand. "Yes?" I smile. "Go ahead."

"You were just telling us how the losers who went running to Westby were never going to make it."

By four o'clock I've got a screaming headache. I know I should go to the health club I picked out in the yellow pages and get a membership, then swim laps and end the day deliciously sweating to death in the steam room, but any activity involving human interaction sounds positively impossible. I can't bear the thought of nodding politely while some beefy guy in spandex shows me how the treadmill works. Medea's the only living creature I can deal with right now. I'm so sick of smiling and saying, "Nice to meet you," and forgetting everyone's names and standing in front of rooms filled with hot, grumpy, sticky people. Oh, man. I just want silence and the cool, fizzy comfort of a vodka tonic.

All day I've gotten the distinct impression that I'm the straggly little mutt among purebred poodles. Most of the other professors are approximately twice my age and are making gallant attempts to take me seriously. I think most of them were fighting the urge to pat my head. My students, it would seem, are undergoing a more delicate process of suspicion tempered by a desire to please. I'll need to perfect a few clever teacherly tricks to get through the week—like learning to dash off cryptic, alarmingly intelligent phrases on the blackboard, or how to lean casually against the podium without sending it smashing to the floor like I did today.

On my way home, I drive past the Owl Club, and there's Clay's bike parked at the curb. No, Claudia. Do not…

I pull over to the curb, park and, taking a deep breath, head for the bar, where Clay is seated.

"Hi," I say, climbing up on the stool beside him. "Didn't know you were a regular."

He smiles. God, that yummy, crooked grin. If only I could capture that look in a bottle, dab a little behind my knees when I need a pick-me-up. "Don't go spreading that around town." He checks to make sure the bartender's not listening, then leans in closer. "The regulars here spend holidays on the psych ward."

"Then I'm in good company," I say. "After today, electric shock sounds soothing."

"That's right. First day at school, wasn't it?"

"Yeah." I'm a little surprised. "How did you know?"

He shrugs, downs a swig of beer. "I just do," he says. Weird. "I bet you blew them all away. If I'd had teachers like you, I never would have dropped out."

"Ha."

"What does that mean?" He catches the bartender's eye. "Mikey, can we have a vodka tonic over here? Actually, make that a double Absolut tonic with extra lime. And another Heineken." He turns back to me. "Seriously, I bet you're fantastic in the classroom."

"You want to know a secret?" He nods. I drop to a whisper. "Dude. I have no fucking idea what I'm doing."

He laughs. It's a big, full-bodied laugh that puts me at ease with its generosity. It's the kind of laugh you want to hear every day. "You see? Any prof who's willing to admit that is already a thousand times cooler than most."

It's 3:00 a.m. and Clay Parker is branding the pale, smooth skin of my inner thighs with a crisscrossing trail of kisses. His lips are hot, and I imagine, a little drunkenly, that I'll awake with tiny, mouth-shaped burns in the morning. Everything before this moment is a blur: C. BLOOM on my office door, the stick-insect woman in pink glasses, me balancing precariously on a stool at the Owl Club, drinking Absolut from a lipstick-smudged highball. It all dissolves like swirls of smoke, leaving only Clay's hands pressing my knees wide, his head bending again and again with each kiss in a series of slow, reverent bows, like a holy man in the midst of prayer.

The room spins slightly as headlights slice through the blinds and dance across the walls in a dizzy web of moving shadows. I'd like to stay here forever, trapped in the heat of our bodies, encased in this dark room, the occasional rumble of a passing car our only reminder that we're not the last human beings on earth. Clay hovers over me, tastes my mouth like he's sampling a rare, exotic fruit. Every kiss, every touch, is infused with the concentration of a blind man. He's studying me. His hands are mapping out my curves, his fingers memorizing the places where my bones jut out, where little dips form shadows, where the flesh is swollen and ripe.

"Please," I say into his ear, cupping his hips and pulling him toward me. "I want you inside me." But he hesitates, lingering, denying us both. Then he works his way back down my body, and I lose myself in the moist world he opens with his tongue: a shuddering explosion of water-muted colors, like fireworks set off on the ocean floor.

CHAPTER 12

Once, when I was very altered on Texas slammers and Mexican weed, I wrote the *Tart Manifesto*. I was twenty-two and in love with myself which, apart from being intensely obnoxious for others, isn't a bad state. I didn't save it; the three pages of largely illegible, drool-stained rantings were way too incriminating. But I do remember the first line: *The dedicated Tart always seizes the day: never put off sex or dessert.*

Not exactly something I'd silkscreen on a T-shirt, but at the time it seemed profound.

This philosophy started taking shape back in high school, when it seemed the rest of the world was in on a secret I'd been excluded from. At sixteen, I was tired of go-nowhere make-out sessions and decided to trade in my virginity for something of real value: experience. My cousin Rosemarie was almost two years younger than me, but she'd had sex twice already in the back of her boyfriend's rusty old Cadillac, so I was in a hurry to catch up. She said it wasn't anything like the movies made it out to be—there was no slow-mo, no searing-hot sound track. According to her, it was all propaganda. "Once you do it, you'll wonder what the big deal is," she'd said. "I was still waiting for it to get good, and then it was over."

Rosemarie was right about most things, but I needed to find out for myself. I checked out candidates for months. I wanted someone who'd know what he was doing, but would also be discreet, and not go bragging about it to the Neanderthals in the locker room. Not that I minded people knowing, necessarily; I just wanted to do the telling. I hated the thought of unworthy punks taking my rite of passage and turning it into their poorly scripted jerk-off fantasies.

I decided on Enzo Belluomini, the Italian exchange student. His skin was a little pockmarked with acne, but other than that he was a lovely candidate. He had espresso-dark eyes, wore the most fantastic, Euro-chic sweaters, and when he was tired he often slipped into Italian, as if his brain were a radio station picking up a distant frequency. I chose him because I wasn't in the slightest danger of falling in love, and he was grateful without being sloppy or sentimental. It worked out well; he did, as luck would have it, know quite a lot about sex—at least the mechanics of it. He'd been seduced by his sister-in-law back in Rome, and they'd been indulging themselves while his brother was away on business for several years. That was why his parents were so eager to send him abroad; if the brother ever found out, it was likely there'd be bloodshed. This story excited me more than a little, and I'd have him narrate the whole tale again, in Italian, while we made it in my father's basement. Even now, hearing Italian or finding myself in the dank, cement-and-boxes smell of someone's basement gets me aroused.

But in general, Rose was right—sex wasn't the all-powerful, magical drug we'd imagined. It was, like anything else, something you had to get good at. You had to learn what made your pulse quicken, and then you had to figure out a way to communicate that, usually without words, so you didn't insult the guy or kill the mood, or come off as pushy.

It was a complicated, subtle language, and even after fourteen years of practice, I wasn't sure of my fluency.

Except with Clay, sex is something else. It's not about guarding his pride, or mine, or sending secret messages. I don't lie there wondering how my body measures up to the airbrushed porn of his fantasies. The two nights I've spent with him have taught me more than all my years of one-night stands combined. With Clay Parker, I don't have anything to prove; it's not an audition, or a performance. It's effortless. I feel his hands on me, his mouth searching my body, and then I'm far above the earth, looking down at the small, remote world, and it's not vertigo that makes me gasp, but joy.

Monday, week two: I'm having a bout of morning confidence. The caffeine buzz is coming along nicely, and I'm wearing my new sky-blue skirt with a cute T-shirt and adorable patent-leather shoes. Over the weekend I broke out the credit card long enough to score a couple of passably decent outfits. I usually avoid credit cards—the massive debt of my early twenties saddled me with a real phobia—but I've got a grown-up job now, so I deserve a little indulgence.

Turning the corner toward my office, clutching a Java House mocha in one hand and half a bagel in the other, I see something that makes me stop so abruptly a splash of mocha leaps right through the tiny hole in the plastic lid and onto my white T-shirt. I stifle the "shit" that springs to my lips and scurry back around the corner. Leaning my back against the wall, I fight the urge to hyperventilate.

It's okay, I tell myself. *He hasn't seen you.*

I peek around the corner with all the stealth I can manage, considering that I'm also scrubbing at the spot on my T-shirt with a napkin while balancing the bagel on top of my mocha. There he is: navy-blue uniform, billy club dangling ominously from a holster, scary crew cut with Nazi origins.

I close my eyes and the bus explodes again. The taste of hot gasoline fills my mouth.

Oh, Jesus, let him go away. What's Westby going to think if she walks down the hall right now and sees an officer of the law pounding on my door? Surely she'd politely inquire if she can be of assistance? Surely he'd reply that he's looking for C. Bloom, car thief, arsonist and cat abuser?

Why am I worrying about Westby? Forget about my *job* or *reputation,* we're talking about my freedom to shower without ten mustached lady cons sizing up my tits.

Maybe I should turn myself in. Don't they lessen the sentence? I'll march down the hallway, dissolve into tears and confess all. Maybe if I offer him a blow job he'll tell his superiors I'm dead.

I nearly drop my coffee when a staticky squawking sound fills the hallway. I peek again and see Scary Cop is gripping his walkie-talkie thingamajigger and striding quickly in my direction. Jesus! Heart racing, I shove against the nearest door and pull it shut behind me. I'm so intent on concealment I turn and trip over a desk, sending my bagel in an arcing trajectory through the air. It lands, cream cheese down, at the foot of a podium.

My relief at having escaped the strong arm of the law is so intense that only when I hear the laughter do I realize I'm standing in a large lecture hall. My eyes dart furtively from the sea of faces to the podium to the person behind it: Ruth Westby.

She clears her throat as I retrieve the bagel. There's a large ring of cream cheese now on the carpet, which I try desperately to remove, first covertly with the sole of my shoe, then down on my knees with my damp napkin.

"Rehearsing a bit of physical comedy, Ms. Bloom?" Westby asks dryly.

"Um…yeah…heh, heh…as usual," I stammer. The stain's still evident, and I look from it to her apologetically.

"Don't worry about it," she says.

As I make my exit, I can't decide if her neutral tone was masking laughter or horror. Probably both.

* * *

Before I know what's happened, it's the third week of school, and my initial panic has given way to a more relaxed sense of general terror. When I'm not dodging the police or enduring the snickers of witnesses to the Flying Bagel Incident, I'm faced with the daunting task of resurrecting the cold corpse of a play-development program. My first mission: find a student-written play worthy of the stage. The good news: I'm determined to put on a stellar debut. The bad news: I have no idea how to actually do this.

I learn more details about my predecessor, a guy named Harlan Wolfe; he was fantastically charismatic and a total fake. Midway through spring quarter, when his official transcripts had still failed to materialize, they realized that his claim to fame—serving for ten years as artistic director of a huge avant-garde theater program in Berlin—was the product of his overactive, coke-addled imagination. He never even graduated from high school. The Festival of New Works he was feverishly directing had to be halted in its tracks; the students were understandably crushed.

Most of this I learn from Mare, the dancer I met the first day. She's been very friendly and supportive these three weeks, which surprises me a little; she's the sort of woman I always want in my corner, but never seem to attract. I'm usually a magnet for the manic-depressive types. Mare's low, husky voice full of wisdom and philosophical musings is the opposite of all the shrill, edgy girls I've hung out with over the years. She's got these eyes that just do not belong in this century—striking, black, haunting. There's a sadness to her, but she keeps that tucked away. Mostly what people see is the huge, joyful grin and the brown hands that are always in motion, as if she wants to sculpt whatever she's telling you out of air and sunlight.

It's Wednesday, which means Thursday is just around the corner, and Friday I don't teach, so Thursday's really Friday, if you see what I mean. This puts me in a vaguely celebratory mood; I settle in after my morning class to sip coffee and read my e-mails. There's always an insufferable pileup of stupid, pointless mass mailings about unions and new babies and pleas to save the women of Uzbekistan. The first week I read each of these obediently, but by now I delete recklessly until something catches my interest. Oh, God, here's one; it's from Westby, and the subject heading looks ominous.

TO: Claudia Bloom
FROM: Ruth Westby
SUBJECT: Evaluating Your Teaching

I sit there for a torturous minute, just staring at the subject heading like a rabbit hypnotized by the shotgun barrel; what could this mean? Has she been brooding over the Ralene Tippets incident or the cream cheese fiasco? Or maybe they've decided I'm not qualified, after all, like poor Harlan Wolfe. They got a call from my sophomore history teacher at Calistoga High, who felt a moral obligation to confess about finding me with Roddy Talbot in the home ec room. No, it's not that, it's even more serious; Scary Cop's called her. "You see, Ms. Bloom, it says right here in the college handbook, 'Faculty members will be summarily dismissed if they steal a boyfriend's bus, drive it cross-country, and incinerate it.'"

Come on, Bloom, just read the damn thing.
Evaluating Your Teaching.
Always hated that word, *Evaluate.* Sounds so stiff and steely, like something only computers can accomplish; though where would be the fun in that? People add the guilt trips and the condescension that makes the whole process so much more human and grotesque.
Read it.
Oh, wait, look, here's an e-mail from Ziv. I'll open his first, just to see—well, he might be in crisis, after all. One can't

always put career before friendship, right? Then you end up a lonely old woman feeding pigeons half your jam sandwich and rambling on to yourself about the time you got the Teacher of the Year award.

TO: Claudia Bloom
FROM: Ziv Ackerman
SUBJECT: Oh Yeah.
Bloomie, my darling, I just have to tell you: roomie's name is Attila. I'm not kidding. He's hilarious, in a very deadpan, slightly stupid way, and you know I hate people who are smarter than me (present company excepted) so we get along swimmingly. When he tells people he's from Transylvania, and they respond with the inevitable Texan vampire cracks, he reassures them solemnly that the people of his country only drink the blood of animals, not humans, and only occasionally, for health reasons. The funny part is, he's not kidding. It's a good thing you took Medea with you.

So it's working out quite well, so far. Of course, you know that you're the princess of all roommates and that a hundred thousand Jude Law look-alikes could never replace you in a million years.

How about you? How's this married sex machine you so alluringly alluded to? And murderous wife? Sounds very cozy. And please, write immediately to clarify about the yurt. The OED said something about nomadic tribes of Mongolia. Surely you haven't taken up with a married nomadic Mongolian, have you?

"Want to get a bite to eat?" I look up and see Mare leaning against the doorway. She's wearing her usual threadbare leotard and wide-legged cotton sweats. I don't know how dancers manage to make such ratty old things look so sexy. Ever since *Flashdance* I've longed for that sort of grace, but on me it all looks insufferably frumpy.

"I'd love to," I say, springing up from my chair. "I'm famished."

Well, what? I can't starve myself, can I? Westby's hateful e-mail will still be here when I get back; if she *is* firing me, I may not have an appetite for days, so it's essential that I fuel up on carbs now.

As we're walking the tree-lined trail to Porter College, I let the beauty of the afternoon take my mind off my imminent unemployment for a few minutes. UC Santa Cruz has a campus that inspires dreamy forgetfulness. It's huge, nestled at the top of a hill, and most of it's wild. There are acres of redwoods, wispy eucalyptus groves, yawning meadows of summer-blond grass where the hippies had legendary nude picnics "back in the day." There are amazing views of the ocean at every turn—vistas that make you catch your breath and shake your head. We round the corner and are confronted with an in-your-face panorama of the Pacific. It's like a Monet: a million dots, variations of blue, green, gray and white. A cluster of darkish rain clouds is moving our way, dragging a voluptuous shadow across the water.

Inspired by a quick, bracing wind on my face, I take a deep breath and study Mare's profile. "Suppose you got an e-mail from Westby with the heading 'Evaluating Your Teaching'…what'd be your first reaction?"

"Exhaustion. I hate those things. After you get tenure, you only have to do it like every six years or something, but in the beginning they put you through the wringer."

"So it's like…standard procedure?"

"Oh, yeah, of course." She laughs. "Claudia, you look like I renounced the death sentence. Haven't you ever been through it before?"

"No. I never taught before I came here," I say, feeling a bit shy.

"That's right. I keep forgetting. You seem like such a natural. Well, I wouldn't worry about it. I'm sure your students love you."

We order sandwiches at the Hungry Slug Café and look around for a table. As we survey the room, I recognize the woman I doused with coffee the first day; she's sitting with the Costume Design professor, Esther Small. I've got very few names memorized at this point, but Esther's the sort of woman you remember. She's six feet tall, close to seventy years old, and she dresses like a twenty-two-year-old fashion slave from L.A.—tight jeans, platform shoes, suede jackets trimmed with mounds of fur. The two of them look up from their salads; they smile at Mare, but when they see me trailing a couple steps behind, their faces go blank and they pretend to be engrossed in conversation.

"Did you see that?" I whisper.

"What?"

"Those women you said hi to—they hate me."

Mare laughs. "Claudia. You're a little paranoid today…."

"No, seriously. I spilled coffee on the little one weeks ago. She still hasn't forgiven me. Every time I see her on campus, she gives me serious stink-eye."

"Monica?" Mare sighs. "She's not an easy one to figure out. We've both been here ten years, and I still haven't got a clue about what makes her tick. I hear she's going through a divorce, so she's probably not in the best mood."

"Is she faculty?"

"Yeah—haven't you met her yet? She's in our department. She teaches Asian theater and that sort of thing. She's really into Noh and Kabuki and—I don't know—shadow puppets, or something."

There are distant alarm bells going off in my brain. Monica…where have I heard that name? "So she's, um, getting divorced?"

"That's what I heard."

I can feel the beginnings of nausea in the pit of my stomach. "What's her last name?"

"Parker," she says before biting into her sandwich.

"Par-ker?"

"Uh-huh."

"Of course," I whisper, and the blood goes out of my face.

She looks up, still chewing. "What's wrong? You're all white. Are you sick?"

"Oh, nothing. Or maybe—I don't know—actually, I do feel a little sick," I say, wrapping my sandwich back up.

"I thought you were starving."

"I was, but…" My neck and face are starting to perspire. "Maybe something I had for breakfast didn't go down right."

Or maybe it's someone I went down on three weeks ago. Jesus, Claudia.

Just then Monica and Esther get up to leave. Over Mare's shoulder, I watch Monica in her pale-yellow, raw-silk pant-suit; she's very pretty, in a petite, dark, hyperpolished sort of way. Very Nordstrom's. She looks like the kind of woman who sorts her underwear into neat, color-coded stacks. She catches me watching her and shoots me a quick but withering glare, followed immediately by Esther glancing in my direction with pursed lips. She puts one hand on Monica's back protectively and guides her toward the stairs as if she's some sort of invalid.

"Listen, Mare," I say, "I'm going to head back to my office. I've got a lot to catch up on."

"Honey," she says—she's the only woman I've ever met besides waitresses in the Deep South who can pull this off, "you really do look ill. Maybe you should go home. Are you okay to drive?"

"I've got another class to teach. No, I'll be okay."

"You might have that flu that's going around."

"I doubt it," I say. "It's just PMS or something."

I walk unsteadily back to my office, gripping my sandwich with a shaking hand.

Parker. Goddammit, Clay.

This is the second time he's done this. When we met he was deliberately evasive about being married; now he's failed to give me vital information about his wife—namely, that I

work with her. I can picture him sitting there on his stool at
the Owl Club.

"That's right. First day at school." He was wearing such a
smug little smile.

"How did you know?" I asked, my skin even then prick-
ling slightly with premonition.

"I just do."

Yeah, you just did because it was your goddamn wife's first
day, too. What in the hell is he trying to do? Brand me with
a scarlet letter?

Get a hold of yourself, Claudia. Maybe you're mistaken.
Parker is a common name, after all. Here—just look at any
phone book. Let's see: Paoli, Paris, Parker…see. There must
be sixty of them. My eyes scroll down the page. Lots and
lots of them, even in a smallish town like this. It's like Jones
or Smith or—oh, God. There they are. Parker, Clay and
Monica. I slam the phone book closed, drop it on the floor
and collapse into my chair. "This is not happening. This is
not happening," I tell myself again and again, like someone
reciting Hail Marys. "Not…happening…not…happening."

"Professor Bloom?"

I spin around so quickly I nearly give myself whiplash. It
takes me two seconds to recognize her. I haven't seen her in
two or three years, at least.

"Oh, my God. Rosemarie. What are you doing here?" I
jump up with delight and surprise, rushing toward her.

"Checking in on you. From the looks of things, you
could use a little checking."

"Come in, come in." I tug at her hand, excited. "Look at
you. You've lost so much weight."

She's still got that rich olive complexion, the brown, impish eyes, still wearing the neo-hippie garb—a patchwork
dress in jewel tones, a big denim bag with Grateful Dead and
pot-leaf decals all over it. But she must have lost fifty pounds
since the last time I saw her. Years ago she was thick and
curvy, now she's slender, almost willowy. We hug and her

body feels insubstantial in my arms. "My little cousin. And jeez, you sure are little now."

"Yeah…I dropped a lot of pounds after…Jeff and I…did you know we split up?"

"Oh. I heard about that." Jeff is Rosemarie's old boyfriend. They had a baby together about four years ago, but she died when she was only two. I heard from my mom that Rosemarie went a little crazy then. She was in an institution for six, seven months. Something like that.

"I had a hard couple of years," she says, reading my face. "But I'm okay now."

"Sure. You look great. Look at you." She does a little spin. Rosemarie. I realize suddenly that I've missed her. "You look fantastic."

"I guess crazy kind of suits me," she says, her eyes shining.

"It always did."

"So," she says, "Do you have time to hang out?"

"Oh—oh, my God." I say, looking at my watch. "I'm going to be late. I've got to teach in two minutes."

Her face falls. "I'm sorry. I shouldn't have come."

"No. Don't be silly. This class is over by three—want to meet me here?"

"Yeah. Okay. What time is it?" Rosemarie never has worn a watch. I remember her patiently explaining when we were twelve that time didn't exist, and she refused to pretend it did. She's been true to that; I've waited for her so often, I stopped imagining it was possible for her to be anything but late. When she finally shows, she always wears such an innocent, childlike expression, and she's so quick to recount her dreamy adventures. It would be maddening with anyone else, but somehow with my cousin it's hard to stay angry for long.

"It's 1:30. Meet me here in an hour and a half."

"Right on," she says. "I'll go braid my dog."

Since I'm already running late, I don't bother to follow

up on this intriguing announcement. I run off to the theater, quickly lead them through some routine warm-ups, then distribute scenes I've selected for them to rehearse. Once they're safely tucked into the various corners of the room, practicing their lines in stiff, unnatural voices, I sink down into one of the red velvet chairs and think about Rosemarie.

When was the last time I saw her? God, it was when her baby, Jade, was still alive; we were at my Mom's house in San Rafael. Aunt Jessie was there and she was stupid drunk on a bottle of my mother's merlot; she kept trying to be cheerful in that sour, sloppy way she had. Rosemarie was still breastfeeding—Jade was just a tiny thing. I remember Aunt Jessie pulling the poor baby from Rose's arms and dancing around with her in campy glee, twirling like some ridiculous pantomime of a happy grandmother, until she stumbled over an ottoman. Rosemarie swiped the baby back, shushing her furious cries with "It's okay, honey. Your granny's happy to see you, is all."

Rosemarie was always so patient with her mother. I never could understand how she managed, when Aunt Jessie was so flaky. Every few months they moved someplace new; most of the time Rosemarie never even made it to the local school. They just bounced like a couple of pinballs from town to town. Aunt Jessie might hold down a job pouring coffee at a truck-stop diner or selling sunglasses in some mall—whatever she could find. She pumped gas in Hattiesburg for a month or two, delivered flowers in Pensacola. But then whatever man she'd taken up with would get too possessive or too lazy or too anything, and Aunt Jessie would stuff their ragtag bunch of belongings into their old, decrepit van and they'd drive until they ran out of gas. That was how they decided where to live next; when the van wouldn't go any farther, it was time to get out and see the town. When the money ran out, it was time to get a job.

I'd always loved Rosemarie. We were both only children,

and we'd bonded like sisters. Even as toddlers we got along,
as if there was a code of empathy in our blood. I felt sorry
for her, getting dragged around by Aunt Jessie, never having
much of a home, and at the same time I envied her amazingly placid, gypsy-ease with the road and everything it
brought. Rosemarie was the kind of kid who could eat pea-
nut butter from a spoon for dinner and a piece of gum for
dessert without a word of complaint. She could talk to just
about anyone, make friends with girls who had swimming
pools and shiny blond hair or with men who lived in cardboard boxes—it was all the same to her. She liked people,
period. And people liked her.

"Um, Mrs. Bloom?"

I resist the urge to look behind me for my mother.

"Yes?"

"I'm like *so* not into this today." It's Beach Barbie, the girl
I bummed a tampon from at the Owl Club. Actually, her
name's Sarah, and she's a real pain in the ass, but I like her.
At first I was startled by the coincidence—running into her
at the Owl Club, then having her in class—but I'm realizing quickly just how small this town is. My students bag my
groceries, they cut my hair, they serve me burgers at the
drive-thru. I felt the first pangs of claustrophobia when I
went to get a bikini wax and discovered I was about to have
my pubic hair yanked out by a girl I'd just a given a D to.

Sarah flops into the seat beside me and blows her bangs
off her forehead. "Would you hate me if I left early?"

"Probably."

"I've got cramps so bad I think I'm going to faint."

I fight a smile. Sometimes Sarah reminds me of myself.
We both have a tendency to lean a little too heavily on gy-
necological excuses. "You need some Advil?"

She shakes her head. "I already took like seven."

"Seven? Doesn't that constitute an overdose?"

She grabs a section of her long blond hair and begins examining it carefully for split ends. "You know what I think?"

"What?"

"I think I want to be a professor like you. How old are you, anyway?"

"Twenty-nine."

She squints at me. "Really? God, I hope it doesn't take me that long."

I chuckle to hide my despair. "What's that supposed to mean?"

"I mean, twenty-nine? That's like—middle age."

I slap her playfully on the shoulder. "Sarah! Go on, get back to your scene work. I want to see a really brilliant Antigone next week, okay?"

"What*ever*," she whines, dragging herself back to the stage.

I let out my breath, my body deflating like a withered balloon. Oh, my God. I'm fucking ancient. In a couple months I'll be thirty. What did I do to deserve this? My worst fears are confirmed; I'm old and I'm alone. I spent the night with a married man before I'd been in town twenty-four hours and now all the women want me buried alive. I'll have to leave Santa Cruz before they drive me out. I'll wander the country in my unreliable Volvo and have serial flings with emotionally unavailable men. I'll pump gas, deliver flowers, mix Carlo Rossi Chablis with Kool-Aid and call it sangria, like Aunt Jessie.

By the time class is over, I've convinced myself that being flattened by a bus abruptly and painlessly is the best future I can hope for. I trudge back to my office through the first splattering drops of rain and stare at my e-mail in-box blankly, wondering what the point is. Monica Parker hates me, and so will the rest of the faculty once the word gets around. Ruth Westby just wants to complete the formality by evaluating my teaching so she'll have an official list of my inadequacies when she fires me. "Ah, yes, Claudia, here are the results: Sluttish, Lazy and Ancient. That wraps it up. Please remove your belongings by Monday."

I haven't even noticed that Rosemarie is twenty minutes

overdue until she comes running in, out of breath, clutching a leash attached to an enormous, braided Thing. "What," I ask, "is that?"

"You mean *who,* Claudia. This is Rex. He's part Saint Bernard. Aren't you, Rexy?" Rex is drooling happily on a pile of my student papers. He's the size of a small horse, and he's sporting so many tiny braids he looks vaguely ethnic.

"Rose, I don't think they let dogs in here."

"What? It's your office, isn't it?" She looks around, as if she expects to spot a supervisor she'd overlooked.

"Yeah, I just mean—come on, let's get out of here. I need a change of scene."

Just as I'm ushering Rosemarie and Rex out of my office, Monica Parker comes striding down the hall in her lemon-yellow pantsuit. She's got a little white sack in one hand and a stack of papers in the other. I see Rex's nose twitch, as if in slow motion, and then I watch helplessly as he bounds toward Monica, making a beeline for that sack.

"Rex!" I cry, lunging for his leash, but he's free and he knows it. Before I can do a thing he's forced Monica into a corner, where she holds the white sack as high as she can. Unfortunately, she's not very tall, so Rex takes on the challenge; he balances on his hind legs and presses his muddy paws against her torso for balance, his tongue coming dangerously close to the coveted bag.

"Hey—stop that," Monica's sputtering. "Get off me, you stupid mutt."

"Come on, Rexy." Rosemarie, thankfully, has sprung into action, a little late as usual. She takes hold of Rex's leash and gently yanks him away from his victim. Monica is pale with fear, and tiny beads of perspiration are breaking out along her hairline.

"I'm so sorry," Rosemarie says. "He's just friendly."

"Friendly? You call that friendly?" she spits out.

"Really, he'd never hurt anyone."

"What a *dog* is doing here in the first place is *beyond* me,"

Monica says, shooting a look at me, then at the skid marks Rex's paws have left on the lapel of her yellow blazer. "This is a university, you know. Not a zoo."

"Look, lady, I'm sorry," Rose repeats. Rex gets away from her for a second and nuzzles Monica's crotch before he's yanked back again. I see Rose is about to laugh at Monica's mortified expression, so I chime in.

"Come on, let's take him outside. Really sorry about that. It'll never happen again."

"No," Monica says, her voice full of warning. "It won't."

As soon as we get outside, I groan and Rosemarie bursts into giggles. "God," she says, shaking her head. "What's up her ass? You'd think she'd never seen a dog before."

"Well, he did kind of maul her."

"He was just saying hello, weren't you, baby?"

"Plus, she doesn't like me," I say. "In fact, she hates me."

"Why?"

"Because I'm in love with her husband."

I don't know why I say it; it just slips out. Maybe because I've been so alone for so many weeks, constantly trying to be more than I am. Maybe it just sounds better than "Because I've been giving head to her husband." Anyway, it's just a slip of the tongue—I'm sure it couldn't be true.

It just couldn't.

CHAPTER 13

Top Eight Reasons Why Rosemarie Lavelle Is the Best Cousin Ever:

1) She combs my hair when I'm sad.
2) If there are two guys coming onto us, she never leaves me with the ugly one.
3) She lets me borrow anything, even her underwear, though normally she doesn't have much to lend.
4) In restaurants/bars/parties she doesn't sneak looks over my shoulder at interesting strangers.
5) Her idea of luxury is a day at the river when you never put your shoes on and there's a cooler of beer with real ice in it.
6) If asked to be quiet, she will, and doesn't taint silence by sulking.
7) Her hands are soft and pudgy, even now that she's skinny.
8) She just is.

It's funny how you don't notice what's missing from your life until you get a taste of it again. Sitting with Rosemarie

at the Front Street Pub, nursing a pitcher of IPA and waiting for our food, I wonder how I've made it these two and
a half years without seeing her. She's so alive; her eyes sparkle and her expression changes every few seconds, like a little kid. Hanging out with her always reminds me of being
little, the way a whiff of suntan lotion invariably sends me
spinning back through a hundred beach days gone by.

She catches me up on her life since she "finished being
crazy," as she puts it. Jade's death, the months at the Napa
State Hospital and her breakup with Jeff are all boxed up
somewhere, but the rest of it she takes out with twinkling
eyes: her torrid love affair with a tantric guru in Port An-
geles, the three months she spent growing pot in British Co-
lumbia, her "Summer of Bees" on Orcas Island, when she
lived with a balding beekeeper and fought off his pesky advances. Underneath the bubbling enthusiasm, I can feel the
other stuff tugging at her smile; it's unsettling, like resting
for a moment in the ocean, waiting for the undertow to kick
in.

It doesn't, though. Rosemarie just keeps riding on the
slick surface of light anecdotes. She barely touches the salad
she's ordered. She drinks glass after glass of water and goes
on about inheriting Rex from a junkie in Oregon, working at a health food store in Arcata, 'shrooming at Reggae
on the River.

It's not her style to skim the surface like this. When we
were kids, Rosemarie could never hide a thing; the family
nicknamed her Stormy because every emotion she went
through had the intensity of a hurricane. She could be sobbing one minute and laughing hysterically the next. Now
it's all blue skies and fluffy little white clouds; it makes me
wonder what sort of thunderheads are looming on the horizon.

"What about the hospital?" I ask gently, when I can't
stand it anymore. "How long were you there?"

She shrugs, looks away. "I don't know. Months. Too long."

She picks up her fork and pushes lettuce leaves around on the plate, takes a bite out of a cucumber, then mixes it back up with the lettuce. "It was an endless acid trip. Except there weren't any good parts."

"Why'd you end up there?"

"The usual reason. I lost it." She tries a brave smile, but then thinks better of it and bites her lip instead.

"Did Aunt Jessie take you there?" I ask.

She nods.

"What's she doing now?"

She lets out a quick bark of joyless laughter. It comes out louder than she meant it to, I think. Several heads swivel in our direction, and she stares at her lap, letting the curtain of brown hair swing down around her face. "Didn't your mom tell you?" she asks, without looking up. "My mom's in jail."

"Oh, my God. You can't be serious," I say. When she still doesn't look at me, I reach across the table and grab her hand. "Rose, why? What did she do?"

Finally she raises her eyes to meet mine. Her fingers are icy. "Third DUI in like, I don't know—five years. They show no mercy when you fuck up three times. Plus, she caused an accident and left the scene."

"How long has she been in?"

"Over a year."

"What?" Now it's my turn to make heads turn. "Rose," I say, forcing my voice to a quieter register. "Why didn't anyone tell me?"

She shrugs, slips her hand out of mine. "You were in Texas. Your mom probably didn't think it was all that—I don't know—"

"*Important?* That her sister was in *prison?*"

"*Is* in prison," she corrects me. She smears a trace of butter on a piece of bread, takes a bite, looks at me. My face must still be registering disbelief, because she says, "Aunt Mira's weird that way. She's—well *you* know, she's *your* mom—"

"She's what?"

"Secretive." She almost whispers it, and I can tell by the look in her eyes that what she really wants to say is "Fucked up." An irrational instinct to defend my mom flickers through me, but I realize it's stupid to pretend with Rose. She knows everything.

"Yeah," I say. "She is." There's an awkward pause. "Anyway, when does Aunt Jessie get out?"

"You know what? I don't have the slightest idea. I'm just so tired…." Her eyes go glossy with tears. She puts the piece of bread down and rests her head in one hand. "I swear, I could fall asleep right this second."

"Hey, Claudia." I hear my name and flinch slightly in surprise. There's Clay, hovering over our table in a pale yellow T-shirt, looking freshly scrubbed and adorable. His hair is slightly damp and messy, his cheeks are tinged with pink; in his arms he cradles his motorcycle helmet. For a good three seconds I forget about everything: Rose and Aunt Jessie, my neurotic mother, Monica Parker—

Wait a minute. Monica Parker.

"Hi," I say coolly. Then I look out the window.

"Everything okay?" he asks.

"Sure. You?"

"Fine. Sure." He looks uncertainly at Rosemarie, but I don't introduce them. He sticks out his hand. "I'm Clay," he says.

"Hi." She beams up at him. "I'm Rosemarie, Claudia's cousin."

"Really? I didn't know you had family here," he says to me.

"Oh, I don't live here," she says. "I'm just—visiting." For some reason she blushes. "We haven't seen each other in forever, so I decided to look her up." She nods, as if agreeing with herself on this point.

Clay nods back. There's an awkward pause. He shifts his weight from one foot to the other, and I'm vaguely aware that this is where I'm supposed to ask him to have a seat. Our eyes lock for an instant and I can feel my heart pound, but I don't open my mouth. Two words, I tell myself: Monica Parker.

He clears his throat, as if he's read my mind. "Well, I guess I'll push off. Uh—good to meet you, Rosemarie."

"Don't hurry off," she says, smiling her best smile, all white teeth and pink lips. For a second, I feel like I'm drowning. "Why don't you join us?"

Clay looks at me. Oh, God. He's so irresistible. The Monica Parker taboo only makes me want to ravish him more. That's so fucked up. I need therapy. I have to confront him and I can't with Rose here and she's *flirting* with him, for Christ's sake. What am I supposed to do? Kick her under the table?

I kick her under the table.

"Yeah," I say weakly. "Pull up a chair."

Ugh. Why am I like that? Why couldn't I just say look, buddy, not only are you married but your wife is gathering the villagers as we speak, preparing to stone me in the town square? Or better yet, why can't I stand up and slap him cleanly across the face like Audrey Hepburn would? Why am I such a puddle of jelly under his blue gaze?

As I silently self-flagellate in my seat, Rosemarie and Clay strike up a conversation about music, and within minutes they're laughing ecstatically and exchanging intimate little jabs when they disagree. Rosemarie is suddenly luminous. When she was fifty pounds heavier, she always had this Rubenesque charm to her—a voluptuous earth-mama charisma that made plenty of men weak-kneed. Now that she's whittled herself down to this nymph body, her appeal is more ethereal and—let's face it—way more Kate Moss. Watching her with Clay, I get this slightly sick feeling in the pit of my stomach. The vibrancy of Rosemarie's smile, the light in her eyes that had all but gone out just seconds before he appeared, is nauseating me more than a little.

What are you up to this time, Bloom? Getting possessive about someone else's husband?

"Oh, abso*lutely*," Rosemarie's saying. "They're awesome. Some of their stuff makes me want to slit my wrists, but I'm a huge fan, anyway."

Groupie bitch, I think. Then a pang of guilt shoots through me, and I feel like sliding under the table in a pool of remorse.

"Have you ever heard Gillian Welch?" Clay's asking.

"She drives me *crazy*."

"I really like her."

"No way!" Rosie practically screams. "She's this fake hillbilly from L.A. *Please.* I'll take Patsy Cline over her any day."

They go on like this for a good fifteen minutes. I gaze out the window. I'm just a conduit. My fate is to bring unlikely pairs together, then disappear without a trace. Jonathan and Rain. Clay and Rosemarie. Who knows, maybe Monica and Esther will embark on a wild lesbian tryst, set off by their mutual hatred of one Claudia Bloom. The thing with Clay and me was just a fluke, like everything else in my life. I'm destined to roam the earth in unreliable vehicles and watch other people skip off into the sunset.

"You're awful quiet, Claudia."

I turn to face him and try to smile, try to think of something witty and light to banter with, but my mind goes blank.

"Everything okay?" His eyes are so startling—green with streaks of gold that make them look blue in certain lights.

"Yeah. Sure. Anyone want more beer?" They look at each other like a couple that's been together so long they can read every nuance with just a glance.

"Okay," they say in unison, then laugh.

Aargh. What a hideous Wednesday. I go to the bar and order us another pitcher, not minding when the bartender takes his time about it. From across the room, I watch the sunlight bringing out the reddish tones of Rosemarie's silky

brown hair. Her slender arms gesticulate, dancerlike. Allegedly, her father was Italian; no one except Aunt Jessie re-
members him. I believe it, though. Rose has always had that
Italian magic to her—expressive, passionate, totally uninhib-
ited. Now she pushes Clay playfully in the shoulder and he
breaks into a boyish grin.

*Oh, Clay. I should have known. You're just a ten-year-old kid
living in a circus tent, aren't you? Your wife is now your mother and
you're out looking for a good time with the girls.*

I deliver the pitcher and take a seat. I pour us three glasses
of the light, golden beer and down mine before they've
touched a drop. They're talking architecture, now, feng shui
and the effects of round structures on the psyche. Christ,
next they'll be organizing a drum circle. Isn't this why I left
California in the first place?

"Claudia, you know what I'm talking about," Clay says,
as if suddenly remembering my presence. "Wasn't the yurt
much cooler than you thought it was going to be?"

"Sure. I guess." I pour myself another beer—my third—
and gulp down a swig.

"Oh, come on. Admit it. You loved it," he says, beaming at me.

I look across the table and notice that Rose is wearing a
quizzical expression; I see her connecting the dots, and I
don't think she's pleased with the picture.

"So you've...been to Clay's...yurt?"

A weird, sweaty little pause. "Uh-huh. Just once."

"Oh. And you liked it?"

"Sure. It's cute."

Clay scoffs. "Cute?"

"Hold on," Rose says, her brow furrowing. "Where did
you two meet, again?"

"I know." My tone is bitter and sarcastic. "It's confusing.
Let me explain. One day Clay saved me from an exploding
bus. Then he took me home to his cute little yurt, where I
met his wife—granted, I was naked, which was slightly awk-

ward, but we worked it out. Oh! I almost forgot. Clay's wife not only works at the same university as me, but in the same department. Isn't that great? She's the one your dog attacked this afternoon. Small world, huh?"

Clay looks sincerely stunned. I might as well have slapped him.

"Claudia," Rose says softly, her voice full of apology. She's finally getting the picture—late as usual.

I reach into my wallet and pull out a twenty. "Here. This should cover it. I'm going to take off."

"Wait—I'll go with—" Rose stammers.

"No. You guys are having fun. Stay." I get up and quickly dash out the door, eager to get away before the tears start up for real. I can already feel them stinging at the back of my eyes. That's a humiliation I just can't stomach tonight.

I've turned the corner and am halfway down the block when Clay catches up. "Hey," he says. I keep walking. He falls in step next to me. "Can we talk?"

"Not right now." I sniff and will the tears to hold off for two more minutes.

"Claudia. Please. Will you talk to me?"

"About what?" I'm walking faster. The tears are in my voice now, and I'm dangerously close to losing it.

"About—you know what."

I turn and face him. "Why didn't you tell me?"

"I already explained the situation with—"

"Leaving out some very pertinent details."

"Okay. You're right." He looks a little sheepish. "I should have told you. I just didn't want to make things worse."

"Oh, but why not? You're so good at that."

"Claudia, be fair—"

"Fair? None of this is fair." I stand there with my hands on my hips, glaring at him. He looks away. "I really like you, Clay."

"I like you, too. A lot."

I butt in before he can say more. "Still, this is ridiculous. I may not be the most mature person on the planet, but I think I can do better than this. I mean this whole thing just feels—juvenile. You know?"

"You're so quick to assume the worst," he says, stuffing his hands in his pockets.

"Then prove me wrong. Maybe then I'll stop assuming." And with that I stride off down the street, letting the tears fall at last.

I'm halfway through my second mason jar of merlot and I'm smoking a stale, hand-rolled cigarette in the bathtub when Rosemarie arrives. After pounding for several minutes on the door, calling out my name and getting no response, she figures out the door's not locked, lets herself into my apartment and proceeds to follow the scent of cigarette smoke. I can hear Rex close behind her, his toenails clicking on my hardwood floor. When she finds me, she shakes her head, puts the lid down on the toilet and takes a seat. Rex collapses at her feet. Together, they stare at me for a long minute with mournful expressions, taking in the pathetic spectacle. Last I checked, my skin was all splotchy-red and my smeared mascara had turned me into Joan Jett circa 1980.

"It's a good thing this turned out to be your apartment. I hate stalking strangers."

I finish my merlot and pour myself some more.

"Mind if I get a glass?" she asks.

"Sure. Help yourself."

She disappears for a minute. I can hear her banging around in the kitchen, discovering Medea, making a fuss over her, telling her how pretty she is and would she like some milky-wilky? "All right if I give your cat a treat?" she calls.

"Okay," I answer, knowing I haven't answered loudly enough.

"Claudia? Mind if I give your kitty a—"

"Fine," I yell, my voice coming out raw and belligerent, like some boozy old hag. Rex frowns at me. There's silence for a moment in the kitchen, followed by some quiet murmuring, some cat-spoiling via milk and maybe even tuna. She comes back holding a Mickey Mouse cup, which she fills with wine before resuming her position on the toilet seat.

"Did Clay tell you where I live?"

"Mmm-hmm." She takes a swig and fixes her eyes on my face. "Come on, Claudia. I didn't know he was the guy you—" I give her a look of warning "—well, I didn't. You acted like he was the last person you wanted to see."

"He was. He is."

"But why? I thought you said you were in love with him."

"I was being…sarcastic. Or something. I don't know."

"No, you weren't," she says, reaching over and taking the cigarette from my fingers. She smokes it like a joint, a tight-lipped toke, then hands it back. "I didn't know you two were involved, or I would never have—"

"We're not *involved*. He's married."

"He's separated."

"His wife lives like three feet from him. It's complicated." I drink more wine and take a long drag from my cigarette, which tastes perfectly disgusting.

"He's married to that bitch we saw today?"

"She's not a bitch," I say. Rose just raises her eyebrows at me. "Even if she is, we shouldn't call her that. I feel guilty enough as it is."

"Okay," she says. "He's married to the personality-challenged whore we had the pleasure of bickering with this afternoon?"

I smirk but try to maintain my scolding tone. "Well, your stupid dog did jump all over her."

"Is it his fault she was taunting him with that smelly paper sack?" She reaches down and pets his matted braids.

"She'll probably sue me. That's the second time I ruined one of her perfect little outfits."

Rose hugs her knees in like a little girl and looks gleeful. "What happened the other time?"

"I spilled coffee on her—that white blouse looked like a mechanic's rag."

She's giggling hysterically. "I wish I could've seen her face," she squeals happily.

I can't help laughing a little, too. "No you don't. It was terrifying."

"She doesn't deserve a guy like Clay, anyway," she says. "I bet she tricked him into marrying her."

"Oh, come on. She's probably really wonderful."

"Claudia. Give me a break."

"She's smart," I say weakly. "She teaches...Noh."

"No?" She giggles. "What the hell is no?"

"It's like...Japanese. You know..."

"No," she cries, getting totally silly now. "I don't *know no.*"

"Well, she teaches it. And...puppets."

"Oh, great." Rose practically howls. "Puppets. Obviously she's a genius." When she finally calms down a little, she says, "Look, he's not going to stay with her. He's way too cool for someone like that."

"You liked him?" I can feel my smile fading a little.

"Are you kidding? He's *so* sexy."

"He is?" I'm torn; half of me swells with an irrational pride—he *is* sexy, see? The other half of me goes all hot and sticky with jealousy. "So you...really got along, didn't you?"

"Claudia," she says firmly. "I didn't know, all right? As soon as I figured it out, I backed off. Really. I'd never do that to you."

"It's not like he's *mine* or anything."

"You like him. That's all I need to know."

"But he liked you, didn't he?" I stare into the bath, trying to sound amiable. "He seemed to, anyway. He sure was flirting with you."

"Don't. He was only being polite because I'm your cousin. As soon as you left, he was beside himself. He's into you—I'm sure he is."

"Ooh, shit," I say, pouring us both more wine. "Shit shit shit shit shit."

"What?"

"What do you mean, *what?* It's catastrophic. He's *married.*"

"No problem," she says, fingering her Mickey Mouse cup. "They'll get divorced, you'll have a little surfer baby and get free records for the rest of your life. It's awesome. A Santa Cruz fairy tale."

"Yeah, right."

Medea noses her way through the cracked-open door, slinks over to the toilet and deftly leaps into Rosie's lap. "Hey, speaking of Santa Cruz," she says, stroking Medea with one hand absently. "I've got something I want to ask you."

"Yeah?"

"Oh, just… I was wondering. How you would feel…?" She pauses, looks up at me, then back down at Medea.

"What? How would I feel about what?"

She leans over, takes the bottle and adds a little more to both of our glasses. "It's probably not the best time to bring it up. You've had a hard night."

"Rose. Come on. What is it?"

"It's just…" She reaches under Medea's chin and strokes her there, sending her into a purring frenzy. "I guess things aren't going so great for me in Arcata. I was staying with a guy who—well—he kind of died."

"Died?"

"Yeah." She nods.

"How?"

She shrugs. "They think he OD'd. Not really clear if he meant to or not."

"Oh, my God. What was he on?"

"Um, they found a lot of shit in his system—sleeping pills, lots of booze, some heroin. But that's a really long story." She looks up at the ceiling. "The point is, I just don't think I can go back there. You know? All my friends there are so...high-strung."

"Uh-huh," I say, trying not to sound shocked or anything. Christ, he *died?* Did she find the body? I restrain myself from this morbid line of questioning.

"I need to be around good people right now. People who love me."

"Of course you do, Rose."

For the second time this evening, I see tears sparkling in her eyes. "You're all the family I've got left, Claudia."

I reach over and put a damp, wrinkled hand on her knee. Medea bites gently at my knuckles. "I'm so glad you came to see me, Rose."

She smiles slightly, licks her lips. "Well, here's the thing. I'm not just visiting. I was hoping I could...move in."

CHAPTER 14

I would like to know what heinous crimes I committed during my years as a student to deserve Ralene Tippets now. At the moment she's gazing at me over her pink glasses with a pained expression, as if I alone am responsible for her ill-fated outfit of lavender polyester, her bony figure, her undoubtedly fat, cheap-domestic-beer-drinking husband, and her dismal deficit of talent.

"I just don't see how tongue twisters are going to help me *perform*," she pouts.

"Your body is your instrument, Ralene. You have to get your mouth open and loose. It's like warming up your car before you drive."

"That's a mixed metaphor if I *ever* heard one."

"Let's keep going, everyone. Topeka Topeka Topeka Topeka Topeka. Wee-wa, Wee-wa, Wee-wa, Wee-wa—good. Use both your lips. Le-le-le-le-le-le-le-le-le-laaaa."

"I can't work like this." Ralene throws up her hands and stomps away from our circle. The rest of us continue. Rule number one, Ralene: do not be a prima donna before anyone gives a shit.

For the first few weeks of the semester, Ralene's resistance to virtually everything we did in class caused me considerable discomfort. I would frequently wake in the wee hours, already hyperventilating about the ninety minutes I would soon be forced to spend in her presence. I had nightmares about those huge pink glasses and watery gray eyes following me wherever I went, her long, bony neck swiveling, like a cast member from *The Exorcist*.

Now that we've reached the coveted week seven, the end of the quarter is in sight, and I've started feeling more frivolous about everything. Ralene Tippets? Ha. I eat middle-aged women in lavender pantsuits for breakfast. The fantasy of winter break, filled with weeks of Ralene-less hours, has begun to intoxicate me. I long to get up in the morning and not even give the woman a thought. I dream of relaxed, mocha-studded breakfasts when the vision of her wicked-witch eyebrows doesn't turn the caffeine and French toast into a civil war. Teaching is incredibly bad for one's digestive tract. I won't get into the details; suffice it to say I'm considerably more explosive since I became an academic, and Ralene Tippets has everything to do with it.

Aside from Ralene's typical warm-up tantrum, the hour and a half passes uneventfully. The students divide into their scene groups and rehearse, some of them belting out each line furiously, the others whispering in voices so tiny and meek, they sound like throat-cancer survivors. I come around and offer tactful pointers like, "Jesus Christ, Misty, the audience isn't *deaf*—tone it down a little. Jason, is this charades? I can't even *hear* you, and I'm standing close enough to feel your spit."

It's my last class on Thursday, so week seven is effectively over. As I'm getting ready to head to my office, I congratulate myself for all I've adjusted to in the last two months: Ralene, a door with my name on it, prolonged celibacy,

Monica Parker's subtle but relentless attacks, Rosemarie's hair clogging the shower, Rex filling my apartment with the powerful scent of himself. It's an impressive list. "Grace under pressure" is an apt cliché for my performance these weeks. Well, okay, medicating myself heavily with vodka tonics at night and keeping a pillow in my office for emergency silent screams is not the dictionary definition of *grace,* but both help me keep up appearances.

"Hi, Claudia."

I look up from stuffing my sweater into my bag and see Miranda, my favorite student and the primary reason teaching hasn't rendered me a vegetable thus far.

"Miranda. Hey, what's up?"

She tugs at the straps of her backpack, her stance wide, one foot toying with her skateboard, rolling it back and forth, back and forth. Her dark violet hair looks freshly colored, a nest of purple, Betty Boop curls. She's extremely pretty, though she goes to great pains to throw people off the scent with a rigorous series of piercings, lurid dye jobs, and a theatrical, tongue-in-cheek wardrobe. One day she wore a mechanic's jumpsuit with a name tag that read "Al." Another afternoon she skated to class in a slightly torn, lacy vintage slip, vinyl knee-high boots and a feather boa. She rarely smiles, and from the dark circles under her eyes, I'd guess her life hasn't been a picnic, but when she does flash her toothy grin, it's like winning the lottery.

"I heard you were taking scripts," she says, pausing in her constant fiddling with her tongue piercing long enough to get this out. She's got on a bright red T-shirt that says Suck my Dick across the chest, and a pair of piss-yellow satin bell-bottoms.

"You're going to choose one for winter quarter, right?"

I'm scheduled to direct a new play in a few months, a "world premiere," if you will, and I've got a growing pile of submissions, all of them destined for the recycling bin.

"Yeah, I am. Got something for me?"

She nods, digs in her backpack and produces a tattered plastic binder with papers sticking out of it randomly. As she offers it to me, it slips from her hand and the pages explode everywhere. "Shit," she mumbles.

"Mmm, well, you might want to work on presentation a bit," I say. "No one wants to have to hunt for page 103, you know?"

She scrambles around to gather the pages and I make some attempt to help. Just then Ralene marches over, lips pursed in her customary I-have-something-to-say-you-don't-want-to-hear look. I swear she goes home and complains to her fat husband that I'm a juvenile delinquent and she's got to keep me from corrupting every youth I encounter with radical dogma. She could have dropped at any point, but she relishes her self-appointed obligation to educate me on how to educate.

"Claudia, listen," she hisses in a half conspiratorial, half accusing tone. "I think you should know there are some very—" she looks at the ceiling, searching for the right word "—inappropriate developments in your class. You may have missed them, but I find it all intensely—" again, she looks upward, as if checking in with God for the right euphemism "—disturbing."

Although my instincts tell me to run screaming from this conversation, I just glance at Miranda with a "hold on one second" look and turn back to face Ralene. "Okay, enlighten me. What seems to be the problem?" Since I started this job, I frequently give myself the creeps by blurting out sublimi-nally stored teacherly remarks I never even knew were in my vocabulary. This particular phrasing is courtesy of Mr. Clem-ens, a high school civics teacher I despised, whose memory I managed to suppress until this moment.

"It's about Benjamin," she says. "He has no boundaries."

Ben Crow is this absolutely beautiful twentysomething fireman with a body that makes you embarrassed to look at. He's half Cherokee, half Abercrombie & Fitch model. I do have to agree with Ralene, in a way; his sex appeal is—particularly in my current celibate state—disturbing.

"What sort of boundaries are we talking about, here?"

"Emotional boundaries, Claudia. Psychic boundaries," she says, clutching at her blouse, "physical boundaries—every kind of boundary there is. He crosses them." Her painted eyebrows wriggle toward each other with concern. "It's definitely inappropriate."

I asked Ben and Ralene to work on a scene from *The Glass Menagerie* for their end-of-quarter projects. I figured a mother-son thing could work well between them, age-wise, and I knew that Ben, being slightly older than most of my students and patient as a monk, would be the least likely to freak out and drop the class at the prospect of being ordered around by Ralene. I was right; he's been an absolute prince, putting up with her antics with such good-natured generosity, I frequently wanted to hug him. Never mind that "hugging" is the only G-rated item on the long list of things I'd like to do to him, if only I weren't his professor.

"From what I see, you two have been working together very productively," I hear myself saying. Suddenly I remember Miranda, and turn to her, grateful that her presence will give me an excuse to cut this conversation off sooner rather than later. "Miranda, I'm sorry—can you wait just two more minutes?" She nods, and I face Ralene with a let's-make-this-quick expression. "Are you saying he makes you uncomfortable?"

She snorts. "Very."

"Sometimes theater itself can be disturbing, you know? Doing scene work can be quite intimate."

She looks slightly aghast. "Don't you want to know what's happened?" Before I can answer, she leans in very close and whispers, "He asked me out." She pulls back, smug and wide-eyed. "On a date."

"Well, I'm sure he didn't—" I begin, and stop myself. *Didn't what? Didn't have the remotest intention of touching an old scarecrow like you?* "Maybe you misunderstood. People do get together outside of class and—you know—rehearse, or discuss the material. It's not uncommon."

"Claudia, what are you running here? An academic course or a dating service?"

I hear Miranda stifle a giggle behind me.

"I'm not saying that you have to go out with—"

Ralene's gaze flicks to Miranda quickly and back to me. "You know, there are laws now about sexual harassment— not just between professors and students, but among the students themselves. If I feel no action is being taken to protect me from inappropriate sexual advances, I won't hesitate to bring this to Dr. Westby."

I sigh. The last thing I need is a student complaining to Westby. She's been very cold these days. I'm sure Monica's been doing what she can to cast me in the worst possible light, so I'm creeping around on thin ice. "Look, Ralene, I'll talk to Ben on Tuesday, if you like—I'll get his perspective on it. Would that make you feel better?"

"'Get his *perspective* on it?'" She looks at me with withering disbelief. "Just tell him to knock it off. I'm a married woman. I didn't come back to college after all these years so I could be stalked by some fireman." My God, I think, can she really be this delusional? "Boundaries," she says, her voice as pious as a nun's, "are essential." With that she spins away from me and stalks off, her skeletal legs slicing the air like scissors.

I turn to Miranda, and resist the urge to indulge in catty remarks. "So, about your script…"

"What a bitch," Miranda observes, her eyes following Ralene's retreat. I hide my smile unsuccessfully. "*Vindictive,* too. Glad I'm not stuck with her."

I feel delightfully validated by Miranda's diagnosis. I mean, sure, anyone can tell Ralene's got issues, but it's also her unique gift to make me wonder if *I'm* a little crazy. It's good to hear someone else say what I can't.

"Yeah, well, anyway. Tell me about your play."

"I suck at summarizing. You just have to read it."

"Okay. I wasn't kidding about presentation, though. Directors don't want old binders with unbound pages. Get it all in order, three-hole-punch it, use brads. It's good practice."

She blushes. "Yeah, I know. It's just, I stayed up all night writing it, and I was so stoked about it, I wanted you to see it right away."

I smile. "Did you write the whole thing in one night?"

"Oh, no." She looks horrified. "I stayed up all night for like, three nights doing it." She shrugs, tugs at the ring in her left nostril. "It probably sucks. I don't know. But yeah, I'll get it together and give it to you next week."

"Good. I can't wait to read it."

This is partially true. The scripts I've flipped through so far have been so patently miserable I didn't get past page three on any of them. I've divided them into two piles: terrible, self-involved drivel in which absolutely nothing happens, and over-the-top, TV-inspired drivel in which just about everything happens. Miranda's, I think, will be different. But I hate to get my hopes up.

"I'm an insomniac," she says. "Writing is what I do to keep from going crazy at four in the morning."

"A teacher of mine used to say, 'If your writing doesn't keep you up all night, how can you expect it to keep your readers up?'"

"I can sleep when I'm dead." She fidgets with her bracelet, and I notice for the first time the jagged, faded scar on the inside of her wrist. I try to look away, but she's caught me staring. She laughs—a sharp, percussive bark of a laugh—and stuffs both hands in her pockets.

A long, embarrassing pause ensues, which I break with self-conscious small talk. "Any big plans for the weekend?"

"Sure," she says sarcastically. "Nonstop disco." Then she gives me a little wave, mumbles "Later on" and skates off.

Miranda. Funny kid. Wish I knew what made her tick. Or maybe I don't.

Driving home, I unbutton my skirt and turn up the boom box as loud as it will go without getting all fuzzy. Sometimes I feel so confined by my professor-wanna-be clothes and my need to placate the Ralene Tippets of the world. Today I just want to be an animal. I mean yes, I am an animal, technically, but I want to be the breed of animal that doesn't comb its hair (okay, actually, I *don't* comb my hair, but that's because it would go seventies Afro on me if I did, not because I am blissfully unaware of my appearance). Stuck in traffic, I fight the desire to pull over, tear off my clothes and race for the hills. I want to tromp about in the mud and hide in a canopy of leaves. I want to stalk something smaller than myself, pounce with lightning speed and tear into its quivering flesh…

Actually, forget the quivering-flesh bit. That's repulsive.

As I let myself in, I see Rosemarie sitting in lotus position on the floor, while Rex sprawls hugely nearby, his dreadlocks rising and falling as he snores. Medea eyes both of them reproachfully from my futon. Rose springs to her feet as I enter, her face aglow with excitement. "I've figured out what I'm going to do with my life," she cries. "I really have this time."

"Mmm. Let's hear," I say, kicking off my clogs and heading for the fridge. This may seem like a lackluster response to such a monumental announcement, but you've got to understand that this, varied occasionally with the gushing description of her life-partner-of-the-week, is altogether routine.

"Claudia, I mean it. It's so absolutely *me* I can't believe I didn't think of it before."

She pauses as I open my yogurt and nod at her. "Go on. I'm listening."

"I'm going to manage a band. I know, I know, it's not loads of money coming in right away, but—"

"What band?"

"I don't know yet, I have to find one, but in the meantime I can cocktail at the Catalyst, because so many groups play there—and then I'll find, like, the absolute perfect band of my dreams that might be really hot but nobody's ever heard of them because they don't have any business sense (creative people usually don't) and I'll make them really awesome posters and book all their gigs and recruit homeless kids to hand out flyers (all these fifteen-year-olds on corners, they need work). And it'll just be so, so great. I know it will." She chews a strand of hair, looking dreamily out the window. "Maybe once I get good at it, I'll take on more bands, start like this super-hip PR firm (for musicians only— and just good ones—I'd never touch sappy commercial shit, just the cool geniuses). Isn't it so perfect? I can't believe we never thought of it. Isn't it totally me?"

This is the delicate part: first response.

"Well, it does suit your personality," I begin cautiously. "You're very charismatic."

She nods solemnly. "It's true. When I was six, my mom caught me selling blueberry Popsicles to half of Portland."

"You made blueberry Popsicles when you were—"

"Just blue food dye and water. But I convinced them. Music's like that."

"Like blueberry pop…?" I begin, but she interrupts.

"The actual music's only about five percent of what makes a band hot—image is the other ninety-five. If owning a certain CD will make you feel more amplified, sexier, then you'll buy it. Music's an aphrodisiac—we use it to turn each other on."

"Sounds right to me," I say, having no idea, since music's never been a priority for me. I probably spend more on tin foil annually than I ever have on CDs. "And cocktailing at the Catalyst's not a bad idea. You could walk to work and tips are probably decent. You'd meet cool people."

"Guys, you mean."

"Yeah, well, that doesn't seem to be a problem for you." Since she moved in last month, she's been through four soul mates. Three of them lasted only forty-eight hours.

Rose cocks her head to the side and smiles at me quizzically. "You think I treat guys like shit, don't you?"

"No. You're very sincere, in the moment."

"I am. I just can't seem to maintain the high. I love the buzz when you first meet someone. Too bad it wears off."

"Mmm. Yes."

"And it's like that with jobs—I'm so stoked and then…I don't know…I lose my steam." She studies her split ends sadly, then suddenly drops the strand of hair and smiles at me brightly. "But not this time. This is definitely it. I can feel it in my bones." She darts off to the bathroom. Rex looks at me for a moment, then turns and follows her, nearly tangling himself up in her long brown legs in his eagerness. He senses I'm not his biggest fan, and consequently avoids being alone with me.

Rose calls from the bathroom, over the sound of running water and apparently through toothpaste, "Should I go buy some more vodka to celebrate?"

More vodka? What happened to…? I go to the freezer and see that the big bottle of Absolut I bought on Monday is now down to a thin film coating the bottom. Either Rose is taking little medicinal nips from it almost hourly, or I'm a sleepwalking party animal.

"If you want, I'll cook," she offers.

I *do* want. This is Rose's major bargaining chip, and she's playing it for all it's worth; I pay for the food, she transforms it into a gorgeous homage to California produce. She can do magic with fresh tomatoes and basil. My stomach growls just thinking of it.

After I've handed over sixty bucks and the flat is blissfully empty, I drain the last of the Absolut and collapse in the patch of sunlight warming my futon. Medea slinks over and makes herself comfortable on my belly. How did this happen? Just a couple years ago I was a free-and-easy honorary Texan with a fabulous roommate (who paid his way—usually more—plus furnished endless espressos) and a little black book bursting at the seams with easy-to-access past-and-future one-night stands. Things were simple then. Now I'm a former fiancée (oh, the shame—can't believe I fell for it), a car thief and accidental arsonist, a celibate, crabby professor and the unwilling patron of a lovely but unstable neo deadhead in the midst of an enthusiastic, slightly overdue quarter-life crisis.

If this is what it means to grow up, I want a one-way ticket to never-never land.

The phone rings, and I gently shove Medea off to answer it. As I cross the room, I fantasize briefly that it's Clay, then remind myself that Clay is married, dishonest and—well, married and dishonest.

"Claudia. It's me, Mira." When I was thirteen, around the time my dad got custody, out went the word "Mom" and in rushed "Mira." She also changed her last name from Bloom to the rather eccentric invention, Ravenwing, though she ditched that as soon as she started marrying again. I think she was embarrassed by Ravenwing almost immediately; it was the kind of thing that only seemed cool for a very brief spell in the eighties.

"Hi."

"You sound tired. Are you getting enough iron?"

"Yeah, I should think so. Rosemarie's been cooking me loads of spinach—doesn't that have iron in it?"

"You should get some supplements. Or eat more steak. Why is Rose still there? I thought you were making her get her own place."

I sigh. "Well, she doesn't have a job yet."

"Oh, Claudia…" I can hear her lighting a joint and taking a long toke. "Christ. That flake. Let me guess; she's got hundreds and hundreds of leads, but nothing ever turns into actual work. She cooks for you, and she's a great help, but she's showing no signs of paying rent or leaving."

"How did you…?"

"Claudia, you've got to wise up to Lavelle women, okay? You know Aunt Jessie's just like that. There are family traits—" she lets out a long sigh, and I can almost smell her killer Humboldt weed through the phone "—most of which are inescapable."

"Yeah, but you're a Lavelle and you're not like that."

"Well," she says. "I try."

My mother's voice always contains a potent mixture of bitterness and amusement.

I suspect her reefer habit helps keep her amusement quota up, and perhaps the bitterness down. Unfortunately, it also wreaks havoc on her short-term memory. I've often thought it was lucky she became a stoner long after my infancy, or she would have left me in a grocery store. ("Let's see, I got the butter, milk, oranges…what *am* I missing?") Probably stunting her awareness of the immediate past is precisely why she gets stoned every day, though; she was supposed to leave her husband Gary last spring when she discovered he was sleeping with the voluptuous landscaper, only somehow this item lost rank on her to-do list. I think bitterness is slowly winning out over amusement, except it's a deeply resigned sort of bitterness, the kind that makes you tired rather than motivated to seek revenge.

"I can't bring myself to give her the boot," I tell her.

"Who?"

"Rose." I say, exasperated. "She's so sweet and sincere and—"

"Broke."

"Well, yeah," I say, a touch defensively. "That's part of it. I don't want to see her on the street."

"Right. Empathy is a Bloom trait—can't take credit for that. Your father was always too nice for his own good."

This is true. My dad is the kind of guy who'll pick the runt of the litter, or even the saddest fruit on display, because he feels sorry for it. He's pathologically attached to the underdog. I suspect he wasn't very popular as a kid; nowadays, all the most picked-on creeps at Calistoga High flock to his shop classes in droves. He's like a beacon of hope for the pimply and the greasy-haired.

"Speaking of your father, I hear he has a girlfriend."

"He what?" My dad hasn't seen anyone since Sandra the Dental Assistant left him ten years ago.

"You heard me." She coughs a deep, rattling cough. "Margie Standish told me he's dating the new librarian at the high school. Word is she's anorexic with one foot in the grave. Sounds like your father's type." I resist the urge to remind her that *she* was once his type; of course, that was before she divorced him and transformed herself so thoroughly I couldn't even call her Mom anymore. "You should go see him, by the way. I think he's hurt you haven't visited since you found a place."

"Did Margie tell you that, too?" I wonder why she doesn't urge me to come visit *her;* we haven't even shared a meal together since I moved back to California.

"It's just a suggestion," she says. "Anyway, I have to run. Emily's got to find an outfit for her big date tomorrow night." Emily is my spoiled stepsister—a terminally cute teenager who owned more designer shoes at age ten than I ever will.

"Is she seeing someone?"

"Didn't I tell you? She's going out with—" and here she lowers her voice to mention a very prominent musician, someone so huge even I know who he is, though admittedly he was much bigger six or seven years ago.

"She *is?* How old is he?"

"I think he's thirty. Early thirties, anyway."

"Emily's only sixteen."

"Oh," she sighs. "Yeah, I know. It does look a little suspect. But she's her own person. I mean we couldn't stop her from seeing him, right?"

"Why not?"

"Claudia." She clucks her tongue at me reprovingly. "Haven't I taught you anything? Don't you know that we can't control other people? If it's her destiny to have her heart crushed by—" again, she lowers her voice to mention him by name, which is one of those absurd one-word stage names, making the impact even weirder "—then our interfering would only…interfere. Haven't you read *Romeo and Juliet?*"

It's my turn to sigh. "I think I've heard of it. Still—sixteen and thirtysomething?"

"She's got decent judgment," my mother says, in an I-can't-be-bothered-with-this-right-now tone. "All right, Em, I'm coming!" she yells away from the phone. Em. She never had cute little nicknames like that for me.

After we hang up, I trudge back to my patch of sunlight and curl up, wanting chocolate and a thoroughly escapist book. I don't want to think about my mother or the explanation she offered when I asked why I shouldn't call her Mom. ("I've spent thirteen years being Mom, and now I'd like to be Mira Ravenwing for a change.") I don't want to think about the cell-phone-wielding, perky-breasted Em and her rock star boyfriend. I want to melt into the soft release of bitter and sweet on my tongue. God, chocolate and sex would be nice, wouldn't it? Wonder what Clay's doing—

Bzzzzzzzzz.

Dammit. Who's that? Did Rose lock herself out again?

I open the door, prepared to tease her about her forgetfulness and pounce on any chocolate products she's bought, when I find myself face-to-face with a very broad-shouldered, hulking man with a vast bald patch in the midst of his crew cut, dressed in—oh, God, no—a police uniform. *Catch your breath, Claudia. Maybe Ziv has sent you one of those awful male strippers to cheer you up; he's going to produce a little boom box blaring "You Sexy Thing" and start unbuttoning any second now.* But he's got all these little ominously sheathed gadgets and—Jesus, a gun—strapped to his waist, and he's not, frankly, the type who would inspire lavish tips if he took off his clothes, because his skin is pretty pock-marked and he's got several layers of flab hovering near the gun and he doesn't look even remotely like a good time.

"I'm looking for Claudia Bloom," he says. He's got a voice that is weirdly high and girlish, like he's been sucking on a helium tank, which disturbs me. Of course, I'm already disturbed, since I'm about to be dragged off, shrieking in terror, and thrown into solitary confinement for thirteen years, where I'll take my meals of lumpy gruel squirming with larvae through a tiny slot in the door, going slowly insane as I sit motionless in the pitch black, dreaming of Clay Parker. I wonder if they let you have a vibrator in solitary confinement? Probably not; you might use it to gouge a guard's eye out. "Ma'am? Are you Claudia Bloom?"

"Oh. Um…" I consider bolting, but even if he does have a voice like Little Orphan Annie, he's the one with the gun. "Yes." I try a light, innocent laugh, but it comes out more like a hyena on crack.

"I'm Officer Cordell. I'd like to ask you a few questions."

"Oh, sure," I say casually, as if cops come to my door all the time, looking for conversation. "Come on in."

As he follows me inside, I see my apartment through a stranger's eyes, and I feel a shiver of embarrassment at the sullen clutter of it. I still haven't got much in the way of furnishings. There's my futon in one corner, surrounded by books, stray socks, a lacy bra. In the other corner is Rosemarie's old Mexican wool blanket stretched out over a bare mattress. She's set up a small shrine with tiny figures of pan-Asian gods and goddesses, feathers, crystals and even a glow-in-the-dark Virgin Mary, all cavorting together on a milk crate draped in velvet. Her backpack is propped against the wall, oozing underwear and tie-dyed skirts. Christ, this is not the sleek, hip flat of a bohemian scarf-wearing professor. This is the grotty little hideout of a car-thief arsonist and her messed-up drifter cousin.

Of course, there's no place to sit, and we both look around in awkward confusion. Somehow I can't see the two of us comfortably kicking it on the futon or the bare mattress, and he doesn't look limber enough to fold himself onto the floor without damaging something. Then again, if he pulls a muscle, my odds at a successful escape increase dramatically.

"Not much furniture yet," I say. "Been too busy." He nods, unsmiling. "Um, there's a café next door. Should we talk there?"

He hesitates—am I being too chummy?—but then takes another look around my chairless studio and nods his assent. "A cup of coffee sounds good. I'm near the end of my shift—starting to drag a little." Thank God. Maybe he'll be slow on the draw.

Once we're settled at a table in the Java House, him with a cup of black coffee, me waiting for my decaf mocha (I fear caffeine might inspire me to lunge for the gun), he gets down to business, pulling a notepad from his pocket and jabbing his ballpoint pen into the poised position.

"Now, it seems there was a vehicle reported missing last week in Austin, Texas, by—" he pauses to study his notes "—Jonathan Van Zandt." I do the math in my head: I nabbed the bus two months ago, at the beginning of September; Jonathan's friend Perry, the appointed bus-sitter, wasn't scheduled to get back from Chile until mid-October; some confusion must have followed, phone calls were made, and they finally reported it stolen last week. I feel perversely comforted by my ability to visualize this timeline, as if it indicates I've got a modicum of control here.

"We recently matched the vehicle identification numbers of the stolen bus with the numbers found on the remains of an abandoned vehicle—a bus that caught fire in—" he's squinting at his notes—why is his voice so *weird?* "—September, on Highway 17." I nod to show that I'm following, and try to keep my expression perfectly blank.

"When we informed the owner of the situation, he gave us your name, indicating that you had recently moved to this area from Austin. Also, that you were one of the few people in possession of a key. Ms. Bloom, are you all right?"

"Sorry?"

"You're pale, and you're—" he hands me a napkin "—perspiring."

Oh, Lord, I am such a miserable criminal. I might as well be wearing a neon sandwich board that reads "Take me, I'm guilty."

"Decaf mocha with whip," the barista yells, and I jump up, mopping my forehead with the napkin quickly.

"Be right back," I say, and turn to eye the exit. Would he shoot if I ran? Probably not, but better not to push my luck when the prize is a bullet between the shoulder blades. I walk to the counter and pick up my mocha, taking my time about it. This could very well be my last steps as a free woman.

I sit down with Officer Cordell again, determined not to make a scene. "So," I say pleasantly. "You were saying?"

"Look, Ms. Bloom, I don't want to upset you. You're not under arrest or anything."

"I'm not?" I can feel my face lighting up with glee, then realize how bad this looks and backpedal. "I mean, I'm not," I say, going for sane and reasonable.

"When someone—say, a partner or, you know, ex-partner—takes a vehicle, it's not really a legal issue unless someone decides to press charges. In this case, Mr. Van Zandt. So far, he doesn't seem inclined to do so." He puts his notepad down and sips his coffee. "But we did feel it was important to follow up, given the circumstances. The vehicle in question was really—well, in plain terms, it was toast." His mouth curls up at the corners and I realize this is his version of humor, so I giggle; it comes out much more nervous and high-pitched than I'd hoped, but he seems not to notice. "Of course, we suspected whoever was driving had escaped unharmed, but there was always the possibility that they hadn't, which would not be—" he taps his pen against the coffee cup "—good." He takes off his glasses and wipes them with a napkin. "Ms. Bloom, was it you in that vehicle?"

Okay, stay calm. He's already said you're not in trouble. Right? You're almost certainly not going to spend the rest of your life in solitary confinement—he practically promised you that. And let's face it, Bloom, your lying skills suck.

"Yes." It comes out as a squeak.

He leans toward me. "I'm sorry? Can you speak up?"

"Yes," I say, too loudly this time, and several students swivel their heads in my direction. Oh, God, one of them is *my* student. It's Miranda. I nod at her in greeting and turn my attention back to Officer Cordell. "It was me."

"That's what I thought." He puts his glasses back on and pushes them onto the bridge of his nose, scribbles something in his notepad and nods at me.

"Am I in big trouble?"

He shrugs. "Like I said, it's unlikely that Van Zandt will press charges. We don't like to interfere in cases of domestic—" he smiles at me "—or in this case, semidomestic, disagreements, unless we have to. But in the future, when the vehicle you're driving explodes on the side of the road, give us a call, will you please? We like to know about these things." He gets up. "Been a pleasure," he says, tucking his notepad back into his pocket. "You take care now."

He walks out, leaving me staring at my mocha in silent awe. Shit, maybe I should steal my exes' cars more often. If I'd known it was this easy, I would've gone into crime a long time ago.

CHAPTER 15

I take another healthy swig of my mother's organic merlot and wonder if there is a god in the great pantheon of deities who could save me today. I mean, come on, there's a god out there for everything, right? Surely one of their job descriptions includes looking after emotionally stunted neo-new-age families who attempt to have Thanksgiving together.

At the head of the table is Gary, my mother's husband. I can barely look at him without wincing. He's short and Yul Brynner bald with a thick black mustache and furry nostrils, dressed in a white cotton tunic and Guatemalan-print pants. Around his neck are several strands of large wooden beads. The weird thing is, you could put him in a used-car salesman's suit and he'd look a lot more natural. Every time I'm with him I see a guy from New Jersey who took a wrong turn in 1985, ended up in Mill Valley, California, and has been passing himself off as a guru ever since.

Across from him is my mother (Mira, if you want to keep your head intact) with her long, glossy brown hair and her

big, Carly Simon mouth painted a matte orange. She's looking a touch hefty these days; her boobs were always huge
and she's naturally got a Venus de Milo figure (plus the arms,
of course), but today she looks a little bloated, and the skin
around her eyes is slightly bruised with exhaustion. Tensions
are running unusually high between her and Gary. Their
only exchanges have been terse, monosyllabic ones. Even
when she smiles, there's a sadness in the curve of her lips.

Next to her is Emily, who is also a touch chunkier, though
in her case we're talking about a toothpick filling out to a
pencil. The last time I looked she had long blond hair, but
now it's dark brown and cut close to her head, which looks
really feisty and sexy on her. She's wearing a tight pink
T-shirt, sparkly pink eye shadow, and she's sporting a tiny little diamond in her nose.

On her right is my father in a grass-green Izod shirt, fiddling nervously with his horn-rimmed glasses. Under the
table I think he might be holding the hand of Didi, his first
girlfriend since Sally left him. Didi is, as my mother reported, the librarian at the high school, and she looks the
part; she's painfully thin with a graying bob, and silver reading glasses dangle from a chain around her neck. She watches
everything with alert, intelligent eyes that give me the feeling I'm going to end up in the principal's office any minute
now.

Next to me is Rose, who's just radiant in her favorite, sky-
blue cotton sundress; her right hand keeps snaking out to
caress the long black hair of her latest soul mate, Marco from
Rome, who is admittedly a sweet guy, though his English is
halting at best, so it's hard to know where he stands on most
issues. He's a giant—six-five, with a head the size of a wa-
termelon. One can't help but wonder about sex with him;
his hands look like they could crush boulders.

My jeans already feel too snug, and my discomfort in
them is heightened by the positively balmy weather.
Thanksgiving should be outlawed in California. Why tor-

ture ourselves by openly gorging on cellulite-inducing foods when it's still so warm you'll be expected to don a bikini that very weekend? These jeans will have to be surgically removed if I eat all the butter and turkey fat quivering on my plate. If it weren't for Gary, I'd be at home getting pleasantly shit-faced with Rose and Marco, probably nibbling on popcorn and listening to demo tapes of Marco's awful band, Total Eclipse. It was Gary who thought it would be "special" and "karma-cleansing" to bring the whole extended divorced-but-civil clan together for the first time ever. See, in other states, broken families accept that there's nothing to salvage from the wreckage; it's only in California that people feel compelled to get all chummy with their exes and *heal the emotional wounds,* like bingeing on carbs together somehow means all is forgiven.

Gary is currently espousing the virtues of his Spine Aligner, and I'm getting progressively more involved with my merlot.

"You see, what most people don't understand is that the sacrum is the center of our existence, the place from which well-being springs."

"Excuse me, did you say the *sacrum?*" Didi asks.

"That's right—the base of the spine."

"I know what the sacrum is," she says, tight-lipped. "I wasn't sure I heard you correctly." She pronounces each syllable with the crisp enunciation of a *Learn English in Twenty Days* tape.

Gary turns to Marco, an easier audience than Didi; Marco's MO is to nod vigorously at every word in order to camouflage his total lack of comprehension. "The kundalini lies coiled in the sacrum, ready to arise once awakened. It's like a sleeping cobra. The Spine Aligner gently prods it into action." Gary smiles his mournful, constipated smile, showing his enormous yellowing teeth, which are sporting bits of broccoli. "It's really a fascinating process."

He looks at Rosemarie, who, much like Marco, can't help

but look sweet and interested in even the most vacuous bullshit. "I've seen women who couldn't even look at themselves in the mirror turn into savage goddesses." What this means, exactly, in Garyspeak is anyone's guess, but it's obvious he's caressing Rosemarie with his creepy, hypnotic voice, and Marco slips his massive arm over her shoulder, for once not nodding.

"Anyway, how's your job at the Catalyst going, Rose?" asks my mother, her voice barely concealing a low buzz of irritation. If she doesn't divorce Gary in the next couple of weeks, I suspect homicide is a realistic possibility.

Rose blushes prettily. "I, um—don't work there anymore."

"Oh, really?" She shoots a very quick glance at me—so quick even I can hardly read the *I told you so* subtext, which I hope Rose doesn't catch. "Did something happen?"

"Well, I met Marco and started managing his band." She looks dreamily at his profile as he devours an enormous mound of stuffing. "Which is a lot of work, you know. It's pretty much a full-time job. And that was my career plan, when I got on at the Catalyst—to find a band to manage."

"Good for you," my mother says, but her tone sounds like Rose just offered her a cockroach.

"You're a musician?" Emily asks Marco, perking up. Little groupie, I think. Keep your paws off this one. Okay, so maybe my Lolita sensors are working overtime, but I've seen Emily flirt, and she's had a take-no-prisoners style since before puberty. Much to my relief, Marco doesn't look up from his plate, and Rose answers for him. When there's food involved, Marco frequently misses his cues.

"Yes. He's a wonderful bassist. They're called Total Eclipse. Isn't that a great name?" Actually, I think it's about the worst name I've ever heard, though not exactly a misnomer, as Marco's band does totally eclipse any desire to hear more.

"Sounds kind of…eighties, doesn't it?" Emily says scornfully.

Rose's smile fades. "No, it sounds poetic. They're into

their lyrics, they don't just throw random BS together, like most bands do these days."

"Are the lyrics in Italian?" Mira asks, and I can't tell if she's being arch or not.

"No. The lead singer's Irish," Rose says, looking at Emily triumphantly. She thinks this is her trump card, as if having a lead singer from the U.K. automatically makes her Brian Epstein.

"Have you heard of—" And here my mother lowers her voice slightly, in deference to the band of the Unmentionable Rock Star Emily is "dating," whatever that means.

"Mom," Emily says, suppressing a smile, in a fake how-could-you tone that really says yes-yes-go-on. But it's not her tone that makes me nearly choke on the cranberries I've just shoveled into my mouth, it's that one-syllable word. How can Emily possibly call Mira Mom? She's not even blood, and here she's using the very term of endearment I've been denied since I was thirteen. The presumptuous little cow.

I wait for my mother's face to register something—anything—surprise, disgust, disdain, but no, she just goes on chewing her food serenely, her jaw working with dogged determination. As I'm staring at her with God knows what sort of expression on my face, her eyes catch mine for a fraction of a second, but then she turns back to Emily and *puts a hand on her hand*.

"Oh," says Didi, with disdain. "Them. What a lot of noise." This earns her daggers from my mother and Emily.

"Yeah," says Rose, her voice more neutral. "Of course I've heard of them."

"Emily is dating—" and my mother whispers Rock Star's name.

"Mother," says Emily, half whiny, half smug, and I can't help it, I push my chair back and rush for the door. I can hear Rose calling after me faintly, but my vision is blurred and I feel that woozy panic, like when you're in the fourth grade and the milk in your thermos is sour but you don't realize so you drink it, anyway, and suddenly you're going to throw up all over the schoolroom floor.

I lunge my way out of the sliding glass doors onto the sprawling deck. I find myself surrounded by Gary's meticulous Japanese gardens and flowering trees from Tokyo. I lean against the railing and breathe steadily until I'm pretty sure I'm not going to puke. My skin is cold-clammy, though, and I stand there for a few minutes trying to think clearly. Mira-fucking-Ravenwing. Most of the kids I knew with divorced parents lived with their moms, and some even became the prized jewels in bloodthirsty custody battles. But Mira Ravenwing just flew off, careless as could be, flitting from husband to husband, purchasing skunk weed in bulk, learning to finger-paint her chakras, delving into her past lives as Korean prostitutes and Swedish clockmakers. Why did she never think twice about her past life with me? Didn't she think I'd miss her, defending myself against Sally the migraine-suffering stepmother and dealing with my father, the pussy-whipped patriarch?

"Claudia?" Rosemarie's warm hand is on my back. She leans on the railing next to me, tucks a strand of hair behind my ear and tries to get a good look at my face. I just keep staring down at Gary's prized koi swimming aimlessly in their tiled, kidney-shaped pool. "What's up?"

"Nothing."

"Hey. You can tell me."

Something in her voice forces me to come clean. "My mother doesn't love me," I whisper, and I feel so childish saying it I can't even look at her.

"Shh. She does, too."

"She never even let me call her Mom."

"Listen, Claudia, Aunt Mira has serious issues, okay? Of course, my mom does, too. But it's not our fault. It's got nothing to do with us."

I turn to her; she's so lovely in the mellow November light, with her warm olive skin flushed slightly from the wine and her dark eyes full of concern.

"I figured that out a long time ago," she tells me, cupping my shoulder with her palm.

"But why can she be so warm with stupid little Emily, who's not even her kid?"

Rose thinks about this for a second. "Maybe she's grown up some, and now she's a better mom. I don't know. You could ask her."

I scoff. "Yeah, right. You know Mira. She'd change the subject—fast."

"Yeah, probably."

I sigh, casting a glance over my shoulder back at the house. "How embarrassing. I feel like a pouty little kid."

"Family," Rose says, shaking her head. "Look at the bright side. At least your mom has kind bud. Maybe she'll share with us for dessert."

I laugh. "Yeah, that's all I need, to be stoned and paranoid on top of depressed." I turn and stare at the sliding glass doors, so slick and clean, reflecting the compulsive grace of Gary's garden, created and maintained by his Australian mistress.

"And Gary," I grumble. "Yuck."

"You can say that again," Rose whispers. "You tried to warn me, but shit, he really is smarmy, isn't he?" She presses her lips together tightly to suppress a giggle. "That Spine Aligner shit? Is he for real?" We laugh a little, trying to keep it down. It's like having the sister I always craved—someone to giggle with in conspiratorial secrecy, someone who'll remind me I'm not the crazy one when the adults all behave like mental cases on acid.

When we've stopped laughing, she touches my hair affectionately and cocks her head in a question. "Ready to face the enemy?"

"As I'll ever be, I guess."

So we march back inside, putting on brave, cheerful faces. Except nobody notices, because by the time we get back to the table, Thanksgiving dinner has gone from pretty-bad-but-under-control to total anarchy.

★ ★★

"He is *not*." Emily is screaming at Didi. "He's only thirty-eight, okay? So fuck you."

"Whoa," Rose mutters, touching my arm.

"Emily," Gary says, his eyes wide. "What on earth are you...?"

"Sweetheart." Mira reaches for Emily's hand again, and my stomach contracts slightly, but not as bad as last time.

"And it's a *good* band," Emily continues, her tone seething and belligerent. "It's like totally out-there music, and nobody expects a stupid, uptight bitch like you to get it, all right?"

"Wait a minute, young lady," my father says, squinting at her over his glasses. "Maybe nobody here cares about your manners, but—"

"And what's that supposed to mean?" growls Gary, offended.

"Obviously she gets away with murder in this house—"

"And your daughter was a perfect angel, I suppose?" Gary glances at me before returning his hostile attention to my father. Wait a second. What exactly did Mira tell him about me?

My father looks at me, confused, and sputters, "Claudia's got nothing to do with this—I'm only saying—" *Thanks, Dad, for that heartfelt defense.* "I'm only saying that Emily should not be allowed to scream obscenities at Didi, here." He puts a shaking hand on Didi's shoulder.

Gary takes a deep breath and returns to his creepy swami voice, addressing the ceiling. "We've raised Emily as a fully conscious being with a vast array of choices before her. She makes those choices on her own. If she expresses anger—"

"She's out of control," my father protests.

Gary sighs dramatically and widens his eyes at Dad. "Please, let me finish. She's expressing her anger at Didi's hostile attitude toward the man she loves. Is that so wrong? Isn't that exactly what *you're* doing?" he says, pointing a finger at Dad. "Expressing anger because the woman you love has been insulted?"

My father swallows, clearly at a loss.

"I just think Didi's a fucking bitch," Emily offers helpfully.

"Emily," Mira says, but there's very little venom in her bite.

"I can't help it. I'm totally hormonal today, all right?"

Marco leans over and whispers to Rosemarie, "What is it? 'Hormoonal'?" This sets Rose off giggling, which sets me off, and pretty soon we're helpless with laughter, clutching each other's hands under the table, while Marco looks hurt, and everyone else stares at us like *we're* the crazy ones.

"Fine," Emily huffs. "Laugh if you want to. No one's going to be laughing when they find out I'm pregnant."

Well, actually, she's wrong. This just sets us off even worse. Tears are streaming down our faces and my stomach is starting to cramp, but neither of us can stop.

"Pregnant," Mira says.

"You're *pregnant?*" Gary echoes, for once not sounding like a constipated guru.

"Yeah, and I have been, for like three months," she says, her bottom lip trembling. "If anyone in this house ever bothered to *look* at me, you might've noticed."

"My God," Mira says. "Why didn't you say some…?"

"Because I knew you'd both tell me to just kill it, you— *liberals!*" And with this she runs from the table, sobbing.

Rose and I finally manage to squelch our hysterics. There's a long silence at the table that *awkward* doesn't begin to describe.

Finally, Marco breaks it with the phrase he practiced all the way here in the car, repeating after Rose until I thought I'd go mad. "Thank you for a lovely Thanksgiving dinner." Everyone turns to gape at him, and he beams at us, his enormous, chiseled face looking pink and eager.

"Christ," my mother says. "I need a bong hit," and she gets up from the table.

Rose and I glance at each other, then get up to follow her, ready to collect on our hard-won dessert.

★ ★ ★

On the drive home, Marco's crashed out in the back seat, while Rose and I, stoned and stuffed, laugh about the whole fiasco to keep from crying.

"That Emily's a piece of work," Rose says.

"Yeah, well, you've got to feel sorry for her," I say.

"Why? She's rich, she's young, she's sexy, they let her do whatever she wants (including supplying her with top-notch chronic) and now she's set for life with a rock star's baby. If he doesn't want her, she could do the talk-show circuit and make millions." Rose is braiding her hair into cornrows; when she's not braiding Rex, she's doing me or Marco or herself. She's got this thing about braids that's positively compulsive. She says it relaxes her.

"She's had it rough, though," I say, surprised to find myself defending the little wench. "When she was six, her real mom died of cancer."

"That's tough. There are worse things than losing a parent, though." And for a long minute, I know we're both thinking about Jade, but we don't say anything.

"Not to bag on the dead," I say, trying to lighten the mood, "but Emily's real mom must've been as out there as Gary. You know what they named her?"

Rose looks at me, mystified. "Emily's not her real name?"

"It's her *middle* name. Her full legal name is Aphrodite Emily Snyder."

Rose explodes with laughter. "No shit."

"Seriously."

"Man, that's wild." Once she's stopped laughing, she gazes out the window with a pensive air.

"Do you, um, miss Jade a lot? Like during the holidays?" I ask, wondering if there's a less awkward way to bring it up.

"What made you think of that?" she asks, and suddenly her face looks ten years older.

"I don't know. I was just wondering...."

"Of course I miss her. All the time." She takes a tiny rub-

ber band from her pocket and ties off the braid she's just finished. Then she glances in the back seat to make sure Marco's
asleep, and I wonder if she's finally going to talk to me about
Jade's death, and what it did to her, and how she can handle
waking up in the morning. But instead, she changes the subject, like she always does. "Hey, maybe if Total Eclipse doesn't
work out, I could groom little Aphrodite. She could be the
next one-name wonder."

"Maybe."

Rose looks out the window again and doesn't say a word
the rest of the ride home. Every time I think she's fallen
asleep, though, I see her fingers braiding with rapid precision, like someone performing an intricate ritual, praying
wordlessly to vague gods in the dark.

CHAPTER 16

Now that we've almost reached the end of the semester, I'm more determined than ever to get Clay off my mind. Monica's been tracking my every move with her glittery little hawk eyes, and she's clearly chummy with Ruth Westby, the department chair. It's been emphasized from the beginning that I'd have to be really stellar and indispensable if this position is to become permanent. It's a long shot no matter how you look at it, but I'm definitely out of the running if I build up more faculty hatred by sleeping with Clay.

Not that he's exactly beating down my door. It's been seven weeks to the day since I stormed out of the pub and told him to stop mind-fucking me. He's complied with maddening thoroughness—haven't seen or heard from him at all. And I refuse, though I've been sorely tempted on more than one occasion, to just happen into Viva Vinyl like a love-struck adolescent. No, siree. I haven't come this far only to give into pubescent urges. I am a mature professional now. I have my own travel mug, which I fill with coffee in the faculty lounge, thanks very much. I own a scarf, and though I haven't had the occasion to wear it just yet, it looks very chic on me.

I am not dying for a decent fuck.

Yes you are.

Am not.

"Professor Bloom?" God, I love the sound of that.

"Yes?" I swivel in my desk chair to see Ben Crow in the doorway. Mmm. Talk about fantasy material. Dark brown hair to his shoulders, high cheekbones, deeply tanned skin. He's got just enough rock star in him to justify long hair— on most boys it looks girlish or sixties goofy, but on him it looks über-masculine. He's wearing a threadbare white T-shirt that shows all his muscles and a loose-fitting pair of chinos. I could eat him with a spoon.

"I wanted to talk to you," he says, and the concern on his face makes him even more edible. "Do you have a minute?"

"Yeah. Sure."

He comes in and closes the door behind him. It's categorically discouraged to meet with students behind closed doors, since it supposedly increases your vulnerability to sexual harassment charges. Still, I can't bring myself to get up and open it.

He sits very close to the edge of my desk and speaks softly. He's got a wonderful, resonant, reach-the-back-row sort of voice, so he's practically got to whisper to avoid being heard all the way down the hall; his timbre makes my chest vibrate slightly. "It's about Ralene," he says, and sighs. "I really tried to be patient with her, but it's gotten out of hand." He leans back in the chair and rubs his hands together, a nervous gesture that makes me fixate on his fingers, which are dark and strong and—

Get it together, Bloom. Student. Off-limits.

I can see his abs through that T-shirt—washboard city— and he smells of sandalwood, which normally turns me off but on him is the height of earthiness, conjuring images of long, delicious massages, glistening oiled limbs…

"She kept coming on to me," he says. "And then she acted like *I* was into *her.*" He gives me a look that conveys just how absurd this notion is. "It was embarrassing."

"But your project's done next week—you won't have to work with her after that." *And could you please take off your shirt so I could just look for a while?*

"I know, I know. But here's the deal. I guess she told Professor Parker that I was—whatever—'harassing' her, and that you refused to do anything about it. So then Parker told Westby." He runs a hand through his hair and looks miserable. Now I'm the one who's nervous. "Westby called me in yesterday, started asking a lot of questions. It's all blown out of proportion. I mean all I did was try to be nice to the woman."

Oh, God. Goodbye, tenure track. Hello, want ads. Well, look at the bright side. You could molest this kid without any ramifications.

"Professor Bloom?"

"Sorry. What did you tell Westby?"

"I just explained how it happened—Ralene complaining about me, how you asked me for my side and all that. I mean, what were you supposed to do? The woman's a nutcase."

"And did Westby believe you?"

"I don't know. She's pretty hard to read." He looks like he wants to say more but decides not to. "Anyway, I just thought you should know."

"Yes. Thanks for telling me." I try to look poised and mature, rather than flustered, scared and so in need of a good fuck that I'm about to ravish him.

"You okay?"

"Who, me?" My voice cracks, and he smiles. He's probably used to women sweating in his presence, but that doesn't make it any less humiliating. "Yes. Fine. Oh, by the way, I want you to read this script." I fumble through my bag until I locate a copy of Miranda's play, *Heirloom.* "We're producing it next quarter, and I want you to read for it. Check out Ray. It's a good role."

He looks pleased. "Cool. Thanks."

"Yeah, and thanks for letting me know."

"No problem. I really like your class, by the way. You're the only teacher here I can relate to, you know? Everyone else seems so—" he looks down at the floor, trying to find the right word "—old," he finishes, and then, dissatisfied with that, he adds, "or stuck in their ways, or something." I feel a ridiculous flush of pleasure. Ben Crow likes me. "You're more spontaneous. That's the way theater should be, don't you think? You shouldn't have to plan every little detail like it's some sort of military operation."

"No," I agree. "You shouldn't. You know, you should read this book—I think you'd really like it. Have you ever checked out David Mamet?" He shakes his head, no. "Totally incredible playwright." I dig through my bag once again. "He writes essays about theater that are just—where is that?" I heave my bag onto my desk and dig some more. I pull a binder out and a tiny swath of material flutters onto my desk, landing inches from Ben's elbow. For a confused beat, we both just look at it, perplexed, and then I realize with horror what it is.

My leopard-print thong.

Christ, Bloom, you've really done it this time.

I reach for it, but Ben, who is quicker and closer, has already picked it up. Realizing what it is, he drops it like it's a rattlesnake, blushing scarlet.

"Panty lines. Just hate them," I blurt out, then cover my eyes.

He makes a small, embarrassed sound in his throat.

"I—I was going to go swimming on campus, so I brought—" I stammer, seizing the offending item and stuffing it back into my bag. "A change of clothes," I finish meekly. "Anyway…" I can feel his eyes on me, and I fumble in my bag more frantically than ever. "Jeez, where is that stupid book?"

Professor Arrested for Forcing Student to Study Thong.

There's a knock on my door. "Come in," I say, relieved to be rescued from this moment. The doorknob jiggles, and then I remember that our office doors lock automatically. I get up and open it, expecting to see Miranda, since we're supposed to talk about *Heirloom* this afternoon; instead I find myself face-to-face with Clay Parker.

"Hi." Having just barely cooled from my stinging embarrassment seconds earlier, I now feel my face burning afresh.

"Good, you're here." He looks over my shoulder and, seeing Ben, goes serious and curt. "You're with someone—sorry. When are you free?"

"Oh. Um—"

"I was just leaving," Ben says. "I'll see you next week, Professor Bloom."

"Okay." I return to my desk and sit down, trying to get my bearings. "I look forward to your final project," I say as Ben and Clay scoot past each other in the doorway. I hope I've struck that perfect professorial tone—encouraging but cool, not a trace of tart—because now that Clay's here I suddenly feel incredibly culpable and transparent, as if he can see with a glance that I've been tossing my panties around recklessly.

"See you," Ben mutters, and disappears.

"Listen," Clay says, shutting the door. I try to calculate whether sexual harassment risk exists with a fellow faculty member's husband. *Professor Convicted of Home Wrecking.* "I'm sorry to bother you here. I know you don't want anything to do with me, but this is sort of an emergency." He sits where Ben did, his legs in a wide V, his elbows propped on his knees. I wonder how I ever could have gotten worked up over Ben Crow, even with his cut abs and his sandalwood oil; he's nothing compared to the symphony of crooked and straight that is Clay Parker.

"That sounds a little scary."

"I'm not trying to be alarmist," he says, "I just figured you should know. Ruth Westby?" I nod, completely mystified about where this is going. "She's, um, she's got a bit of a problem with you right now. You can talk her down, but she's not happy."

"Actually, Ben was just telling me—"

"Was *that* Ben? The guy that just left?" I nod. "Huh. Okay." He appears to be working this into the equation, making calculations. "Well, Westby's under the impression that you're playing favorites with him. That you deliberately ignored some very serious complaints about him by other students because you're fond of him. Maybe even— too fond."

"Too fond?" I repeat weakly. Oh, my God. I'm a child molester. They've planted a microchip in my brain and have monitored every lustful spasm that passes through my quivering, sex-deprived cells.

"Monica's encouraged the notion. She's talked to a bunch of your students, and now she's got Westby semiconvinced there's something scandalous going on."

"Wait," I say. *Breathe. Go on—inhale, exhale. You can do it, Bloom.* "Are you saying they think I'm like—they don't think Ben and I are…?"

"Let's just say it's crossed their minds, okay?" I look at him in horror, and he just shrugs. "Welcome to academic politics."

"But how do you…?"

The phone rings. I stare at it blankly, my heart pounding, then pick it up with damp palms and croak, "Professor Bloom." Usually just saying this cheers me up, but today it sounds absurd, like a little kid with a toy gun lisping, "Bond. Jameth Bond."

"Claudia. Ruth Westby here." She sounds very cheerful, not at all like someone about to accuse me of lewd and immoral conduct. "Have you got a minute?"

Have I got a minute? A minute to be sacked? A minute to be prosecuted as a sex offender? "Sure? What's up?"

"I wonder if you could stop by my office. I'd like to have a chat." A chat. God. Beware the Chat.

"Sure. Like in…" I look at Clay. "Oh, ten minutes? Will that do?" He's rubbing his forehead as if he's got a migraine.

"Sounds perfect. See you then." Her voice rises on "then" with an almost shrill effervescence, and for a moment I wish to God she was a gruff, patriarchal man-boss, the sort who barked, "My office, Bloom. Now."

I hang up and stare at Clay, feeling sick and not bothering to hide it. "She's going to fire me, isn't she?"

"It's not that bad—really—she wouldn't do that. All she's got is Monica's allegations, which were all gathered from your students—"

"Students, or student?" I ask, hating Ralene Tippets with such passion I'm convinced I could commit homicide with a smile.

"I don't know for sure. Someone went to Monica and then she started snooping around, but she hasn't got any hard evidence."

"I'm not sleeping with Ben Crow," I whisper. "You know that, right?"

He shrugs. "It's none of my business—I just thought you should be armed with information."

"Oh, my God," I say. "Of *course* I'm not sleeping with him—I'm not sleeping with *anyone*." I bite my lip. Oops.

He grins at me, maddeningly cool in the face of my panic. "Is that right?"

"Yes, that's right, Mr. Smiley, and don't look so smug about it, either. If it weren't for you—" I glance toward the door and consciously lower my voice, leaning toward him to hiss, "If it weren't for *you,* I wouldn't be in this mess. So stop gloating."

"I'm not gloating. I'm trying to help."

"Yes. Okay. I see that. Sorry." I start gnawing at a cuticle, terrified. "I told you I'm not cut out for this. I can't believe Monica would turn my students against me."

"She doesn't want you here. I've never seen her like this. She's gotten ruthless since that—" He hesitates. "That morning."

A pulse of heat throbs through me at the thought of our limbs braided together, but then the reality of Monica's revenge cools it. "Did she come right out and tell you she's trying to get me fired?"

"I know some people in the department—they tipped me off. When I confronted Monica she didn't deny it, exactly, she just tried to spin it all professional and businesslike."

I can feel my face contorting with this fresh wave of information. "So other people think I'm—that Ben and I are—does the whole department assume…?"

"Rumors, okay? That's all it is right now—just hearsay. So explain your side to Ruth and stick to your guns."

The urge to hyperventilate assails me, but I take a deep breath and close my eyes. He's right. I haven't done anything wrong. Monica Parker and Ralene Tippets can go fuck themselves. I'm a good teacher—maybe a little raw, a lot to learn, but I've got an instinct for it, and I'm compassionate, which is more than I can say for Monica Stick-Up-Her-Ass Parker or Esther Too-Tall Small. What did Ben just say? He said I'm spontaneous—and he's right. I've got that on my side. Half the geriatrics around here wouldn't know a fresh idea if it French-kissed them. Now go defend yourself.

"Okay," I say softly, standing. "I better go. She's waiting."

"Right. You'll do great. But…Claudia?" He looks painfully uncomfortable, all of a sudden. "There's one more thing I should mention, before you talk to her." He stands and shoves his fingers into his Levi's pockets, letting his thumbs hang out; he won't meet my gaze.

"What is it?"

"I wanted to tell you this before, but I didn't know how you'd take it." There's a long, elastic pause, as our eyes meet and a thousand impulses pinball between us—sparks leaping and spiraling off, like little meteors—urges without names, only salty flavors and tangy smells.

"You know—Westby?" he says finally.

I nod. Of course I know her—what is he...?

"She's my mother."

"Claudia, come in. Have a seat. We haven't really talked since I did your evaluation."

Hearing that word, I have to wrestle with a powerful instinct to run screaming from the room. I barely made it through that without pissing my pants. There was Ruth Westby in her fashionable tortoiseshell glasses, her short hair gleaming silver in the back of my classroom, her perfectly unreadable face reminding me of my father's—her eyes every bit as cryptic, her mouth a flat line of infinite variables, which no equation can yield.

And after the classroom observation was over, I'd waited a week for the results. When summoned, I'd trudged to her office with quick-drying concrete in my belly, sure she was going to give me my walking papers ("You call this thing you're doing *instruction?*"), I tried not to whimper profuse apologies and excuses. I just knew that the careful mask she'd worn as she watched me flailing and striving before my students would fall away as her office door clicked shut, and I would be face-to-face with her naked scorn.

Instead, in her mild, expressionless way, she had given me her stamp of approval. At least I think she did. She suggested I use the board more. She liked how I "got everyone involved" (although no one could have missed Ralene's moping reluctance to participate in nearly everything, except the critiques—Ralene loved to critique). In short, she signed my evaluation and effectively labeled me satisfactory until proved otherwise.

Still, I couldn't shake the eerie sense that Ruth Westby was the sort of woman who revealed exactly nothing, and therefore praise or criticism were all the same, falling from her lips. Everything she said was opaque; she used her words to hide rather than reveal, always with the same polite precision.

I would have preferred a good whipping.

"So. How are you getting along here? Do you like it all right?"

I start to answer, but it comes out as a squeak, so I clear my throat and begin again. "I do. I love it here."

She leans back in her plush leather desk chair and folds her hands neatly in her lap. She's wearing a pale blue suit—wool gabardine, I believe—tasteful lipstick (muted rust) and pearl earrings. I try to imagine her giving birth to Clay Parker: knees splayed wide, panting and moaning, glazed all over in sweat, his slippery head forcing its way into the doctor's latex grip.

"And your classes are almost over, of course—are you eager to start winter break?" She arranges her mouth into a small, conversational smile.

"Well, it's a good time to recharge, reorganize, I guess." Translation: to lie around and stuff my face with See's candy.

There's a pause as she gazes at me over her glasses, and then her right eye blinks furiously—as fast as a hummingbird's wing—before resuming its previous, unblinking pose, making me think I've imagined it. But no—there it is again. It flutters with remarkable speed, while the rest of her face remains motionless and composed, apparently unaware of the rogue eye's resistance to frozen order.

Is she nervous? Somehow this thought injects me with a tentative dose of courage.

"So," I say, leaning forward a bit. I hold her gaze. The language of deference is intricate—I have to show her I'm not cowing, nor am I challenging. Every actor knows that our faces and bodies are perpetually negotiating the balance of power. Who's on top now? Who's on bottom? "What did you want to see me about?"

Again, a long, icy pause. Her eye does its thing and I feel another surge of confidence.

"Am I in trouble?" I ask, sounding more irreverent than contrite. Well, shit. Does she have to torture me like this?

"Are you familiar with William Ball's *A Sense of Direction?*"

"Sure." I thumbed through it when I found it on Jonathan's dresser once. Promptly fell asleep.

"Do you recall his emphasis on unity as the defining characteristic of art?"

I just nod. I actually sort of do remember that. It was on the first page, I think. Maybe Westby didn't get very far in it, either. Why doesn't she just come out and *ask* me: are you fucking Ben Crow?

"Well, I look at my department in a similar light. I see everyone teaching here as the various components of an ongoing performance. And when Bill Ball talks about *unity,* he's not just talking about the performers working together, he's talking about the audience believing in what they see so that actors and audience alike are caught up in—" and here she slows down, hitting each syllable with great emphasis, like a drummer pounding out the final notes of a song "—the same, unified spell."

She takes off her glasses and squints at me. "In our case, the students form the audience—they must believe in us, because we believe in our performance. We are professionals. We are not *pretending* to be professionals. We actually are. At least we are when we step foot on this campus." She has gradually inched her way forward throughout this speech, until she's flattened herself against the edge of her desk in what appears to be a painful position. "Do you consider yourself a professional, Claudia?"

"Sure." Gulp. Scary woman. Very Scary.

"And are you comfortable with the responsibilities this entails?" There goes the eye again—a prolonged flutter this time, a spasmodic moth caught in a too-tight space.

"Dr. Westby, if you're referring to the incident involving Ralene Tip—"

"I am referring, Claudia, to professionalism, unity and responsibility. Are you comfortable with each of these concepts?"

"Er—sure. I guess so."

"Do you guess so, or do you know so?"

I clear my throat and say, in the clearest, calmest voice I can manage, "I know I haven't violated any tenets of professionalism, if that's what you mean."

"Excellent." She forms her features into a half smile, tight-lipped and void of joy. "So glad you could come by for this little chat, Claudia. Good luck with finals, and I hope you return refreshed from your break."

CHAPTER 17

After we've turned in our final grades, Mare takes me out to celebrate Santa Cruz-style: we go to a yoga class that makes me feel like a defective human pretzel, then soak in her chlorine-free hot tub until our fingers prune up. Her house is nestled in the Santa Cruz Mountains, about thirty minutes from mine. It's one of those huge-windowed, redwood-deck-type places, and her walls are filled with black-and-white photos of feet.

"You must like feet," I say, studying a huge blowup of a big toe.

"My son," she says. "He did those."

"Oh, I didn't know you had kids. How old is he?"

She hands me a cup of tea. We're in our towels, standing in her kitchen. There's a leaning tower of dishes in the sink and the tile floor could use a good sweeping, but somehow the mess enhances the atmosphere rather than detracting from it. "He's twenty-two. I had him pretty young."

"Any others?"

She wraps her long brown fingers around her mug and

her ancient eyes turn a shade darker. "My daughter, Kayla, died last year," she says, her voice low.

"Oh, my God. I'm so sorry, Mare."

Her eyes flit to me, then back to the floor. "She was, um, in Colorado. On a river-rafting trip. She drowned." This last part is barely more than a whisper.

I shake my head, unsure of what to say. Finally, I resort to a cliché provided by years of absorbing bad TV. "How awful for you."

We drink our tea and listen to the crickets starting up outside in the dusk.

"Anyway," she says, "enough about me. Come in here, sit down and let me grill you about all the juicy gossip I've been hearing."

"Oh, shit," I laugh and follow her into the living room. She tosses me a thick, spa-style robe while she throws on her usual dancer-sexy threadbare T-shirt and sweats. We settle into the big suede couches.

"First things first. Are you or are you not having a torrid affair with the fireman?"

I scream, "Are you kidding?"

"Of course I'm not kidding. And tell me the truth, because if you're going to lie, I guarantee you I can get five or six much more interesting lies at the next faculty meeting."

"Mare! He's a student. Of course not."

"Scout's honor?"

I sputter indignantly, "What do you take me for? A child molester?"

"Okay," she says. "I believe you. Now, question number two. Are you making it with Monica's ex?"

"No," I say, but she looks at me so skeptically I feel compelled to elaborate. "Okay, here's the deal. I met him before I knew anything about Monica, and we got a little bit involved, and then as soon as I found out he was married, I totally backed off."

"But you like him?"

"Mmm. Yes and no." I stare out her big windows at the redwoods backlit by flaming pink sky. "I like him, but not enough to alienate everyone around me."

"You sure about that?" She looks like she's trying not to laugh.

"What do you mean?"

"Well, I hate to say it, but from the way Monica's been acting, the damage is already done."

"I know," I say. "She hates me."

"Did you know they're divorced now?"

"No. Really?"

"Well, practically. Monica got the papers like a month ago. She must have signed, unless she wants to take him to court."

"Oh. I didn't know that." I don't want to dwell on this information right now; I'm already in dangerous waters. It hardly seems appropriate to clap my hands and cry, "Great. Now I can bed her ex!" though I do a feel a pang of something—relief, or excitement. But as much as I like Mare, and instinctively trust her earthy, wise, makeupless face, I've learned to keep a layer of secrecy around me when it comes to colleagues. Fat lot of good it does me; they fill in the blanks with their own pornographic fabrications.

"Are you and Monica friends?"

She shakes her head. "No. She got mad at me four years ago because I didn't cast her nephew in the spring dance show. She's still holding a grudge. I heard it from Esther." She takes a sip of her tea. "Monica's okay, but I don't think she's big on forgiveness. Not to be dramatic, or anything, but I would watch your back."

Later, after Mare has dropped me at home and I'm lying in the dark with Medea, listening to Rose and Rex snore a sweetly off-key duet, I think about Clay Parker.

Divorced. He's practically divorced.

And he's got the cutest butt in Levi's I ever saw in real life.

He did come to my office specifically to save my ass last week.

And he did tell me the truth, voluntarily, about Ruth Westby being his mother.

Sure, it took him three months, and naturally the information was supplied well after she had time to hate me for home wrecking, like everyone else on faculty, except with more intensity, since it was her son and daughter-in-law's home I'd wrecked, her future grandchildren's existence I'd trampled on and crushed like yesterday's cigarette butts.

I listen to the train and to young, girlish laughter on the street, someone calling out to someone else, "Hey, give my cigarettes back!"

I think of Monica, and try to imagine how she felt when she saw those divorce papers waiting for her signature, a slash of ink to blot out years of her life, to undo the future she must have tasted when she stood in a puffy white dress and said, "I do."

How can anyone believe in marriage in the twenty-first century? Didn't we all listen to our parents bicker while we turned up the volume on *Hawaii Five-O?* Didn't we learn the fairy tale was dead when we found half our parental unit shoving their socks and underwear into a suitcase while the other half spit out vile insults?

Cutest butt in Levi's ever—swear to God.

Very cute out of Levi's, too.

I mean, look at my parents. Years of misery together, followed by years of misery with others. And still they bravely marry—can you imagine? As if they've no choice in the matter.

My mother's voice: "Claudia, I don't marry because I *want* to, I marry because I find it impossible not to."

A tiny sound reaches me, bobbing up through the layers of canine and human snoring, through the hum of the refrigerator and the frantic techno throb of the club two blocks away, tugging me from my random collage of hypnagogic thoughts and fixing me on this: *Tap. Tap. Tap.*

I sit up.

The window. Someone's tapping on the—

There's a flash of something bright in the streetlight—a darting glimmer—then the little tap again. Hail? But it's been one of those days that make California so freaky, eighty-five degrees and dazzling in mid-December. No, not hail. Too sharp and distinct to be leaves. Miniature kamikaze bats? Even I have to admit this is unlikely.

I sleep naked when Marco's not over, but I do keep a pair of old boxers and a tank top near the bed. I glance quickly across the room to confirm it's just Rose and Rex here tonight, his huge paws draped across her dark spill of hair on the pillow, then, slipping the boxers-and-tank ensemble on, I make my way to the window, crouching low.

Just as I reach the glass, another tap. Looks like a—penny?

I'm down on all fours as I peer over the windowsill. On the sidewalk below stands Clay Parker, one hand in the pocket of his jeans, the other poised to toss again. He does, just as I'm opening the window, and the penny hits me hard in the forehead.

"Ouch," I cry.

"Claudia. Is that you?"

"Almost put my eye out."

"Claudia," he calls again, and I can tell from the wobbly joy in his voice that he's drunk, though I have to confess a little storm of confetti erupts in my chest just the same, a no-one's-ever-thrown-pennies-at-my-window giddiness.

"Yes, Clay?" I say, trying to sound calm, anyway.

"I'm divorced."

I stand there. What's the proper response to this declaration? *Excellent—come inside and let me do you?*

Rose creeps up behind me and watches over my shoulder. "What did he say?" she asks in a groggy, amused voice.

"He said he's divorced."

"Huh. He's cute, isn't he?"

"Uh-huh."

"You going to ask him in?" she says, chewing on her hair.

"You think I should?"

"I would."

"He gets me in a lot of trouble," I say.

Medea comes over, leaps onto the windowsill and peers down at Clay blinkingly, looking unimpressed. She lets her tail twitch frenetically, though, giving away her memories of those hands on her fur.

"Everything fun's a lot of trouble," says Rose through a yawn, and goes back to bed.

"Hold on," I call out to him. "I'm coming down."

"Oh, no," he says. "Don't—please, no."

"Why not?"

"I stink. My hair's all—" He gestures vaguely at his head. "I might throw up." As if to emphasize this point, he stumbles off the sidewalk into a large clump of bamboo, rights himself quickly and stands up very straight, as if nothing's happened. "Gotta go. Just wanted to tell you."

"Clay. You're not driving, are you?"

"Y'kidding?" He adds something to this that sounds like "mash sticks."

"What?"

"Not driving," he says. "Crash at Nick's. Just wanted to…" And then he shrugs helplessly, as if it's all too much for him, and starts off down the street, putting one foot in front of the other with self-conscious deliberation, like someone taking a sobriety test.

"Wait," I say. "Let me just come down there for a—"

But he's already walking away.

I watch his precious sagging Levi's for a couple of seconds as he totters off. Then he steps into the shadows, and though I stay at the window for several more minutes, he's gone.

WINTER

PART 2

CHAPTER 18

My thirtieth birthday falls on a Monday, which only compounds how depressing it is. Rose tries to convince me that since I'm on winter break and she's unemployed, this negates its Mondayness, but I disagree. I secretly suspect it's a sign that the decade ahead will be packed with the spirit of Mondays: drudgery, dread and coffee-guzzling existentialism.

I don't want to hate aging. It's so un-tart to buy antiwrinkle serums and curse the mysterious, insectlike facial hairs that crop up with the years. Somehow, though, in my *Tart Manifesto,* I never got around to considering myself at thirty, or—Jesus—forty. I was filled with the drunken buoyancy of *Me Me Me,* which leaves no space for the future. I vaguely imagined I might die at twenty-seven, like Kurt Cobain, Janis Joplin and Jim Morrison. I doubted I would ever actually *be* a rock star, but I figured I could probably manage to die like one.

Rose is trying to be enthusiastic; she's dutifully baked me an incredibly dark, intoxicatingly chocolate cake with cream-cheese icing and strawberry trimmings. She also

drew me a picture of Rex and Medea, which is slightly fic-
tionalized since she's portrayed them sitting side by side
peacefully, which would never happen. Rex and Medea
have a dysfunctional relationship that mostly involves de-
nial of each other's existence, occasionally disrupted by ex-
citing episodes of goofy pursuit on Rex's part and violent
counterattack by Medea.

In spite of Rose's sweet and solicitous birthday smile, I
know she's seething. She's not mad at me, but at God or fate,
whichever is responsible for the whiplash-inducing ride that
is her life. Total Eclipse decided last week that their career
was stagnating in Santa Cruz, and just like that they moved
to L.A., not even bothering to invite Rose along. She and
Marco had a terse, clipped goodbye—couldn't expect much
else, given their language barrier—and that was that: bud-
ding career and soul mate whisked off together in a dilapi-
dated Volvo.

I'm a little worried about Rose, to be honest. Vodka continues to evaporate around her, she hasn't worked since her
two-week stint cocktailing at the Catalyst, and though she
cooks like a glutton, she eats like a bird. Her once Botticelli-
esque body is now catwalk-thin, and though she may look
extraordinarily good in Levi's (buttless works for women,
too), when she strips down to her underwear she looks a little too concentration camp for my taste. I can't shake the suspicion that Jade's death is lurking like a bad dream just under
Rose's skin, forcing her to dart restlessly from one distraction to the next.

Jade isn't the only subject she's silent about. There's Aunt
Jessie, stashed away in some New Mexico prison. Neither
Rose nor my mother are inclined to talk about this at all, as
if one's immediate relatives often do time and there's no
point in discussing it. I know Aunt Jessie's an alcoholic, and
yes, Rose has good reason to resent the random, gypsy childhood she endured in the name of Jessie's freedom, but all
the same, shouldn't someone be doing *something?* Maybe

prison break is out of the question, but one of us could visit, or write? A couple times I've started letters to Jessie, but I ended up feeling ridiculous; what's there to say? *Hi, sorry you're such a boozer, hope prison dries you out for good. By the way, your daughter keeps stealing my Absolut on the sly. Much love…?* Besides, it would upset Rose if I wrote; she's so defensive whenever I raise the subject, like I'm accusing her of abandonment just by mentioning Jessie's name.

"Come on," Rose says as we're lying around on the couch we scored at a garage sale, moaning about having eaten too much chocolate cake for breakfast. "There must be *something* you want to do."

"There's only one advantage to having your birthday three days before Christmas," I say. "You get the two worst holidays out of the way all at once."

"You're being so negative."

"I'm not. This is the bright side," I insist. "If I go out and get really ripped on my birthday, I might just sleep straight through to New Year's. I'd consider that a good year."

"Maybe we should go to the beach?"

Medea and I regard her with appropriate skepticism. Outside, a torrent of rain lashes against our windows, as it has for days. It's like living in a car wash. I rather like it, actually. It gives me an excuse for gloom.

"Okay," she says. "Maybe not the beach. How's about we go thrifting? We'll get really groovy, totally tasteless dresses and wear them out tonight."

"Out where?" I ask listlessly. It doesn't help matters knowing that if we go shopping, it'll have to be my treat. Ditto for night on the town.

"Out *anywhere.*"

"Rose," I begin, and then I hesitate, which tells her everything she needs to know.

"You're mad cause I don't have a job," she says. "You think I'm a parasite. You wish I was dead."

I smile. "That's not exactly the sentiment," I say. "But

we're both pretty broke. You know I blew most of my paycheck at that stupid salon."

Last week, in a mad attempt to achieve the ever-elusive
bohemian scarf-wearing professor look, I took Ziv's suggestion and went to a fancy salon in San Francisco for a complete makeover. Ziv's ex-boyfriend runs the place, and it's
the sort of joint where they offer you espresso in the delicate, eggshell-thin cups that remind me of Ziv, and everyone looks so glam you feel utterly revolting as soon as they
plop you in front of the mirror. When I left there I looked
like an albino bushman. The stylist encouraged me to embrace my Afro rather than fight it, bleached it bone-white
and ordered the cosmetologist to do my makeup in porce-
lain geisha-tones. Clownish is, unfortunately, a very apt adjective. I spent three hundred dollars on the makeover and
$2.75 on a box of Kleenex for the ride home.

"Claudia, I suck," Rose says. "I've totally and completely
let you down."

"I'm not saying—"

"No, I *have,*" she says emphatically, sitting up. Medea blinks
at her, and Rex comes trotting over, his toenails clicking,
sensing the possibility of a walk. "I just realized—the only
present I can give you is to go out and get a job."

"Rose…"

"It's true." She stands up. "I'm going. And I won't be back
until I'm employed."

My instinct is to stop her, and I think she wants me to,
but the truth is, her sudden resolve is very welcome. Living
in Santa Cruz isn't cheap, and having to support a vodka-
swilling housewife has swollen my cost of living to the brink
of serious debt. Debt is one of my biggest phobias, right
alongside monogamy and venereal warts.

She stuffs a few things into a big straw bag, grabs her car
keys, swipes her lips with Chap Stick and heads for the door.
"Later on," she calls, and with that she and Rex are gone.

Rose can be surprisingly adept at leaving, when the mood

strikes her. Usually she dawdles, like me—changing her clothes five times, braiding and rebraiding her hair, jumping in the shower at the last second because she's suddenly decided she reeks. When the two of us are headed somewhere, it takes us hours to get out the door. But Rose also possesses this uncanny knack for bolting impulsively every now and then, practically midsentence. Probably the legacy of her drifter childhood. Aunt Jessie often demanded immediate escape; if Rose wasn't ready, she might get left behind with the bulkier furniture and the stray animals they'd adopted for the month.

This instinct for ill-planned flight is one strain of the Lavelle blood that's always disturbed and fascinated me. It's most pronounced in Aunt Jessie, but Mira's got a dash of it, herself. How many mothers could surrender custody of their thirteen-year-old daughter, pack up and move to a town they'd barely driven through, shed the moniker of "Mom" and reemerge as Mira Ravenwing? I was showing my Lavelle blood when I went to Austin, led by vague cowboy mirages—and again when I came here, come to think of it. Stealing one's ex's bus and promptly incinerating it en route could certainly fall within the bounds of "ill planned."

The rain's stopping, or at least slowing to a drizzle, and the chocolate cake for breakfast is turning to something sludgy and unpleasant in my belly, so I decide I'll walk to the post office and check my box. If you have to turn thirty, better to start the decade moving, rather than moping prostrate on your tatty old couch, waiting for your thighs to transform into varicose-veined cottage cheese.

Once I'm outside, the ocean-scented drizzle makes me feel something like happy—or alive, anyway, which I'll settle for today. The cloud cover is giving way in the south, and I can feel the sun burning through the blue to reach my face.

My mother once said that her life didn't really begin until her thirties. Considering that she left me with Dad when she turned thirty-three, I guess it's obvious why this inspires more bitterness than hope.

Walking to the post office, though, I try not to fixate on my mother or my rapidly bulking thighs or my thirties. Instead I concentrate on a chain-link fence half consumed by an unruly burst of passionflowers; their exotic, otherworldly centers are dripping with this morning's rain. Half a block later, there's a toddler digging in the mud while her mother smokes in her bathrobe. As I pass, the girl offers me a fistful of slime and cries with extreme pleasure, "Eeeee." I smile without meaning to, and it feels good.

Claudia's Thirtieth Birthday Mail Call:
1) Phone bill. Outrageous due to two-hour emergency conference with Ziv on the Friday morning after Clay's penny-tossing divorce announcement. Also, tearful hour-long Ziv debriefing post clownish makeover.
2) Hallmark card from Dad with check for fifty dollars. Card pink (hate pink) featuring daisies and daft-looking cartoon butterfly. Message inside reads: For a special girl, on her special day, who brings great happiness my way. Hate the word special.
3) Flyer for new pizzeria opening half block from apartment. Wonderful. Fresh new ways to achieve alluring, dimpled-thigh look.
4) Letter from Aunt Jessie.

When I first see the return address in her spidery, lefty's scrawl, I assume it must be for Rosemarie, but there's my name, smack in the middle of the plain white envelope: Ms. Claudia Bloom. Unable to endure my curiosity for the six-block tour home, I duck into a café and order a mocha. There's a grim, midmorning need-my-fix working crowd in Café Roma, sharing the quaint little space reluctantly with a few boisterous students who forgot to go home for winter break. I take my mocha to a seat near the window, as far as I can get from the students, and slice open my letter with a butter knife. Unfolding the carefully creased binder paper, I can almost smell the sadness wafting up out of it. I smooth it out on the table and read.

Dear Claudia,
I'm hoping this will reach you on or before your birthday. I have ample leisure time now—hours and hours to remember the occasions of joy I'm missing out on. I don't mean to whine. Unlike everyone else in here (you'd never believe how many "innocent" people are incarcerated—it's scandalous), I recently realized that I'm here because of my own stupid tendency to magnetize filth and squalor. Every man I ever slept with was the perfect embodiment of this.

Anyway, on to brighter subjects. I'm studying astral projection. I plan to spend as much time as possible outdoors, and soul travel will save in the end on both sunscreen and gas. This is a life skill that will come in handy long after my release date, so my time here's not wasted. So far, I've managed only a couple of lucid dreams, but from what I've read, this is the beginning stage. I hope to quench my lifelong thirst for liberty.

I have many things I'd like to tell you, but I'm not sure it would be in your best interest.

I wonder if you know the whereabouts of Rosemarie? I worry about her. Of course, your mother must have told you about Jade's death. None of us will ever be the same. And Rose is strong in some ways, but delicate in others. She tends to latch on to the wrong people, and lets the right ones breeze past her without a second glance. I fear she inherited my gift for attracting the Scum of the Earth.

If you see or hear from her, I hope you'll tell her that I love her. Please look out for her well-being in whatever way you can manage. I've sent letters to her old address, but they just come back to me.

Claudia, you were always the promising one. You've got all the grit. Rose is like an ephemeral nymph, only tentatively bound to earth plane. If you're there for her, I'll know it in my bones, and sleep easier.

> With love and despair,
> Aunt Jessie

I lean back in my chair, one hand absently caressing the crease in the paper, the other wrapped around my mocha for warmth. *With love and despair,* I think. That so perfectly captures Jessie. Full of love, but also so busy trying to jerk free of her own fucked-up web, she's never really nurtured anyone. Maybe that describes all the Lavelle women. We're spazzes when it comes to love, too caught up in our own phobias to do anything really well but run.

"Mind company?" Wouldn't you know it? Clay Parker. And me barely out of my pajamas.

"Oh—um—no. Have a seat." I stuff Jessie's letter back into its envelope and into my pocket. Clay sits down with two paper cups and smiles uneasily. He's looking even more attractive than usual in a wool fisherman's sweater and those trusty Levi's.

"Your—hair," he says haltingly.

I duck my head instinctively and smooth my hand over my platinum disaster, as if I can make it go away. "Yeah," I say. "I cried."

"No, it's very…" I want to die as he searches in vain for the adjective. "Bold," he settles on at last. I appreciate that he doesn't lie and tell me I look like Cameron Diaz.

"Drinking for two?" I ask, nodding at his twin beverages, eager to move on to brighter subjects.

"One's for Nick."

"Oh. How's he?"

"Crazy. Yesterday he called this teenage boy a cock-sucking maggot."

I smile. "Cock-sucking maggot. That's a new one. Do you think he meant faggot?"

"Hard to say. He's not very linguistically precise. But you know, it could be worse. I could have an employee who spouts all kinds of clichéd bullshit, like 'have a nice day.'"

"Yes," I say. "That would be tragic."

"I feel like an idiot, by the way," he says. "About the other night."

"What do you mean?"

"I don't usually get all drunk and toss pennies at peoples' windows."

"I thought it was kind of seductive, actually." *Bloom, what are you doing?*

"Well, I'm not in the habit of seducing anyone. Obviously, I need practice."

"Obviously." I'm unable to keep from smiling.

"Ouch." It comes out barely a whisper; he doesn't look like he's in any pain.

We hold each other's gaze for a long moment, long enough for a tremendous heat to gather force inside me. I think about spontaneous human combustion and wonder if this is how it starts.

"Well," he says, standing up and retrieving his paper cups. "I better get back. No telling who Nick's calling a cunt as we speak." He hesitates, as if he'd like to say something more, and the gray-tinged sunlight filtering through the plate-glass windows makes his eyes even brighter than usual. "I guess I'll see you around. Merry Christmas. If you're into that sort of thing."

"Not really," I say, suddenly awash in loneliness. "But same to you."

It's my birthday, I want to scream. *Love me. Ravish me.* But thankfully, I'm spared my own version of Tourette's. I just wave pathetically as he navigates the Monday crowd and vanishes out the door.

CHAPTER 19

Christmas puts me in a black, desperate mood. These seasons when families are supposed to go all gooey with affection totally freak me out. Any warmth I have for my parents goes cold under all the pressure. This year, I spend the actual day with my father and the Vegetarian Girlfriend, Didi. We sit together in his tragically sterile tract home and exchange weird, well-intentioned gifts. I get my father a book he already owns and a weed-eater he no longer needs, since he long ago hired a gardener, unbeknown to me. He gets me a gift certificate to a clothing store in Calistoga that specializes in T-shirts featuring hand-painted kittens. Didi and I are even less successful; she gets me the *Sound of Music* video, and I give her a fantastic bottle of wine, only to learn that she's active in the local AA.

After this embarrassing ritual, we settle in for an hour or two of TV, which inspires in me a powerful desire to slit my wrists. I haven't watched TV since I left home twelve years ago, and the sound of the laugh track makes the little hairs on the back of my neck stand on end.

Eventually, I escape, and brave the drunk-driver-packed highways until at last I'm safe in my flat. It may not be chic or elegantly furnished, I tell myself, but it's definitely more bohemian than my father's snowy-white couches and his alphabetized DVD collection.

What greets me when I open the door is definitely on the extreme side of the bohemian spectrum: Rosemarie is half naked, handcuffed to the refrigerator, and a very short, ropy-muscled gnome of a guy in boxers is dripping wax onto her nipples.

I'm not a prude, you understand, but this isn't exactly the scene I expected to come home to on Christmas.

"Oh—Claudia." Rose struggles to free herself of the handcuffs, but only succeeds in yanking the refrigerator door open. "Bruce, c-can you...?" she stammers, jerking harder on the cuffs.

Bruce is relatively nonplussed; he merely looks from her to me and back to her again. I try not to stare at the embarrassing bulge in his boxers.

"*Bruce,*" Rose practically shrieks, blushing crimson. "Get the key. This is Claudia. My cousin." When he still doesn't react, she adds, "This is *her* apartment."

"Sure," he says, his voice petulant and distant. "Whatever you say." He struts past me to a large backpack on the couch, retrieves a small key and unlocks Rose before putting on a pair of tattered black jeans.

"I'm really sorry," Rose whispers to me as she's throwing on her clothes. "I just—we met downtown and I was— we were..." She looks at Bruce, who's eyeing me in a slightly predatory way, probably plotting out a cousin sandwich. "I think you better go," Rose tells him, her tone apologetic.

"Doesn't your cousin like to party?" he says, his bloodshot eyes on mine.

"I'm sorry," Rose says to me, "I didn't think you'd be back tonight."

"Hey, cuz," he says in a booming voice, as if from a great distance. "Everything's cool, right? It's Christmas, after all."

"Listen, no offense," I say to Bruce. The guy's really giving me the creeps. "But I'd like you to leave."

Still, he hesitates. Rex edges closer to Rose and fixes Bruce with a fierce, wild stare, a low growl issuing from his throat. For once, I'm grateful to the mammoth mutt. Bruce seizes his pack and stalks out, mumbling something about stupid bitches under his breath.

When the door's slammed behind him, I lock it and turn to Rose. "What was that?"

"I'm so sorry, Claudia—"

"Did you seriously like that guy?"

"Don't be mad—I can't stand it if you're mad," she says, slumping into the couch, her shoulders hunching over like a gawky teenager's.

"Was that another soul mate?"

"It's Christmas. You were gone. I was lonely…."

"I asked you to come with me. I begged you." Just this morning I stood here and practically bribed her to help me face my father; she said she wanted to stay home and take a bath.

"Yeah, but you have a family." She bursts into tears; her hair forms a curtain around her face. "I have—Rex."

"Rose, *I'm* your family," I say, sitting down next to her, trying to ignore the smell of candle wax and acrid sweat. "My family *is* your family." Thinking of the pathetic gift exchange I just endured, I add, "For whatever that's worth."

"I miss Jade," she says, and makes a strangled little sobbing sound in her throat.

"Shh," I say, wrapping my arms tightly around her. "Shh. It's all right. Of course you do, sweetie. Of course you do."

"Sometimes I can barely remember her face. Or her smell. I used to love her smell so much."

I just hold her and stroke her hair, wishing I could do something more. I rack my brain for some brilliant insight to offer—a one-liner that will induce a movie-of-the-week epiphany, but nothing occurs to me except trite clichés, so I whisper those instead.

After she's cried for the better part of an hour, I make us both strong martinis, which we carry carefully up the fire escape to sit on the roof and share a hand-rolled cigarette, a secret little vice we like to indulge in when things get desperate.

We sit together sipping our drinks, staring out over downtown, watching the leaves of sidewalk-planted maples shimmer in the streetlight.

"I think it's good for you to talk about Jade," I say.

She shakes her head. "I don't know. It doesn't seem to help."

"Yeah, but you keep so much bottled up—about your mom, too. That can't be good."

She stiffens. "Claudia, don't take this the wrong way, but there are some things you couldn't possibly understand."

"I know that. It doesn't even have to be me you talk to. Maybe a therapist."

"I had enough therapy in the hospital to last me a lifetime."

"Maybe," I say, passing her the cigarette. "But I think if you could talk about all this heavy shit you're carrying, it might make things easier."

"How do you know what would make things easier?" Her brown eyes are flashing a warning.

"Okay," I say, backing down. "You're right. It was just an idea."

I consider telling her about Jessie's letter—I've been looking for the right moment since I received it—but something tells me not to bring it up. Even mentioning Jessie puts Rose instantly on the defensive.

We sit there for a while in silence. The soft, bluesy moan of the train floats on the air, along with the smoky smell of winter—or what passes for winter in California, anyway.

There's a couple down on the street walking hand in hand, a tiny dog yapping at their heels. Rex sticks his big nose out of the window and barks at them halfheartedly.

"Claudia?"

"Yeah?"

"Merry Christmas." She barely whispers it, peering at me sadly over her martini glass.

"Merry Christmas to you, Rosemarie," I say, and take another drag off our cigarette.

CHAPTER 20

Number of Hours Since I Last Had Sex: 3,366.

But who's counting?

Jonathan and I had tearful, achingly tender sex on the Fourth of July—all locked eyes and whispery caresses, both of us muttering soul-binding promises just before we climaxed. Three days later, he was packing his bags for New York City, the glamorous mecca we'd always planned on venturing to once we were married, while Rain, with her mouth full of starlet teeth and her neatly waxed brows, waited in a taxi outside.

For some reason I wake up on Friday the thirteenth with this memory clouding my brain like a hangover, and an empty sensation in the pit of my stomach no breakfast can cure. All I want to do is hide under the covers and flip through J. Crew catalogs, but I've got too many things to do before rehearsal. We're already two weeks into February; we've got barely three weeks until opening night, and the stupid creatures aren't even off book yet.

Miranda's play, *Heirloom,* has proven the ideal distraction from my involuntary celibacy; it's so demanding, and the cast so talented yet challenging, they drain me of all sexual energy and then some. There are only four actors, but each one is such a head case it might as well be a cast of thousands. There's Sarah Lundy, aka Beach Barbie of the Owl Club. She's playing the lead role of Olivia, and she's constantly amazing me with her stellar talent and her emotional instability. Every other day she's in crisis.

Then there's Ben Crow (my hot hunka burnin' love, if you believe the rumors). It was a risk, of course, to cast him, but he read beautifully for the role of Ray, Olivia's shy, introverted brother, and it was criminal not to cast him because of vindictive gossip. He's proved to be a challenge in his own way. He's perfectly adept, but he's never really performed before, and he's got the worst case of stage fright I've ever encountered. I have to talk him down from his phobias every time we rehearse.

I personally discovered Cheryl Spratt, the fortysomething sociology grad student I cast as Olivia's mother. She's frighteningly intelligent and great on stage, except she's got this eensy-weensy voice you can barely hear. She'd be perfect for film, but unfortunately we're performing in a theater that seats over five hundred, so the back row (who am I kidding? the front row) is going to be pissed if we don't fix her projection problems pronto.

Which brings us to Mr. Seth Grumm, the former off-off-Broadway actor who never tires of reminding us that he met Sam Shepard once at a party. I'm convinced he was put on the planet specifically to torture me with egomaniacal episodes. He's good—sure he's good—technically speaking, he's practically flawless, but the time I save in not teaching him technique I more than make up for curbing his rampant attitude. He's constantly bickering with me about directorial choices, he can't respond to the simplest request without dishing out hyperacidic sarcasm, and he's perpetually hitting on Sarah, which adds an ominous layer of incestuous sub-text I keep trying to eradicate from their scenes together.

I guess I should count my blessings. At least this quarter I don't have Ralene Tippets in any of my classes, and she didn't audition for *Heirloom*—not that I would have cast her. She was a nightmare, but now that I don't have to deal with her in class, I sometimes wonder why I let her get to me. Once the Ben Crow scandal was drained of its juice and she saw that her complaints hadn't gotten me fired, she went from rabid to de-spondent and then, once she was no longer my student, she became almost conciliatory. At the end of the quarter, she left a jar of homemade jam outside my office, which I found ut-terly mystifying. The note said simply, "Thinking of you."

And there are other blessings to count this quarter: Mi-randa, thank God, has been my comrade, collaborating with the maturity and poise one wouldn't automatically expect from someone sporting purple hair and (her latest addition) a bone through her septum. As the playwright, she attends rehearsals often, hunting for clues about the script's weak-nesses and revising accordingly. When we discuss the play she offers her insight with humor instead of the usual writer's ran-cor. Even working with Jonathan, back in the early days when he was trying to get in my pants, there was never this smooth synergy in our collaborations; he and I had to fight it out whenever our visions forked. Miranda and I, miraculously, see eye to eye on just about everything, and though she's not super verbal, I've gotten so I can read her face pretty well.

Tonight we're working on a crucial scene between Olivia and her father, Gus. Unfortunately, Sarah is in the throes of near-fatal PMS, according to her, and though Seth isn't fir-ing as many sarcastic shots as usual, he's been giving me with-ering looks all night.

"Olivia, get me a cup of coffee," booms Seth.

"Sure." Here Sarah disregards the blocking and clutches her abdomen, a grimace momentarily rendering her pretty features grotesque.

"Goddammit," Seth shrieks, after Sarah's recovered from her spell of cramps and has mimed handing him a cup. "This is cold. You know I despise cold—"

"Jesus, Seth," she says, breaking character. "Do you have to scream? You're damaging my eardrums."

"Sarah," I scold. "Focus."

The one good thing about Seth being smitten with Sarah is it keeps him from snapping back at her. Heaven forbid if anyone besides her critiques his "work," including me. He practically removed my jugular with his teeth when I suggested he stop convulsing during his death scene. It's *hard* to die convincingly; even someone who met Sam Shepard once has to work on it a little.

"Seth, can you sit a little farther upstage, please?" Again, I earn a venomous glance, but he does as I say. "Good. Perfect. Okay, Sarah, just take it from there."

"Okay, Dad. Sorry. I'll warm it up." Sarah takes the cup from him again, mimes putting it in a microwave. Then she takes it out and mimes adding the cyanide. This, obviously, is a defining moment, since it's in this beat that Olivia impulsively decides to go through with the crime she decided two scenes earlier she wasn't capable of, but Sarah enacts it in a bored, listless fashion, as if murdering her father is just another item on an endless to-do list. Buy Saran Wrap, call dentist, commit patricide…

"Sarah," I say, my voice betraying my fraying patience. This is the fifth time in half an hour we've rehearsed this particular beat, and I'm developing a nasty case of life-threatening PMS myself. One side effect of spending so much time with your cast: the women's cycles tend to sync up, making for some serious collective mood swings. "How's the audience supposed to know this matters?"

"I don't have the poison yet," she bristles. "I'm doing the best I—"

"You're going through the motions. Don't blame it on the

props. You look utterly uninvested," I say, tapping my pen against my clipboard. I sigh and try a different approach. "Why are you doing this? Why do you want your father dead?"

"Because," she says, looking pointedly at Seth, "he's an asshole."

"And what makes you decide, right here, right now, that you can kill him, when just ten minutes ago you told your brother you wanted to but you couldn't?"

"Because he yelled so loudly he, like, damaged my hearing?"

"Is this Sarah talking, or Olivia?" I ask.

"Sarah is hemorrhaging, okay? You're lucky Sarah's even here."

"To hell with Sarah," I say, "I'd like Olivia to show up." I mean it to be playful, but it comes out more like a threat.

"Oh yeah? Well, to hell with you!" she yells, and flounces off stage right, slamming the back door as she goes.

"Okay, then," I say. Miranda and I exchange a look. "Guess we'll have to work this scene another time."

I look at Seth, who's cradling his face in his hands, Ben, who's asleep in the front row, and Cheryl, with her head retracted deep into her shoulders like a frightened turtle. All of a sudden I feel way too exhausted to move. I desperately want to call it a night, even if it is dangerous precedent. I don't want them thinking they can pull a prima donna anytime they want out of rehearsal, but then again, a collective nervous breakdown won't help the show.

"Look, everyone's tired—have a good weekend. Run your lines like crazy. We'll be working act three again next week, then we'll start over at the top."

As Miranda and I are trudging through the halls on our way to my car, a poster on one of the bulletin boards catches my eye:

```
Viva Vinyl and Medealovesmotorbikes, Inc.
                      presents
      The First Annual Anti-Valentine Ball
                 for cynics only
                      Come:
         ·Resist the Hallmark Holiday,
                but party anyway
              ·Shake your Moneymaker
    ·Get drunk enough to surf in the buff with
              fellow anti-Valentiners

      DJ'ed music from nine till whenever
                   BYO Whatever
         It's Beach, Valentine's Night
```

The lettering is cut from newspaper headlines, like a ransom note, and photocopied a little sloppily, giving it a rough-hewn, indie-production charm. At the bottom there's a sketch of a cat driving a Harley, all puffed up and wild-eyed. I stand there, beaming at it like an idiot.

"What is it?" Miranda asks, peering over my shoulder.

"Oh. Nothing," I say, snapping out of it and walking away. "Where's It's Beach, anyway?"

"On the west side, you know, where the hippies play bongos on Sundays."

"Oh," I say, having no idea what she's talking about. "Okay."

I give Miranda a ride back to her dorm; she keeps her skateboard and her backpack piled in her lap, even though I insist there's plenty of room in my back seat. She's got this weird thing about her stuff; I figure maybe she grew up poor, because she clings to her few ratty possessions with noticeable intensity.

I'll admit I've been increasingly puzzled by the enigmatic Miranda, the more I spend time with her. I've even resorted privately to hammering away at an equation I've always argued is irrelevant: the old "which part is real?" game people can't resist playing with writers. *Heirloom* is about a wealthy CEO who terrorizes his family until Olivia, his daughter, finally poisons him. The father's a closeted homosexual who enjoys secret trysts in public bathrooms and then goes home to yell at his wife for buying books written by "faggots." Though Miranda seems incredibly different from her rich-girl protagonist, Olivia, it wouldn't surprise me if her real-life family had a few dark secrets. She's just got that feeling about her; she holds herself like someone who grew up tiptoeing around violence.

She stares out the window in pensive silence, and when we arrive at her dorm, she says, "Do you think Olivia's insane?"

I give myself a moment to consider before answering. "I think she's disturbed… I mean, her family's got serious problems, obviously. But in a way she reacts sanely to an insane situation."

"Exactly," she says, slapping my dashboard happily. "I let my brother read it, and he thought Olivia was totally certifiable. He said it didn't work, because nobody could like her."

"I like her," I say. "I like her a lot."

She nods and, as she moves, the streetlight plays on her purple curls. "I like her, too," she says. "Thanks for the ride. See you Monday." And with that she hops out, hitting the pavement and skating toward the dorms, looking scrappy and agile as a sprite.

Her parents named her Miranda, the sappy innocent who gets the guy, but if I ever do *The Tempest* here, I'd cast her as Ariel in a heartbeat. She's got that androgynous, impish thing going. Then I remember that I probably won't be here past this year, so I won't be doing *The Tempest*—or working with Miranda again.

Back in September, I wondered how I'd make it through the year. Now that I'm more than halfway there, I'm beginning to wonder how I'll manage to leave gracefully. As much as I hate to admit it, I'm starting to hope against hope that Westby will decide I'm worth keeping.

Well, she could. Monica's backed off some, since I haven't molested her ex recently, and my student evals were fairly glowing—aside from Ralene Tippets's contribution, anyway. They're supposed to be anonymous, but even with the comments typed, I recognized Ralene's signature bitchiness instantly:

Professor Bloom (if you can even call her a professor) is consistently unprofessional and inappropriate. She frequently shows up late, clutching a muffin and looking frazzled, then tries to make it up to us by offering us bites. Please. She flirts with her pets while berating the rest of us. More than once I've caught her examining a Victoria's Secret *catalog while the students rehearsed. You call this an education, Ms. Bloom? I think not. Please buy your underwear on your own time.*

I was a little discouraged, I'll admit, especially considering that none of Ralene's allegations were bald-faced lies. I am late sometimes, I do frequently show up with a muffin, and yeah, I've been known to peruse *Victoria's Secret* when things were slow. I'm not perfect, God knows, but I prefer to focus on my more encouraging evals, such as this two-word one: "Bloom rocks."

As I drive home, my mind drifts from teaching to my default setting: Clay Parker. So he's planning a little anti-Valentine bash. My curiosity is definitely piqued by his sweet little flyer, but I remind myself to be cautious. He's almost definitely in the throes of a post-relationship-give-me-the-antidote delirium, or the Big Swing, as Ziv used to call it. Practically everyone does it: you get out of a relationship with a neat freak, you find yourself crazy about a lice-infested grease monkey with fourteen rotting cars in his yard. After a week of gazing adoringly at his mountain of laundry, you come to your senses and flee. It's the way we are. Clay is fresh off the Monica boat, so naturally he'll find me irresistible. She's a tightly wound, overachieving, expensively groomed and probably (deep down) tender brunette. I'm a disheveled mass of walking blond chaos with a battered little peach pit where there ought to be a heart.

The all-too-predictable Big Swing forecast: Clay will binge on me for two weeks, become seriously nauseated, purge, and then begin his search for a healthy, normal relationship with a saucy little redhead who completely defies the whole Monica/Claudia dichotomy. Meanwhile, I'll lose my job, my self-respect and my battered little peach-pit heart.

No thanks.

21
CHAPTER

Rose didn't get a job on my birthday, like she wanted, but she did find one in early January, and amazingly, she's still at it more than a month later. Sure, the pay is scandalously low, but then she isn't exactly orchestrating corporate mergers or finding the cure to cancer; she's the gofer girl at Wabi Sabi Tattoo, although she prefers the more upwardly mobile if somewhat archaic title, apprentice. She's determined to be a tattoo artist, and I figure this is as likely as anything else.

Rose is better, lately. She hardly ever sneaks vodka anymore, she's eating more carbohydrates, and she hasn't hooked up with a soul mate for two solid weeks. Not that going without soul mates is a good thing, strictly speaking; it's only that, in the case of Rose, soul mates have become an addiction, so cutting back is a sign of improved mental health.

When we're having breakfast on Valentine's day—delicious strawberry crepes she threw together on a whim—she surprises me by announcing, "I don't need a man, Claudia. I've decided I'm going to be more like you."

"Like me?" I sip my tea and wonder where this is going. "How so?"

"I'm not going to get caught up in all that 'is he The One?' bullshit. It's passé. Way too eighties."

"But, Rose, I thought you were looking for your soul mate."

She spears a strawberry and shrugs. "So? Maybe I was wrong. There's probably no such thing." I give her a look, and she cries, "Why are you looking at me like that?"

"Like what?"

"Like 'poor Rose is delusional?' I'm saying you're right, I'm wrong. Hello!"

"But," I protest, "you're so good at finding soul mates. As long as you limit yourself to one or two a month, who cares if they don't last?" She just stares at me, mystified, and I try to gloss over the absurdity of what I just said with "Besides, you've got to have a certain constitution to be as jaded and unromantic as I am. You have to be hardhearted."

"Oh, please," she scoffs. "You are *not* hardhearted."

"Of course I am."

"Claudia, do you remember when we were eleven and you gave me not only your Walkman, but your Run DMC tape?" I smile, remembering. "They were your favorite band, and it was your only tape, but Mom and I were leaving for Mississippi, and you were scared I'd be bored. That is not a hardhearted girl."

"Maybe not," I say, "but that was twenty years ago. A lot's happened since then."

"Uh-huh," she says, unconvinced. "And look at you now. Putting me up without complaining. Staying up all night over casting decisions because you're terrified of hurting your shittiest students' feelings. Pining away for Clay Parker."

"I am *not*," I shriek.

"Oh, yeah? Then why haven't you had sex in the past— what?—three months?"

"Four," I mumble, "and nineteen days. But who's counting?"

"See?" she laughs. "You're pining."

"I'm just in a dry spell. And anyway, I thought you started off by saying I don't need a man, and that's what you like about me."

"Ahh," she says. "The paradox."

"What's that supposed to mean?"

"You don't believe in soul mates, but your soul mate is tormenting you. I've always believed in The One, but I'm stuck with sordid flings. Well, not anymore. I'm changing. In fact, I'm going to try being a lesbian."

I practically spit out my tea. "Rose, I don't think that's the sort of thing you just try on."

"Why not?" she asks, all innocence.

"You're talking about your sexual orientation here, not a pair of shoes."

"Oh, come on," she says. "How hard could it be? I already like women better. Now I just have to learn how to have sex with them." She gives me a sly smile. "I've already picked someone out."

"Who?"

"This girl who comes into the studio to get ink. She's so great. And I think she's sort of bi, like me." She stares off into space, evidently dreaming of bi-girl.

"So now you're bi?"

"Oh, I don't think I could give up men completely," she says solemnly. "I'm just not that disciplined. It's like cigarettes. If you tell yourself you can never smoke another one forever and ever, you go crazy. You have to allow yourself a little treat now and then. It's cosmic law."

"Right," I mumble. "If you say so."

I can't quite bring myself to tell Rose about the flyer at school, but I do manage to find out exactly where It's Beach is, and to get us there around eleven o'clock on Saturday night. I figure showing up before then would just be asking for humiliation. After four months and nineteen days of celibacy, I have to take every precaution not to come across as sex-starved and hysterical.

There's already a pretty big crowd gathered. Santa Cruz may be a magnet for dreamers, but evidently the jaded population isn't lacking, either. I'm glad. The crowd makes me feel anonymous and safe.

I have additional insurance against being ferreted out, though. Earlier today, Rose and I were wandering through downtown aimlessly, drifting in and out of shops, making sarcastic remarks about the poor saps searching frantically for Valentine gifts, when we came across a glossy black wig in a novelty store. It was one of those smooth, chin-length bobs a la *Pulp Fiction,* and the second I saw it I fell in love. "Try it on—try it," Rose urged when she saw the gleam in my eye. I did, and it looked fantastic. Goodbye bone-white blond, hello Cleopatra. I shelled out the fifty bucks and I haven't taken it off since.

My new mantra: Let there be wigs.

So here I am, incognito in a red Chinese silk shirt, black bell-bottoms, cherry-red lipstick, dark glasses and my cherished raven-black bob. I probably look like a lunatic, but I feel like La Femme Nikita.

It's a really stunning night, I have to admit, the sort of scene that could lure you into the romantics' camp, if you're not vigilant. There's the thinnest sliver of moon suspended above the horizon, its reflection warping this way and that in the waves. The air smells like salt and reefer. *Everything smells different under the stars,* I think, and a weird nostalgia seizes me. How can I be homesick for someone I've probably spent a total of twenty hours with—several of which we wasted sleeping?

Rose sees someone she knows from work and becomes engrossed in conversation with him. He looks like Jerry Garcia, minus a few teeth, and he's wearing assless chaps; I'm hardly crushed when he ignores me after our introduction in favor of regaling Rose with a lovingly detailed description of his latest motorcycle accident. I catch a couple snippets of their conversation over the music: "sliced to the bone" and "intestines hanging out." Tales of medical trauma have always riveted Rose, but I just get queasy.

Just then I see Clay at the base of the cliffs, lit dimly by a wad of bulky Christmas lights, a few tiki torches and a red strobe. He's half obscured by two turntables and multiple milk crates filled with records, fading out on "Should I Stay or Should I Go?" and starting in on something frenetic by Dee-lite. A small group of barefooted dancers, many of them scantily clad in spite of the chill and most of them female, let out a squeal and shake their butts harder to the two and four.

The man knows how to please women.

I stand there watching him, toying with my options as I dig my bare feet into the cool, dry sand and feel it filling up the space between my toes. I didn't exactly plan to come in disguise, it just sort of happened. Now that I'm unrecognizable—which I'm pretty sure I am, since two of my students just walked right by me without a second glance—I have no idea how to proceed. An awkward moment for 007.

For now, I'm savoring watching him from afar, seeing his face emerge from the shadows and retreat into them again, his expression lined with concentration, his fingers tapping the air while the rhythm takes off, sometimes head-bobbing when it gets going really good. Once in a while he flips through the records with practiced speed—searching, finding. It never dawned on me before now, but a DJ's omniscient; he's a puppet master, yanking at the limbs, hips and heartstrings of his audience, pumping us into a frenzy, slowing us to a crawl, slamming us through the decades at dangerous speeds.

Unfortunately for me, omniscience is way too sexy. Especially on Clay.

One of the barely clothed dancers breaks from the writhing pod and saunters over to him. Her face is lit by the tiki torch she stands under. She's very petite, with enviable bone structure and the same halogen-bright smile Rain's got. In fact, she looks a lot like Rain, with dewy skin, silky black hair to her butt and a miniature body that makes me feel twenty pounds overweight just looking at her.

She leans in close to Clay, balancing on her toes as he bends down obligingly, so that his ear nearly touches her lips. I see this all as if in slow motion, through a close-up lens: the tiki light illuminating her strong, sweat-glazed clavicle; her full, pink mouth whispering; his face, tense with listening at first, and then his eyes lighting up, his head nodding in fervent agreement to whatever she's suggested. Now he sweeps her hair away with the familiar intimacy of a lover and says something into her ear for what feels like hours. Unable to look away, I watch with sick fascination as they both crack up, and he pulls her into a tight, laughing embrace.

I turn away, nauseous in my bones. The crowd around me, which has thickened in the last ten minutes, suddenly fills me with an intense jolt of claustrophobia. The Thai food I had for dinner is threatening an encore, and I'm overcome by the need to escape the forest of swaying bodies all around me. Now, I think, now now now. Gogogogogogo!

I'm halfway up the stairs that lead to the street when I remember Rose, and turn around to see if I can spot her. I scan the crowd and find her standing near Clay, right where the Rain-clone was three minutes ago. Just as my eyes land on them, Rose starts pointing and waving at me; so does Clay. In a mad panic, I turn back to the stairs, charging up them as quickly as my mules will allow.

Just as I've reached the safety of the sidewalk, I hear Deelite fade out. When Greg Brown starts up, I stop dead. His rich, smoky voice tugs at me like an undertow. *With your pretty dresses and your ragged underwear.* I turn halfway around and look over the cliff at the partiers littering the beach, see the dancers puzzling over the DJ's selection; there's no driving beat to animate their hips, and I giggle a little as they flounder.

I've just taken two steps toward the stairs when I see Rain's doppelgänger grab Clay's hand and spin him around with her so her scarlet skirt fans out like a flower. I remember her lush pink mouth hovering so close to Clay's exquisite earlobe, and realize I just can't get any closer to that.

I turn back around and keep walking.

I am not a jealous person. Sure, I've had my episodes, but I find the emotion so repugnant and lowbrow, I've managed to squelch it. Mostly. When I was fifteen, I did knock Chelsea Gibbon's front tooth loose when I caught her heavy petting with Jason Pritchard, but that was in my hormone-addled youth. Since then, I've navigated mostly micro-flings, and in doing so I've never had time to work up much jealousy— at least not the terrible I-think-I'm-going-to-be-sick variety.

Besides, jealousy is totally un-tart.

Of course, when Jonathan was scrambling around the apartment his last afternoon in Austin, stuffing a paperback, some dirty socks and a Walkman into a plastic bag, having already packed the bulk of his belongings and now just furtively grabbing at the leftovers, I'll admit that the sight of Rain's gloriously dark hair in that taxi made me feel murderous and limp and murderous again in such rapid succession it was all I could do not to collapse.

And all right, in the early years of my tart enthusiasm I got in over my head with the first and last bona fide cowboy I could scrounge up. His name was Clint Martin and he wore an actual Stetson, no kidding. I got a little too attached (I was nineteen, give me a break), and when I found him in the kitchen getting cozy with Ziv's sister I pretty much lost my shit. There were broken plates and a sprained jaw involved (his)—nothing serious.

So maybe I do have a tiny jealous streak—just a streak, mind you, not a vein or a bone, only a minuscule thread of the stuff lurking in my blood. Like most things I can't control, I blame it on the Lavelle DNA. My mother can be a jealous fiend; when she found out that Dad was giving it to the dental hygienist she took a sledgehammer to his '57 Chevy. It took him six months and several thousand dollars to get it cherry again. Jessie's obviously got it in her, too. At least ninety percent of the times she fled any given town it was because her beau-of-the-month showed signs of straying. She hardly ever waited for the actual betrayal, since she was always much more preemptive than that. All it took for her was a *feeling*—the sense that a man was slipping from her grip—and she was out of there.

When it comes to men, I'm more Jessie than Mira. I'm not as nomadic as my aunt geographically, but I have moved from bed to bed with a drifter's agility, and I've adopted her leave-before-you're-left stance in most cases. If only I'd followed through with Jonathan and dumped him when I got restless, I never would have felt that sickening rage and weakness, staring at Rain's dark hair in that taxi.

I'm almost home, now. I've walked a mile or so, and I can feel blisters welling up, one on each big toe. The air is cool, but I've worked up a sweat from the exertion, and my scalp itches under my wig. The whole disguise thing turned sour the second I saw Clay clutching his nubile little dancer. It started as a frisky adventure, but now it strikes me as a pathetic plea for attention, and I feel disgusted thinking of Clay seeing me like this. The only reason I haven't yanked the offensive black bob from my head is because trudging home with a fistful of hair is the sort of thing that attracts all the derelicts and freaks within a ten-mile radius, and Santa Cruz is a gold mine of derelicts and freaks.

Only a couple blocks from home, a bar called the Ghost Orchid catches my attention. It's unusually festive tonight, with live blues pouring out through the front door, its plate glass windows rattling with bass. I can see people dancing on the blue-lit floor. The band's playing "Mustang Sally," and everyone's really into it; they look drunk and happy. It makes me homesick now for Austin and my twenties, so recently deceased, and all the barhopping I used to do on a Saturday night such as this, back when I was confident and tart. Impulsively, I pay the somewhat extortionate cover charge and swagger in, trying to shake off the events of the evening and the haunting stigma of a woman at a bar alone on a Saturday night.

It takes me a good ten minutes to catch the eye of the sassy blond bartender with the Buddha tattoo. She's really adorable; she's got on a lime-green, strappy tank, hip-hugger jeans and her cheekbones are sparkling with pink glitter. I swallow hard when it occurs to me that this town is filled to capacity with naturally beautiful twentysomething hipsters. Clay is now an official divorcée; after years of dragging around the ball and chain, can I blame him for wanting to sow his proverbial oats in this fertile oasis? Why would he look twice at a has-been like me with a bad dye job, weird wigs and more cellulite on my little finger than these betties have on their entire, taut little bodies?

By the time Miss Sassy gets around to me, I'm so depressed I order two shots of Jack Daniel's and down them both. Then I plow my way out onto the dance floor and get to work.

Let me just say: I'm a very good dancer.

There aren't too many skills I can list on my résumé without feeling a bit like a spin doctor, but this is one I can bullet with absolute confidence. When the music is pulsing in my veins and I've got a fresh buzz on, I'm practically spectacular. I'm not saying I go out there to *Saturday Night Fever* it—people don't stand back and gasp—but my body takes on a personality that transcends the regular, fumbling Claudia Bloom. I become something more graceful, less earthbound. I forget about what my ass looks like or what my hair's doing and I turn into the snap of the snare drum, the quivering throb of bass.

If I don't look as good as I feel, I don't want to know. Dancing, bathing and sex are my few opportunities to lose myself in something vast. I'd hate to sully any of them with my usual neuroses.

I must look okay, because after I've been dancing alone for three or four songs, this Hugh Grant look-alike wades through the sea of anorexic surfer chicks and asks in a charming British accent if I'll dance with him. No kidding. I just nod, and suddenly my night takes a turn for the sexier. Not only is he ridiculously cute, but he's got the whole dance-floor seduction thing down to an art. He starts off with distant, take-all-the-space-you-need floor sharing, moving into let-me-just-enjoy-your-beautiful-erotic-hips-by-occasion-ally-cupping-them-with-absolute-reverence. Then he progresses to more advanced partner stuff (which hardly any guys know, and those who do know are often pushy, so someone who just pulls this out at the last minute casually, like, "By the way, want to tango?" is scoring huge points), during which more intimate, body-pressing maneuvers are welcome and pulled off with tremendous flair. By the time the band plays their last number, I'm glossy with sweat and feeling like I own the place. Even the sassy little bartender with her Buddha tattoo is giving me turf defending looks. Goodbye, aging jealous wench in wig. Hello, goddess of Tart.

As the band packs up, we've only got a few minutes before last call, so we scramble to get ourselves cocktails and to find out who we've been dancing with for the past couple hours.

"I'm Merrit," he says, holding his hand out. "And you're…?"

It's quite bizarre exchanging niceties after you've been pressing your sweaty pelvic bones together and gyrating so intimately you could probably draw pictures of each other's anatomy.

He smiles winningly. "You do have a name?"

I start to introduce myself, and then I remember my disguise and change my mind. "Cleo," I say, "Cleo—" I scan the room madly and blurt out the first thing I see "—Coors."

"C'ours," he says, adding something elegant to my ridiculous christening. "Is that French?"

"Yes," I say. "I'm impressed. Most people think it's a beer."

For this I earn a hearty chuckle. My God, he even laughs with a British accent.

In the ten minutes before Sassy Buddha kicks us out, I learn he's a writer with an arts grant, working on something set in Santa Cruz. He's here from London to soak in the atmosphere and to finish a first draft. I tell him I sell lingerie at the mall. Why not? It's the sort of thing Cleo Coors would do.

I'm both intrigued and repelled by the writer part of his intro. I want to believe I learned something from Jonathan: namely, writers suck. At the same time, Merrit's incredibly cute and we're both arty, after all, which should at least justify further investigation.

In the end, I take his phone number and chalk it up to a maybe.

Walking home, I have to admit this isn't like me. The old Claudia Bloom would be at his place by now, shedding her clothes and shucking off his, eager to get back in the saddle. I mean, what? I haven't had sex in like (give me a minute) 3,407 hours. The guy lubes me up with hot dancing, has a gorgeous British accent, looks like Hugh Grant and is obviously gagging for it himself (to borrow a fave Brit phrase), but I'm walking home to my grungy little flat that reeks of Big, Braided Dog?

The only explanation, as much as I loathe it, is I've been Clay Parkered. Big-time.

Fucking tragic.

22

CHAPTER

Three days before *Heirloom* opens, just as I'm breaking out in hives and enduring the worst case of tech-week insomnia ever, my mother shows up on my doorstep in tears, insisting that Gary has ruined her life. I want to say, "And you're just figuring this out *now?*" but I'm so floored that she's actually turning to me in a crisis, I pull her into my kitchen, make her a cup of tea and watch in awe as the floodgates open.

"He's having an affair," she says, and an avalanche of mascara rivulets breaks free from her lower lids, making her look like tabloid material.

"I thought we knew this." I try to make my voice as warm and caring as possible. "With the Aussie landscaper, right?"

"A *different* affair," she wails. "With a *girl*." Visions of Rain's nineteen-year-old butt dance in my head for a couple of seconds before I banish them.

"Who?"

She shrugs. "Some aerobics instructor. Did you know he's doing aerobics? He says the 'youthful energy cleanses his aura.' *Youthful energy.* Twenty-two-year-old piece of ass, more like it."

"Twenty-two?" I gasp.

She clenches her jaw and for a moment I sincerely fear she'll kill him. "He's scum. I'd like his balls in a vice."

"Just leave him, Mom—Mira." We both pretend not to notice my slip. "Revenge isn't worth it. Sue him for adultery and take him to the cleaners, if it'll make you feel better, but don't stay."

More tears run down her cheeks, streaking her face with fresh black rivers. "I would," she says, "I would have left him when I found out about the gardener-slut. But…"

"But *what?*"

"It's Em," she says, so softly I can barely hear her. "I can't leave Em. And if I leave him, he'll keep her from me." She stares into her tea.

I wonder if she knows how much this hurts me. Does it occur to someone like Mira that abandoning your real daughter at thirteen, then enduring hell to keep mothering a stepdaughter is a little…odd? Does it cross her mind that this makes me feel like hopelessly damaged goods replaced by New and Improved?

She looks at me, and for a wobbly, weird moment our eyes lock. It feels like it does on stage when someone goes up on a line and the world is all unscripted silence; seconds last for years.

She breaks the moment by asking for a tissue. I get up and, finding no Kleenex anywhere, return with a roll of toilet paper. Mira takes it in stride. She and Gary may live in an oasis of immaculate pan-Asian tastefulness, but she's not big on rigorous hygiene, if left to her own devices, so she doesn't judge people who neglect to purchase facial tissue.

I guess that's one thing she's got going for her.

When she's successfully cleaned her face of most the mascara, she pulls herself together a bit, even takes a small compact from her purse and applies a layer of mauve lipstick.

"Em is six months pregnant, you know." She studies her reflection wearily, then snaps the compact closed.

"Yeah. I was there when she announced it."

"I don't care if Gary is a fuck-head—I just can't disrupt her life right now."

"Uh-huh." I'm afraid the bitter taste in my mouth will seep into my words, so I don't trust myself beyond these two syllables.

"There's something I want to ask you," she says, in a tone that is classic Mira: brusque, subject-changing, recklessly disregarding the need for a segue.

"Oh?"

"I talked to Jessie. She told me she wrote to you."

"Yeah," I say. "I haven't written her back, yet. I feel kind of guilty ab—"

"What did she tell you?" she interrupts. "What did she say in her letter?" There's an edge to her voice that I don't quite recognize.

"Not much, really. She asked me to look out for Rose, mostly."

She searches my face with an intense scrutiny that's unsettling. My mother never pays this much attention to me.

"Why do you ask?"

She shoves the compact back into her enormous leather satchel and tries a tentative smile. "Just curious. Listen, Jessie's not well. You know that?"

"How do you mean?"

"You know what I mean, Claudia—she's an alcoholic, she's depressed—"

"She's incarcerated," I say, wanting to defend her, for some reason. "It's depressing."

"Okay, fair enough. My point is, if she writes you again, and she tells you anything…bizarre? Just know that she might be a little confused right now. Do you see what I mean?"

I don't, really, in fact I can't for the life of me figure out why my mother is saying all of this, but I just nod because interrogating her at the moment seems less than compassionate, and I don't want to screw up this incredibly rare opportunity to be my mother's confidante.

"Good. I knew you would," she says. "How are things with you?"

"Um, okay."

I think of telling her about Clay, while we're on this little heart-to-heart jag. I've got to start sharing stuff with her, right? If I don't try telling her things, how will we ever get close?

"I've been sort of interested in this guy."

She reaches into her bag and pulls out her cell phone, checks the screen. "Yeah? What sort of guy?"

"He's really great. But when I met him he was married."

She stuffs her phone back in her bag. "Claudia," she says, her tone full of reproach.

"He's not now. They're divorced."

"Don't be a rebound girl."

"I know. I don't want to be stupid," I say, suddenly really sorry I brought it up.

"Then don't be," she says. "It's as simple as that." Then she gets up, and I follow her to the door.

She puts her hand on the knob, then turns back to me. Briefly she wraps her arms around me, but it's over so quickly I don't even have time to return the embrace, if you can call it that. "Thanks for the tea."

"Anytime," I say, swallowing down the thickness in my throat.

"Oh, by the way, I just got this wonderful new grass—you want a little?" She reaches into her bag, pulls out a film canister, pops it open and hands me a healthy joint, meticulously rolled.

"Sure," I say, smiling. "Thanks."

And then she's out the door, leaving me with the fragrant spliff.

I can't resist the urge to go and watch her from the window, my eyes following the smooth lines of her convertible Saab in retreat, until the brake lights flash a glowing red goodbye. Then she turns left and disappears.

It's the view I remember most of my mother: the back of her head, leaving me for someplace better.

There's a neighborhood in hell devoted just to directors; it's called Technical Difficulties, and there, well-intentioned theater artists tear their hair out and gnash their teeth, raging against the machine.

It is not a good place.

I am there now.

Deep in the bowels of a parallel hell (though his agony must be less—it's not *his* debut, and he's got tenure, for Christ's sake) is Sam Bogue, the five-foot-one, grumpy, recently divorced, chain-smoking tech guy. We're the oddly paired duo in this fight against the apparatus, and I fear we're losing the battle.

The problem: we open in five hours, and our light board is defunct.

Not just faltering, not just finicky, but totally, irrevocably, dead.

My rash is spreading. Yesterday, it was an isolated island of tortured pink just to the left of my belly button. Now it's a hideous, scaly continent that spans the better part of my torso.

I set my coffee cup down on a nearby stool and rub my stinging, sleep-deprived eyes. "Okay, Sam. Let's just go through this again. We have two options, right?"

"Right. We could try to get a new light board—"

"Which is virtually impossible, at this point?"

He nods. "Pretty much. Or we could move to another venue…"

"Which means leaving our set behind. Totally unthinkable. I mean, all the work Matt and Lisa put into—"

"I know," he agrees mournfully. "I know." He fingers the pack of Pall Malls in his shirt pocket.

"Plus, the atmosphere will be shot."

"And I'm not even sure we could *get* another venue, at this point," he says, taking the pack out and tucking a cigarette behind his ear. "There are so many student projects."

We sit in gloomy silence for a long minute, staring at the dead light board, willing it to resuscitate itself magically. It doesn't. All my ambitious hopes for this play—that it'll grant me instant genius status on campus, eclipse the ugly rumors about me and Ben, undo all the damage I incurred hooking up with Clay—are stamped out by this huge, ugly, lifeless hunk of knobs, levels and toggle switches. A powerful urge to kick it makes my leg twitch.

"Wait a minute," I say, feeling a distant lightbulb clicking on. "What if we used the board in the black-box theater, and ran wires from there to here?"

"But how would I work my cues? I have to see the actors."

"We'd have you on headset, of course—"

"But even so—"

"We could hook up a video monitor, so you could see everything," I say, warming up to the idea. "It'll be fine. We'll have Josh in here giving you cues, in case anything goes wrong."

He looks at me, and a slow smile creeps over his terminally scowling features. I hardly recognize him. "That's a possibility…" he says. "We'll have to round up some serious extension cords, but I can swing that."

"You think it'll really work?" I'm so giddy with relief I bounce on my toes and clap my hands together.

"If it does," he says, "I'll be the first to buy you a beer."

CHAPTER 23

Heirloom is glorious. No, I mean seriously—it kicks ass. Sarah nearly scratched Seth's eyes out when he tried to cop a feel backstage, and Ben puked into a garbage can just before his entrance, but I learn all of this after the curtain call, so throughout the actual performance I sit blissfully ignorant in my red velvet seat, lost in the world of Olivia Speer and her beautifully fucked-up family.

It's often struck me that everything we love in drama we despise in life, and vice versa. I guess we'll pay to watch a miserable, repressed sixteen-year-old girl murder her hypocritical father because it thrills us to see others suffering more than us. Sick but true. I can tell the audience is into it. The house is three-quarters full, and they're a perfect mix of what I call hyenas and hummers. The hyenas scream with laughter at Miranda's rich, dark humor, and the hummers make soft, perceptive "hmm" sounds that fill up all the right pauses.

Sitting with Miranda on one side and Rosemarie on the other, I feel a deep, thrumming satisfaction. Miranda's squirming in her seat, thumping one foot on her skateboard when things are going well, and Rose keeps squeezing my hand when the audience reacts, a tiny pulse of congratulations that makes me love her with fresh enthusiasm. At intermission, the three of us sneak out the side door and smoke Miranda's clove cigarettes; they taste vile, but it's fun, anyway.

When the show's over, we go backstage and hug everyone in the cast. They're chattering a mile a minute, still high off the standing ovation. You can almost smell the peculiar brand of stage adrenaline coursing through their veins. Even Sam Bogue is giggly with relief; our light board plan worked seamlessly, and he keeps slapping me on the back, saying, "I just can't believe we pulled that off, Bloom. I really can't believe it."

Afterward, Rosemarie, Miranda and I go to Café Pergolessi to sit outside under the March stars and share two celebratory slices of mocha mud pie, Rose's treat. I shovel a forkful of the dark concoction into my mouth, savoring the bittersweet fattiness of it. There's a glow you get after an opening night that reminds me of the postcoital kind. It's like you've been holding your breath for weeks and all at once you get to breathe a special, oxygen-enriched air that gives everything a soft, luminous sheen.

Rose is acting a little funny. She's been gushing nonstop since the curtain fell, which isn't entirely out of character, but I should think she would have eased up by now, since it's been almost two hours. She keeps tucking her hair behind her ear, and doing this cute little pouty thing with her mouth when she's not talking. In short, she's acting exactly as she would around a devastatingly attractive man, so I keep craning my neck to see which table her future soul mate is eyeing us from, but there's no one but balding ponytail types and pimply students.

"Oh, my God," Miranda cries, staring at Rose with her blue eyes wide; she looks more like Betty Boop with a bone in her nose than ever. "I know where I've seen you."

"You do?" Rose asks coyly, tucking her hair behind her ear for the fiftieth time.

"Wabi Sabi Tattoo, right? Don't you like work there or something?"

Rose nods and does the pouty thing with her lips again. Oh, Jesus—not...? Is Rose flirting with *Miranda?*

"I'm in there whenever I have money," Miranda tells her, so excited she's bouncing on the edge of her seat. "Ian is such a genius."

"Oh, he's good," Rose purrs. "He does the most amazing work."

Miranda unhooks the leopard-spotted cape she donned for the occasion and yanks at the neckline of her T-shirt. She exposes most of her left breast to show Rose the neon-green-and-magenta gecko tattooed there. It is a pretty one, I have to say—the gecko, I mean, not the breast. Although, as breasts go, I suppose it's fine. Oh, God, now I'm assessing my student's left breast. I really should not be here.

"Wow," Rose breathes, not even disguising the mixture of shyness and lust mingling in her throat. "I've never seen anything more beautiful."

I'd be lying if I claimed that Miranda's sexual orientation never occurred to me as a subject of interest. She's such a quirky, one-of-a-kind girl, she really doesn't lend herself to simple categories very readily. She's not butch at all; her delicate features and her doll-like face are way too femme for that. But her skinny, adolescent body, her ever-present skateboard, her silver-and-bone-studded face, and her bowlegged walk all have the flavor of a defiant tomboy. Her clothes—well, her clothes are just incredibly weird, alternately hyper-girly and super boyish, often a mix of both. With other students she's always standoffish and shy, so I haven't had much chance to see her flirting with anyone. Now, watching her practically undress right here on Café Pergolessi's patio to show Rose the collection of amphibian tattoos she's covered in, I suspect this is her way of flirting.

She's lifting the hem of her skirt to expose an indigo tree frog on her inner thigh when I clear my throat and say, "You know what, guys? I'm suddenly beat."

"Fantastic," Rose says, as if I haven't spoken. "Look at those webbed feet—such detail."

"Um, here. Let me just pitch in for the tip," I say, stuffing a couple dollars under an ashtray.

"Have you gotten any yet?" Miranda's asking. I've become invisible and mute, apparently.

"I'm just going to walk home," I say, getting up. "Congratulations, Miranda. See you at home, Rose."

They both glance at me briefly, and I can see they're anything but sorry that I'm going. "'Night," they say in unison, then "Jinx." (Also in unison.)

I slip away as they erupt in girlish giggles.

The buzz hits the street after our opening night, and the rest of our shows are sold out, both weekends. It's a smash hit—one of those magical runs when the cast, the script, the set, the costumes all come together and strike just the right chord with each audience. Even our light board fiasco shifts from a serious crisis to an amusing anecdote, and by the second weekend, the original board is replaced. For once, other faculty members are saying hello to me with something other than disdain, and I realize how thirsty I've been for that approval. Even Monica Parker grants me a quiet, tight-lipped compliment when we find ourselves awkwardly trapped in the faculty lounge one afternoon. I'm waiting for my microwave popcorn to stop popping when she comes in, hesitates for half a second, as if thinking about turning around, then heads for the refrigerator.

"I understand *Heirloom* got a good review," she says, retrieving a red-lacquered lunch box. "Congratulations."

"Thanks," I say. "Did you see it?"

"Yes, I did. It was very promising."

Promising. Okay, well, could be worse.

"Thanks. I think Miranda's a really talented writer. The students here are so fun to work with."

"Yes." She pours some coffee in her cup and spoons in some sugar. "It seems you're quite a hit with them, as well." There's a niggling little edge to her voice, but I try to ignore it.

"How's your quarter going?"

"Not bad. Can't complain, I suppose." Her tone conveys she has very much to complain about, but her red-painted mouth smiles, anyway. She's so impeccably groomed. I've always found that a great mystery—how some women manage to maintain such incredibly high standards in their personal hygiene. She hasn't got a single stray hair, her makeup is flawless, and her suit is so pressed, the creases look dangerous.

"Will you be directing anything this year?" I ask, trying very hard not to stare at her perfect, manicured toes as they peek out from her open-toed sandals.

"Oh, no. I don't direct. I do have a book in the works, though, a treatise on shadow puppetry."

"Brilliant," I gush. "That's wonderful."

She shrugs. "We'll see."

"I want a signed copy," I say.

"See you later." Her smile is passably genuine as she clicks out in her high-heeled sandals, clutching her coffee and her shiny lunch box.

Maybe she's not as grim as I imagined. I wander back to my office, munching popcorn thoughtfully. Sometimes a man wedged between two strong, capable women can distort the whole picture. I've probably jumped to all sorts of conclusions, and she's really a wonderful, funny, vibrant woman I'd actually like if I gave her a chance. Maybe we'd be best friends, except we got off on the wrong foot.

I sit down at my computer and check my e-mail, all the while entertaining visions of Monica and I sharing a salad at her kitchen table, laughing chummily over a bottle of wine. We'd have people in stitches, telling the story of how we met. "And then I—" giggle giggle "—stormed into the yurt…" "While *I* clutched at the sheets." "And I was so angry, I practically decked her right there—" Everyone dissolves in sobs of laughter.

My little fantasy explodes in a spasm of smoke when I see the following words glowing in my in-box:

From: Ruth Westby
Subject: Unfortunate Situation: Urgent. Please Read.

My palms are instantly slick with sweat, and my mouth's so dry I swear I taste dust. I try to force my hand to drag the mouse and click on those terrible words. Instead I remain paralyzed with dread as my mind rearranges them over and over like a crossword puzzler on PCP.

URGENT. WESTBY. UNFORTUNATE. PLEASE SITUATION. READ RUTH. URGENT WESTBY. PLEASE PLEASE PLEASE.

"Claudia?"

A tiny scream—more a whelp, really—escapes my lips, and I spin toward the door, spilling my popcorn in all directions. There, looking at me with steely calm over her tortoiseshell glasses, is Dr. Ruth Westby.

"Yes?"

"Can I see you in my office?" she says, crossing her arms.

"Now?" I reach down and scoop up a handful of popcorn from the floor, toss it at the garbage and miss.

"If you don't mind."

"Certainly."

The walk down that poster-laden hall has never seemed so long. I move like a prisoner toward the gallows, my feet dragging heavily. I notice a piece of popcorn clinging to the sole of my shoe and try to kick it free, unsuccessfully. I decide to ignore it. A thin trickle of perspiration snakes its way down my spine, and I'm fighting for control of my sphincter. Relax, I order myself. So what? You've done nothing wrong, and if Westby thinks you have, you'll just set her straight, like last time.

When we're both seated, she takes off her glasses and cleans them with a scarlet handkerchief that matches her blazer perfectly. "I expect you read my e-mail," she begins.

"No, I—er—I mean, I saw the subject heading, but I didn't get a chance to. Yet."

She raises her eyebrows at this. I feel like a terrible slacker and resolve to scan my e-mails every two minutes from now on in the off chance that she might send me one. "Right. Well, I'll try to be simple and to the point. It's about your play—or rather, your student's play, *Heiress*. It seems—"

"Heirloom," I interrupt, and instantly regret it.

"Excuse me?"

"Heirloom," I mumble. "It's called *Heirloom*."

"Ah," she says. "Well, I hear it's wonderful. So that's good news." She flashes me the most unconvincing smile I've ever seen, and my throat constricts with pure, unadulterated terror. "The not-so-good news is your student—Miranda Wilkes, is it?" I nod. "Her father is…well, he's an extremely wealthy, powerful man. In fact, he owns—" and here she mentions the largest tennis shoe manufacturer in, oh, probably the world, say, if not the universe, along with a line of clothing that every teenager from here to China covets. "He's also an extremely generous benefactor of the university. He's donated—well, suffice it to say, *a lot* of money."

"Uh-huh," I say, a little surprised that Miranda comes from such deep pockets, but still not getting what the big deal is.

"Mr. Wilkes saw the play yesterday. He's…" She licks her lips once, and the rogue left eye starts twitching like mad. "He's less than enthusiastic about it."

"But why? Miranda's a wonderful writer—"

"He's threatening to sue." She puts her glasses back on,

presses them tight against her face and stares at me through the thick lenses. This does little for her appearance, as it only magnifies the twitch tenfold. "I have our legal team looking into it. He most likely doesn't have much of a case, but nonetheless, making Mr. Wilkes unhappy is not advisable."

"He wants to sue?" I say dumbly. "But why—?"

"Let's just say he finds the father figure inappropriate and offensive." She clears her throat. The situation becomes illuminated with the blinding white glare of a nuclear blast inside my brain. He's the father. Miranda's Olivia, only she didn't get her revenge with cyanide; she's getting it now.

Little Miranda. Why didn't I see this coming?

But even if I had, would it have made any difference? Is autobiography a crime?

Through a whirling kaleidoscope of thoughts shifting rapidly in my brain, I faintly hear Westby's clincher: "Of course, we'll cancel the performances for this weekend."

"What?" I barely recognize my voice; it sounds much too hostile to be mine.

"Claudia, I'm very sorry, but there's absolutely no way, considering the circumstances—"

"Cancel my show? After all the hard work we—the cast will be crushed. You can't do this."

"You'll have to think of something to tell them. A technical difficulty, perhaps. We don't want to give the wrong impression. And neither, of course, does Mr. Wilkes."

"But what about Miranda? This play means so much to her—"

"Miranda will receive a difficult lesson, and sometimes that's what we as educators are forced to provide."

I swallow hard, feeling woozy and unsure.

"I see."

"Really, Claudia, I hate to do this." She looks almost vulnerable for a moment, her dark eyes going from blank to pleading for a split second. "I know you've worked hard. And the students—I know all that. But my hands are tied."

How can this be happening? It doesn't even make sense. And here's Westby, calmly pronouncing the death of my precious show, as if it's unavoidable. "Who is he going to sue, anyway? His own daughter?"

"The university, of course. He insists we're providing a venue for defamatory material."

"That's ridiculous!" I can't, in my confused state, recall the legal definition of *defamatory,* but I'm sure we haven't committed it, whatever it is.

"Perhaps." She looks empathetic for an instant, but then her voice becomes hard again, precise and cutting. "Unfortunately, given his position, I have no choice but to take the threat quite seriously."

A red streak of anger shoots through my chest and then, from out of nowhere, a lucid calm comes over me. I meet Westby's gaze. Her left eye spasms crazily, looking dangerously out of control. I almost feel sorry for her, with that weird little tick revolting against her gallant efforts to be made of ice.

"I won't do it," I say.

"I'm sorry?"

"I'm not going to lie for you. It's—it's censorship," I say. "I'm still too young and stupid to sell out just like that."

"Claudia, I really think you should reconsider—"

"Why? You've already made it clear I'm just a stand-in. It's not like I have that much to lose, anyway."

"Actually," she says, "given how promising this production is—these unpleasantries aside—the department is seriously considering extending your contract."

"Well, I'm not considering your offer, if this is how you run things."

She stiffens. "It's not an offer. It's just a possibility."

"Well, then, all I'm losing is a possibility." I stand and make my way toward the door.

"Claudia?"

I turn at the door. "Yes?"

"I respect your ideals. Really. But there is simply no way you're performing this play again. I absolutely forbid it."

A tiny smile plays on my lips, though I try to repress it. I can't help myself; I'm about to deliver the line I've waited for all my life. "Try to stop me."

CHAPTER 24

After a sleepless night, five o'clock finally brings dawn. I'm pacing the floor of my apartment in my boxer shorts and wife-beater tank top, nursing a cup of English Breakfast with the phone glued to my ear. "Okay, let me get this straight. You're saying, if I make a big enough stink—"

"Become their worst nightmare—"

"They'll let me do the play and they won't fire me?"

"Right." Ziv is getting excited now. He lives for this shit. I close my eyes and visualize him: bony white knuckles gripping his cell, a cigarette burning almost to his fingertips; balanced precariously on the porch rail beside him is his third demitasse of homemade espresso. "It would make them look bad in a *very* public way, and open them to a lawsuit they could lose. If it comes to that, I'll represent you." He laughs explosively and a powerful wave of nostalgia washes over me, making me wish more than anything that I was there, sitting on our porch in the Austin spring light, sipping his magical espresso.

"And you really think Miranda's dad will back down?" I try to squelch my longing by focusing on the task at hand.

"Of course. He's freaked out because she basically outed him."

"And made him look like a hypocritical fuckface his own family wants dead."

"Which is probably all accurate, judging from his reaction."

"Shit," I sigh.

"Come on, Bloomie. This is what you drama queens live for."

"You don't get it, Ziv. We like *make-believe* drama. Not the actual, job-threatening live-action kind."

"I don't believe that for a second." I make a tiny, scared whimpering sound in response, and his voice goes soothing. "No worries, okay? You've got the law on your side."

"Yeah, maybe, except my enemy's got all the money and power. You really think the First Amendment's going to stand up against that?"

"If not, then the First Amendment's got to be amended. Just remember—" He speaks slowly and distinctly now, like a coach drilling his star player. "Make it as *public* as you can. The press is your friend. Turn this into the biggest scandal since OJ."

"Ha." I chip polish off my toenails and let Medea gently gnaw on my hand. "Unfortunately I don't have racial tension, organized sports, stardom, gender issues, billions of dollars or a bloody glove to spice it up."

Ziv makes a dismissive sound and I can hear him taking a drag off his cigarette. "So improvise."

Westby issued my warning Monday at half past one; by Thursday afternoon I've got the ACLU behind me, every newspaper in the area alerted, and a small army of student organizations ready to storm the castle as soon as I give the signal. I was wrong, actually, when I whined to Ziv about not having gender issues on my side. Evidently, Miranda's backed by the Gay, Lesbian, Bi and Transsexual Resource Center. They see this as a bi-questioning author being silenced on important issues of sexual politics. As a result, they've galvanized all their affiliated organizations, including (but not limited to) the Down with Heterosexism Clan, the Kidz of Queers Club and the Jewish Transgender Organization. I've also got Students for Civil Liberties, Theater Students for Anarchy and the Slug Chess and Games Club (precisely why this last group cares, I'm not sure, but who am I to second-guess political fervor when it's on my side?).

So far, Westby hasn't actually issued anything to publicly cancel the show; the only proof that she wants to censor it is our private conversation. So, going on Ziv's and the ACLU's advice, I'm proceeding as if that conversation never happened. Only if they try to bar our performance Friday night will we rally the press and our ragtag army of radicals.

I've been so busy e-mailing, phoning and researching I don't have a spare minute to feel sick with remorse until Thursday evening around six o'clock. This is when it hits me: I've pitted myself against the University of California, Corporate America and somehow (though I've only the vaguest notions of how this happened) heterosexuality in general. I've probably pitted myself against God, as well, though I'm too tired to consider this possibility at the moment—Ruth Westby's bad enough.

Now that everything's in place, the twenty-four hours that stretch out before me are too intolerably suspenseful to bear. I figure I've got two options: put a bullet in my head or walk the streets of Santa Cruz until my muscles cry out for mercy. Then—only then—when I'm on the verge of collapse, will I draw a hot bubble bath, have a cigarette, a vodka tonic and two of Rose's sleeping pills to get me through the night.

The sun's been down for a while when I hit the streets. The sky's taken on that ethereal hue of blue that washes everything in ocean shades and makes even the mundane sidewalks surreal, dreamy. I want to wash my brain in that color—drown out all the blinking red warnings and flashing green lights that have guided the congested traffic in my psyche all week.

I stop at my favorite, passion-flower-covered fence and inspect one of the blossoms, marveling at its insectlike stamen and its wild splay of purple fringe. Passion flowers are tart. They're eccentric, edgy and sexy. They disregard convention and refuse to be tamed.

About an hour later, as I'm meandering along the bluffs, I try to concentrate on nothing but what's around me. The seagulls surf the evening breeze, scan the ground for food and occasionally erupt in grumpy squawks. I look out over the darkening ocean. There's a billowy white fogbank easing slowly toward town, and I can smell the sweet, waffle-cone and cotton-candy perfume of the Boardwalk. As I stand there, watching the lights blink on along the coastline, it occurs to me that fighting for Miranda's play is the first thing I've ever done that isn't just about me. Sure, my ego's invested; the righteous rebel suits me, so it's not selfless. But there's also this little kernel of something else in there. For once, I know what it's like to fight for something bigger than the immediate gratification of my petty little needs.

Walking home in the dark, listening to the waves crashing at my back, I think: maybe this is what tart tastes like at thirty.

Friday at three, Westby summons me to her office and for once I go willingly, almost eagerly, aching for an end to the suspense.

"Have a seat, Claudia," she says crisply. I do as I'm told but sit perfectly erect in the hopes that my posture will make up for the disadvantage she's created by opting to pace while I remain glued to my seat. It's the oldest ploy in the book: place your opponent lower than yourself, and I'm surprised someone as slick as Westby would resort to such parlor tricks.

"How are you?" I ask. This throws her off guard.

"I'm fine, thank you." She takes off her clip-on earrings and stashes them in the pocket of her silk blazer. "These earrings are driving me crazy," she says, in an oddly human moment. Then she gets down to business. "Well, things have taken an interesting turn."

"Have they?"

"Yes, they have. I'm referring of course to—well, who am I kidding? You know what I'm referring to."

"Heirloom?" I ask innocently.

"Yes. And more specifically, your choice to back Mr. Wilkes into a corner with the threat of negative publicity. When he caught wind of your little scheme, he was irate. It took us hours to calm him down." She pauses at the window and I watch as green, rain-drenched branches lash about behind the glass. It's a windy day and has been raining on and off since I woke up at dawn. When I look at her face again, she's wearing an odd expression. As usual, I can't read it any more than I can Farsi, but I can see it's loaded with meaning.

"You're a clever woman, Claudia. Frankly, I never expected such violent convictions from you."

I'm aware of a subtle insult embedded in this praise, but I ignore it and mumble, "Thank you."

"No doubt, at a different, less liberal institution, your choices this week would lead to dismissal. But on this campus, we're very serious about artistic freedom. We don't take accusations of censorship lightly." She paces back to her desk and sits down. "So you're fortunate. You happen to work for a university that values what you value."

"Do I?" I ask, sitting up even straighter, eyebrows arched.

"You do. Which is why we've decided to stand by you in this awkward situation and defend your right to express yourself artistically without hindrance."

"Meaning, the show is not canceled?"

"Correct." She smiles, and though it's a twitchy, tense, hardly warm expression, neither is it completely poisonous. "The show, as they say, will go on."

An hour later, Miranda and I have our heads bent over my desk, the door locked, not daring to raise our voices above the level of joyfully hissed whispers.

"I talked to my mom last night," Miranda tells me. "She said Dad's lawyers finally convinced him that he'd better shut up about the whole thing or he'd risk being exposed even worse than he already is."

"Oh, my God," I giggle. "I can't believe it worked."

I jump up and do a little victory dance, then sit back down when I hear footsteps in the hallway.

"What? Is that Westby?" Miranda whispers, wide-eyed with anxiety.

"Probably not—I just heard someone, is all." I shrug sheepishly. "This whole thing's made me a little paranoid."

Miranda laughs. "Join the club." Then she looks down at her Doc Martens and says, "Claudia?" Her eyes shimmer with tears, and she tugs at her hair shyly. "Thanks."

"For what?"

"For being on my side. Hardly anyone ever is."

I reach across the desk and hug her awkwardly. She smells like incense and clove cigarettes and I think, if I ever have a kid, I hope it turns out as cool as this little freak.

SPRING

PART 3

CHAPTER 25

The first day of spring falls on a Saturday—my first official day of spring break—and I sleep gloriously late. It's the kind of sleeping in where you wake up every hour or so after eight o'clock, squint groggy-eyed at the sunlight, consider slippers and a cup of coffee but opt instead to snuggle deeper into your soft, body-warmed sheets and drift back down the stream of lazy half dreams.

At eleven, however, there's a knock at my door. I open one eye and the empty place confirms that Rose and Rex are at work. Medea stretches luxuriously and blinks at me like, "What, you think I'm getting it?"

I roll out of bed, pull on my boxers and a crumpled camisole, stumble toward the door and, still too comatose to remember things like hurriedly examining my hair, open it. There, in a faded yellow T-shirt and a pair of blue board shorts is Clay Parker, beaming at me.

I shut the door.

He knocks again. "Come on, lazybones. Let me in."

"I'm not awake," I groan, leaning against the door in agony. "You didn't just see what you saw."

I wait to hear rapid footsteps indicating he's fled in horror, but no such luck. Eventually, I open the door again and try in vain to flatten my hair as I shuffle to the couch and sink into it, wanting to disappear. "You're not really here," I say as he follows me. "I'm dreaming."

"Oh, yes, Ms. Bloom. I am very much here. And you're coming with me."

"Get out of here." I laugh, throwing a pillow at him. This is too weird. Clay Parker in my flat, with me half dressed and breathing the worst morning breath in the history of mankind.

"I've decided there's only one way to deal with you," he says, flopping into a chair as Medea, the little slut, leaps into his lap, wiggles her rump against his thigh and purrs.

"Oh, yeah?"

"Yes. You're a very naughty girl. I insist you do as you're told."

I laugh, then cover my mouth, afraid he can smell my breath from over there. "Tell me what you have in mind."

"No." His voice is matter-of-fact, but his eyes are sparkling with mischief. One of his lovely brown hands is absently stroking Medea into an embarrassing state of ecstasy. She arches her back as a string of drool slowly snakes through the fur on her chin. "Now, get dressed. I'll close my eyes if you like, but I'm not leaving. You have five minutes."

"Five? That's not even enough time to change my under—"

"Five. And that's final." He looks at his watch. "Starting…now."

Let's face it: *take charge* is a turn-on. Don't get me wrong; I despise machismo, and if anyone tried to get masochistic on me I'd take my chances with the nearest blunt object, but that's not what I'm talking about here. What I'm talking about is a man with a calm, commanding voice cutting through all the indecision, polite conversation and general crap that normally fills our days with orders as sharp and precise as scalpels. What I'm talking about is Clay Parker driving up Highway 1 until we arrive at a place where the artichoke fields end abruptly in cliffs and sea, getting out, nodding at the three surfboards strapped to the rack of his truck and saying, "Pick one."

"Wait a minute here."

"Go on," he says, his eyes and voice both insisting that I've got no options. "I don't care which one."

"Clay." I gasp, incredulous. "I don't *surf.*"

"Yet. All that's about to change."

"I can't. I can't—swim." I put one hand on my hip in a "take that" stance, but he's unfazed.

"Uh-huh. And that story you told me about trying out for the diving team was…?"

"All lies?" I try, cringing.

"We don't have all day. You already slept through the prime surfing hours. Now pick one out and let's go."

"But how am I supposed to know which…?"

"God. Are you always like this?" He yanks the straps off the big turquoise one and hands it to me, then grabs the pale yellow one for himself. He shoves a wet suit under my arm, grabs a big backpack stuffed so full the zipper looks ready to give and starts marching across the street toward a dusty path carving through the vegetable fields. I just stand there, slack-jawed. "Hurry up," he calls, not turning around. "Last one in's shark bait."

"Whose wet suit is this, anyway?" I ask an hour later, after a fierce battle with the breakers that looked to me like tidal waves but which Clay claimed "weren't even chest-high." Now we're bobbing in the calm stretch just beyond the chaos, straddling our surfboards and contemplating the landscape of pale blue sky meeting navy-blue sea. A harbor seal's black, shiny head pops up ten feet from me and I scream. Clay laughs.

"It used to be my sister's."

"You have a sister?" I ask, trying not to think about sharks.

"Three. Well, two full sisters and one half. Now, listen, you want to watch the shape of the swells as they roll in."

"What were you saying earlier, about shark bait?"

"Don't think about it," he says. "You eat shark?"

"I have. It's delicious."

"Don't do it again. It's bad luck."

"Seriously," I say, craning my neck to peer down into the opaque depths. "Are there great whites out here?"

"You're more likely to be killed by a terrorist."

I try not to fixate on the fact that he's still avoiding the question.

"Okay, check this one out. This is a little more ridable, yeah?"

I turn and notice for the first time a tsunami steadily gaining bulk as it swells in our direction.

"Ahh. Clay—what do I...?"

"Turn around—there you go. Now, lie flat—hurry—chest to your board." He gives me a mighty shove toward the shore. "Paddle!" he screams, just as I feel the fat part of the wave rising under me. "Paddle!"

I do as I'm told, cutting into the icy-cold water with my hands and pulling as I feel the suck of the tube just behind me. I can sense the wave preparing to crest, tugging me toward it. My heart is pounding like a teenager's too-loud car stereo. I want to scream, but I'm concentrating too hard on staying ahead of the foam and now—it's a miracle—I'm sloping down the face, white-knuckling the board with both hands, pressing the length of my body against it and riding the magic power of it, screaming at last, "Heeeaaaaa!" the taste of salt in my mouth and the white spittle of the sea frothing all around me until finally I flop triumphantly onto the sand, beaming.

The ankle-deep beer foam now reverses its direction, sizzling and popping and pulling slick black pebbles with it in a bubbly, percussive retreat. I just lie there on my board, tingling with pleasure.

I turn, and Clay's still where I left him, past the breakers, nodding his approval. I pull myself up off the board and jump up and down to demonstrate my glee.

Now I watch in horror as a *huge* wave—my tsunami times three—builds behind Clay. I scream a warning and brace myself for his terrible, waterlogged death. Instead he paddles nonchalantly, pops up to a standing position and surfs the great blue beast practically to the sand, carving and sliding with the cocky, effortless grace of the ocean itself.

Yeah, yeah, yeah. So you're good, I think. *What else is new?*

Taqueria Vallarta is packed. Aside from the huge mural on one wall painted in vibrant, rich tones, it looks like a million other no-frills taco joints in California. But from the second we walk in the door I can tell this place is one of a kind. The line snakes straight back from the counter to the entrance, and the smell that fills the air is sublime—carnal and steamy. As I look around, it's clear the patrons are divided into two classes: those who are ecstatically eating and those who are anxiously waiting to eat. I watch as a lanky guy with thick black dreads and full lips lifts a taco to his mouth. Oh, God. I work hard at suppressing the impulse to beg and drool at the nearest table until somebody takes pity and tosses me a scrap.

"Ever been here?" Clay asks, standing so close I could graze his hip with mine if I swayed ever so slightly. I just shake my head no, mute with desire. "It's one of my favorite places—especially after surfing."

"Why does being in the water make me so unreasonably ravenous?"

"I know. I'm starving." His eyes rest on my lips for a second, and suddenly all I can think about is that time at my place when he made me scream with a piece of ice. I bite the inside of my cheek gently, willing the vision away, but when our eyes meet it starts up all over again: his big, solid hands spreading my thighs with gentle reverence, the wolf-ish smile tugging at the corners of his mouth as he clenches the dripping ice cube between his teeth.

"You did really well out there today," he says softly, tucking a strand of saltwater-crazed hair behind my ear. "You're a natural."

"Yeah," I scoff, grateful for the distraction from the pornographic film strip looping through my brain. "What about when I almost drowned?"

"Happens to everyone," he says. "Teaches you respect for the power out there."

"Oh, I respect the ocean," I say. "I'm not so sure she respects me, though."

On the drive here I learned that, in addition to running the record store and DJing occasional gigs, Clay shapes surf-boards in his spare time. It's a labor of love, though he thinks it could turn into some pretty decent money if he keeps up with it. There's an old shaper named Vince who's a regular underground legend among big-wave surfers—the guys who go up against towering skyscrapers of water that make my adventures today seem like kiddie-pool stuff. Clay's been learning Vince's tricks for five years now; he's got a shop at home and a bunch of regulars.

Why is it that everything I learn about Clay Parker makes me want him more? I take that back; finding out he was Monica's hubby and Westby's son didn't exactly stoke my lust. But everything else about him is maddeningly sexy: every little anecdotal tidbit and offhand remark, the way he tugs gently at his boxers or licks his slightly chapped lips— it all stirs me to ridiculous levels of arousal. It's not the way I used to imagine falling for someone. Back in my Barbie-playing days, I always made sure Ken was a rock star or a race-car driver. Before I pressed their naked plastic bodies together in a hopelessly vague attempt at anatomically inaccurate sex, I made sure Ken had wowed her with flowers and dinner and a gallant rescue from the lethal edge of my bed. No one prepared me for the effect minute details can have on your system: the gently swerving nose; the muscle that pulses at his jaw now and then; the tiny, crescent-shaped scar close to his ear.

After we order, there is a harrowing ten-minute wait during which I summon every ounce of willpower in me to resist prying a steamy burrito from the hands of a ten-year-old girl sitting so close I can smell the chicken on her breath. At this point I'm so hungry I feel dizzy. Luckily, we've ordered Coronas with lime, and a long pull from this takes the edge off my hunger, though I still feel as if the room is spinning slightly.

Clay lifts his bottle and says, "To the Little Surfer Who Could."

I clink my Corona against his and take another swig. When I look at him again, he's staring at me with these bright blue saltwater summery bedroom eyes, and I feel positively nauseous with longing. I know he's taking off my clothes as we sit here—slipping the elastic neckline of my peasant blouse down my shoulders, kissing his way from my clavicle to the salty aureole around my nipple, licking—

"Clay. Don't *look* at me like that."

"Why not?" He smiles shyly, and his fingertips sweep along my forearm with a feathery touch that makes my mouth go dry.

"I cannot, should not, must not, *will* not sleep with you."

Just then a little visor-clad guy arrives with a tray full of our steamy food. He's attempting unsuccessfully to hide the huge smirk on his face by ducking his head slightly. We take our food from him, nod our thanks and Clay digs in, but I'm so embarrassed by my outburst, I've momentarily lost my appetite.

"Why's that?" he asks through a mouthful of taco.

"Because. Your mother's my boss, you're freshly divorced from my colleague."

"So?"

The full aroma of my *carnitas* tacos suddenly overwhelms me, and my moment of appetite-killing mortification passes. I squeeze lime over everything and stuff a huge bite into my mouth. Oh. Heaven is a taco, a beer and a beautiful man after surfing.

"You're missing the point," I say, after I've recovered enough from my first few bites to speak. "I'm so totally on probation. Your mom thinks I'm the worst shit-stirrer ever."

"I know," he says, "I heard."

"What did you hear?"

"That you threatened to sic the ACLU and two-thirds of the campus on that dickhead dad if he didn't back down."

"Who told you that?"

"My mom. And listen, I'll give you a little inside tip— one thing my mom likes is a woman with balls, if you'll pardon the expression. You may have pissed her off momentarily, but in the end that round scored you points. At least now she knows you're a force to be reckoned with. That's one thing she never liked about Monica—too much of a brownnose." He reaches across the table with a napkin and wipes a bit of something from the side of my mouth. With most men I'd find this humiliating, but with Clay it's perfectly natural—sexy, even.

"You've run out of excuses, Ms. Bloom." His voice is confident and brusque. "As soon as this meal's over, you'll be forced to come home with me and perform unspeakable acts."

"Great, and drive right past Monica's cottage on our way?"

"I don't live there anymore," he says. "I got a place in town."

This information does please me, but I try to hide my pleasure with a highly skeptical stare.

"What?" he demands. "Why are you looking at me like that?"

"Don't you agree that getting involved with you is a terrible career move on my part?"

He leans back in his chair and considers this. "Not really. I mean, unfortunately—and I do apologize for this—you became the other woman in Monica's mind the day you rolled into town. I know I should've said something right away. It's just that...I really liked you. Like you, I mean. I didn't want to scare you away."

"Clay..."

"And if you're thinking that it's a low-return risk for just a careless little rebound-fling, forget it. I don't know what your intentions are, but I have a distinctly long-term plan in mind."

I scoff. "That's a little bold, don't you think?"

"You're a very naughty girl, Ms. Bloom. If I take you on as my pupil we'll have to be very committed. There'll be rigorous lesson plans, and spankings will be administered regularly. Probably hourly, based on what I've seen."

I almost choke on my beer. When I've regained my composure and finished my last bite of taco, I ask, "What are we really talking about, here?"

"Your education. So, what do you say?" He drops a couple of bills on the table, stands and offers me his hand. "Are you ready for your first lesson?"

Looking up at him, all of my carefully constructed reasons for resisting Clay Parker dissipate and float away like ocean mist. When it comes down to it, that hot little command central between my thighs makes every last decision for me.

"Sure," I say, taking his hand and following him to the door. "I live for spankings."

"I guarantee you'll get more than you ever dreamed of," he says, opening the door for me and resting the other hand firmly on my hip.

"Mmm," I murmur, walking so close I can smell the salt water on his skin. "I feel a terrible bout of naughtiness coming on."

Top Ten Reasons to Have Sex with Clay Parker:
1) Puzzle Bodies: extremely rare. Previously considered mythical, but now understand is factual. Possible for two physiques to fit with such precision, everything goes suede and cashmere. Unbelievable.
2) He smells like a July morning.
3) Teeth: some boys bite like horses or nibble like kittens, the worst ones suck like vampires seeking blood extraction through pores. Clay strikes perfect balance. Teeth are highly evolved surgical tools employed solely for pleasuring purposes.
4) Pulls hair. Just right.
5) When whispering in ear, says things that make even tarts blush.
6) Spankings as promised.
7) Precoital foot massage, complete with Skin Trip lotion and between-toe action.
8) Postcoital ice cream orgy: Häagen-Dazs Dulce de Leche. Almost as good as coital itself.
9) Bathroom tidy, toilet seat down, emergency afterpee does not induce desire to vomit.
10) Could be due to dry spell immediately preceding, but climactic scream even louder than gaudiest porn-star-style forgeries.

26

CHAPTER

It's April Fool's Day, and Rose insists we celebrate. We actually have plenty to be giddy about. Spring quarter's just begun, signaling the home stretch leading straight to summer, with its promises of laziness, debauchery and unemployment. Clay and I have been shamelessly, deliriously happy for one week and five days now. We're drunk on each other's flesh, floating in that anti-gravity state that Hallmark cards enshrine and pop songs worship: love. It's a terrible, embarrassing thing. If I weren't so intoxicatingly happy, I'd have to shoot myself.

And Rosemarie has been promoted this fine Thursday from gofer girl to receptionist at Wabi Sabi Tattoo. There's a nominal raise involved, increased access to learning the trade, and it's the first job she's held down for three months straight in her whole life, so I'm really proud of her. She looks good tonight, dressed in the retro polka-dot halter top and the suede skirt we found her at a consignment shop last week. She's finally reversed the frightening trend toward skeletal and has put on enough pounds lately to soothe my anorexia alarms.

We're sitting at a table toward the back of the Poet and Patriot Irish Pub, sharing shepherd's pie, French fries with vinegar and a couple of pints of Guinness. I've resurrected my Cleo wig from my underwear drawer. Rose is determined that we should get quite drunk tonight, and I've decided that going out undercover is the only way I can comfortably get shit-faced in this town, where there's a student or colleague lurking under every rock. So I'm fidgeting with my slick black bob, and Rose is attempting to explain to me how she and Miranda managed to break up before they even made it to their first kiss.

"Okay, let me start again," she says, stuffing another fry into her mouth and downing it with a swig of beer. "You know how when you're in a relationship with a guy, you sometimes get the urge to talk about heavy stuff—analyze why he dreams about his mother, that sort of thing?" I nod. "And he wants to watch football?"

"I don't sleep with guys who watch football," I say. "But I know what you mean. Women are more verbal. We like to talk shit out. Guys are generally monosyllabic."

"Exactly. Now, imagine a relationship where nobody wants to watch football. It's pure, twenty-four-seven analysis. There's no, 'you think too much, let's fuck' here. That's why Miranda and I didn't get anywhere. It was all conversation, no action."

I have to say this comes as a bit of a relief to me. They'd been meeting for breakfasts and lunches and post-work cheesecakes (probably the reason Rose has put on pounds) for weeks now, and I dreaded the moment when Rose would waltz through the door with a Cheshire cat grin plastered all over her face. It's not that sex between women is unsavory; it's sex between Rose and Miranda that unsettles me. Somehow my favorite cousin getting carnal with my favorite student seems incestuous, and I worried that Rose's inevitably detailed recapping would make me profoundly uncomfortable.

"But if you weren't even *in* a relationship, what did you spend all your time analyzing?" I ask, still mystified.

"You see, that's the thing, we were too busy discussing what we might theoretically be like if we were, theoretically, to have a relationship. We dissected the whole thing before it happened."

"I still don't see how—"

"I'm telling you, we seduced, became disenchanted, betrayed each other and broke up before we'd even gotten around to holding hands. It was pathetic." Rose shakes her head, and then I watch the canvas of her sweet, expressive face go from disappointed to spellbound in under two seconds. I look over my shoulder to see what she's staring at; there's a monstrously tall, tattooed guy with a shiny, shaved bald head and a dimpled smile taking a seat at the bar. I look back at Rose.

"What? You know him?"

"Oh, my God. Claudia. I'm tingling all over. What's wrong with me?"

"Soul-mate radar activated?"

"Don't tease. I'm serious," she whispers frantically. "Do I look okay? Is my nose all shiny?"

"You look fantastic."

"Do I look edgy enough for him?" she says, messing up her hair a bit.

"Wait a minute, I thought you were determined to get with a girl."

"Kismet," she says. "Out of my control. What do I do? Should I go talk to him?"

I sneak another covert look over my shoulder. "What's the tattoo of?"

She sighs dreamily. "It's a giant bat biting the head off a goat."

"And the radar's still…?"

"He's perfect. Look at him. He's got to be huge. Check out the hands on that guy. And the feet. Christ…"

"If it weren't for the dimples, I'd say he looks dangerous, but he does have a very sweet smile."

"I'm going to talk to him," she says, yanking the neckline of her dress an inch lower. "Otherwise, I'll kick myself for years. You don't mind, do you?"

"Of course not. Who am I to interfere with kismet?"

She kisses me quickly on the cheek and stands up. I shift my chair slightly so I can watch her stalking the bar out of the corner of my eye. I try not to be too obvious, but through undercover glances I'm able to confirm that giant goat-eating-bat-tattoo guy is obviously delighted.

It's at this moment that everything shifts drastically. One second I'm filled with a subtly blossoming Guinness buzz, indulging in French fries, watching my cousin make the moves. The next my heart is sliced in half and is flopping around sloppily inside me.

Clay Parker walks in the door.

With his arm around a girl.

And not just any girl. Wouldn't you know it? The shoulder his lovely brown hand is cupping would have to be the shoulder of my nemesis: Little Miss Practically Rain from the Anti-Valentine Party. She might be twenty-one, no more, and her hair is just as long, just as glossy-black as Rain's, her teeth just as impossibly white. Her lips are painted with ruby-red gloss and her eyes are shining with the pleasure of a girl whose twenties are still stretched out before her like an endless, shimmering highway. She's smiling as if she knows she's getting laid tonight. Or perhaps this is a post-coital pint, the nonsmokers' version of a cigarette in bed.

I wait in paralyzed horror for Clay to see me and either vehemently deny my existence or stammer lame excuses at me. He does neither. His eyes slip over and past me casually, without hesitation. Then I remember I'm wearing a wig and horn-rimmed, pink-tinted glasses; it's small comfort, but at least I'll be spared the humiliation of a barroom brawl. For a fleeting second I consider torturing myself by sitting perfectly still, watching them. They've chosen a cozy booth in the corner that allows me a decent view of their gleeful profiles facing each other, their animated mouths jabbering on about God knows what. But then I feel the shepherd's pie, vinegar-soaked fries and Guinness sloshing together in grisly communion. I have barely enough self-control to bolt into the bathroom before kneeling over the toilet and puking it all up.

That should teach you, Bloom, I scold myself as I kneel over the pinkish-gray mess in the toilet and heave again. *Haven't you seen enough of love to know it's toxic?*

Rose comes in as I'm flushing the toilet. "Claudia? Babe? You okay?"

"Sick," I mumble, coming out of the stall with my hand over my mouth.

"But you've barely had a pint."

"I'm not drunk," I say, splashing cold water on my face to disguise my tears. "It's Clay. He's out there with some vulgar little slut. Why does everyone leave me for Lolita?"

"Oh, God," she says. "I'm so sorry. I didn't even notice."

"It's typical." I yank angrily at a paper towel, dampen it slightly and pat at my splotchy face. I will myself to be brave and just shut up about it, but when I catch sight of Rose's face in the mirror, watching me with her eyebrows forming an inverted V of worry and empathy, I turn around and fall sobbing into her arms.

"Shh," she says, patting my back. "It's okay. He's not worth it."

"He *is,* though," I cry incoherently. "If anyone is, *he* is."

"Not if he's stupid enough to prefer some tacky little bimbo over you." We go on like this for a few minutes, me crying and slobbering into the crook of her neck, she murmuring mindless, reassuring assertions of my supremacy, Clay's blind stupidity, and the nameless slut's totally skanky vileness.

"Do you think he saw you?" she asks when I've managed to pull myself together a bit.

I pull at a strand of my wig. "I'm Cleo tonight, remember?"

"Oh. Right. I forgot."

"God, I want a cigarette," I moan.

"Okay, look. The night can be saved. I'm going to go get Tim, and we'll all sneak out the back, okay?"

"Don't worry about me," I say. "I'll just walk home. You two have a good time."

"No way. You are not going to mope about this, Claudia. We're leaving this stupid pub, and we're going to go get properly sloshed at a bar that doesn't serve scumbags like those two out there. Got it?"

"He's not a scumbag," I whine, hating myself for such weakness.

"Claudia, listen to me. Anyone who two-times you, the most brilliant, beautiful, seductive cousin alive, is scum. Is that clear?" I hesitate, then nod obediently. "Good. Now, slip out the back—I'll meet you there in ten seconds."

"Rose—"

"Do it. And we'll get you a cigarette, first thing. Then we'll pour so much liquor down your throat, you won't even remember his name."

Morning After. Ugh. I wake up in a slice of sunlight so sticky-hot and oppressive, I somehow find the strength to sit straight up and peel my shirt off. Then I flop back down and my head clouds with pain. There's the headache, yes— that's a given—but there's also a searing, throbbing spike in my ankle. I prop myself up gingerly on one elbow and peer down the length of my body at the puffy, swollen mess at the end of my leg. It looks like someone amputated my own bony white ankle in the night and replaced it with a fat girl's thick, puffy one. It's an angry red and I swear I can see the pain throbbing from under the skin.

Christ. What…?

I notice a note written hastily on a paper towel on the pillow beside me.

C,

I called in sick for you. I told them you had laryngitis and also that you'd sprained your ankle. I'm pretty sure the last part is true. Meet me at Pergolessi tonight at five for an update and emergency mud pie.

R

P.S. Do not—I repeat—do not call Clay. He deserves nothing. If you've forgotten, I'll explain all tonight.
P.P.S. If Tim's still there when you wake up, don't freak. He's a really really really nice guy. He carried you home, too, so we owe him one.

I moan softly, roll over and carefully peek at Rose's mattress in the corner, dreading the possibility of a stranger's large, bald body there. Nope. Coast is clear. Then I hear the toilet flush and wince as goat-eating-bat guy appears, drying his face with my favorite fluffy blue towel. He looks away, mumbling, "Sorry—didn't realize…" at which point it occurs to me that I'm shirtless in boxers before a stranger. I frantically scramble back into my tank top as he politely averts his eyes.

"How you feelin'?" he asks once I'm decent, a little too cheerfully and definitely with more volume than I'm prepared for.

"Errmm" is my eloquent response.

"Sorry," he says, lowering his voice. "I know how it is. If it's any consolation, you were impressively wasted last night. I'm surprised you can face the light of day."

"Time?" I say, looking around for a clock.

He consults his watch. "Twelve forty-five. Hungry?"

"Eugh," I say. "Don't think so."

"No. But you will be. Can I get you some water?"

"Um, this might seem rude, but who are you again?"

He laughs. "Tim Frank. Nice to meet you. Last night we were fast friends, but I guess everything's different in the morning." He finds a mason jar in the cupboard, fills it with ice and water and hands it to me. I sit there, blinking in the sunlight. The cold glass feels wonderful in my hand and I gulp down half its contents, making greedy slurping noises and belching when I'm through.

"So listen," Tim says. "I'll give you your privacy. I just wanted to stick around until you woke up, make sure that ankle's not giving you too much pain."

"It hardly hurts at—ouch," I cry as I try to wiggle it and am rewarded with a red-hot poker stabbing into my ankle-bone.

"Could be broken," he says, examining it. "But probably not. Do you want some aspirin?"

"You mind?"

"Not at all." Much to my surprise, he produces a leather briefcase from Rose's corner, pops it open and pulls out a bottle of Extra Strength Tylenol. This guy's a trip.

"So," I say, when I've popped three of his pills and summoned enough strength to sit all the way up. "You don't have to be at work today?"

He grins. "You really don't remember last night, do you?" I shake my head no and blush, imagining myself swinging from some chandelier. "No, I'm a freelancer. I do graphic design. Pretty good gig—make my own hours, that sort of thing. I should be out of here pretty soon, though. I was going to get a bagel before I head down to Carmel. I need to meet with a client around three. Do you want me to grab you a couple bagels and drop them by? It's no problem, and you'll be hungry soon."

"Oh, don't bother—"

"No, really," he insists. "I don't mind."

"Well, okay. If you say so." I start to get up so I can scrounge up some cash, but putting weight on my ankle causes me to shriek with pain. "Motherfucker. What the hell did I do?"

He tries very hard not to laugh, but it's no use. "You, um. Well, let's see…you were dancing with this guy, I think his name was…what was it? Something unusual…"

"Clay?" I ask hopefully.

"No. Something else. You were ranting about Clay most of the night, but the guy you ended up with had some other name. Oh. I know. Malcolm. No, wait, that's wrong. Merrit. He seemed to know you. You know a Merrit?"

"Vaguely," I say.

"Well, you got to know each other much better last night."

"Oh, God." I bury my face in my hands. "Why me?"

"He was cute," Tim offers. "Funny accent."

"British?" I ask.

"Yeah, exactly. See? You do know him."

"Whatever. Um, if it's not too grisly, do you mind saying what I did with him?"

"Like I said, you were dancing. Pretty close. Lots of tongue action, from where I was standing."

"Fuck," I mumble.

"And then you got up on the bar."

"Fuck, fuck, fuck."

"Which was okay—I mean, you know, it was April Fool's Day, you were in the spirit of things. Except then…"

"Please," I cry, pulling at my hair. "Just get it over with. What did I do?"

"You fell off. Or possibly, you dove—it's debatable."

"No."

"And then, when Merrit tried to help you up, you sort of…" He cringes.

"*What?* Tell me."

"Puked."

"No. What did he do?"

"Seeing as the projectile landed more or less on his very pricey-looking shirt, he mostly tried to get it off."

"Oh, God." I flop back down on my futon, utterly destroyed. "Just tell me. Was my wig still on?"

"Yes."

"Thank you, Angels of Mercy," I sigh. "At least Cleo's the alcoholic slut, not me."

"Except you did give this Merrit character your phone number."

"Yeah," I laugh. "And I'm sure he'll be calling right away."

"Oh, he already did," he says, handing me a slip of paper with a phone number on it. "I told him you'd call as soon as you're feeling better."

I do the only thing I can do, of course: I get the hell out of Santa Cruz. Even if it *was* Cleo who made an ass of herself, I need a change of scene or I'll wilt with regret and humiliation. I'm so desperate, I actually visit my father, who's a good sport and takes me to the movies, but I feel like a loser, sharing popcorn with my dad on a Friday night, watching gorgeous people fall in and out of love on the big screen. Saturday, I go to my mom's and savor the sight of Em eight months pregnant, looking considerably more swollen and less perky than usual. But watching my mother dote on her, asking every five minutes if she'd like more ice cream or a cool rag for her forehead is too depressing, so I end up leaving early Sunday morning. I stop in the city to hobble around aimlessly on my half-healed ankle, fingering the cheap trinkets in Chinatown and longing for the expensive shoes in North Beach. When I drive past Clay Street a debilitating wave of melancholy and jealous rage breaks on me; I have to pull over because the tears are making my contact lenses all foggy.

When I get home Sunday night, Rose tells me that Merrit called twice. "And...?" I press hopefully.

"And what?"

"Nothing," I say, crushed.

There's a long pause as I drag my duffel bag in and heave it onto my futon.

"Okay," Rose says, as if she's been holding her breath. "I won't lie. Clay called, too."

"He did?" I hate to admit how my voice wobbles with hope and happiness.

"Three times," she confesses grudgingly.

"Really?"

"But, Claudia, let's face it. The guy's a two-timing weasel."

"Maybe it wasn't him at the pub—or, maybe that girl's just a friend…."

She shoots me a deeply sarcastic look, and I flop onto my futon in despair.

"You're right. I'm pathetic."

"Just forget him, okay?"

"Ha. Easy for you to say."

"Not easy for me to say. I liked him a lot—I thought he was perfect for you."

"You did?" I sit up, a goofy grin on my face.

"*Until* I saw him with that prepubescent skank."

I flop onto my back again. "You're right. He's in rebound mode. Making up for lost time. I won't call him back."

"You definitely will not. And I think you should call Merrit. He's adorable. You love Brits."

"Hmm," I say doubtfully. "I puked on him."

"He's still interested, obviously. And he'll help you get your mind off Clay."

"Maybe."

"So call him," she says, bringing me the phone and the scrap of paper with his number on it. Rex comes, too, and stares at me mournfully, huffing his dog breath into my face. He's been freshly braided and looks like Bob Marley.

"Not tonight," I say.

"Why not?"

"I'm busy," I mumble, clutching a pillow to my chest.

Rose gives me a look, and so does Rex, but they both back off and head for the bathroom together. "Okay. If you say

so. I've got to shower fast. I'm meeting Tim downtown in
a few minutes. You want to come?"

"No, thanks. That's great, though. Is he as soul matey as
you suspected?"

She just shrugs mysteriously and fights an impish grin.
"He's pretty fantastic. But I don't want to jinx it." Then she
shuts the bathroom door and turns on the shower.

I lie there, listening to the water running through the ancient pipes, hearing them groan and grumble deep in the
walls. I wish Rose was going to be around to chaperone me,
make sure I don't do anything stupid like binge on Häagen-
Dazs or dial the seven little numbers that would deliver up
Clay Parker's irresistible voice. *You've got self-control,* I tell myself; *you just stay right here, Bloom. Clay Parker? You don't need
no stinking Clay Parker, you've got better things to do with your
time.*

With this mantra looping through my brain, I settle in for
a long night of staring at the ceiling.

Around eleven o'clock, as I'm digging into my third bowl
of Dulce de Leche, I actually pick up the cordless and punch
in the first five digits of his number. What makes me put it
down again isn't willpower, sadly, but my fear of the hello
I'll hear: that bubbly, twenty-one-year-old sassy brunette
voice—an echo of the tart I once was.

27

CHAPTER

First faculty meeting of spring quarter, all in attendance, and I'm so bored I'm covertly listing everything I can think of. I start with "Ten Worst Fashion Faux Pas in This Room," then move on to "Best Orgasms of My Life" (as soon as I realize number one was with Clay Parker, I abandon this endeavor). Eventually, I opt for the much safer "Rose's Soul Mates Since August," which I attempt to order chronologically. I'm on number thirty, circa New Year's, when out of the gray sea of acronyms and the never-ending slosh of budget concerns, something of interest bobs to the surface.

"Speaking of guest artists, guess who's here in Santa Cruz as we speak? Merrit Russell. Can you believe it?" The faculty responds to Westby's announcement with the appropriate collective gasp. I bite my lip.

"*Serenade*'s up for a Tony," says Monica, and she's so front-of-the-class crisp in her Liz Claiborne separates, I almost feel sorry for her. She keeps shooting Westby needy, approval-seeking glances. I wonder how Clay ever made it through seven years of marriage to such a kiss-ass. "I read in the *New Yorker* that he's in town for a few months."

"Monica and I have been racking our brains trying to find him, but so far we've had zero luck." Westby turns up her palms.

"He's quite a recluse, from what I understand," Monica says. "Even so, we wanted to get him up here for *something*— a guest lecture, anything. It would be a shame to let him go without even meeting him." And then, perhaps afraid this sounds too groupie-like, "Our students would really bene-fit—they come in contact with so few award-winning writ-ers." I cringe, knowing what's coming next. "When I was at NYU…" She starts every other sentence this way. Mare steps on my toe under the table and I suppress a giggle. "…there was a constant flood of top-notch writers, direc-tors, actors. On my first day of grad school I met Tony Kush-ner. Imagine." If she says another word about the vastly superior cultural benefits of New York, I'm afraid I'll puke all over her pressed yellow blouse.

Before I can stop myself, I blurt out, "I can get Merrit Russell."

Monica slips her glasses down slightly on her nose and peers at me. I swear she studies Westby and copies her ges-tures precisely. Pretty soon she'll be doing the mad-eye twitch. "What does that mean, exactly? You can 'get Merrit Russell'? Are you familiar with his work?"

"Of course I am." Okay, not a lie. I didn't realize he was a playwright, let alone up for a Tony, but if rumors are to be believed, I French-kissed him, or Cleo did, anyway. "We're friends."

Monica clears her throat. "Is that right?" I know she doesn't believe me. Every head in the room is turned toward us now, gawking like rubberneckers at a grisly car crash. "Then why did you fail to respond to the faculty e-mail I sent out, requesting any information that might help me contact him?"

Gulp. She's got me there. "I don't always, um, read. Every. E-mail?"

"Right," she says, her eyes darting first to Esther Small, then to Westby.

Mare steps in. "We really do need to cut back on the e-mails. The other day I came in and found fifty-nine new messages."

"Good point, Mare. And that's interesting, Claudia—you know Merrit Russell." This from Westby, who's wearing one of her many cryptic expressions and tapping the tips of her fingers together lightly.

"Sure. He's working on a play set in Santa Cruz. That's why he's here."

Monica barely stifles a choking, incredulous sound. She tries to disguise it as a cough, but nobody's fooled.

"Catching a cold?" I ask her icily.

She smiles. "Of course you're aware that Russell's work has always focused on issues of class in eighteenth-century England?"

I swallow hard and nod. Is it possible I've got the wrong Merrit Russell? Could I be talking about the perverted barfly Merrit Russell, while Monica's referring to the Tony Award nominee?

"I just find it curious," she continues, "that he would take a sudden interest in little old Santa Cruz."

Around the table, there are chuckles and exchanged glances as the tenured crowd savors the comic relief I've inadvertently provided; their collective smugness makes me want to scream.

I dig my nails into my own thigh and announce in what I hope is a calm yet commanding voice, "We could do a staged reading of his new play."

Westby sits up straighter and gives me what I think might be an encouraging look. "Could you arrange that?"

"I'm pretty sure," I say. "He's a totally cool guy." *Note to self: stop saying "totally" and "cool" at faculty meetings.* "He'd probably go for it." *Also, nix "go for it."*

"Excellent. Would you direct it?"

"Love to."

Monica's shooting poisonous darts from her eyes, and Esther Small's mouth looks like she just bit into a lemon, but Westby's obviously pleased and maybe even a little proud. "Keep me posted on that. It sounds like a very good plan." She glances at Monica. "This may not be NYU, but we can occasionally provide glimpses of culture here."

I concentrate on repressing a savage cry of victory when I see the look on Monica's face.

And then I realize: I'm now forced to ask a Tony nominee to save my career—a Tony nominee I recently puked on.

Okay. Mega-panic. It's moments like these I wish I were a Valium addict. My heart has migrated from its usual spot in my chest and is now performing a naughty little samba in my throat. I'm sitting (scratch that: Cleo's sitting) at a sunny table in the Java House, waiting for Merrit Russell.

After I called yesterday and we set up a time to meet, I was faced with a terrible dilemma: to wig, or not to wig. I went around and around for hours, putting it on and yanking it off, until Rosemarie finally saved me with "Look, just wear the stupid thing or he won't recognize you. Take it off later if you feel like it."

"Cleo." I jerk my head around so violently, my Cleo hair nearly flies across the room, but thanks to the wonder of bobby pins I'm still a brunette when I rise to meet him.

"Merrit."

He hugs me with surprising force, then kisses me on the cheek. This could be interpreted as merely European, though it feels decidedly intimate and even nuzzly, which is a little disturbing.

"How *are* you?" I gush, backing up awkwardly and successfully knocking over my chair. I blush and he quickly rights the chair, chuckling fondly, as if this is a private joke between us—you kiss, I knock things over.

"I'm fine. Wow, look at you. You're even lovelier in the light of day."

I clear my throat and wish to God I had some memory of our night spent groping, just so we'd be on the same page. Then I recall the dancing-off-bar-puking-on-shirt part and figure that blackout is preferable in this case.

We sit down and I sip my water. "I'm really sorry about that night," I begin, as my cheeks burn.

"What do you mean? I had a great time."

"Did you?" I ask, not bothering to hide my disbelief.

"I never liked that shirt, anyway," he says, looking very serious. Then his eyes go bright and he laughs and I start to loosen up a touch. "Actually, all my friends back home are shameless alcoholics. Imagine how relieved I am to find out not all California girls live on wheatgrass and tofu."

"Wheatgrass, tofu and tequila," I say. "The three basic food groups."

We banter. We flirt. We talk books, movies, London, music, California, food and celebrities. It's not exactly relaxing; I feel decidedly on the spot, but he is the epitome of charm, and I do get a little buzz off his flirting.

Eventually, I've got to work the conversation around to the hard part, namely why I'm here, in a goofy *Pulp Fiction* wig, pretending to be Cleo Coors who sells underwear at the mall, when really I'm a bad dye-job blonde trying to manipulate him into handing over his play.

Unfortunately, there's no natural segue into this kind of thing, so after an hour of torturous foreplay, I finally opt for the element of surprise. "By the way," I say, yanking off my wig, "I'm not really a brunette."

His eyes widen.

"And…well, my name's not Cleo, either."

"Let me guess," he says. "FBI."

"No, but I like that. Um…I know, this is totally weird. I just—I wore the wig a couple times as a lark, and I happened to run into you."

"Both times."

"Yeah. Then the name was—I don't know, something I threw together. That sounds so lame."

He reaches across the table and squeezes my hand. "It's okay," he says. "I'm a writer. I like interesting people."

"Interesting. That's a good euphemism."

"Okay," he says. "I like crazy people. So what's your name, if you don't mind my asking?"

"Claudia."

"Lovely. Claudia what?"

"Bloom."

"Ahh," he says, nodding knowingly, as if this explains everything. "Claudia Bloom."

"I don't sell underwear at the mall."

"Don't you, now?" He looks increasingly amused, which I suppose is better than incensed.

"No, I don't. I teach theater at the university. Mostly acting and directing."

This elicits a single arched eyebrow. "Interesting," he murmurs.

"And, well, I have a favor to ask."

"Uh-huh…?"

"I would be absolutely and completely indebted to you if you would please, please, please let me do a tiny staged reading of your play. The one you're working on. Any part—I don't care—it could be nothing but the footnotes. I mean seriously, it would just help me out in this totally important way because I'm such a complete idiot I got myself into this huge bind and I—"

"No problem."

"What?"

He's smiling at me the way you smile at a retarded child who's just done something very touching, albeit idiotic. "I said, no problem. I finished a draft last week. I'd love a chance to see it on its feet."

"You're kidding. Really?"

"Really."

"Oh, God, Merrit, I can't even tell you how much I appreciate this."

"I can see that," he says, his smile going a little wolfish around the edges. "And don't think for a minute I'm above exploiting that."

I'm lying on my couch with Medea curled snugly on my chest, thinking about Clay, unfortunately. I keep swinging back and forth between the kind of longing that makes your stomach drop pleasantly and the kind of jealousy that makes you want to vomit or break things.

I've been avoiding his phone calls for weeks. He finally showed up on my doorstep this morning, demanding an explanation for my disappearance. The sight of him there almost made me give in—I wanted to press myself against him so desperately, smell his fragrant heat—but then I thought of my dark-haired replacement, and his arm slung over her shoulder. I refused to make a scene, so I just told him that things weren't working out. I babbled on about not wanting to be exclusive, about seeing other people. Every single trite breakup cliché that popped into my head came flying through my lips. I think I even used that tired old line "I just want to be friends." It was pathetic.

He looked sad, then angry, then his face went sort of blank, like someone who doesn't speak English. I wanted to tell him the truth—about seeing him with that girl, and how it made me throw up, I was so upset—but my pride kept me rattling off vague phrases about "needing space" and "not being ready for a commitment." Eventually, he just shook his head at me, like I'd really disappointed him, turned around and left without a word of goodbye. That pissed me off. As if I was the one who'd screwed up. It wasn't me who decided to test drive a younger model.

After replaying this scene twenty or thirty times, I force myself to think about this afternoon; I'd spent it strolling through the redwoods with Merrit, discussing our plans for his play, *Organically Grown*. Half a mile into our hike, he lit a cigarette, took a seat on a mossy stump and confessed he wasn't much of an outdoorsman. After the cigarette, and a breath mint, and a long, reasonably pleasant kiss, he put his hand on my breast, and I removed it. I can't remember the last time I removed the hand of someone I was willing to kiss.

And there, in the presence of warm April sunlight streaming through branches and the hush of all those ancient, towering trees, I covered my face with my hands and started to cry.

Conveniently, Merrit assumed I was overwhelmed by my attraction to him and started babbling nervously about "No pressure" and "Just enjoying every moment."

I had no desire to tell him the truth: that I was crying because I wasn't twenty-two anymore, and because I'd finally fallen in love—me, who doesn't even believe in love, most days—and because I was no longer thrilled to kiss someone just because his mouth tasted different from the last mouth I kissed.

Medea looks up, blinks at me and inches closer to my face. She stretches her neck until her tongue is tracing tiny sandpaper trails along my cheek.

Only then do I realize I'm crying. Again.

28

CHAPTER

May Day, Em gets impatient and decides to have Baby Rock Star nine days before it's due. Well, to be fair, I guess Baby Rock Star does the deciding. My mother calls me in a panic and insists I meet them at the hospital in Mill Valley as soon as I can. It's a Saturday, and all I had planned was an afternoon matinee at the Nickelodeon with Rose and Tim, so I readily agree. I'm excited both by the prospect of seeing Em in excruciating pain and by the novel idea that my mother, the great Mira Ravenwing, needs me.

But when I get there and hurry into the birthing room, guided by a mousy nurse and the sound of Emily's shrieking, my desire to see her in pain instantly evaporates. She looks so young and vulnerable in her little paper gown, with her sweaty hair plastered to her forehead and her feet clamped into those medieval stirrups. I feel a tremor of anxiety when I spot my mother hovering at her side, looking pale and sweaty herself, shouting, "You're okay, just breathe."

The rest of the evening is a blur. At one point, the baby's heart slows down on the monitor, and I have to pull my mother away, shove her into the corner with a Dixie cup of water and mumble trite, soothing things while the doctors and nurses rush around in a quiet, efficient panic. Pretty quickly, though, they get the heart rate back up and the C-section crew disappears.

Amazingly, Emily goes completely au natural from beginning to end. I'd be screaming licentious threats at anyone with the power to knock me out then and there. But little Em is a lot tougher than I could have guessed.

What can you say about watching one human being give birth to another? It lasts for hours—so much longer than I ever thought possible—and it's the most barbaric, beautiful thing I've witnessed in my life. Nothing in movies or books or baby shower anecdotes prepares me for it. Emily is alternately a little, whimpering girl and a powerful, raging beast. She's so caught up in the struggle, nobody else exists in the world, and we have to call out instructions as if she's very far away. Outside the din of her own thundering pain, though, beyond the chaos of the nurses and the monitors and our feeble encouragements, I can see this strange, determined peace in her face, something that can't be touched by anything around her.

Molly May Snyder is born at 9:20 p.m.; she's an ugly, primordial little shriveled-up thing and at the same time she's exquisite. Her toes are like pink, barely unfurled fiddleheads, and her head smells so sweet I want to press my face against it for hours, hording that strange, intoxicating scent like a fiend sniffing glue. In a word, she's mesmerizing.

When an exhausted Emily holds the tiny, wailing Molly in her arms, both of them damp and still glistening, I find it hard to speak.

"You," Emily says, touching her baby's nose with one finger, and just like that both Mira and I are crying uncontrollably. It's moving in a way that transcends even art; standing so close to something so ancient and powerful humbles even cynical me and my jaded, maternally disinclined mother.

★ ★ ★

The next day around noon, when Emily and Molly are both sleeping, my mother and I drive to a Mill Valley café and try coming back to the earth plane. Our ticket back: double lattes and huge, beautiful salads heaped high with avocado, roasted chicken and sunflower seeds. For a while we don't say anything, we just dig into the mound of greens in busy silence, chewing with great zeal. Eventually, when my hunger's not so fierce anymore, I sit back in my chair, nursing my latte and looking around at the Mill Valley fashion show; understated, impeccably tasteful women in linen and cashmere tote around men they obviously dressed themselves in manly earth tones and expensive sandals. Normally it would all seem nauseatingly bourgeois, but today I'm filled with an unexpected generosity toward the human race.

I watch a pretty brunette in red pedal pushers and a white tank top wipe a crumb from her lover's mouth; I think of Clay, and for the first time in a month, I don't feel sick with jealousy. Instead, I just miss him, and wish violently that I could sit with him right now, study his eyes, reach across a table and touch his mouth.

"You okay?" Mira asks.

This is highly unusual—my mother rarely inquires about how I am, and I'm so shocked I don't take full advantage. I just shrug and mumble, "Fine. You?"

"Sure."

"So, what's the story with Molly's father?" I ask. "Is he going to be involved?"

Mira shakes her head. "No. Em says she didn't want him in the picture."

"Really?" This surprises me. I never would have pegged Emily, with her platform shoes and her sexy little hip-huggers, as the do-it-yourself single-mom type. Then I remember that deeply calm look on her face between the contractions—maybe I've just got her all wrong.

"She says he's a crackhead, and she doesn't want her baby growing up around that."

"What do you think?" I ask.

"I support her decision. Who needs some high-rolling druggie for a dad? Molly will be better off without him. Besides, Em is so young and pretty—she'll find someone when she's ready. In the meantime, Gary's lawyer has ensured she'll get more than enough child support."

There's something weird about Mira today. Her eyes are glassy and distant. I can understand, in a way; ever since yesterday, I've been feeling like I'm under the influence of a powerful hallucinogen. My theory is that contact with birth jolts you out of pedestrian mode for a while, into the realm of acid trips. But what I sense from Mira isn't just a disconnection from gravity. I get the feeling there's something she wants to tell me; it's on the tip of her tongue every time there's a lull in the conversation, only she keeps changing her mind and opting for banal small talk, or silence.

"What was it like when you had me?" I ask, beating her to the punch this time with a silence-breaker of my own. I never ask her stuff like this; I guess I'm still altered. After you see someone grunting and sweating a new life into existence, discussing the merits of buying versus renting is just too jarring.

I'm not prepared for the look she gives me. Her jaw is clenched as if she's furious, but her brown eyes mist over instantly.

"That bad, huh?" I say, trying to make my tone light.

She stares at the ruins of her salad and says in a sorrowful, thick voice, "I can't talk about this right now."

A tiny shoot of niggling anger springs up in the pit of my stomach, then grows and unfurls, until I'm sitting there in the silence she's resumed, studying her pained face, thinking, "Why was it so terrible being my mom? What did I do to make you regret that day so bitterly?"

I don't even realize I've said anything aloud until I see the shock on her face and hear her stammer, "Claudia—it's not like that."

But I'm off and running now, since the unspeakable has been said. I hear my own voice pressing on with a force and determination that can only be attributed to the latte hitting my system. "You just left when I was thirteen. *Thirteen.* Do you have any idea how hard it is to be swimming in hormones and have your mom decide she's no longer Mom, she's Mira Ravenwing? Do you know how it hurt when you said you'd never been happier? You were so busy unblocking your chakras, marrying every Tom, Dick and Harry, you barely even noticed that *you left me.*" Without any consent from me, my face crumples into tears—not silent, pretty tears, but full-on hyperventilating sobs. The coiffed Mill Valley crowd is politely trying to absorb themselves in their meals, but a few of the less refined ones gawk. I hear a toddler say loudly, "Mommy, why is that lady crying?"

"Listen, I do know," Mira says. "I probably seemed oblivious, but I do realize that I hurt you. I just—I had to do some things for myself. It's so complicated, Claudia."

"It's not that complicated. You hated being a mom. I just wonder why you even had me." I brush the sunflower seeds off my napkin and use it to mop up my tears, which are thankfully no longer making me gasp for breath.

"I didn't—" She stops herself.

"You didn't *what?*" I ask coldly.

She hesitates. "I didn't know what was involved. But I didn't *hate* it. Just—as it turns out—I was never that good at it."

"Then why are you so devoted to Emily? If you're so bad at being a mom, why take it up now?"

"Em is..." She hesitates again.

"Oh, I see. Em is different. You didn't hate being a mom. You hated being *my* mom."

She looks so helpless there, opening and closing her mouth in mute, listless protest. A fresh round of sobs rises from within me and I dart toward the door in a panic. Just as I'm making my escape, I hear from somewhere behind me, "But *why* is she so mad, Mommy?"

Why *am* I so mad? The entire drive home, I grip the steering wheel so tightly, my knuckles look ready to burst through the skin. When I hit traffic just before the Golden Gate Bridge, I lay on my horn and yell obscenities at my fellow Sunday drivers; their puzzled, California-mellow expressions only enrage me more. When I learn it's an accident holding us up, I curse the inconsiderate motorist who had the poor taste to flirt with death right in the middle of my route home. Tonight of all nights.

I get to Santa Cruz and drive straight to Clay's house. It's like moving in a dream. My rage has made me untouchable, incandescent. I slam my car door and kick at a piece of newspaper that wraps itself around my ankle in the wild May wind. Goddamn stupid fucking newspaper. I stomp down the garden path and up the stairs to the garage apartment he's rented. Then I bang on the door with furious, balled-up fists. Clay answers in a pair of board shorts and a ragged hoodie. I want to scream at him for being so juvenile and beautiful.

"Just what do you think you're doing?" I spit at him, my fists clenched.

"Claudia—"

"Why would you fuck with me like that?"

"What are you talking about? You're the one who broke up with me."

"Ha!" I force the syllable out, but it's more like a karate chop than a laugh. "You never gave a shit about me. Why bother to keep up the pretense? You think I'd just fall for it, like your stupid little teenybopper girlfriend?"

At this, Clay looks utterly mystified; he literally scratches his head. "Teenybopper? What are you…?"

"Ohh," I growl. "Lies, lies, more lies. When is anyone *ever* going to be honest with me? Huh? Is that so much to ask? First my mother, who doesn't even *like* me, let alone love me, and now you." For the third time in the last twenty-four hours, my words dissolve into a series of hiccupping sobs. Even in my fury, it's mortifying for Clay to see me like this, gasping for breath and wiggie-haired, splotchy face convulsing. Jesus, why did I come here?

But now he's folding me into his arms—love those arms—and he's lifting my face to his and kissing my tears. A part of me still wants to spit and hiss like an indignant cat, but now that his lips are branding hot little scars on my cheeks, I find I'm immobile. When his mouth finds mine I moan a little under my breath at the taste of him. His hands pull gently, then harder at my hair, tilting my head until my neck is exposed. I can feel the edge of his teeth as he kisses my neck. My whole body throbs in response, and when he pushes me against the wall of the entryway, pressing himself forcefully against me, I can feel the outline of his cock against the fly of my jeans.

"I missed you," he sighs. "I've been missing you so much."

"I miss you, too."

"Come inside," he says, looking into my eyes and smoothing my hair from my face. "We need to talk."

Though he says it in a tone of tenderness and, under that, innuendo, those words make my mouth dry with fear. I see Jonathan sucking at one of his hand-rolled cigarettes, pale and wan with nerves. I'm standing on the balcony; behind me, two stories down, is Rain waiting in a taxi. Even her shadow is luminous. "Come inside," he'd said, his voice cold and resigned. "We need to talk."

I pry myself out of Clay's arms, the light of my fury burning white-hot again, more searing and explosive than ever now that the gasoline of lust has been added. "You…" I say, my eyes narrowing into slits.

"Claudia, get a grip. What's going on?"

"You," I repeat, this time forty decibels louder. "Fucking child molester!"

"Is this what happens with you?" He's yelling now, too, rearing up to meet my tantrum halfway. "Everything's great—everything's fantastic—then one day you wake up, decide your man's a perv, steal his rig and drive cross-country?"

"You were never my man, okay? And you are a perv, and I'm nobody's little Lolita substitute. You got that? Not now, not ever."

He folds his arms. "Fine." He spins away from me and kicks the wall so hard I suspect his toe is not recovering well. "You've got a royally fucked-up way of letting a guy off the hook."

"Yeah? Well, you're off. No obligations here."

"Fine," he says, tears glistening in his eyes. He turns, stalks into his apartment and slams the door.

"Fine!" I yell, just as it bangs shut, and start to stomp back down the steps.

When I'm halfway to my car, he opens the door again and yells at my back, "I just want you to know, Claudia, I have no idea what any of this is supposed to be about."

"Yeah, right," I scream over my shoulder.

"And you need help. Serious psychological help."

I want to douse his smug little motorcycle with gasoline and light a match as it mocks me from the driveway. Instead, I fold myself into my car, clinging to the paltry vestiges of dignity I'm left with, and start the motor with a shaking hand. I can't resist the wild-animal instinct to make noise, though—the last noise in this last exchange with Clay Parker. I pull away from the curb in a mad rev and try to peel out, but the effect is more like a lurching teen with a learner's permit trying desperately not to stall.

29

CHAPTER

I prefer "affirmation" to "lie." If there's one thing I learned growing up in the New Age eighties, it's that what other people call Full of Shit, we in California call Creative Visualization. Therefore I maintain that when I told Merrit Russell I adore cooking, that I live to peel garden-fresh basil from its stalk and pry garlic from its skin to chop and sauté, I was merely taking the first step in *becoming*. Ask any guru in Santa Cruz: you must *believe* before you can *be*.

Unfortunately, this particular affirmation forced me to beg Rose one Wednesday night in May to please, please, please not go to San Francisco tonight with Tim as planned but to stay home and cook with me. *We'll make it a double date,* I enthused. *It'll be a blast.* She wasn't exactly pleased, but seeing as I'd promised Merrit I'd cook him my specialty, homemade gazpacho and stuffed portobello mushrooms, even though I'd never advanced beyond Pop-Tarts, she pretty much had to bail me out, or find a new place to live come morning.

The night turned out okay. We pulled off a sort of Cyrano de Bergerac of the kitchen, me pretending to give orders and her playing at the clueless prep cook, all the while secretly subverting disaster each time I actually dared to touch the food. At one point—about four glasses of wine in—I got carried away with my role and, slipping into a Julia Child accent, nearly scorched the mushrooms, but Tim saved me by inviting Merrit to join him outside for a predinner cigarette. Later, I got a little paranoid when Merrit didn't take a toke off Tim's medical-grade grass—suddenly I feared we were coming off as hedonistic losers, as opposed to fashionably indulgent sophisticates. By the time dessert plates were cleared, though, I was far too wasted to make the distinction myself.

Even in this inebriated state, I couldn't work up much sexual enthusiasm for Merrit. Every time he kissed me, Clay's face flashed strobelike through my brain and I ended up pulling away. Merrit is still under the impression, invented on his own but not discouraged by me, that I suffer from chronic shyness and need time to ease into my awe-inspiring attraction to him. For all I know, he thinks I'm a thirty-year-old virgin.

"We have such a connection," he keeps cooing. "I know that, given time, we'll just flower."

Merrit is fond of plant metaphors. In fact, his play is so packed with them—pulsing stamens and flesh-eating orchids, love that wilts and passions that go to seed—I'm tempted to suggest he weed some of them out. Except, of course, he's a Tony nominee, and I'm just a temporary, last-ditch replacement with barely a shot at tenure track, let alone fame or fortune. I decided long ago to keep my suggestions to myself when it comes to Merrit.

Not that he's unreceptive, precisely. It's just that, when I suggested that the ingenue's fixation on finding the ideal zucchini might be a touch heavy-handed unless he's going for laughs, he merely flashed me a patronizing smile and said, "You forget just how thick the audience can be, Claudia."

Sure, if he says so. I mean let's face it: who really cares if *Organically Grown* is a hit? He's the one everyone's coming to see. The reading is a thin excuse for people to check him out, and tell their snooty waiter friends in Manhattan they went to the world premiere of Merrit Russell's newest effort.

In the end, our somewhat disastrous double date only confirmed what I had long suspected: getting over Clay Parker is essential, but Merrit Russell isn't the man to aid me in that heroic effort. I'm just not that attracted to the guy. Sometimes, to be honest, he makes me feel a little queasy. He's so different from Clay. He smells like expensive cologne sprinkled into an ashtray. Kissing him only makes me long for Clay's smell, which is impossible to describe, but somehow contains sea salt, sun-baked hills, and the icy air that fills your lungs when you're staring up at the stars.

I'm unreasonably, sickeningly nervous the night of the reading. It's scripts-in-hand—not a big deal, really. Minimal rehearsals, black-box venue, just a chance for Merrit to hear it all the way through. A glorified rehearsal, really. But the department—well, Ruth Westby in particular—was very generous about getting the word out. My publicity budget for this was twice what they gave me for *Heirloom,* and mysteriously, announcements have been popping up on the radio and in the papers that I don't recall orchestrating. By the time I arrive at the theater the night of our show, I can't say I'm shocked to see a long line snaking out the door. Still, my heart picks up its tempo until it's practically a death-metal anthem.

"Professor Bloom—thank God you're—did you hear? What will we…?" Ben Crow runs up to me in his requisite staged-reading black, out of breath, with his usually golden-brown face geisha-white.

"What happened?"

"You haven't heard? Sarah had a nervous breakdown."

I put a hand on his shoulder. Ben is still particularly vulnerable to preshow nerves, and Beach Barbie's still masterful
at squeezing maximum drama from her allegedly tumultu-
ous personal life. I seriously doubt there's a real emergency
here. "Sarah has a nervous breakdown every day," I tell him
soothingly. "Where is she?"

"That's just it. She's in L.A."

"But she came to rehearsal last night," I say, still unwilling to believe there's a problem. "Come on, this is some kind
of joke…."

"I'm serious. She's not here. Everyone says she was sleeping with Merrit, and today she found out he's not going to
marry—"

"Wait a minute. Who was sleeping with Merrit?"

"Sarah is—or was. Until he broke up with her this morning. Then she had a nervous breakdown and her mom
bought her a ticket to fly home to Bel Air. The point is, what
are we going to do? Who's playing Juliana in—" he looks at
his watch "—forty minutes?"

Fuck. Fuck fuck fuck. Why did I cast Sarah again? She's
got wonderful expressions and she read so well at audi-
tions—I loved the Valley Girl twist she added to the otherwise insipid ingenue, Juliana—but I should have learned by
now she's volatile as a Molotov cocktail. And Merrit, the
head case. What is it with men? Do they suddenly become
raging, hormone-driven beasts the second they see a nineteen-year-old with nice tits?

Okay, Claudia, think fast. Script in hand, not a big deal,
who do you know that could pull off Juliana with only forty
minutes to prep?

"Hey, Big Director Lady." I turn and Rose crushes me in
a warm, patchouli-scented hug. When she pulls away, she
hands me a big bouquet of passion flowers and nasturtiums,
their stems braided and tied with twine. "I had to steal them
from the neighbors," she confesses, smiling at the flowers.
"But I knew they were your favorite."

"Rose. You've read Merrit's play…."

"Of course. I can't wait to see it."

"Well, I kind of have a really enormous favor to ask…."

I have to watch most of the show from the doorway, holding Rex by the collar, straining to keep him from bounding down the aisle or peeing in protest on my leg. Rose has agreed to play Juliana, in exchange for my promise not to be doggist and to let Rexy see his mommy-wommy snatch her fifteen minutes of fame. Tim, forever the good sport, relieves me from my post after intermission, so I get to watch act three from a seated position.

And Rose—my God—she's glorious. She's never acted in her life and here she is, performing circles around my best students, sending chills down my spine with her spot-on inflections. She takes Juliana—a flat, uninteresting heroine, hemmed in by unrealistic dialogue and absurdly phallic vegetable obsessions—and turns her into a funny, vivacious little sprite. Her diction is perfect, her timing impeccable, and she adds humor where there was melodrama, sparks of insight where there was listless overwriting. She's made for it; I can hardly sit still, I'm so thrilled for her.

The only unfortunate part of all this is she makes *Organically Grown* seem like a passably decent, maybe even promising play, though I decided weeks ago it sucks. I'm even more convinced I hate it now that Merrit's been revealed as an inconsiderate, ingenue-fucking oaf; how could I ever have kissed that weasel? The skirt-chaser. The smarmy, egomaniacal—writer.

After the show—after Westby's pulled me into a spontaneous, totally unexpected embrace, and a reviewer from the *Sentinel* has patted me energetically on the back and the cast has filled me in on how Ben puked before the show yet again—I run up to Rose and squeeze her so hard she loses her breath. "Thank you, thank you, thank you," I squeal. "You were the best Juliana ever."

"You think?" she asks modestly. "I wondered if I was loud enough?"

"Oh, my God, Rose, you stole the show."

"Is that a good thing?"

"Yes," I say. "It's a very, very good thing."

Tim is there, beaming at her, his bald head shining and his face filled with adoration. "You're a regular Audrey Hepburn," he says. She turns to him with a dreamy expression before kneeling and kissing Rex, who is pulling so hard at his leash only someone as mammoth as Tim could possibly restrain him. I decide I like Tim and Rose together, even if monogamy is an evil plot and all men turn out to be helplessly drawn to jailbait, in the end. In spite of these strikes against him, I suspect he loves her almost as much as I do.

I'm in my car, fuming halfheartedly about Merrit. He skulked off during the curtain call, the yellow bastard. No doubt he figured I'd heard about his ingenue-fucking when I barely spoke to him at intermission. Perhaps he's booking the next flight to London right now, having figured out that Santa Cruz women aren't exactly generous when it comes to teen molesters. Good riddance. He can take his lukewarm kisses and his nauseating vegetation references right back to that fog-ridden city—see what I care.

Oh, shit. I left my bag backstage, and it's got my wallet in it. Dammit. Now I have to trudge back, unlock the theater, disarm the security, dig around in the inevitable post-show mess until I find it.

When I open the door to the green room, I hear a low murmur of voices and I freeze. No one's supposed to be in here—I locked everything before I left. Instinctively, my stomach constricts and the horror-movie score swells in my mind, the sort they inevitably play right before some hapless chick gets decapitated. I can already see my obituary: *She lived for the theater, she died in the green room.* But then I hear a soft, girlish come-hither giggle, so I figure maybe Frank the janitor's treating his date to a little backstage tour. While I don't exactly relish the idea of interrupting Frank's secret seduction, I do need my purse, and I can't find it without lights. I cough twice, pray they've had time to beat it to the dressing rooms, reach for the switch and flood the room with light.

The vision that greets me makes me gasp in horror, then blink in surprise. It's Merrit Russell, with his expensive-looking camel trousers bunched around his ankles and his bare ass, white as milk, thrusting frenetically; a pair of shapely legs are wrapped around his waist, looking weird and disembodied at first glance. Then I see he's got whoever she is propped up on the makeup counter, her back against the mirror. He jerks with a start from his trance and I see his reflection lit by the blindingly bright bulbs around the vanity—there's a fleck of spittle at the corner of his mouth, and his eyes are buggy with surprise. He kneels down to yank up his pants. Only then do I see the flushed face of his latest victim: Monica Parker.

CHAPTER 30

Once the reading is behind me and the semester's nearly over, I expect to be filled with intoxicating relief and almost-summer elation, but mostly I'm listless and insecure. I haven't talked to Clay since our crazy fight over a month ago. I guess that's not surprising. I still have no idea why I went there—what I was hoping he would say or do. Sometimes I feel like a wisp of lint being tossed this way and that by the random force of my own manic impulses. One second I'm bursting with love and compassion for the human race, the next I'm homicidal. No wonder Clay hasn't called; I'm the psycho his mother warned him about.

On the last day of finals, I turn in my grades and try to feel celebratory, but I can't seem to shake the heavy layer of doldrums weighing me down. It's a stunning day. The June sky is a vibrant blue and the sun's pouring gold on every-thing. Thin tufts of fog clinging to the Pacific have kept the air cool, even up here on the hill. I decide to walk around campus and see if I can absorb the twentysomething party-animal vibe—ecstasy by osmosis. Tomorrow's graduation, and fresh-faced students are rushing around on bicycles, pulling each other into "will I ever see you again?" embraces, lighting reckless joints in the woods, screaming post-finals screams. There's a reggae band singing the praises of Jah near the student union, and someone in a red Miata parked in front of the bookstore is playing "Californication" at maximum volume. As I walk, I soak in the familiar landmarks: the sunshine burning gold into the glass facade of the library, the spray-painted wisdom on a concrete slab: *This is where natives pissed, where angels spit.*

I walk and walk. The campus, as usual, is so stunning, so pristine and idyllic. Usually, walking around here makes me feel pleasantly light-headed. Today, every postcard-worthy vista makes the dull pain in my head a little sharper. It's a fragrant, shimmering utopia, and all I can do is feel sorry for myself.

Maybe it's better my last days here are melancholy; it's unlikely I'll be asked to stay, even as a part-time lecturer, so I might as well start packing up mentally now. *Organically Grown* won me points with Westby, and my student evals were all pretty good (Ralene Tippets aside), but I doubt these little victories can overcome the shadow of scandal that's clung to me since day one. I showed up determined to reinvent myself as a sophisticated, scarf-wearing professional. The year is over, and I'm exactly what I was: a scattered, wannabe twenty-two-year-old tart saddled with thirty-year-old crow's feet, half-finished manifestos and a stunning knack for fucking everything up.

By the time I get in my car and cruise down the hill to the post office, even the great sweep of ocean laid out before me can't make me smile. When I unlock our PO box and discover a thick envelope with Aunt Jessie's return address on it, I cringe with guilt. I had meant to write her ages ago. When did I get her last letter? It was on my birthday—almost six months ago. I'm a self-absorbed beast.

At home, I use a butcher knife to cut the letter open

and accidentally slice my finger in the process. At first it looks harmless as a paper cut, but then blood rushes in, fills the groove and drops in a bright red flower splotch onto the envelope. I curse, wrap my finger in a dish towel, then sink into the pile of cat fur on the couch. Reluctantly, I unfold a daunting thirteen pages of cramped, crazy-looking writing with weird little sketches of toads, lilies and dragonflies in the margins. I'd forgotten about Jessie's artistic aspirations; once she painted a mural on an old bus someone gave them. It featured dolphins, mermaids and—seeing her doodles reminds me— a family of toads. It was a bit hideous and Day-Glo, but Jessie was bursting with pride over it. Rose was thirteen; I thought she was a saint when she just smiled at her mother indulgently rather than covering her head with a paper bag.

I was fifteen at the time. They stayed for most of June and July that summer. It was their longest visit. Rose and I went to the city pool almost every day. We lived on Eskimo Pies and greasy buckets of popcorn at the double-feature matinees. I remember it vividly, not just because it was my only summer with Rose, but because it was the longest period of living with my mother since she'd left me two years before.

It's also etched in my mind because she and Jessie sometimes fought, and I don't think this happened during the other visits. They'd start at five o'clock with martinis and end up with cheap red wine at midnight, slurring their words. Rose and I huddled together in the guest room waterbed, listening to their confusing tangle of accusations as the bed sloshed gently beneath us. It was usually something about my grandmother—Claudia Lavelle, the one I'm named after. She died weeks before I was born, so I never met her. I gather she was depressed and not very warm but capable of occasional bursts of creativity. One year, when Mira and Jessie were in their teens, she made an enormous tile mosaic in their garden—a huge sprawling depiction of the zodiac. It sounded amazing.

Sometimes, when I'm trying to sleep but my mind keeps springing from one fretful, morbid subject to the next, I try to imagine that mosaic and it calms me. I see it sparkling in morning sunlight, surrounded by irises and bluebells, a circle of creatures, some mythical, some real: the golden lion, the ram with curly horns, the scorpion with its twisted tail and the centaur yanking back his bow. I wish I could have seen it, but maybe it's better this way; the real thing could never be as magical as the one I've put myself to sleep with for years.

I flip through Jessie's letter, reading snippets here and there: *…can't even eat the food…your grandfather was a stingy bastard…I wanted to shoot myself many times.*

"I just can't right now," I tell Medea, who is licking her paw meticulously on the windowsill. "I'll read it later, I promise." And then I stuff it between my dictionary and a dog-eared copy of *Franny and Zooey* on my makeshift bookshelf.

"Later," I repeat, when Medea glares at me accusingly. "I'm just not up for someone else's pathos today."

I decide I can face Jessie's epic letter if I get my hands on some serious caffeine. I wander into the Java House and order a double espresso. I'm in too bitter a mood for the childish sweetness of a mocha; today I want to taste the bean. The barista with red ringlets and blue nails does not disappoint. When I sit down at a sunlit table in the corner and take my first sip, it's almost too intense for consumption. It makes my lips pucker against the bitter black, but as soon as I've adjusted, I want more.

Maybe this is what crack's like, I think. Except with crack I hear the top of your head blows off. This is only my mouth imploding.

I tell myself to stop delaying—time to read Jessie's letter. Instead, I sit and watch an old man wearing a khaki beret and baggy purple sweats trying to pick up a girl with a crew cut. She's got dark, liquid eyes—espresso eyes—and a beauty mark so perfectly positioned I wonder if she painted it on. The Beret Guy isn't getting very far. She's trying to turn her eyes back to her book, but he keeps prolonging the conversation, and she's too polite to ignore him outright. The war of the sexes, I think. Sometimes it's a gentle little struggle in a café, sometimes it's tooth and nail.

As much as I try to resist, my mind drifts stubbornly back to the fight I had with Clay. I remember his eyes went from sea glass to navy just before he kissed me. I try to think about other things: the grain of the wood table under my elbow, the Beret Guy and his valiant, annoying efforts, the taste of my double espresso as it burns a hole in my intestines. Nothing works. I just sit there, getting increasingly agitated as the caffeine works its way into my blood, wanting Clay Parker.

I tote my letter back home, telling myself I'll be able to concentrate better there. I hear Rosemarie's scream before I even get to the stairwell. My pulse races and I feel cold, then hot, then clammy, too scared to move. I know it's some streety freak she's dragged home and now he's raped and murdered her in our apartment; when I get there she'll be dead and then he'll have to rape and murder me, too.

I force my legs to pound up the stairs and my arms to throw open the door. But the room isn't splashed with Rose's blood, and there's no stringy-haired, homicidal stranger crouching in the shadows with a hatchet. In fact, the scene that greets me might almost be sweet if you could mute it. Rose is on her knees, clinging tightly to Rex's mangy neck, sobbing wordlessly into his fur. Her shoulders are shaking and her hair is hectic with static; several strands are clinging to his disgusting, matted coat.

"Rose?"

She looks up at me with bloodshot eyes, then buries her face in his fur again, sobbing with fresh conviction.

"What is it? What's happened?"

She just shakes her head and goes on crying. When she gasps for breath, I worry she'll suffocate in all that ratty dog.

"Come on," I say gently, taking her hand and attempting to tug her toward the couch. "Come sit down and tell your cuz what happened."

"He's dying," she spits out fiercely, yanking her hand away to clutch again at Rex. "He's dying, okay? Just like everyone else I ever loved. They all fucking die on me."

"Who, Tim?"

"Rex," she screams, as if I've asked the stupidest, most insensitive question ever. I look at Rex, and he glances at me nervously. He's clearly not sure what to make of his imminent death or Rose's response to it.

"Now, Rose, come on. How do you know he's dying?"

She wipes her nose on her sleeve and attempts to catch her breath long enough to explain. "Manny—that guy who reads tarot."

"A tarot reader told you Rex is dying?"

"Yes. And he's never wrong. He told Ian his girlfriend was going to marry someone else, and he told Sandy about his motorcycle accident two weeks before it happened."

"Sweetheart…" I look at her tear-streaked face and sit down beside her on the floor. With one hand, I try to smooth her staticky hair into some semblance of order. "Rose, listen. It sounds like this Manny fucks with people." I search my brain for any scrap of information I've gathered about tarot. I remember something my mom's astrologist told me. "Aren't the cards really just symbolic? I mean there's a death card, right? But it doesn't necessarily mean *death*. Maybe Rex's inner puppy is about to die."

Rose's face goes from vulnerable to hard so fast, it's scary. "You're laughing at me."

"I'm not."

"You are." She shoots to her feet, and suddenly she's towering over me and Rex, her face stony with anger. "You don't know what it's like. Everything works out for you."

"That's not true."

"Yes, it is. Ever since we were little. You got the refrigerator that made ice cubes and the VCR, and I got my stupid mom who couldn't stay in one place for five minutes. You've got your fancy job and your master's degree, and what have I got? A dying dog. That's what I've got."

"Rose, he's not dying." I try to sound empathetic, but it comes out irritated instead. I try to compensate by half-heartedly patting Rex's head. He follows my hand with his eyes suspiciously.

"You think I'm delusional, don't you? You'll send me to the bin, like Mom did." Her hair is bristling and her fists are clenched. Her rage is electric.

"She was probably worried about—"

"Mom should worry about herself—alcoholic bitch." After so many years of Rose gently tolerating Jessie, it's foreign and disorienting to hear the venom in her voice.

"Maybe if you just gave her another chance…" I suggest tentatively.

"Give her another chance?" She places bitter emphasis on each syllable. "You have no idea. You had it easy, okay? You should just count your blessings."

"I'm only saying, maybe if you get in touch with her, you could work things out."

She laughs. It's a weird, hysterical sound and I feel suddenly cold. "Why don't *you* work it out with her, Claudia? Let's see *you* try to make peace."

"But she's not my mother," I blurt out.

She narrows her eyes at me. "Yes, she is."

For a second I feel dizzy. The walls swim unsteadily and the floor dips like a carnival ride. "What?" I whisper.

"Jessie *is* your mother. Mira only took over because Jessie was too fucking irresponsible to deal. And if you ask me, you got the good end of the deal. At least you got the VCR."

"What are you talking about?" I pull my knees in to my chest, and Rex sniffs sympathetically at my ear.

"Mom told me when she was drunk. They made me promise not to tell. Mira never wanted you to know."

"You're crazy," I say, pushing Rex away and standing up. She only turns away and shrugs.

"That's insane!" I'm yelling now. "You're lying!"

"Ask Mira," she says coldly, still not looking me in the eye. "See if she has the guts to deny it."

CHAPTER 31

I'm driving past the Boardwalk, and the streets are crawling with tourists of every variety: portly families with cotton candy, Harley dudes in head-to-toe leather, Japanese teenagers in platform shoes. They're all determined to be hit by me; I keep slamming on my brakes as they dart or stumble into my path, drunk on the freedom of June.

Jessie's my mom? What the fuck?

I'm entangled in a maze of one-way streets and dead ends. Every time I try to turn in a direction that will lead me away from this vortex, I'm faced with Do Not Enter signs or chain-link fences. I can't even park—the sidewalks are packed with tourist buses belching black clouds of exhaust, station wagons and minivans unloading more tourists. I just circle, directionless, my heart beating faster and faster with claustrophobic rage.

"Get out of the way, freak!" I'm horrified to hear my own voice screaming out the window with glass-shattering volume. The woman looks at me over the hood of my car without blinking. Her hair is as matted and crusty as beached seaweed. She's got a scarf around her neck tied tightly, like a child bundled too thoroughly by her mother. Her green eyes are sad, but with detachment, as if she's remembering something that happened long ago. She reminds me of Jessie.

I want to get out and apologize profusely, drive her somewhere, buy her won ton soup or coffee or something. But already she's moving on, one foot in front of the other, making slow, deliberate progress toward the opposite sidewalk.

Shit. Now I verbally abuse the homeless, too. A couple of middle-aged women frown at me, and I squint at them threateningly. They scurry down the sidewalk.

Mira, I think. I'll go to Mira, and she'll tell me how wrong Rose is. Maybe she'll even go pro on me and hypnotize me with psychobabble until my fight with Rose is as distant and impotent as a half-remembered dream.

As soon as this thought occurs to me, I turn left, and the road leads me smoothly away from the carnival music and the stench of waffle cones, toward my mother.

My mother, I remind myself, weaving through the traffic. *Mom.*

I sit facing Mira in her new-age living room, hugging my knees on her organic cotton couch. She's in the ergonomically designed meditation chair, with a Quan Yin-adorned fountain burbling in the corner behind her. I notice for the first time an enormous statue of a laughing Buddha on a shelf, and a large glass pyramid on the coffee table. My eyes keep darting from one object to the next in a desperate attempt not to take in the look on Mira's face.

"I never wanted you to know," she's saying. "I didn't think it would…" She stops, midsentence, and starts again. "You've always been a sensitive girl. I thought it could damage you."

"Damage me," I repeat, my voice hollow and soft.

"And there was the question of when—after we'd gone so many years under the assumption."

"Yes," I say. "The assumption…"

"I was afraid you'd hate me for keeping it a secret." She pauses to wipe some tears with the back of her hand. "But Jessie's become obsessed with the idea, lately. She's got nothing to do now but stew in regrets. She hates that she wasn't together enough when you were born to…" Again she stops herself.

I stare at a title on the bookshelf, *One Hundred Ways to Awaken the Heart Chakra*. "How did it happen?"

She sighs and recites the tale in a distant, uncertain voice, like she's reading from cue cards she can't quite make out. "Jessie was eighteen when you were born. I was twenty-six. I'd been married to Simon for five years. Your nanna had just died and Jessie was out all the time with this guy. He was an actor, or so he said—he'd done some radio stuff. He was much older than us, in his early forties, I think. Jessie was crazy about him—she thought he hung the moon." I'm surprised at this turn of phrase. Mira Ravenwing never uses old-lady expressions. "Anyway, she got pregnant, but the man—Ray—died before you were born."

"He was my father?"

She nods.

"How did he die?"

Her lower lip trembles slightly, and she bites it, then murmurs, "His liver. He drank."

For a fraction of a second I'm stupidly gratified. So I'm not the spawn of Simon, with his blinding white socks and his Pine-Sol. My father was a radio star, a boozer—it's so much seedier and more glamorous than the shop-teacher story. I think of poor Simon, struggling to keep our lives alphabetized after Mira left us for the nirvana of Mill Valley. He always looked so perplexed and unsure, like he just woke up one day and found he was a neurotic single dad, with no idea how he'd gotten there.

"When you were about two months old, Jessie left town with a roadie. She started moving around all the time, and she never really stopped. When Rose was born, she asked if we'd take her, but you were two and—well, we had our hands full."

"Why'd you take me? Why not just put me up for adoption?"

She shrugs and stares out the window. The sunset has turned the stretch of sky above Gary's bonsais a bruised purple. "I couldn't have kids. We'd been trying for five years. I saw you as—I don't know—my one chance, I guess."

"Why didn't you take Rose, too, if you wanted kids so much?"

She stares at her lap. "I was young. You were a difficult baby, could have been Jessie's drinking—I don't know." Great. I'm brain-damaged, on top of everything else. "Anyway, motherhood wasn't really what I'd pictured." She makes a weird sound—half giggle, half snort—and looks at me helplessly. Tears stream down her face and her nose is running. "I guess that's a terrible thing to admit. I wouldn't blame you if you hated me for saying that."

I feel numb. I wish for tears, for hysterical rage, for anything but this pretzel of disbelief in my stomach. I want to pick up the ridiculous coffee table pyramid and shatter it against the wall, roll around in the shards just to see my own blood and know that I'm not dead or dreaming.

"Do you think you'll ever forgive me?" she asks.

I look at her blankly. "For what?" Impersonating my mother? Ditching me when I hit puberty? Making my life a lie? Which one, I wonder, does Mira Ravenwing imagine is forgivable?

"For all of it," she says.

I think about this for a long couple of minutes in silence. I know it's cruel, but I find myself actually enjoying the tension that mounts in the room, making Quan Yin's gentle bubbling sound ominous rather than soothing. "I don't know," I say, finally. "I'll have to think about it."

"You're probably in shock," she says. "Do you want some tea? Valerian root, maybe? Or a bong hit? Might take the edge off."

"No," I say, unfolding my legs and standing. "Thanks, anyway." I start for the door.

"Where are you going?" she asks, her eyes on the carpet. It's hypoallergenic. Gary breaks out in hives around anything synthetic.

"Don't know."

"Maybe you shouldn't drive. You could sleep here tonight."

I shrug. "I'll be okay."

She concedes a little too readily, and I know she doesn't really want me to stay. Upstairs somewhere, Molly starts to cry, and I hear footsteps above us, then Emily cooing baby talk and pacing in circles as Molly wails louder.

I wish I could cry like that. Her lungs must fill like little balloons, taking up half her body; I can hear her pausing for breath before a fresh shriek pierces the air. Babies cry like they're dying. When do we forget how to do that?

I walk stiffly to the door. One foot in front of the other. I don't look back at Mira as I make my way down the stone steps.

"Call me," she says to my back.

I get in my car without answering and drive away.

CHAPTER 32

The constant blast of wind on my face is fragrant with sage. The Mojave is still kissed with the cool of night, but I can sense a suffocating heat getting ready to pounce. I've got all my windows rolled down, and my hair's Afroed so thoroughly I look truly demented. I'm beyond caring. The road's been disappearing beneath my wheels for seven hours; it's now almost five in the morning, and the sun's thinking about coming up over the scorched hills.

I've stopped four times for gas, cheap coffee, obligatory visits to repulsive bathrooms, but never for sleep. In this surreal, half-dreaming state, I don't have to think about much. When memories threaten to ambush my placid world of dashboard, yellow lines and headlights, I just turn up the radio on my boom box louder. I keep it tuned to whatever emerges from the static—mostly Top Forty country, the perfect distraction. I moan in disgust at the crappy, sentimental slow songs and sing aloud with the honky-tonk anthems, especially the ones that involve drinking oneself into a stupor.

At Barstow, I head east on 40. The sun comes up around Needles, just as I'm crossing the Colorado River. The sky is a brilliant pink, and the sun splashes yellow brilliance across my windshield. A sign reads: Welcome to Arizona.

My mother's in prison, I think by accident.

She didn't want me.

I concentrate harder on the girl wearing tight jeans in the song. She's at a bar, telling the bartender to pour her another shot of whiskey. *Good,* I tell her. *Drink more. Forget everything.*

Drive home drunk and then do it again and again. Sit in a New Mexico prison and write letters to the people who are ashamed of you.

No, wait. Find some Orson Welles-wannabe stranger with a starved look in his eye and get him to shell out the fifty bucks for some run-down, anonymous hotel. Squeeze his hips with your thighs and ride him like a stallion. Ride him like a fast train to oblivion.

Then wake up pregnant, with your Orson Welles motionless beside you, a big bottle of Jack Daniel's flung haphazardly onto the sad shag carpet, the smell of stale vomit in the air.

No. Don't do that, either.

Stay at the bar. Keep feeding the jukebox and dance until you're dripping with sweat. When the sun comes up, drive and drive. Just keep your hands on the wheel and the road will swallow your thoughts. Soon you'll be a hollow girl in tight jeans with one cowboy boot on the gas, and as long as you never stop driving, nothing can get you.

In Flagstaff I stop to pee and nearly run over a fat old woman walking a pit bull, so I decide I'd better sleep soon if I want to live. I pull into the shady corner of a McDonald's parking lot and fall asleep to the smell of French fry grease and the sound of semis moaning on the interstate. I dream I'm in Texas, wandering along a highway, looking for a baby that fell out of my car. I'm sure it'll be a pulpy mess when I find it, and I'm sick with anxiety.

I wake to sharp, irritated knuckles rapping on my window. The car's so hot it's unreal. I sit up and see a stocky, red-faced man in a brown uniform and a visor; he's smoking a cigarette and peering in at me with a stern, unfriendly look creasing the corners of his mouth. When I roll down the window, he tells me I can't sleep here. I mumble, "Fuck you," under my breath and start the car.

Apparently, in addition to oral sex, sleeping in one's car is now illegal in most states. I feel a bland, unfocused hatred for the world at large.

Los Lunas. The moons. I wonder how this Albuquerque suburb got such an exotic name. It's the plural that adds such intrigue—invites visions of Galileo eyeing Jupiter with a primitive telescope, laughing joyfully at the multiple orbs circling the planet slowly. When I check into a Motel 6, though, the sweet-faced Mexican boy in glasses responds to my query about the name with a smile and a shrug. As I start for the glass door with my plastic key in hand, an old woman pushing a cleaning cart says abruptly, "Los Lunas. You asking about Los Lunas?"

"Yes," I say, turning to her.

"It's a family name. Old family here. They got a big house—you can go see, if you want."

"Oh. Thank you." She starts away from me with her cart, and I blurt out, "I'm actually here to visit the prison."

The elderly couple with the RV taking up four spaces outside frown and inch closer to each other. The boy behind the desk goes on smiling sweetly. The cleaning lady squints at me; her face is withered and brown, like a rotting apple. Her eyes twinkle darkly from the folds of skin. "Why you want to…?" she begins, but then she glances at the nosy old couple in their matching plaids straining to eavesdrop and jerks her head toward the door. I hold it open for her and we cross the parking lot to sit down on a pink adobe bench in the shade of a tree that's already shed most of its yellow flowers. She pulls a small wooden pipe from her pocket, stuffs it full of stringy brown tobacco and lights it. I watch her old, puckered lips suck hungrily at the stem and feel suddenly thrilled to be here.

"Why you want to go out there?"

"My—" I hesitate a second but plunge on bravely, "My mother's out there."

She cocks her head at me like a bird. "She work there?"

"No. She's an inmate."

The woman only nods her head slowly and smokes some more, apparently thinking this over. "My nephew out there," she says grimly. "But he get out soon."

"Oh. I thought it was a women's—"

"What?"

"I assumed it was only women."

"They got both," she mumbles, the corner of her mouth still clamped on the pipe. "Men, women. Some people out there very bad—killers, thieves. But they got not-so-bad, too. Just a little messed up. Like my nephew." She winks at me. "And your mama."

"What's your name?" I ask her.

"Luz Alvarez," she says, her tone suddenly formal. "You?"

"I'm Claudia Bloom," I say, sticking out my hand. "Nice to meet you."

She wipes her palm on her apron quickly and grips my hand with surprising warmth and force. It's probably because I've been trapped in my car for two days, delirious with desert heat and sleep deprivation, living on mini-mart coffee and Corn Nuts, but the feel of her fingers in mine floods me with a jolt of sweet relief. When she smiles, her teeth are yellow-brown and jagged as a jack-o-lantern's; her eyes nearly disappear in all that skin. She's quite beautiful.

She tells me how to get to the prison. When she's sure I understand her directions, she goes on about a place the locals call Mystery Mountain, where there's a rock with ancient Hebrew writing on it. Then a clap of thunder makes my throat vibrate and a dark gray rain cloud opens up like a faucet, instantly soaking us both. She swears good naturedly in Spanish, laughing, and moves toward the lobby. We wave goodbye in the parking lot; then I run to my room, and she ambles back to her cart filled with Windex, paper-wrapped soaps and fresh towels.

I wake at 3:46 in the morning to a nuclear war. I cower under the cheap, synthetic covers for ten minutes before mustering enough courage to rise, roll myself a cigarette, free a glass from its paper doily and pour a couple fingers of vodka with a shaking hand. I figure, if this is the end, I want to go out with a buzz. I creep outside onto the balcony that overlooks a leaf-strewn pool and wait for the world to end.

As it turns out, it's only another thunderstorm. It doesn't really matter; I can't shake the apocalyptic dread that's lodged itself inside me. I watch the rain hammering ripples into the neglected pool, lit a dingy yellow by streetlights. I wonder for the four-thousandth time if Clay Parker is having sex with his thin, dark-haired mystery girl right now. I wonder what she sounds like when she comes, and what he sounds like, and whether they talk afterward or stare at the ceiling together in wordless communion. I wonder what it means now that my aunt is my mother and my mother is my aunt and my father isn't my father, he's a white-socked stranger who got suckered into raising the abandoned daughter of a dead alcoholic.

I hate waking up in hotel rooms in the middle of the night. It's like your skin's been peeled away, and all the dark thoughts you shield yourself from in sunlight finally swoop in to feast on your exposed flesh.

I finish the first glass of vodka and pour myself another. I smoke my cigarette slowly, savoring the dirty sensation of smoke invading my lungs. I will myself not to think, just to watch the patterns the rain makes in the pool and the shapes the smoke forms as it reaches toward the stars.

★ ★ ★

In the morning, I eat *huevos rancheros* in a little Mexican place Luz recommended and drink strong black coffee that tastes shockingly divine. Since I haven't eaten anything but Corn Nuts, Sweettarts, beef jerky and shitty coffee for days, this meal is like heaven on my tongue. When I've gotten enough food in me to think straight, I open Jessie's letter. The young, round waitress wearing a hairnet and red lipstick pours me more coffee and I smile at her. Then I skim the first page and the second and the third. It's the fourth page that makes my heart thump with manic fervor in my chest.

> Mira never wanted you to know, but lately I'm convinced risking her hatred is worth it. I've wanted to come clean for years. Now I've got so many empty hours and no wine to soften things, and I feel if I don't tell you, I'll die. Claudia, I'm your real mother. Mira took you because I was too young. Please don't consider yourself a mistake. I've always watched you with a mixture of pride and pain. You're everything I'd want in a daughter, and it makes me sick to know that if only I'd been stronger, less confused, less stupid, you could have been mine.

And later, on page six:

> Your father was a complicated man. He knew how to love—too much, I think. It killed him.

Finally, on the last page:

> If there's one thing I desire most in the world, it's to be, in some small way, a mother to you. I know it will take so much to forgive me, and in writing these things I risk losing the only family I've got left: you, Mira, and

even Rose. But if I sleep one more night with the secret inside me, I know I won't wake up in the morning. Please forgive me.

Your mother loves you.

Jessie

I sit with the letter shaking in my hands while tears fall
uncontrollably, slipping off my chin to pool on the red For-
mica. *Your mother loves you.*

Which one?

The waitress comes and takes my plate; I avoid her con-
cerned gaze, stare out the window at a big Ford truck pulling a U-Haul trailer. I consider getting in my car, turning
the key and speeding away from this town with its multiple
moons and its cleaning lady named Light and its sublime
huevos rancheros. I could drive to New Orleans, live in the
French Quarter, tend bar in some smoky place where people order hurricanes to go. I could call myself Eva or Jen-
nifer or Daisy and choose a last name by opening a phone
book with my eyes closed and seeing where my finger lands.
I could. Why not? What's stopping me?

Instead, I pay my bill and follow Luz's directions until I
get to the Central New Mexico Correctional Facility. I take
a deep breath, put on some lipstick and go to face my
mother.

CHAPTER 33

Jessie looks bruised around the eyes from lack of sleep, and her graying, curly hair is even more chaotic than mine. I notice for the first time details that escaped me in the past. Her eyes are the exact same stormy-green as my own. There's a patch of freckles spread across her nose that matches the one I've cursed in mirrors since I can remember.

When she sees me waiting at a picnic table in the visitor's yard, the joy that lights up her features almost negates the tired pallor of her skin. Though she looks worn and a little thin in her baggy prisoner's uniform, the two years she's spent drying out have given her back some vitality. She's not as bloated anymore, and her complexion's lost that yellowish tint that always made her look slightly seasick.

"Claudia," she says, and pulls me into a fierce hug. My arms are pinned awkwardly to my sides. I can smell the sweet fragrance of cheap shampoo in her hair. She pulls away and holds me at arms' distance, studying my face. "I can't believe you're here," she whispers. She looks like she might cry.

All of a sudden she becomes abruptly embarrassed and

lets me go. "Have a seat," she says, gesturing to the other side of the picnic table, overly formal now. "I'm so glad you came."

We sit opposite each other. There are other women in the yard, meeting with husbands and lovers and children. A couple at a table in the corner are arguing. The woman's about my age, and she keeps picking at her cuticles savagely as the man leans in and hisses inaudible accusations at her, his face livid.

I look back at Jessie and try to smile. "So," I say, and my mind goes blank.

"So…" Jessie echoes. There's an awkward pause. Finally, she says, "You must have gotten my letters."

"Yeah."

She looks like she wants to say something, stops herself, and asks instead in a light, conversational tone, "Have you heard from Rosemarie?"

"Uh-huh." My voice sounds funny. "We're living together in Santa Cruz, actually."

"Really?" Her eyebrows arch in surprise, then she smiles. "That makes me happy. I was so worried about her."

"She's okay." I nod for emphasis. "She's going to be fine. I just wish she'd talk about Jade once in a while. She acts like nothing ever happened."

"Rose has always been like that," she says, shaking her head. "She won't deal with anything until it comes crashing down around her." She smirks. "Don't know where she learned that."

"Everyone's a little that way," I say.

Another awkward silence. The couple in the corner are getting louder. "They're your fucking sons, Carla. Wake up," the man's saying. "They won't just go away."

I study Jessie's profile. She's staring off at a mesa in the distance. It's getting hotter, and I can feel a trickle of sweat inching down my back where the sun's burning a hole between my shoulder blades. A slight breeze stirs, lifting several curls from Jessie's forehead. I can feel my own curls shifting, too.

"So I guess you know," she says, still staring into the distance.

"Yeah."

"Are you angry?"

I swallow hard. My mouth is suddenly dry and I long for a cool glass of water. "I don't know. More numb, I guess. Confused."

She nods. "I would have told you a long time ago. Mira thought it was better this way." She sneaks a glance at me and our eyes meet briefly. Then she goes back to gazing at the mesa and I watch a young black woman cuddling a toddler in her lap. "I hate living with secrets. I just figured that I owed it to Mira. She did so much for me."

"She never really got into the mom thing," I say.

"No." Jessie smiles sadly. "Lavelle women have trouble with that." She looks at me. "You won't, though. If you want that, I mean. You're different."

"How so?"

She shrugs. "You just are. You can do whatever you want. I've always known that, since the day you were born."

Something long ago frozen in me melts in a rush, like an ice cube in boiling water. There's a warmth in Jessie's eyes that pierces all the arctic space in me and liquefies what's been solid and jagged for years.

"You really think so?" I say, my voice cracking.

"Absolutely," she says. "You can do anything." She looks up at the sky. The clouds have drifted west, leaving a big, vivid stretch of blue above us. "Your father was an amazing man. He was an artist, like you."

After that, we talk about other things—when she expects to get out (September, maybe), what she misses most (wine and Brie—though she's determined to stop drinking), what I'll do now that the school year's over (who knows? Maybe tend bar in New Orleans). At noon, the guard comes over and tells us our time is up. In a way, I'm relieved. It's been hard coming up with things to say, and every time we're through with one topic, I feel a tiny lurch of fear that an unbreakable silence will descend.

We hug again before they lead her back inside. This time my arms aren't pinned to my sides. We're almost exactly the same height, I notice.

As the guard hovers nearby, she whispers into my ear, "I'm sorry."

I just nod.

She doesn't want to let go, I can tell. The guard murmurs, "Come on," and then she says into my ear with quiet but furious intensity, "I love you."

I'm too mute with clogged emotion to produce an answer, and luckily she doesn't seem to expect one. Anyway, the guard's getting antsy and takes her by the arm.

Driving away, a roadrunner scrambles along next to my car, moving with amazing speed. It makes me laugh.

On the way back to the freeway, every single light I hit is green.

How do you rearrange the family tree when it's not some distant cousin you've misplaced, but yourself? How do you make peace with that tangle of confused branches? Here's where I thought I was, here are the people who raised me, and here's the people I come from. Here's the dead father, with a radio mike in one hand and a stiff drink in the other. Here's the man I called father, who organizes his tools alphabetically. My mother is my aunt, my aunt my mother. What do I do with the thirty years I spent begging Mira for the love of a mom?

Rose is my half sister. I think of the mysterious empathy between us, a love that permeates my memories all the way back to graham crackers and Big Wheels. I always thought we were only children, and that we clung to each other because of it. But we inhabited the same womb, grew inside the same skin. No wonder our hands make sense to each other.

★ ★ ★

I stop by the hotel to say goodbye to Luz; it's Saturday, the sweet-faced boy informs me, her day off. I leave her thirty dollars in a small manila envelope and hand the boy five, which makes him beam. He's not yet learned the adult trick of pretending nothing matters.

Studying my Triple A map at a gas station, I decide to loop back through the Grand Canyon. It's a little impractical, but I've never paid much attention to reason, so I figure this is no time to start.

I consider driving through Truth or Consequences, too; it's tempting to the poet in me, but since it's at least three hundred miles in the wrong direction, the poet loses. There are limits to my craziness.

As I drive for hours on a remote highway dotted with one-gas-station towns, I realize my detour isn't about sightseeing at all. I'm not ready to go back. California means Rose and Mira and Simon. I'll be forced to look at their faces and deal with the swirl of unanswered questions. I'll have to interact with them in some reasonably normal way. They've known the facts about me for years. I've known for forty-eight hours; I'm having a little trouble catching up.

At sunset, I pull over in the middle of nowhere. According to my map, I've hit the Painted Desert, and the world around me does look drenched in paint; there are miles and miles of color, from crimson to salmon to stripes of lavender. Lumpy earthen hills rise up from the flat earth and soak up the bloody light of the sun.

I could just stay here, I think. Learn to hunt roadrunners and prairie dogs. Cook them over a tumbleweed fire and drink whiskey under the stars.

A scrappy coyote trots by casually about ten feet from me. In the distance, his brothers start howling like a demented choir. He looks at me, sniffs the air. I change my mind about whiskey under the stars and get back in my car.

★ ★ ★

By the time I get to the Grand Canyon, it's well after dark. I find a campground and decide to stay the night. My legs ache from so many hours in one position, so I walk in a loop around the campsites, clutching my three-dollar mini-mart flashlight but not turning it on. I prefer the sensation of slipping ghostlike through the shadows, spying on each microcosm of the living as I pass: a family of six roasting marshmallows; a couple putting up their tent with great difficulty, shouting out orders in slurred voices; a big party of French teenagers drinking Mexican beer.

I'm not exactly prepared for camping. The air is warm, though, and my car is too small to be comfortable, so I wrap myself in the cheap Indian blanket I bought, lie on the picnic table and stare for hours at the stars. I can't believe how many there are up there. I think of that first night with Clay: the Greg Brown song, the night air perfumed with pine and yarrow, the color of his eyes at the Saturn Café, the silky-hot feel of his naked skin on mine. I kill the sweetness lingering in my chest with the bitter recollection of his arm around that glossy-haired girl. Why do they always fall for the shiny brunettes? Who in the hell suggested that blondes have more fun?

I lie awake with a troubled montage flashing images randomly: Jessie's gray curls stirring in the warm desert breeze; the small, wrinkled hands of Luz; Rose on stage as Juliana; the coyote's eyes watching me suspiciously. I can't imagine how it all fits together. The pictures just come and go like slides that don't belong together; one is hardly even visible before it dissolves abruptly into the next.

Just when I think I'll never sleep and am considering getting back on the road, the last images give way to a merciful black. There are two things I see just before I finally succumb: myself as a baby, naked and crying, and my own hands as they are now, creased around the knuckles, chapped by the desert air, and strong.

* * *

When I wake, it's dawn, and the smell of bacon greets me. I roll over and see a little girl of about four watching me from a crouched position in the dirt. She's trailing one finger in the dusty earth, drawing lopsided spirals. She sticks the finger into her mouth and sucks on it, an impish smile playing on her lips. When she sees my eyes are open, she crouches lower as if to hide. I smile weakly, still groggy, and she starts to wail at the top of her lungs. A middle-aged woman in overalls swoops her up and carries her into an RV.

I get up and go pee, then wash my face with cold water, trying to ignore the clogged hair in the sink. I drive until I find a small corner market, where I pay an extortionate sum for apple juice, a banana and a bag of chips. After driving a little farther, suddenly the earth opens up before me in an enormous, yawning pit of pink, orange and purple. I get out of my car and walk until I'm so close to the edge I'm dizzy with vertigo.

I've never seen the Grand Canyon—never given it much thought, really. Standing in the cool June dawn with all that pastel majesty carved out below me, I wonder how I could have avoided it all these years. It's awesome; it makes you nervous, it's so beautiful.

I know it sounds bizarre, but I'm struck with the insane certainty that I can fly. I see myself backing up ten feet, then running with full force, hurtling myself over the edge and into the enormous space below. For a second or two, I'll freefall, and my heart will pound in my ears. The lavender cliffs will blur as I pass them, making me nauseous with regret. But then I'll put my arms straight out, and my chest will catch on an updraft, and my fall will become a graceful swimming through air. The Colorado River will sparkle like a gold chain beneath me, and I'll float with feather-light bones in an easy, meandering descent.

Gazing out over the emptiness, the vision is so visceral I'm starting to scare myself; maybe I'm having an acid flashback. I walk slowly in the direction of my Volvo. Before I get back in the car, though, I turn back, and look one more time at the huge canopy of sky—half pink, half Easter-egg blue—stretched out over the orange-and-purple canyon.

I close my eyes and whisper, "Please." I don't know who I'm addressing, or what I'm asking for, exactly, but somehow this syllable makes me feel calmer than I have in days.

Back on the road, I watch the canyon shrink slowly in my rearview mirror. The sun beats in through the passenger window, and before long sweat is beading on my forehead. Steering with one knee, I wrap my hair in a red bandanna. My throat's dry, so I drink the expensive apple juice.

After a while, the sound of nothing but my wheels on pavement makes me lonely, so I reach to turn on the boom box I stole from Simon and spin the dial slowly, navigating the static, until a radio station finally comes in. When I recognize the song, I can't help but smile. It's Greg Brown, way out here in the middle of this red desert. *With your heart-shaped rocks and your rocky heart, your worn-out shoes and your eagerness to start.*

I'm ready to go home.

CHAPTER 34

When I open the door, Rose is there, and her head is completely covered in braids so I know right away she's been worrying. She grabs me by both shoulders and launches into a breathless monologue:

"Oh Claudia you're okay Jesus I thought you were dead for sure and it was my fault because I'm such a selfish girl your mother I mean, Christ, Mira keeps calling and she's so mad at me for telling you and I was so terrified for you last night I called every police station from here to L.A. and this morning I was going to call the FBI but—"

"Whoa, whoa. Slow down."

"I was sure you were dead in a ditch," she cries, and wraps me in a hug while at the same time jumping up and down with relief, which jostles me around a bit awkwardly, but I don't mind. "Oh my God we have to call Mira right this second she is so fucking worried she's like bitten through all her acrylic nails and smoked half her supply."

I make my way past her and flop onto the couch. "Hold on. Just let me catch my breath."

"Absolutely I'm so sorry I'm totally overwhelming you. Do you want something to eat?" She scurries to the fridge. "I made tamales and homemade raviolis and gazpacho and there's beer or cranberry juice or wine and I could make you a tofu sandwich or—"

I stare at the bulging shelves. "Rose. Are you going into catering?"

She looks at me innocently. "Of course not. I was worried sick—what do you mean?"

"Why do you have so much food in there?"

She shrugs sheepishly.

"What's that mean?" I ask, suppressing a smile. She's like a little kid sometimes.

"I was worried…you know what I do when I can't concentrate on anything else. I braid and I cook."

I feel a pang of guilt. "I'm sorry," I start, but then Medea springs into my lap and I get distracted for a second, cooing soft cat-greetings at her and petting her until my hands are covered in her fur. "I never meant to worry you."

"Well, you did," she says. "But it was my fault, and now you're okay. So what do you want to eat?"

"A tamale sounds dreamy."

As she busies herself heating up my food, slicing tomatoes, pouring me a crantini and generally fussing over me, I ask, "Don't you want to know where I was?"

"Of course," she breathes. "But I don't want to pry."

"I went to New Mexico. I visited Jessie."

I can see her stiffen slightly; she hands me my plate and sits down on the opposite couch to watch me eat, her face tense. "How was that?"

"Weird, but okay."

"Did she seem depressed?"

"A little, but I think it's kind of good for her, being in there. She says she doesn't want to drink anymore, and she seemed more—" I search the air for the right word "—serene than I remember her." I take a bite of my tamale. It's

wonderful—moist and warm and spiced with Rose's particular gift for flavors.

"Why'd you go?" Rose asks, playing with a braid.

"It was instinctive—I just ran. I needed a few days to think
about everything. And I needed to hear it from her, I guess."

Long pause.

"I have a shoe box full of her old letters," she says quietly.
"Unopened."

"Well, you'll open them when you're ready," I say.

"I guess." She loosens one of her braids and starts it again.
"I, um, I took Rex to a vet."

"Oh, yeah?"

"Yeah. She said nothing's wrong with him. I guess you
were right—Manny really was messing with me."

"That's great, Rose. You must be relieved."

Rex looks up from the floor for a second, gazes with mis-
chievous longing at Medea curled up fast asleep in my lap,
then flops his huge head back down on his paws.

"And I did something else, too," Rose says. "I signed up
for a support group. My first meeting's next week."

"What kind?"

"For people who've lost—you know—a child. Like me
with Jade." She braids faster, her fingers moving so quickly
they practically blur.

"That's so good," I say, surprised. "I'm so proud of you."

She shrugs. "I figure it's about time. And Tim was starting in on me with all the same stuff you'd said—that I was
only running away and all that. I guess it finally sank in.
How's the tamale?"

"Fantastic," I say with my mouth full.

"Do you want dessert? I made brownies."

"Maybe after," I say, already anticipating the rich sinful-
ness of Rose's espresso-chip genius. "I can't believe how
much you did while I was gone."

"Oh. You have messages. Mare called. She wanted to invite you to the beach. And some lady called a couple of days

ago…" She gets up to retrieve a scrap of paper, turns it sideways and squints at it. "Ruby Vest, I think."

"Ruth Westby?" I suggest, my stomach tightening.

"Yeah. That's it. She left her home and office numbers. She said it was really important."

I put my fork down. "Did she say why?"

"No. Who is she, anyway?"

"My boss," I say, my voice full of dread. "Clay's mom."

"Ooh, her. That reminds me, I saw Clay downtown yesterday. He looked really depressed. He asked about you. I almost felt sorry for him, even if he is a two-timing weasel."

"He wasn't with the brunette?"

"No." She gets a brownie and sits down on the couch next to me. "Maybe you should call him."

"What if she answers?"

"Who?"

"The brunette."

"Then ask for him, anyway," Rose says, as if I'm being dense. She takes a bite of brownie and it smells divine. "You're never going to get what you want until you ask for it, right?"

"Wait a sec, Rose. I thought you were totally anti-Clay."

"I was. But he looked so pathetic yesterday. It occurred to me that—I don't know—maybe we were wrong."

"Let me have a bite of that," I say, nodding at the brownie.

She hands me hers and gets herself another. When she's settled with her feet under her, Medea, the little traitor, gets up and curls into her lap, instead. "Isn't it weird that we're sort of…" She falters, and looks away shyly.

"Sort of what?"

"Sisters?"

"No." I tuck one of her braids behind her ear. "It's not weird at all."

CHAPTER 35

"I'm sorry to ask you here so early," Westby's saying. "I know many faculty members need a little downtime after finals."

"Oh. No, that's okay."

"It's just that what I need to speak to you about is really quite important, and time-sensitive as well."

Okay, I think. Here comes the ax. I try to hold her gaze without flinching.

"Obviously, when we hired you, we envisioned your position as a temporary one."

"Yes," I say quietly. "That was clear from the beginning." I will be grown-up, I will not cry. I can go tend bar in New Orleans. I can hunt grizzlies in Alaska. She's handing over my freedom. Rejoice.

"There are fairly strict regulations governing the application process, and we've been taking dossiers all year from a variety of highly qualified candidates."

Yeah, yeah, yeah, I think, staring out the window at the flowering magnolia tree just beyond the glass. *Get to the brutality, Westby.*

"Although usually we conduct the interviews the year before we hire someone for a tenure-track position, this year the budget was shaky and—well, we got a bit behind. So the committee will be meeting with candidates this summer."

Okay, Jesus, get to the point.

She chuckles. "You're thinking, 'Westby, come on, what's this got to do with me?'"

I'm shocked. Fantastic, the woman's psychic. Just my luck.

"Don't look like that, Claudia. It's natural to want to know where you fit in. That's why I wanted to meet with you right away."

Suddenly the door bursts open and I think I gasp, though I pray it's a sound that happens in my brain and never makes it to my lips. Who should rush in with her hair shining black and her face glowing, but Clay's little Rain-clone.

"I'm sorry," she says. "I didn't know you were busy." She looks at Westby with pleading eyes. She really is adorable; I can't blame Clay for choosing her over me. Is she a student here? No, students don't burst into Westby's office—no way. Oh God—they've gotten married. She's Westby's new-and-improved daughter-in-law.

"What is it, Selena?" Westby asks, her tone a touch impatient. Good. I hope they learn to despise each other.

"I got a flat," she says, sticking one skinny hip out to the side.

"On your bike?"

"Yeah. I don't know what happened—I parked it outside the scene shop and when I got back it was totally flat."

"See if you can find Frank."

"I did. For the past twenty minutes. He's not around. I'm *so* late for work!"

Westby picks up the phone and punches some numbers. "Nell, have you seen Frank?"

Selena looks at me. "I'm sorry," she says. "I hate to interrupt. It's kind of an emergency."

I try to smile at her, but my heart is deflating at a dangerously rapid rate. First Westby calls me in to give me the boot, now I'm forced to endure this bewitching little enchantress who's stolen the only guy I ever really wanted. There she is, pink-cheeked in her cute little tank top and shorts, the picture of summer, while I sit here like a death row inmate waiting for the juice, trying to summon the dignity not to whimper for mercy.

"Nell's paging him," Westby says, and to my dismay her tone is indulgent rather than hateful. "He'll meet you by the scene shop."

"Will you call my work and tell them?"

"Yes," Westby sighs. "As soon as I'm through with Claudia."

"Thanks." She shoots one last apologetic look at me and disappears.

"My daughter," Westby says, shaking her head. "She's twenty-one, but sometimes she's forty and sometimes she's still twelve. Full of surprises, I guess."

"Your—daughter?" I say.

"Yes. My youngest." She studies me. "Is everything okay?"

"Not your daughter-in-law?"

"Oh, no. I've only had one daughter-in-law, Monica, and now she's my ex-daughter-in-law. But you knew that, didn't you? Aren't you friends with Clay?"

I blush, and try wildly not to, but it only makes my face burn more. "Sort of."

She takes pity on me and changes the subject. "Anyway, the reason I asked you here is to discuss your future with us. You've done truly excellent work this year. I've been very impressed."

"You—you have?" I stammer, expecting the "however" to crop up any second.

"Yes. Of course. You're an excellent professor, Claudia, and a fine director as well. You have the instincts and the courage to do theater the way it should be done—with balls." I try unsuccessfully not to look taken aback, and she smirks. "If you'll pardon the expression." She takes off her glasses and continues. "That's why I want you to get an application in as soon as you can—this week, if possible—so we can officially consider you for the tenure-track position. Have you made other plans already?"

Just tending bar in New Orleans, but that can wait. "I—no, not really."

"Excellent. I was so afraid someone else would snatch you up." She reaches into her desk and pulls out a folder. "Here's the application. We'll be interviewing mid-July, if all goes well." She stands, and so do I. She hands me the folder, which I nearly drop in my befuddled shock at all that's transpired in the last three minutes.

"I know it's been a curious year for you," Westby says. "I fear not all of us were as welcoming as we should have been. But I'm sure we'll make it up to you, if indeed we're lucky enough to work with you further."

I just can't believe what I'm hearing.

"You're much more talented than you realize," she says, and for the first time since I've met her I think there's genuine warmth in her voice. She shakes my hand. "Good luck. But I don't think you'll need it."

I wander, dazed, into the sunlight and stand there, blinking stupidly at the view. The fog has wrapped itself all the way up the coast and is making its way gradually up the hill toward us.

Did that really happen? Does Westby seriously want me on faculty? Is Clay really—oh, my God—I can't believe I called him a child molester. No wonder he thinks I'm a head case.

"Hey, lady." I turn and see Mare in her dance clothes, leaning against the doorway.

"Hi. What are you doing here?"

"Working on some choreography." She drinks from a bottle of water, her silver bracelets jingling as they slide down her arm. "I called you—did your cousin tell you?"

"Yeah. I'm sorry, I just got back last night."

"Where'd you go?"

"New Mexico."

She looks surprised. "Really? What were you doing there?"

"Oh, I was kind of doing research," I say evasively.

She nods. "Cool. For a play?"

"No," I say. "Not really. More selfish research, I guess."

"Uh-huh. Is there a man involved?" she asks, smiling knowingly.

"Not directly." I pull my sweatshirt tighter against the chill of the coming fog. "But there might be, soon."

CHAPTER 36

"Come on," I say, as soon as he opens the door. "We're going swimming."

"What are you doing here?" he's wearing his boxers and nothing else. His hair is a mess, and he looks adorable. He squints at me, scratches his chest and says in a grumpy, sleep-heavy voice, "I thought you hated me."

"Hurry up. No time for bickering."

"I'm not even awake," he mumbles, letting me in reluctantly. There's an empty pizza box on the floor, a pile of laundry in the corner, but so far, no signs of Woman. Good.

"I can see that, you sloth. Now, get your swim trunks on, grab a towel and let's go."

"Have you tried swimming here in June?" he protests. "It's still cold as shit."

"Listen, if the evil spawn of tourists can get in that water, so can we."

"Spawn of...?"

I put my hands on my hips and hover over him as he collapses onto his bed. "Last week I saw a brood of pasty, clearly

Midwestern kids plowing right in like it was bathwater. Now, come on—where's your local pride? Aren't you a surfer, for Christ's sake?"

He looks out the window with a pouty expression. "It's foggy."

"And…?"

"And," he says, changing his approach abruptly. "The last time you were here, you called me a child molester. Why do you want to go swimming all of a sudden?"

I hesitate but decide to plow ahead. "I will have no more excuses, Mr. Clay Parker. What you do with children is of no concern to me at the moment."

"I don't do anything with—"

"My immediate goal is to drag your lazy, pizza-eating ass to the beach."

He half grins. "'Pizza-eating ass?' Does that imply my ass eats—"

I kick the empty pizza box at him. "You know what I mean. Now, come on. I'm giving you five minutes to get dressed. If you're not in my car by—" I look at my watch "—10:23, I will abduct you and toss you into the waves in your underwear." I glance at his boxers. They're yellow, with little airplanes on them. "Which are hideous, by the way."

He shrugs. "Minor laundry backup."

"Lazy slob," I say, heading for the door. "You now have four minutes and counting."

"Seriously," Clay says when we're bobbing in the surf, our lips blue with cold but neither of us willing to get out first. "What's this all about? Are you trying to make me crazy, or what?"

"There was a misunderstanding," I say, using the agentless passive in the desperate and misguided hope that he'll overlook what an idiot I was. "Anyone could have made the same mistake."

"What mistake, exactly?"

A line of pelicans swoop across the horizon single file. "Do pelicans migrate?" I ask, all innocence.

"Claudia," he says sternly. "What mistake are we talking about here?"

"I thought your sister was your girlfriend."

He looks incredulous. "My—Selena? Are you serious?"

I nod. "I saw you with her twice—once at the Valentine's thing and then downtown one night, at a bar. You just seemed so into her. I assumed…"

"Pretty big assumption," he says.

"How was I supposed to know?"

"You must have a pretty low opinion of me."

"Seriously, Clay." I'm practically pleading with him, now. "Rose thought the same thing."

"Couldn't somebody have asked me?"

"I mean come on, I see you twice with this gorgeous young thing and—well, she looked exactly like the girl my ex left me for, and…" I trail off. "I sound kind of loopy, don't I?"

"Yes." He yanks me gently toward him in the water. Our bodies are suddenly pressed together, with only the thin, filmy fabric of our bathing suits between us. "It does sound loopy. And you might have asked."

"I know," I say, too excited by his proximity to manage more than two syllables.

"It was hell on me. I missed you so much. And I had no idea what I'd done…."

"I'm sorry," I say, and then my teeth start chattering.

"You think in the future we could learn to communicate rather than just shout names at each other?"

"Uh-huh," I say, my eyes on his lips.

"You sure about that? You don't sound too sure." He's teasing me now. I can feel him getting rapidly aroused in spite of the cold. Goodbye, shrinkage.

"I'm sure," I say.

"Because I don't want you showing up on my doorstep

tonight calling me a child molester. The old lady next door wouldn't speak to me for weeks."

"I'm sorry!" I cry. "I said I'm sorry."

"How sorry?"

"Very sorry," I whisper, enjoying the feel of my hard, frozen nipples pressed against him. My teeth have mercifully stopped chattering. "Now, can you shut up about it?"

He does, and when he presses his salty mouth to mine the kiss goes on for a long, electric forever. The current is wrapping around our legs, tugging us first this way, then that. A seagull calls out in shrill joy and I could swear the sound comes from inside of me. Before I know what's happening, Clay is tugging at my bikini bottom and my legs are wrapped around him and he's inside me, filling me up and pulling me to him again and again. I'm trying not to moan out loud; there are kids bodysurfing so close, I can hear their individual squeals. Thank God for the layer of soupy fog, or the big Mormon family unwrapping sandwiches on the beach would get an eyeful.

Something hits me ruthlessly upside the head. All at once, my legs sweep out from under me and I'm being thrashed about in the blue-gray world of salt and foam. I figure it's sad, but at least I'll drown a highly aroused woman.

I land on the beach with my bikini half off and sand in every crevice.

Clay runs over, trying not to laugh.

"You okay?" he asks, bending down to help me to my feet.

"Jesus," I say, and choke for two minutes straight. He pounds on my back gently, but luckily I'm spared the humiliation of puking up all the seawater and stray fish lodged in my lungs.

"Sleeper wave," he says, when I've finally caught my breath. "Sneaky bastards."

By now it's afternoon and we're both starving, so we laugh off our coitus interruptus episode and walk back to our towels, shivering. I produce the paper bag of groceries

I purchased frantically on my way to his house, and pull each item out one at a time.

"Ze French bread," I announce, pulling the baguette out and trying on a ridiculously bad French accent. "Ze French wine."

"Mmm."

"Ze Brie."

"Très bien!" Clay's accent is even worse than mine, if that's possible.

"Pasta sal-ad." As I pull the plastic container out, it leaks oil down my arm, which Clay immediately licks off. This is getting good.

"And," I say, my voice all husky now from watching his tongue on my wrist. "Le pièce de résistance—chocolate *et* cherries!"

Clay's eyes light up with delight, and I take a mental picture of his face like that, thinking if he ever dumps me, I'll torture myself with the memory of this moment.

We demolish the bread, Brie and pasta salad like wolves. Then we pour plastic cups of the merlot and have that with the chocolate. By two-fifteen we've eaten everything but the cherries. We feed them to each other one at a time, stretched out side by side in the warm sand.

"Mmm," he says as I pull the stem from his teeth. He chews as if he's memorizing the flavor, a hedonist taking notes. "That one was so tart."

I brush a few stray flecks of sand from his cheek. "That's right," I say, looking him in the eye. "Learn to love it."

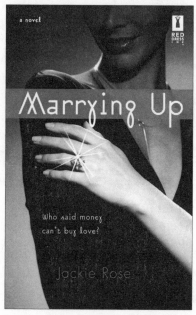

Are you getting it at least twice a month?

Here's how: Try RED DRESS INK books on for size & receive two FREE gifts!

Bombshell
by Lynda Curnyn

As Seen on TV
by Sarah Mlynowski

YES! Send my two FREE books.
There's no risk and no purchase required—ever!

Please send me my two FREE books and bill me just 99¢ for shipping and handling. I may keep the books and return the shipping statement marked "cancel." If I do not cancel, about a month later I will receive 2 additional books at the low price of just $11.00 each in the U.S. or $13.56 each in Canada, a savings of over 15% off the cover price (plus 50¢ shipping and handling per book*). I understand that accepting the two free books places me under no obligation ever to buy any books. I can always return a shipment and cancel at any time. Even if I never buy another book from Red Dress Ink, the free books are mine to keep forever.

160 HDN D34M   360 HDN D34N

Name (PLEASE PRINT)		
Address		Apt. #
City	State/Prov.	Zip/Postal Code

Want to try another series? Call 1-800-873-8635
or order online at www.TryRDI.com/free.

In the U.S. mail to: 3010 Walden Ave., P.O. Box 1867, Buffalo, NY 14240-1867
In Canada mail to: P.O. Box 609, Fort Erie, ON L2A 5X3

*Terms and prices subject to change without notice. Sales tax applicable in N.Y.
**Canadian residents will be charged applicable provincial taxes and GST.

All orders subject to approval. Offer limited to one per household.
® and ™ are trademarks owned and used by the trademark owner and/or its licensee.

© 2004 Harlequin Enterprises Ltd.

RED DRESS INK™

RDI04-TR